THE SUITE LIFE

A Paradise Bay Romantic Comedy, Book 3

MELANIE SUMMERS

Copyright © 2019 Gretz Corp.
All rights reserved.
Published by Gretz Corp.
First edition
EBOOK ISBN: 978-1-988891-23-1
Paperback Edition ISBN: 978-1-988891-24-8
Paperback Colour Edition ISBN: 978-1-988891-25-5

This is a work of fiction. Names, characters, businesses, places, events and incidents are either the products of the author's imagination or used in a fictitious manner. Any resemblance to actual persons, living or dead, or actual events is purely coincidental.

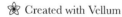 Created with Vellum

PRAISE AND AWARDS

- Two-time bronze medal winner at the Reader's Favorite Awards, Chick-lit category for *The Royal Treatment* and *Whisked Away.*
- Silver medalist at the Reader's Favorite Awards, Women's Fiction category for *The After Wife.*

"A fun, often humorous, escapist tale that will have readers blushing, laughing and rooting for its characters."

~ Kirkus Reviews

"A gorgeously funny, romantic and seductive modern fairy tale…"

~ MammieBabbie Book Club

"…perfect for someone that needs a break from this world and wants to delve into a modern-day fairy tale that will keep them laughing and rooting for the main characters throughout the story.

~ ChickLit Café

"I was totally gripped to this story. For the first time ever the Kindle came into the bath with me. This book is unputdownable. I absolutely loved it."

~ Philomena (Two Friends, Read Along with Us)

"Very rarely does a book make me literally hold my breath or has me feeling that actual ache in my heart for a character, but I did both."

~ Three Chicks Review for Net galley

Books by Melanie Summers

ROMANTIC COMEDIES
The Crown Jewels Series

The Royal Treatment

The Royal Wedding

The Royal Delivery

Paradise Bay Series

The Honeymooner

Whisked Away

The Suite Life

Resting Beach Face (Coming Soon)

Crazy Royal Love Series

Royally Crushed

Royally Wild

Royally Tied (Coming Soon)

WOMEN'S FICTION

The After Wife

The Deep End (Coming Soon)

Dedication

For single moms,
I am in awe of your ability to keep it together under the weight of all that is
parenting. You must have so many balls in the air, it's hard to see the sky some days.
Forget the pro athletes and the YouTube superstars, you are the heroes of this world.
I wish you laughter, peace, and a good night's sleep.
Melanie

Author's Note

Dear reader,

Welcome back to Paradise Bay, where the drinks are always cold and the men are the exact opposite. 😉 I hope this finds you well and that the story you are about to read will make you snort laugh and sigh happily.

The Suite Life is the third book in the series, and although it can be read as a standalone, I'd suggest starting with *The Honeymooner*, then *Whisked Away*, *then* coming back to this one. It'll be more fun that way because you won't miss all the little inside jokes from the first two stories. And my romantic comedies are nothing, if not fun.

My goal when I sit down to write is to give you a well-deserved escape from reality, because let's face it, reality isn't exactly what it's cracked up to be. Reality has shitty things like bills that need to be paid and well-dressed, judgmental parents at your child's school drop-off. I see you, Blair, in your Lulu Lemons with your got-up-at-five-to-look-just-so hair. Go do another set of squats. We'll be over with the fun people.

Oh, that sounded bitter, no? Just kidding, Blair. Good for you for having that thigh gap.

I should stop now before I get really nasty.
Imperfectly yours,
Melanie

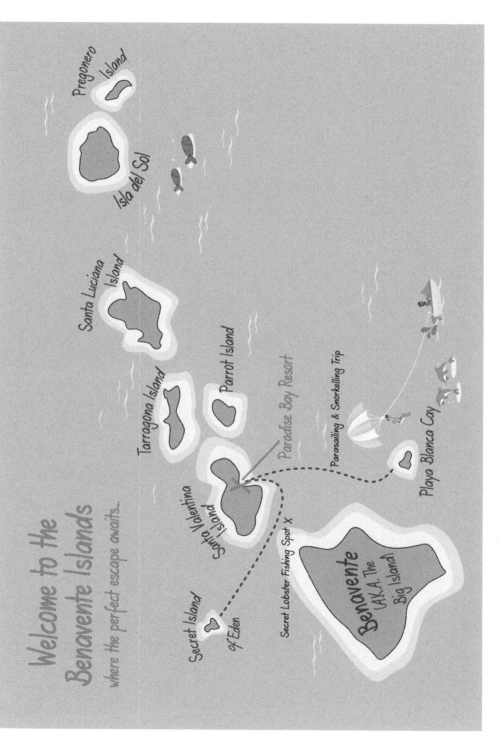

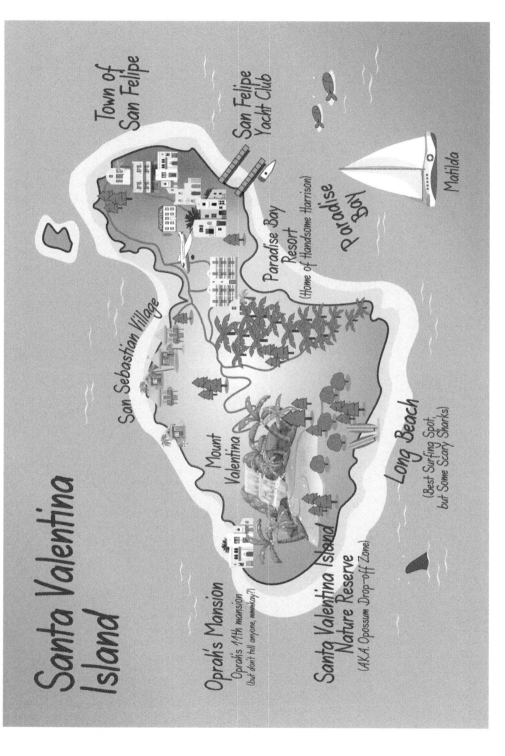

THEY'RE READY TO TIE THE KNOT!

Zidane & Amber

SAVE THE DATE!
Saturday, August 8
Santa Valentina Cathedral
123 Main St. San Filipe

RSVP AT
DANELOVESAMBER.COM

A Math Lesson Courtesy of the Prodigal Son

Leopold Davenport

Paradise Bay, Santa Valentina Island

MOST PEOPLE HAVE it arse backward. They work for forty years or so, usually at a job they hate, wearing down their bodies and minds along the way. At the end of it all, they're too old and decrepit to *really live* (read: skydiving, scuba diving, cliff diving—any sort of diving, really, summiting the K1, making the most of a trip to Rio during Carnival, etc.). I, however, am doing the exact opposite. I've decided to take my retirement first, and for as long as possible, while I'm still young enough to enjoy it all. At some point, should I stumble upon the perfect career, I'll spend a few years doing work I love while bettering the world until I grow tired of it. Then I'll bid adieu to the workforce and go back to the life of leisure.

Up until now, my plan has worked out brilliantly thanks to the generosity of my parents, Lord Alistair and Lady Bunny Davenport. You've probably heard of them. He owns Davenport Communications, the largest media, telecommunications, and something or other company in all of the UK. Or is it in all of Europe? I can never remember because I really don't care. Hmmm, I should correct what I said about my parents being generous. *Mother* is the benevolent one (when it comes to her youngest son—that's me—anyway). Father, not so much. Until very recently, we've managed a peaceful co-existence where he pays for my life and otherwise ignores me while I ride the razor-thin line that exists between complying with his lowest expectations and embarrassing him to the point where he feels he must react.

As a teenager, I developed something called the Alistair Pain Ratio, or APR. So long as my "childish behavior" doesn't exceed a level one, I'm golden. Basically, the APR is an equation used to calculate my father's desire to pretend I don't exist vs. his desire to avoid public humiliation. For those at the back of the room, it looks like this:

Leopold's Latest Screw-up = Level of Humiliation ÷ Ability to Pretend Leo Doesn't Exist

Alistair's Ability to Pretend Leo Doesn't Exist is always a remarkably strong factor of 10 on the scale. Yes, when Alistair sets his mind to something, he seldom falters. If the Level of Humiliation (LOH) is greater or equal to 10, bringing the Leopold's Latest Screw-up (LLS) to a factor of 1 or more, I'm fucked (IF).

Based on twenty-seven years of careful trial and error, I discovered the following brings me to a quotient of 1+ (or IF):

On the front page of the *Weekly World News* = 3
Mentioned on the Avonian Broadcast News Channel (ABN) = 5
His golf buddies aware of LLS = 12
Warrant a conversation with his wife/my mum = Level 15
You get the idea.

Should the IF quotient reach a 1 or more, he engages in an attempt to stop the behavior. This time, as far as I can calculate, I'm at an unprecedented Level 50, which means not only being banned from my parents' home, which has happened dozens of times before, but also a very surprising ban from the entire Kingdom of Avonia for a minimum of six months. As a side note, if you've never been to Avonia, it's a lovely little island just north of Belgium and east of England. You should go sometime. It's quite a lovely place. Like

England, we have our own monarchy, and they're *far* more interesting than those tossers to the left of us.

Anyway, back to this silly ban imposed by my father. Poor bugger thinks this'll break me, which goes to show he really doesn't know his youngest son. Not even the slightest bit. If he did, he'd realize I'd turn this whole banishment thing into an extended vacay in paradise. So suck it, Alistair, because I'm having a marvelous time.

Truth be told, I'll have fun no matter where I wind up. And I'm not just saying that. I once turned an overnight stay in a jail cell in Bali into what the papers dubbed "the party of the century." Even the chief of police had a grand time. In fact, he enjoyed himself so much, he not only had me released at dawn, but he dropped the charges and gave me a lift back to the resort, where we spent the day drinking by the pool. We've stayed friends ever since. Last year, I was one of the groomsmen at his fourth wedding.

For two days, I've been at my brother Pierce and his girlfriend, Emma's, luxurious, ultra-private beachfront villa on Santa Valentina Island. Trust me, there are worse places for a guy to have to live in exile than the Caribbean. I sleep late, then lounge by the pool and work on my tan while Pierce's housekeeper, Mrs. Bailey, prepares my meals and does my washing.

It's been a little dull so far, but only because I haven't bothered to get out there and meet people, and my big bro is a total bore. He's a famous author (yes, *that* Pierce Davenport, the *Clash of Crowns* guy) so he spends all his time holed up in his office, tapping away at his computer—yawn. Emma's a blast, but she's also a very busy chef at the resort her family owns. It's just up the bay from the villa, so she cycles off every morning, only to return late in the evening, needing to get off her feet.

Not that I'm complaining. Santa Valentina Island, known as the jewel of the Benaventes, is one of the most lush, beautiful places on earth. The water is crystal-clear turquoise, the sun is always shining, and the women are always in bikinis. I can *easily* find ways to amuse myself for six months until I'm allowed back home. The trick will be not annoying Pierce so much that he kicks me out, which could be a slight problem, because when I'm bored, I tend to find creative ways to amuse myself. And since Pierce has a giant twig up his arse, he doesn't like people touching his things.

But that's okay because I've decided to spend most of my time enjoying nature, so as not to be tempted to do something ill-advised, like take the Samurai sword off the wall to slice that big, juicy watermelon sitting on the counter at the moment. Just the thought of it is fun, isn't it? Live-action Fruit Ninja. I can almost hear the satisfying swish of the sword as I slice through it in one quick blow. But since that would make a mess I don't want to clean up, and the sword was a gift from the 126th Emperor of Japan, Naruhito, I shall distract myself by going for a swim. After a refreshing dip, I'll have a bite to eat, then a nap by the pool. After which I'll venture into town, find a pub, and turn Santa Valentina into Ibiza for the next six months. Which reminds me, I have to call Mother, because it seems as though my credit cards are frozen, and cash is always helpful at party time. Bunny'll feel sorry for me and front me some play money. But first, a dip in the sea.

I walk down the wide, sunbathed hall toward the kitchen in my swim trunks, a snorkelling mask, and a pair of flippers. It's a bright, beautiful morning, and I'm going to hit the ocean to see what I can find. Hopefully, some gorgeous lost tourist who has wandered away from the resort...

"What the hell are you doing?" Pierce asks from his position behind the kitchen island.

I pop the snorkel out of my mouth. "I'm going for a swim."

Pierce closes his eyes. "And you're planning to walk down the steep steps to the water in those things?" He opens his eyes and points to the flippers.

"Thought it would be a fun challenge." I pop the snorkel back in my mouth and head for the sliding doors.

"At some point, we're going to have to talk about why you're here, Leo, and for how long."

Waving my hand back at him, I continue, my flippers slapping the white tile floor.

Pierce's mobile buzzes on the counter and I hear, "Bunny Davenport calling."

Oh, yay! It's so much better that she's calling me. Now it won't seem like I'm only calling for money. Hello, Amex.

I turn in time to see Pierce pick up the phone. "This wouldn't be happening if you weren't here, you know."

Pierce hates Bunny. But I can't blame him. She favours me in a way that is rather appalling. "Don't move a muscle," he says, swiping the screen.

"Mother, hello." Pause. "Yes, he's right here." Pause. "I have no idea why he's not answering his phone. I'm not his nanny." Pause. "Lovely to speak to you as well."

He rolls his eyes as he walks over to me and hands me the phone.

I pop the snorkel out of my mouth again and say, "Hello, Mum! How's my favourite lady?" I know, I hate myself, too.

"Terrible, Leo. You've dropped a huge clanger this time."

"Yes, I know, and I'm horribly sorry." I'm not really, but she seems to like when I say that.

"No, you're not, but you will be. Your father has never been this angry in all the years I've known him."

"I find that hard to believe. His favourite pastime is being angry."

"The King of Sweden is entertaining meetings with Vodaphone and MTS."

"Seriously?" Shit. This is bad. I've never fucked up so badly that the family biz was affected.

"Yes, seriously," she says dramatically. "Why *her*? Of all the women you could have…*gotten to know better*. She's not even good-looking. Plus, you knew who she was. How could you not think this would happen?"

"I find her quite lovely. Also, I didn't think anyone would find out." Oh, that was a lame answer, wasn't it? The truth is, I was so hammered, I forgot she's in line for the Swedish throne. "Why don't I come back so I can smooth things over? I'll go see her father. Perhaps if I'm man enough to go there in person, he'll change his mind."

"Definitely not. Someone tipped off the press, and they're sniffing around for a story. If you show up anywhere near Sweden, you'll ruin us all."

Good. I didn't want to go anyway, but I have to *act* like I want to fix this so she'll send me some money, and I can stay put. "In that case, how can I make it up to you and Father?"

"You can't. You're completely underestimating the level of rage this time," she says with a sigh. "Oh, my head, Leo. This migraine you've caused is unbearable. I've been in bed in the dark since yesterday morning."

"I'm sorry, Mum." This time, I mean it. I never seek to harm anyone, especially not someone as delicate as my mother. "It was very selfish and stupid of me, and if I could fix it, I would."

"Well, you can't. And I can't help you this time, either," she says, sniffing. "Your father has cut off my wellness fund. He's saying it's because the stocks will fall if we lose Sweden, but I'm certain it's because he doesn't want me to send you any money. I can't live without my wellness fund, Leo. You know how much I need my treatments."

Her weekly spa treatments serve to preserve her like a jar of pickled woman. If my mother could live in a cryogenic chamber wheeled around everywhere to prevent her from aging, she would totally do it. Nothing gets in the way of her regimen—not the time I broke my leg skiing when I was eight and had to have surgery, not even when her own father died. She sent an enormous flower arrangement from the medi-spa in Switzerland in lieu of actually bothering to show up.

"Not your wellness fund!" I roll my eyes at Pierce, who scrunches his nose up in disgust. "But surely after a few weeks, I'll find a way to make it all right as rain, or at the very least, find the loopholes to get you your money back."

"As much as I appreciate the offer, lamb, it won't work. Your father has found a way to close *all* the loopholes this time."

Impossible. There are literally limitless loopholes, and my super-power is finding them and squeezing my way out. "I'm sure I can finesse the situation—"

"Not this time."

Her tone definitely has me worried. "All right, I'll camp out here until this blows over, then come back and ask his forgiveness. It's not half bad, really. I'm getting some sun and helping Pierce and Emma around the house a bit." Eyeing the sword on the wall, I add, "I was just about to cut up some fruit."

"Oh, well, that's good of you," she says, sounding completely caught off guard at the thought of me helping out. "Oh, my darling boy, I'm afraid things are about to get much worse for you."

That sounded a little apocalyptic, no? "What is that supposed to mean?"

I hear a voice in the background. It's Mum's personal maid, Genevieve.

"I'll be right there," Mother says, her voice a little muffled. When she comes back on the line, she says, "Leo, lamb, I didn't realize the time. My massage therapist is set to arrive to help with my migraine, and I must shower before he arrives."

Let's pretend we didn't hear that, okay? "Mother, wait. Can you please tell me why things are about to get much worse?"

"I must run, but your father is sending someone to see you. Do *everything* he says, and things may work out. Kisses!" With that, she's gone, leaving me standing in my trunks wondering what the hell is about to happen.

I flipper my way over to the counter, lifting my knees in an exaggerated fashion with each step, and set Pierce's phone down in front of him.

He narrows his eyes. "That didn't sound good."

"Yeah, not so much. Apparently, I'm going to have a visitor soon, and I'm to do whatever he tells me."

"Are we in a tropical version of *A Christmas Carol?*"

"Christ, I hope not."

2

Stuffed Dates and Tiny Pedos in Bellbottoms

Brianna Lewis

San Filipe, Santa Valentina Island

THE SECRET to life is to never trust anything that can get an erection —a lesson I learned at the age of twenty-one, taught to me by a plus sign on a plastic stick and a vanishing boyfriend who had promised me forever. Don't get me wrong, I don't regret for a moment that I have the world's sweetest, just-turned-four-year-old little girl. I can't imagine my life without Isabelle. It just would have been uber helpful to have, at the most, a loving partner with whom to share my life, and at the very least, financial support for my daughter. I'm not sure if you have children or not, but they are bloody expensive.

You know what else is expensive? Being maid of honour for your sister. I'm learning firsthand how many parties there are that lead up to the big day. Today's is likely the worst. At least, I hope so. It's a themed engagement barbeque hosted by the parents of the groom. Unfortunately for me, the theme is famous couples in history, which isn't the easiest thing to pull off when you're very single.

Because my Great Aunt Dolores lives with us, my sister, Amber, thought it might be fun if she and I paired up for the event. Doesn't that sound terrific? Me and my 71-year-old great aunt dressed as Bonnie and Clyde, or perhaps Cinderella and Prince Charming?

As pathetic as that would have been, it gets worse, because my aunt and my daughter quickly partnered up, leaving me feeling like the clumsy kid who gets picked last for kickball in phys ed. That was me, by the way, so this little moment has allowed me to replay some of the more traumatic parts of my childhood.

Anyway, they're going as Sonny and Cher. If you're wondering who is dressed as Sonny, it's my daughter, Isabelle which meant fashioning a wig/moustache to fit a scrawny pre-schooler. Dolores made them matching faux-fur vests out of a throw from the thrift store. She already had the Cher wig. I do *not* want to know why.

My sister, Amber, and her fiancé, Zidane—Dane for short—are coming as Romeo and Juliet, so that's nice. I'm not sure if either of them realizes it's not actually a romance as much as it's a teenage tragedy ending in a double suicide, but she's going to look gorgeous, and he'll be the height of handsomeness in his sweaty tights under the hot sun.

After much deliberation in front of my closet and computer screen, trying to find some extra cash that simply isn't in my account no matter how many times I check, I've decided to go as Jane Goodall. I already have a light-green button-up shirt, hair elastics for a low pony, and I'm borrowing Mr. Bananas—Izzy's chimpanzee stuffy with Velcro hands so it can stay affixed to my neck. The price was right, and now I have a plus-one. He can't breathe or converse, but that also means he can't lie or pull a disappearing act.

At the moment, I'm dressed in my costume sans Mr. Bananas, wrapping the seventy-five-dollar designer salad bowl from their registry. It was the cheapest thing on the list, which means I'm really screwed when it comes to the actual wedding gift.

Knickers, the calico cat whose tail was flattened by a mail truck when he was a kitten, hops up onto the table to see what I'm doing. He watches intently as I crease the ivory wrapping paper around the box. "Don't even think about it, cat," I say as he reaches one white paw for the ribbon.

He glares at me for a second before returning his attention to my furiously moving hands.

"Oh, fine. Here," I say, cutting off a piece of ribbon and tossing it onto the floor for him. He hops down and starts batting it around like a soon-to-be-dead mouse.

Fold, tuck, tear off a piece of tape and place it just so. I need everything to be perfect today so I can avoid another round of, "Poor Brianna never should have got knocked up before she got married, because now her life is spiralling out of control at a violent pace, but we can fix that with this nice young man we met at the lumber yard so our granddaughter will have a brother and/or sister to play with someday soon." Not my favourite game, to be honest.

Come to think of it, I'm not one for games, anyway. I don't have the time for them. Likewise to going to the hairdresser for a cut and colour, shopping for new clothes, going out for drinks with my besties after work, or sleeping—all of which require money I don't have. Well, not sleeping, I suppose. That one's free, but only if you have the luxury of time. Which I do not.

Take today for example. I didn't get home from my job as concierge at an all-inclusive (read: no-tipping) resort until two in the morning, and by the time I got to bed, it was after three. Izzy had me up at seven a.m. on the dot, because she's an early-to-rise sort of girl. After making oatmeal and cut-up fruit for breakfast, we played her favourite board game, Snakes and Ladders, which to me is merely an irritating string of setbacks reminiscent of my life. Let the snake out of his pants, and you'll quickly slide down the bloody ladder to the start-again square, instead of getting ahead like all of your peers who have already completed law school, passed the bar, and are happily practicing law and buying big houses to which they drive to in their BMWs. But I digress.

After board game time, I let Izzy watch cartoons for an hour while I studied, threw in a load of laundry, did the dishes, and cleaned out the kitty litter. The cats (plural, yes, there are three of them) are not mine. They belong to Aunt Dolores, so when I moved in with her because she could no longer work and I needed someone to watch Izzy so I could go to school/work, we also moved in with Milo, Knickers, and Puddy Tat. Three cats and three people in a tiny two-bedroom house is a LOT, but we make it work. Dolores and Izzy each have a room upstairs, and I sleep on the couch in the living room so I don't wake anyone up when I come home in the middle of the night. It's horribly inconvenient because all my clothes are upstairs in Izzy's closet, and the couch is insanely uncomfortable, but it's only temporary, so I keep telling myself it's not that bad.

But that's a lie because I long for a real bed the way Ferris Bueller longed to have his own car. Every cell of my body yearns for a soft-yet-firm mattress without springs that violate me while I attempt to sleep.

Soon. I just have to stay on track, and before I know it, we'll be moving into an airy three-bedroom home with plenty of space for the cats, the toys, and the woman who's paying for it all to have her own bedroom. I even have the perfect house picked out. It's a bright-yellow two-story English cottage-style home with a nice big yard and an attached garage. The house is shaded by a huge old gum tree with a tire swing affixed to one of the long branches, and the property is only three blocks from the ocean in the nicer part of town. It's not for sale yet, but the owners are getting on in years, and every time I drive by, I expect to see a for-sale sign. I hope it won't go on the market until I'm ready, but if it does, I'm sure I can find something else I'd love almost as much.

The only thing standing in the way of me and the life I want is passing my bar exams. The tests are eight months away, which is both exhilarating (because there's a light at the end of the tunnel) and terrifying (because I'm not sure if I'll be ready in time). I know eight months sounds like a lot of time, but when you work evening shift five nights a week at a busy resort and have an adorable child who needs your love and attention, you find yourself being spread a little thin. And now with Amber's wedding coming up, things are about to get trickier.

Glancing at the clock, I let out a sigh of relief. For once, I'm ahead of schedule, and it finally looks as though the stars are going to line up long enough for me to actually put on some makeup. I set the tape down on our small wooden kitchen table and hurry over to the living room, (which is also my bedroom and Isabelle's playroom), open the secondhand buffet cabinet that serves as our art supply/linen closet/extra dish storage, and find a scrap of pink construction paper and black felt pen.

"Perfect." I'm saving a bit of money by making my own card. I cut the paper into the shape of a gift tag, then use my hole punch to cut a circle to loop some white ribbon through.

"Isabelle?!" I call up the stairs as I rush back to the kitchen table. "Are you almost dressed?"

"Almost, Mummy," she calls down.

Almost. That means she's probably standing in her knickers in the middle of her room playing with her stuffed animals, having completely forgotten we're in a big rush.

"Come right down, honey! I still need to help you with your wig."

No answer. I know exactly what's going to happen. I'm going to have to go up there and finish dressing her, even though she's fully capable of pulling a T-shirt over her head and pulling up a pair of elastic-waist bell-bottoms. Plucking my coffee mug off the table, I take three giant gulps of the sweet and creamy mixture that has now gone cold. I don't even like coffee when it's hot, let alone when it's cold, but it's pretty much what I'm fueled by, so it's either that, or lie down on the floor and have a twenty-hour nap.

The sound of the stairs creaking indicates that Aunt Dolores is on her way down. Dolores is an unapologetic seventy-one-year-old bachelorette. Do not call her a spinster, not if you know what's good for you. Milo and Puddy Tat, the tiny Siamese brother and sister, arrive ahead of her and trot into the kitchen, catching sight of Knickers, who is still bashing the ribbon around. Sighing, I cut two more pieces of ribbon and drop them onto the floor to avoid a catfight under the table.

I quickly draw a set of wedding bells and write:
For the happy couple, Amber and Dane,
Congratulations!
With love,

Brianna, Isabelle, and Aunt Dolores

"Did you finish wrapping the ridiculously expensive bowl?" Aunt Dolores asks, shaking her head and rolling her eyes.

I start when I glance at her because she looks more than a little terrifying with a nylon pinned to her head in preparation for her Cher wig. She's also wearing way too much eyeliner for a woman her age. "Why anyone needs a seventy-five-dollar bowl is beyond me. That thing won't hold any more lettuce than the one I bought at Goodwill for a dollar."

"Yes, but this one is very classy, so when they have guests over, everything will look just so."

"It'll look like they're suckers who wasted the better part of a hundred dollars on a damn bowl." Her gaze moves from the box to me. "Although technically, you bought it, which would make you the sucker."

"Promise me you won't say anything about the cost of the bowl—or their registry. You'll hurt Amber's feelings." I raise an eyebrow at her. "Also, I should point out that she's very nervous about our family meeting Dane's."

"What's to be nervous about? Are they weird or something?"

"Not them. Us," I say pointedly. Amber's a bit of a delicate flower on account of everyone treating her like one since she was born four weeks early. She had a bit of a respiratory problem that she quickly grew out of, but for some reason, my parents remain certain she could stop breathing at any moment. She's skinny and gorgeous like our mum (and unlike me who is built more like our big-boned father), but I still love her. Since getting engaged, the delicate hot-house flower has become a delicate bride-to-be. Unfortunately, Aunt Dolores couldn't care less about coddling my little sister, so the unspoken expectation for today is that I will keep her under control. Since no one has been able to manage that task for seven decades, I really don't have a hope in hell to do it now, but I have to try anyway. "Please, for my sake, just behave today so I won't have to deal with a sobbing bride-to-be."

"I'll try." She sniffs. "But I'm old, and sometimes I get confused."

That's the biggest lie I've ever heard. Aunt Dolores is as sharp as a tack, and even though she most certainly *has* a filter, she chooses not to use it. "Auntie…" I say in a warning tone.

"What? I've got one foot in the bloody grave. I should be allowed to speak my mind. Besides, whatever happened to the days when young people respected their elders?"

"Pretty sure those days were a myth carried down through the ages, like the brontosaurus or decent men. Now, where's your costume? We have to leave soon."

"I know that. I'm not thick in the head."

"I'm not suggesting you are. I'm merely wondering why you're still in your bathrobe?"

"Because I don't want to get my Cher costume dirty while I'm finishing making my cheese people." She walks past me and over to the fridge.

"Oh God. Not the cheese people today, please?"

Dolores's head pops up from behind the fridge door. "And what exactly is wrong with my cheese people? They're a very big hit every-where I go."

In lieu of the more popular hedgehog-style cheese balls, Dolores likes to shape processed cream cheeses into people she knows. Because the people only have four limbs as opposed to a hedgehog having hundreds of spikes, there is a total of four pretzels per cheese person on the plate. So once those are gone, it's just generally two blobs of cheese that sit uneaten until the end of the party. I tried to point that out to Dolores once, but apparently, it's by design, because if no one can eat it, everyone can enjoy her creation the entire time.

She sets the plate down on the table and beams at it.

"Is that…?"

"Yes, it's the bride and groom. I used Velveeta for their faces since they both seem to like tanning so much."

I stand, momentarily transfixed by the terrifying figures in front of me. The bride and groom are both dressed in white from head to toe and have big bulgy eyes made of green olives. Completely ignoring the horror on my face, Aunt Dolores smiles lovingly at her creation. "I took the pimentos out of the olives to make their lips. Kind of a nice touch, don't you think?"

"Oh, it's touched all right. What exactly did you use to make her eyelashes?"

"Oh, those are fake eyelashes. I picked them up at Walgreens yesterday."

"So, people probably shouldn't…"

"Oh, yeah, no one should eat the olives, I'm pretty sure eyelash glue is toxic." She walks over to the fridge again, and gets out some lettuce, then prepares the platter on which she'll set the happy couple. "Is that what you're wearing?" Aunt Dolores asks.

"Yes, you don't think I look like Jane Goodall?"

"Oh, no, *I* think you do. I'm just pretending to be your mother because that's exactly what she's going to say when she sees you've decided to dress as a plain Jane. I want you to have a good comeback."

Dolores and my mother, Naomi, have never exactly hit it off. My mum and my dad were high school sweethearts. She played the clichéd cheerleader to his football star. Petite and pretty, my mum is always well-put-together like one of those 1950s housewives, complete with the pearls. Dolores, who has absolutely no use for all things fashion or frilly, finds my mother a bore.

I pause for a moment, trying to think of a good comeback but coming up blank, which is quite frankly a bit concerning since I'll need to be quick with the retorts if I'm going to argue effectively in a courtroom someday. But since my mother won't be presiding over any of my cases, I should be fine. She's really the one person who can effortlessly get under my skin. "Well, at least I'll be in costume. That's about all she could ask."

The inescapable sound of bass guitar starts up courtesy of our neighbour, Jerry, who reckons he should be the new lead singer of the Grateful Dead because of his sweet licks, his pure vocals, and his name. Jerry is one of the many reasons I need to pass the bar, so I can move us to a nice house without a super loud pothead who walks around outside in his shorty robe all the time.

"Jerry's up early," Dolores says.

I glance at the clock and realize she's right. Jerry normally doesn't wake up and start playing until after noon, and it's only eleven.

Ack! Eleven!

I'm quickly running out of time. "Isab—" I start to call but am interrupted by the sight of Isabelle, who, although technically dressed as Sonny, is sporting glittery eyeshadow, overly dark rouge, and blindingly bright-pink lipstick. She grins widely and does a spin. "See, Mummy? I did it myself with the makeup kit Grandma gived me."

"You certainly did." I plaster a smile on my face even though the sight of my child like this is rather disturbing.

She holds up both hands, displaying the rainbow of nail polish covering her fingernails, not to mention large patches of skin.

"Do you like it? I maked myself pretty."

"Made. You made yourself look pretty. Maked isn't a word."

"Do you like it, Auntie?" Isabelle asks, blinking quickly.

"You're absolutely gorgeous. Don't change a thing." Covering her mouth with one hand, Dolores mutters, "She looks exactly like that clown from IT."

Oh, Christ, she's right.

Dolores pats Isabelle on the head. "Do you know what that outfit needs? A red balloon! Let me see if I can find one in my room. In my purse."

"Auntie, can you please just finish your cheese people platter?" I ask, rubbing the bridge of my nose. "We're running out of time, and I promised Amber we'd be early."

Turning back to Izzy, I lean down a little. "You look really lovely, sweetheart, but we need to take a bit of it off. Sonny didn't wear makeup, honey."

Isabelle's face falls. "She didn't?"

She? Oh, dear, I don't think Dolores explained who Sonny and Cher were. "No. He didn't. But you do get to wear a super fun moustache, so you'll have something on your face anyway."

Gingerly, I take her hand and start leading her up the stairs to begin the massive job of scrubbing her down, realizing I definitely will *not* have time to touch myself up a bit. It's fine, really. I don't need makeup. Now that I think about it, I'm pretty sure Jane Goodall doesn't wear any more makeup than Sonny Bono did. Less, in fact.

. . .

***

Forty-five minutes later, we're finally getting into my ancient Toyota Corolla that has been baking in the sun on the cement pad in front of our house. Isabelle, who is now sporting the light brown mushroom-cut wig and matching 'stache, sits buckled into her five-point harness, kicking her feet with my date, Mr. Bananas, buckled in beside her. After a lengthy scrubbing, she's gone from resembling Pennywise to a tiny creepy 1970s pedo. Not that I'm suggesting Sonny Bono was a pedo. I'm sure he was a wonderful guy. It's just Isabelle is having trouble pulling off his signature look.

I've managed to settle Dolores into the passenger seat in her long black wig with her cheese people platter on her lap. We're now running twenty minutes late, so instead of arriving calm, collected, and on time, I'm going to arrive late, frazzled, and frumpy—my normal state. This will lead to the inevitable, "Why didn't you make yourself up? You'll never catch a man looking like that" lecture from my mum as soon as she sees me. So obviously, I'm eagerly awaiting that moment…

Hurrying around to the driver side, I mutter, "Just get this over with so you can come home and study."

The car door groans loudly when I open it, and I do my silent please-don't-die prayer to the Corolla gods.

"Hey, Bree," Jerry says as the screen door slams behind him and he lights up a cigarette. "Where are you off to in such a hurry?"

"My sister's engagement party," I say, getting in.

Aunt Dolores, who can't stand Jerry and all his bass playing, scowls at him. "You should get a longer bathrobe, Jerry. You don't have the legs to pull off that shorty robe."

Jerry laughs and shakes his head, obviously believing she's flirting when really, she's dead serious.

I slam the door to the car and start up the engine. "That wasn't very nice."

"Well, it's not very nice of him to wear that stupid shorty robe. For God's sake, does that man have no sense of shame?"

"Yeah," Isabelle pipes up from the backseat. "For God's sake, he should get a long robe."

I cringe and give Aunt Dolores a sharp glare, then a matching one for Isabelle in the rearview mirror. "Watch your language, Isabelle."

"God's not a swear," Isabelle says.

"When you use it before the word sake it is," I say, as if that makes any sense at all.

Unrolling the windows, I let the hot breeze in so as to push out the stiflingly hot air in the car. First purchase when I'm a lawyer—a new car with air conditioning that works.

3

The Ghost of Christmas No Future

Leopold

I MUST SAY, that call from my mum has really lowered the fun factor this morning. I'm out here snorkelling in the warm Caribbean Sea, but I'm not enjoying it nearly as much as I should be. Her warning keeps popping into my mind. *Your father has sent someone. Do exactly what he says.*

Those haunting words have an unfamiliar feeling brewing in my gut. I'm guessing it's worry based on what I've heard from other people who experience it. And I don't know about you, but I don't like it one bit. It tags along, no matter how far I swim away from shore.

I know! Booze!

Booze will definitely help rid me of this feeling. Turning back toward shore, I flip quickly through the water until my knees scrape the sand below me. Then I stand and walk, lifting my knees high in the air while I hold my arms out wide to the side to help me balance.

Oh, shit. The visitor has arrived. Turns out it's Seth Hughes, my father's lawyer, and an unidentified woman. Seth, a short, bespectacled man in his sixties and my dad's favourite henchman, is wearing his usual barrister uniform—black suit, white shirt, plain blue tie, patent leather shoes. He looks completely out of place on the beach and is clearly uncomfortably hot based on his red cheeks.

His companion appears to be in her mid-fifties, is wearing a short-sleeved button-down shirt adorned with enormous flowers of various colours over a pair of khaki crop pants. Her hair is stuffed into a dark-blue ball cap, and she's got aviators on, making it difficult to gauge her mood.

Pasting a grin on my face, I tug off the mask and wave, calling, "Hi Seth! Welcome to Fantasy Island!"

He says nothing, leaving his poker face in place while I splash my way toward them. Even from here, I can feel the level of disgust for me he brings everywhere.

I smile at the woman. "I'm Leo. I was just about to make a pitcher of margaritas. Who's up for a little refreshment?"

Seth dabs at his forehead with a tissue. "This is not a social call, as I'm sure you've guessed."

"I did, but there's no reason we can't mix a little pleasure with our business, is there?" I wink at the woman, hoping the old Leopold charm will help lighten things up some. But nothing. She just continues to stare. Gesturing toward the woman with one hand, Seth says. "This is Ms. Jolene Fita. She's the private investigator who will be keeping an eye on you during your exile."

What now?

Right before my eyes, I can see all my lovely little loopholes closing up and disappearing. Before I can say anything, Seth holds up his briefcase. "We'll be in the kitchen. Join us as soon as you're dressed."

***

I sit at Pierce's dining table with Seth, Jolene, and Pierce, all of whom are sipping tea while I skim the contract in front of me. My head is spinning with words like "refrain from sexual contact, alcohol, recreational drugs" and "must find gainful employment and hold a paying position for a minimum of six months. Must not quit, get fired, or change jobs during that time."

As soon as I finish reading the three-page document, Seth sets his mug down. "Do you have any questions, Mr. Davenport?"

"A few, yes.' I nod quickly. "So, I'm meant to get a job—"

"And keep it."

"Find a home to rent and become completely self-sufficient... What exactly does that include?"

"Taking on all the responsibilities of a normal adult human being. Shopping for groceries, cooking, cleaning, laundry, arriving at work on time, staying for your entire shift, paying bills on time..." he answers with just a hint of a smirk. Damn him. He's enjoying this. "It's all laid out in Appendix C."

"Yes, I realize that. Can't I just—?"

"No. You may not live here with your brother."

"But how will I pay for my own house?"

"Your father will front you $500, but it will be given to Ms. Fita. When you find suitable accommodation, that will cover your deposit. You will have exactly six weeks to pay him back."

I glance at her. Still no smiles coming from her direction. She's taken her sunglasses off, and her cold, dark eyes are quite frankly a little terrifying. Looking back at Seth, I fold my arms. "So is she my new nanny or something? Because I am twenty-seven years old, you know."

Ms. Fita snorts. "I'm no nanny. I'm a retired parole officer who is being paid to follow your every move for the next six months."

"Ms. Fita comes highly recommended by the San Filipe chief of police. She's considered the best PI on the island."

"That's right. I am," she says. "And I have a large network of people who will report your every move to me. You won't even be able to pass gas without me knowing about it."

Giving her my winning smile, I say, "You'll find I'm not a gassy person."

Seriously? The winning smile doesn't even work on her? It reduces most women to fits of giggles. All right, new tactic. I blow out a long breath. "I am truly sorry for the trouble I've caused my father. There's no excuse for how I've behaved, and I very much want to make everything right." Holding up one hand, I add, "I solemnly swear to stay on the straight and narrow from now on. No more partying, loafing around, or poorly thought-through sexual relations with any members of any of the royal families. I'll figure out a career path and get right on it, I promise. So you see? No need for this legally binding contract or my very own parole officer—as lovely as I'm sure you are," I say, glancing at Ms. Fita. "*Really* not necessary. Not now that I am voluntarily giving up the shenanigans."

"Your father is in no mood to let you off the hook this time. You either agree to the terms and conditions and you sign the contract, or you will be permanently disinherited as set out by the terms in paragraph four on page two."

My stomach lurches. Permanent is a bloody long time. But if I sign this, I'll have no dignity left whatsoever. Talk about a Sophie's choice situation. A sense of indignant anger builds in my veins. "*Really*, I mean, whose father insists on putting these types of restrictions in place for *their own son*? Opening a bank account and providing monthly statements of all earnings and expenditures? Cooking *and* cleaning? One would be more than enough for me to learn my lesson, don't you think? Submitting to random drug and alcohol testing? It's not like I'm some sort of addict or con man. A little lazy and rather fond of women, yes, but I'm not a *criminal*."

Seth glances at his watch. "I'm due at the airport in exactly forty-two minutes, so you have thirty seconds to make your decision."

"Thirty seconds? No. This is insanity," I say, raising my voice. "I'm not signing that. You can go back home and tell him to return with a more reasonable offer."

"Twenty seconds."

"You can't expect me to make a decision like this in under a minute."

"Fifteen." Dammit. He's not kidding.

"Five."

Fuck.

I pick up the pen, sign, and hand him the agreement. He snags the pen out of my hand and puts the papers in his briefcase, then slides a copy of it to me. Snapping his briefcase shut with a loud click, Seth gives me a smug smile. "Good luck, Leopold. You're going to need it."

4

Tools Come in All Shapes and Sizes

Brianna

WE'RE EXACTLY twenty minutes late when we pull up in front of the Hammers house. Yes, their last name is Hammer, which I secretly find hilarious for many reasons, including but not limited to: A) they own a demolition company, and B) because Amber is changing her name and will forevermore be known as Amber Hammer, which sounds like a really strong cleaning product. Either that or a female wrestler in the WWE. But don't tell anyone I said that, because it would gut her.

I take Isabelle's hand and start up the long sidewalk, following the bright-yellow signs that inform guests to come directly to the back and let the party begin. "Make sure you say please and thank you, and if you don't like the food someone offers you, don't wrinkle up your nose and say yuck. Simply say thank you, but that's not my favourite."

"I already know all of that, Mummy," Isabelle says.

"I was talking to Auntie Dolores," I say, throwing a look over my shoulder and receiving a sharp glare in exchange.

The sound of a speech grows louder as we make our way toward the back gate that stands open. Dammit. The speeches have started. We are unforgivably late.

Another large sign greets us that says:

Come help us celebrate Mr. and Mrs. Fabulously Happy.

A snorting sound coming from behind me tells me Auntie Dolores has also noticed the sign. "That's a bit rich, don't you think?"

I stop and turn to her, shifting the present that is now growing heavy in my left arm. "Seriously. Behave or I'm not buying any bacon when I go to the market tomorrow."

Dolores narrows her eyes. "You wouldn't dare."

Dolores calls herself a bacoholic and brings a baggy of it wherever she goes, just in case she needs her bacofix. Honestly, she puts it on everything from pizza to desserts. Her latest creation is called the bacon weave apple pie.

Staring her down, I say, "I'm hot, I'm wearing a fake chimpanzee in place of a boyfriend, and I've had three hours of sleep. If you want to roll the dice, old lady, go for it."

Isabelle's eyes grow wide, and she makes a gasping sound. Tugging on my hand, she whispers, "You said we're not supposed to call her old."

Bollocks. She's got me there. A flash of guilt has me softening my expression. "Please, Auntie, for Amber. Can we please try to make a good impression?"

"I don't know why you care so much," Dolores sniffs. "It's not like she ever looks past the nose on her face to see what kind of a life you have."

"That's not true. And even if it were, it doesn't matter. She's my little sister, and she's getting married, so I'm going to do whatever I can to make this the best possible experience for her."

As we round the corner of the house into the enormous back garden, I'm greeted by a sight that makes all my muscles tense up. Suddenly, the whole Sonny and Cher thing becomes completely clear. *"It will be hilarious, just go with it, Bree. People will die when they see Izzy dressed as Sonny Bono."*

There, standing at the front of the crowd next to Dane's parents, who are dressed as Fred and Wilma Flintstone, are none other than Sonny and Cher themselves—or as I like to call them, Mum and Dad.

They're both smiling at Dane's dad, Trenton Hammer, who is going on about how they're gaining a daughter.

I purse my lips together and blow a long, frustrated sigh out of my nose, watching as Dolores makes her way over to the buffet table to set down her cheese people. Isabelle lets go of my hand and races to catch up with her, no doubt hoping to sneak some of the sweets off the table before I can get there.

"She really is the perfect Juliet to our little Romeo," Trenton says, holding up a glass of champagne. The sight of Dolores and Isabelle catches his eye, and he fumbles for words for a moment as he glances back and forth between them and my parents. Amber, who is standing arm in arm with Dane, takes note of the second set of matching pop stars, her smile transforming into shock.

Dane's too busy chugging his beer to notice his fiancée is upset. A six-foot-six, hulking specimen, Dane loves two things: smashing things and beer. He's basically a younger version of his dad, who owns the only demolition company on the island. According to Dane, there is absolutely no better feeling than hitting a wall with a sledgehammer, and from the looks of this swanky property, I'm guessing there's some money in it as well. It's got that we-made-it-big-and-we-want-every-one-to-know air about it with the carefully manicured yard filled with randomly placed fountains and Grecian—mostly nude—statues scattered about in the oddest of places. On the far side, there's a large swimming pool and a tiki bar—obviously—with twinkle lights and a giant bust of Elvis Presley wearing a pink and white lei sitting on the bar top. There's so much going on that it takes me a minute to realize several large shrubs have been trained to resemble women in various sexy poses, which is both off-putting and wildly funny. I chew on the inside of my cheek to stifle the laugh that is threatening to come out. The overall effect is quite jarring, really. It's a mashup of gaudy and erotic garden art that begs the visitor to post photos solely to shock their friends.

I stay toward the back, next to a stone statue of a unicorn, not wanting to attract unwanted attention to myself and Mr. Bananas. Dane's mum, Sharon, tugs on her husband's shoulder and whispers something in his ear. Then, much to my horror, she points at me, and his eyes follow her finger until they land on yours truly.

"Oh, she made it, folks! Amber's big sister is here. Come on up here, dear. I'm sure you have a few words for the happy couple."

No. No, I don't. I shake my head and half-whisper, half call, "That's okay, no. I don't want to interrupt."

"Don't be silly," Dane's mum says, gesturing wildly for me to join them.

Oh bugger. I make my way toward them, my feet as heavy as the nudie statues I'm weaving through as the humiliation of this moment sets in.

"Who are you dressed as, dear?" Sharon asks.

"Jane Goodall," I mutter. Turning, I face the small crowd and chuckle awkwardly. "This is Mr. Bananas. He's my plus-one this afternoon."

Amber lets out a loud, phony laugh. "Brianna's such a kidder. Wait till you all get to know her. She is honestly the funniest. Go on. Say something funny."

Dance, puppet, dance. "Well, I haven't exactly been working on my comedy routine lately, so…I don't really have anything prepared."

I glance at Amber's three besties, Kandi, Valerie, and Quinn, all of who have a disdain for me that I happily return. Their faces are scrunched up in disgust as they hang off their boyfriends' arms. Quinn and her date are Cleopatra and Mark Antony. Valerie and her plus-one have gone all classy as Meghan Markle and Prince Harry, while Kandi and her boyfriend, Jared, have opted for the even classier Hugh Hefner with a Playboy Bunny. Not really what I would call a famous couple, but since I'm wearing my date, I probably shouldn't talk.

Off to the side, I hear one of the guests ask, "Is she really a comedian? She doesn't look funny."

My mum, who is aghast at the thought, cuts in. "No, she's just single."

Well, that explains it then, don't you think? Clearing my throat, I say, "Anyway, thank you so much for hosting this super-fun barbecue. I look forward to getting to know you all as we help Dane and Amber unite in holy matrimony." I give a confident nod and smile, hoping that's enough. Apparently, it is, because there's a smattering of polite applause.

Dane's dad nods. "Yes, well, thanks for that, Bridget. Now, everyone please head over to the buffet and help yourselves to some lunch."

Sharon tugs at his arm. "Brianna, not Bridget."

"Right. Sorry, Brianna. I'm afraid I've already had a couple of mojitos."

As soon as the guests start for the buffet table, my mum and dad, Dane's parents, and the guests of honour all zero in on me.

Sharon holds her hands out to me. "Brianna, so lovely to finally meet you. Amber absolutely adores you."

I should hope so. I take Sharon's hand and shake it. "Likewise. Amber is always going on about how lucky she is to have a future mother-in-law as wonderful as you, Mrs. Hammer." That's a lie, by the way. Amber can't stand her because she's unnaturally attached to her son and tries to hold his hand all the time.

"Call me Sharon. When you say Mrs. Hammer, I turn around and look for my dead mother-in-law."

"Ack. We wouldn't want her showing up, now would we?" I say jokingly.

Sharon's face falls, and she gives me a confused expression. "Why not? She was a wonderful woman."

"I only meant it would be sort of strange if she appeared since you said she was…umm…not alive anymore." My voice trails off, and I glance at Amber, hoping she'll save me.

Unfortunately, Amber is far too busy listening to my mum, who is hissing in her ear and pointing to Auntie Dolores and Isabelle. Mum sets her sights on me. "Did you know about this?"

Ha! For once something isn't my fault. "About the matching costumes?" I shake my head. "I had no idea."

"That's because you don't bother to keep in touch."

Oh, there we go. She found a way to make it my fault after all. My mum takes one hand and swipes her long black wig back with a flick of her head, very much resembling a pissed-off Cher.

"Yes, well, I'm not sure if you noticed, but I'm a little busy working full time, finishing law school, and raising a child," I say quietly.

But apparently I'm not quiet enough, because Trenton chimes in with, "Looks like we've figured out who the black sheep of the family is right off the bat." He chuckles smugly, slapping Dane on the stomach. The two of them laugh eerily in time with one another before holding their drinks up at the exact same time and gulping them back.

My mum, Amber, and Sharon also laugh while standing among them wearing phony smiles. Aunt Dolores decides this is the perfect time to appear with her cheese-people platter. "Amber, Dane, recognize these two?" she asks, beaming at them in a rather creepy way.

Dane shakes his head and narrows his eyes. "No, I can't say I recognize them. Can you give us a hint?"

"It's us, Dane," Amber says flatly. "Do you see this one has a veil on?"

"Yep!" Aunt Dolores says. "I used Velveeta for your faces because the two of you—"

I cut her off before she can insult their matching spray tans. "Auntie, why don't you go put that on the buffet table. The guests are dishing up right now, and I'd hate for them to miss out on your cheese people."

Aunt Dolores seems satisfied with this and starts toward the buffet table, leaving me with one very short Sonny Bono to my left and a much taller one to my right.

Trenton peers down at Isabelle. "And this must be Amber's nephew that we've heard so much about."

Nephew? Clearly Trenton is as dialed in as his son. "This is my...Isabelle."

Sharon smacks her husband on the forearm. "You really have had enough mojitos. It's a *girl*." She crouches down and speaks to Izzy in a loud, sing-songy voice. "Hi Isabelle, it's very nice to meet you."

Isabelle, who is used to people treating her like a real human being, wrinkles up her nose a tiny bit, then, perfectly imitating Sharon, says, "It's nice to meet you, too."

My mum, clearly sensing danger in the realm of some sort of

embarrassing exchange, takes Isabelle by the hand. "Are you hungry, sweetie?"

"I could eat. But I don't want any of those cheese people that Auntie Dolores made," she says, cupping her hands to her mouth and whispering, "She said the glue is *poison*."

Mum's voice grows urgent. "Why don't you go with your grandfather and get some lunch?"

My dad winks at Isabelle. "Don't have to tell me twice. Us twin Sonny Bonos are starving, aren't we?"

"You're bloody well right we are," Izzy says as her bell-bottoms sway in time with her steps.

Sadly, preschoolers lack the ability to control their voice volume, so her proper use of the phrase bloody well doesn't go unnoticed by anyone within fifty feet. Swallowing hard, I say, "She heard that on the TV. I'm going to sell it...just sell the whole thing and get her reading instead."

My mum does that little thing she does when she's embarrassed, raising and lowering her eyebrows while she stares at the ground and purses her lips.

Lucky for me, Sharon comes to the rescue. "They all test out cursing at some point or another. Usually later... But never mind that. There's someone I'd love to introduce you to. Our nephew, Evander." She gives me a nudge and a wink. Literally. "He's single, too, and is one of the groomsmen."

My mother's eyes light up, and she gives me the once over, suddenly looking panicked. Clutching Amber's arm, Mum whispers, "Do you have some makeup here?"

"Of course I do."

I shake my head. "No, I don't—"

She ignores me and turns to Sharon. "Wait here. I'll take her inside and get her done up."

"No, thank you. I wouldn't want to upset Mr. Bananas," I say patting the stuffed monkey's head. "You really should leave with the same date you came to a party with."

Amber snickers. "You're so funny, Bree. But seriously, you should meet Evander. He's a nice guy."

I give her a tight-lipped smile. "I'm really not in the market for love at the moment." Glancing at Sharon, I add, "No offense to your nephew or anything. I'm sure he's an amazing person. I'm just so swamped right now, studying for the bar exam and, you know, raising Isabelle."

Sharon's face falls. "Why don't you at least wait till you meet him before you say no."

I open my mouth, but my mum tugs on my arm. "Amber, I'll take Bree inside. You need to stay out here with your guests."

Amber gives me an apologetic look. "I have a makeup kit in my purse, which is in Dane's room."

Traitor.

***

Five minutes later, I find myself in Zidane's delightfully air-conditioned childhood bedroom along with my mother. I'm sitting on his bed, facing a full-length mirror that hangs on the wall next to it. What kind of boy has a full-length mirror? I can picture him as a shirtless fifteen-year-old flexing his muscles and kissing his guns. Yick.

Now that we're alone, my mum is going to talk some sense into me. "I cannot for the life of me figure out why you would insist upon making yourself look so plain. Honestly, it only takes fifteen minutes to blow out your hair and put on some makeup." She digs around in Amber's makeup kit and pulls out an eyeliner.

When she comes at me with it, I snag it from her before she can go to work. "Thanks, I got this. Although I don't really see how it matters. Today is all about Amber, not me."

"What kind of impression are you going to make on the Hammers? They'll think you're some kind of *feminist* showing up here like that." She says the word feminist as though it's the other F word.

"Well, Mum, since I do believe women should have equal rights to men, I guess I am a feminist. Also, like I said outside, I'm too busy for dating."

She opens her mouth and then snaps it shut. Ah, silence.

I put the lightest dusting of taupe eyeshadow possible on my top lids while she watches. I can tell she wants to offer some sort of critique, but thankfully for both of us, she refrains. When she speaks again, my mum goes for the we're-just-girlfriends-having-a-chat approach. "Love's not something you can plan, Brianna. But if you're open to it, you never know what could happen."

"Sure I do. I could end up with two children." I snap the eyeshadow case shut.

My mum grabs it from me and hands me the most terrifying of all makeup devices—an eyelash curler. I take it from her and turn back to the mirror.

"I don't want you to end up old, broke, and alone like Dolores."

"Auntie Dolores isn't alone. She's got Isabelle and me. And I'm certainly not going to be broke, because I'm good with my money, and in case you haven't heard, barristers tend to do pretty well financially."

"Oh, fine, I suppose you know everything, and I know nothing because I haven't gone to law school."

Oh, great, she's going into full-guilt mode. "That's not what I said *at all*. I just don't want to be forced on some stranger because he's the only other single person in the wedding party. Is that so unreasonable?"

"No, but you didn't have to insult Sharon by turning down her nephew without even seeing him. He sounds like a real catch. He's the only one in the family to have gone to university, and now he works as a financial advisor. He's done really well for himself. He drives an *Audi*." She says this like it's a huge selling point.

"An Audi? Why didn't you say so before?"

Mum hands me the bronzer case and a huge fluffy brush. "No need to be sarcastic. I just want to see you happily married for your sake, as well as for Isabelle's. It's not healthy for her to be an only child living with a seventy-one-year-old foul-mouthed crazy person and her man-hating mother."

"I don't hate men. I just don't trust them. It's completely different."

"Well, the end result is the same. You're robbing Isabelle of having a *real* family."

"That is *not* fair," I say, tossing the bronzer back in the bag without using it. "I'm doing *everything* I can to give her the best life possible. So it's a little unconventional? She's happy, she's loved, and she's going to have every opportunity."

"Knock, knock. I hope I'm not interrupting," Amber's best friend, Kandi, says, bursting into the room. Kandi has huge brunette hair that matches her personality. She and Amber have been best friends since grade three, and people call them the tiny twins because they're both so cute and skinny. In fact, most people mistake Kandi for Amber's sister instead of me.

"Hi, sweetie," my mum says, standing to hug her *'other* daughter' as she calls her.

"Hi, Second Mum," she says. "You are *gorgeous.* Cher wishes she looks as good as you. Seriously, you and Mr. Lewis are an *epic* Sonny and Cher."

"Oh, you," my mum says, waving off the comment in spite of the broad smile on her face. "You look beautiful. Cute bunny ears."

"Thanks. It was Patrick's idea," she says, pretending to be annoyed to be wearing her ultra-sexy costume. She turns to me. "Bree, I was hoping we could chat about Amber's hen's party without her overhearing."

Crap. I totally forgot about throwing her a hen's party. How much is that going to cost me? "Oh, sure."

"Now, as the maid of honour, I know it's usually your place to plan it," she says, planting one hand on her hip. "But I thought maybe you'd be okay with letting me take the lead since you're so busy with school and Izzy."

"Thank you. That is *so thoughtful* of you, Kandi." It's not really. She just doesn't trust me to come up with something *epic* enough because all of Amber's friends think I'm a stick in the mud. Which I am, but there are worse things a girl could be. She could be eye Kandi.

"No probs. You've got a lot on your plate, and Amber deserves an *epic* weekend away."

See? I told you.

Kandi gives me a big smile. "Cool. Okay, I'll start a group text of all the bridesmaids so we can sort out the deets."

"Awesomesauce," I say, hoping I sound enthusiastic instead of sarcastic.

Her smile falters for a second, then she says, "I better go find Patrick before he makes some other bunny next month's centerfold."

She spins in her four-inch stilettos and walks off, her fluffy little tail wagging behind her.

***

The sound of Calypso music assaults me as soon as I walk out the sliding door from the kitchen to the back garden. I scan the yard for Isabelle and see she's with Dolores. They're mugging for the camera as the photographer snaps some shots of them over by a naked-lady waterfall statue.

"Here she is now," Sharon calls from across the yard. "Brianna, come and meet Evander."

The pair walk toward me with Sharon practically dragging her nephew, who seems about as enthusiastic to meet me as I am to meet him. He's tall, thin, surprisingly handsome, and is dressed as Sherlock Holmes, complete with the pipe and deerstalker hat. Huh, maybe this won't be so bad after all.

"Evander, Brianna's the one I was telling you about. The miniature Sonny Bono is her little girl." Turning to me, Sharon beams. "Evander doesn't even mind that you have a daughter."

So that's nice...

Her smile falters a little. "Anyway, I thought you two would have a lot in common since you're both studious types, unlike my Dane." She laughs a little and glances back and forth between us. "Okay, well, you two get to know each other. I need to go check on the other guests."

"Hi," I say, feeling super awkward. "Nice to meet you, Mr. Holmes."

He nods, looking uncomfortable as he sips some of the boozy punch through a swirly straw. "Are you Jane Goodall, then?"

"Yes, I am."

"Jane Goodall never wore makeup."

"Tell that to my mother," I say with a little chuckle.

Apparently, he doesn't get the joke, because he frowns a little as he looks me up and down. "She's also very thin."

Okay, we're done here. "Yes. Yes, she is..."

***

Amber's Bitches Group Text

KANDI: Hey, ladies! SO fun today at the bbq, no? Dane's rents know how to throw a party. Anyone else still buzzed from the punch?

QUINN: Me!

VALERIE: Totes!

KANDI: I'm already hungover. LOL

Me: I had to drive home, so I didn't have any.

KANDI: Okay, so I have the most epic plan for the big hen's party! Two words: Las and Vegas!!!!

VALERIE: EEEEEKKKK!!!! YES TIMES A ZILLION!!!

QUINN: What happens in Vegas, stays in Vegas, baby!!! When do we leave?

Me: Sorry to be a Debbie Downer here but Vegas sounds like it'll be out of my budget. I could probably get us an ocean view suite at the resort for a weekend? We could do some spa treatments, relax on the beach, eat at the a la carte restaurants. Anyone up for that?

KANDI (after a twenty-minute pause, which I'm sure was spent with the rest of the bitches texting back and forth privately): *Bree, Paradise Bay is super nice, and it's really generous of you to offer, but we could all use a weekend away from the island—you especially. #singlemomlife #wegotyour-backsister*

VALERIE: Agreed. You don't want to have a party weekend where you work. That would be cray!

QUINN: Totes! Bree, you deserve an amazing fun party. Let yourself go for once! Plus, we've all been to the resort for so many functions already. We should go somewhere new. If Vegas is too expensive for you, maybe we could hop over to Isla del Sol for a couple of days.

KANDI: Great idea, QUINN! Patrick's uncle has a gorgeous villa there right off Coco Beach, so we won't have to drive to get to the bars. It's a total party shack. Hot tub, eight bedrooms. AMAZING. I'll see if we can get it.

VALERIE: Perfect! Done!

QUINN: Is that okay with you, Bree?

ME (After ten minutes of staring angrily at my phone)*: Sounds lovely. Thanks so much, Kandi.*

Brenemies (You know, Brothers Who are Also Enemies...)

Leopold

It's late in the evening, and Emma has finally returned from the restaurant. I'm particularly glad she's here, not only because there's a distinct possibility that she may be able to help me find work, but because I genuinely like Emma. She has an adventurous spirit and is the perfect foil to my very serious, sceptical brother. She brings out something in him that I've never seen before. Empathy.

At the moment, she's stretched out on one side of the long sectional in their living room while he rubs her feet. It's quite something to see my brother like this—in love, that is.

A bottle of wine is open on the coffee table, and Emma sips at the glass Pierce poured for her while she reads over my contract. Emma will know what to do. And she won't find this the least bit funny, unlike my brother, who hasn't stopped snickering since Seth and my parole officer left this afternoon.

Jolene is a real peach, and I mean that in the most sarcastic way possible. I have to hand it to Seth though, he managed to find the one woman in the Benavente Islands who cannot be charmed by a man.

My first attempt to do so was quickly thwarted by her raising her left hand and saying, "I'm going to stop you right there. Your little Prince Charming routine won't work on me. You're not my type."

"Not into younger men?"

"Not into men, period."

Turns out she's happily married to a kindergarten teacher, so when I tried to switch gears, I found out she has absolutely no desire to go pick up women with me.

Emma finishes reading the document, flips the pages back into place, and hands it to me. She gives me a long, sympathetic look. "I'm so sorry, Leo. This must really hurt."

"It does, thank you, Emma. It's nice to know someone cares," I say, glaring at my brother.

"What?" Pierce asks. "Can I help it if I find this hilarious? To be honest, I can't wait to take some video of you working to send to all your friends."

Oh my God, I hadn't considered the humiliation if my friends find out about my little situation. Most of them are truly awful people. They will never let me live it down. My stomach drops at the thought of it. "You wouldn't."

"Oh, but I would," he says, letting go of Emma's foot long enough to pick up his wineglass and have a sip.

"You're such a douche-canoe. I don't know why I came here."

"Because I let you stay, and unlike our other brother, I'm not a total arsehole who lives with a complete witch."

"Aww, thanks, baby," Emma says facetiously.

"Anything for my lady." Pierce makes a kissing motion at her, and I can't help but chuckle at their exchange. Turning back to me, he adds, "But not anything for you, you lazy bellend."

"Try to be sensitive, Pierce," Emma says. "Your father has *literally* hired a parole officer to keep watch over your brother. Their relationship is obviously severely damaged."

"Oh, please," Pierce scoffs. "His relationship with father is no worse than the rest of ours, and look how well I turned out. Besides, it's the perfect opportunity for him to find some direction in life."

"Stay out of it, Pierce. I'm trying to have a conversation with

Emma here," I say, staring longingly at the bottle of wine I'm not allowed to touch for fear that my parole officer will jump out from behind the potted palm in the corner with a tiny plastic cup. "Pierce seems to think there's no way out of this other than to live up to the terms, but there must be some loophole. Anything come to mind for you?"

Emma shakes her head apologetically. "I think he's got you. The resort does have a lawyer if you want to run it by her, but she's pretty expensive."

I'm about to ask Pierce if he could front me some money, but apparently he's on to me, because he shakes his head. "Not a chance."

Bugger. I really may have to get a job. I stare down at the dreaded contract that I must've read over a dozen times by now. "In that case, I guess I have no choice." I pull my mobile phone out of my pocket. "Okay, Google, how does one find a job?"

Emma and Pierce exchange a glance, then she says, "Perhaps I can help you. The contract doesn't say anything about not working for someone you know. I'm sure I can find some sort of position for you at the resort."

"Really?" I ask, feeling a hint of relief for the first time today.

"Sure. What kind of work experience do you have?"

Pierce cuts in with, "I made him clean up after himself once in a while when he lived with me."

"The wax-finger figurines?" I ask.

He nods.

"Oh, Christ, cleaning was awful. That sucking machine was horribly loud. I don't want to spend six months doing that."

"Okay," Emma says. "What else have you done?"

Tapping my index finger on my bottom lip for a moment, I rack my brain for anything I've done that would qualify as work experience. "Does maintaining excellent personal hygiene translate into anything useful in a resort setting?"

"Not…not really," she says, attempting to hide a troubled expression. "That's all right. We do on-the-job training so it should be fine. What would you say your biggest assets are?" Emma asks.

"As an employee, Leo," Pierce says in a warning tone. And it's probably a good thing, too, because I *was* about to say something inappropriate.

"Well, unlike my brother, I'm a people person. I'd say I am very fun most of the time, and I know how to show other people a good time. Are there any jobs like that? Perhaps director of entertainment or some such?"

"Uh, no, but friendliness is definitely important in the hospitality industry."

Suddenly an idea hits me—a terrific idea. I snap my fingers. "I could be a bartender. Pierce and I learned to mix cocktails for our alcoholic nanny when we were small. I'm actually quite good at it." Oh, yes, I can see it now—me behind the open-air bar shaking a martini while I flirt with lovely guests and bring in all those sweet tips. I wouldn't even mind if my friends found out I was an ultra-cool mixologist taking a new woman home to my bachelor pad each night.

Crap on a stick, I can't. I've agreed to the no-women clause. Bugger, that would have been terrific fun.

Emma nods apologetically. "Yeah, bartending is pretty much the job everyone wants, so it usually takes at least eight years to move into that position."

Eight years? To work your way up to being a *bartender*? "Really? So people work that long?"

Pierce's nose wrinkles up in disgust. "Yes, Leo. Most people work for the better part of their entire adult lives."

Might as well wind Pierce up a bit while I'm at it. "I think you should check your facts, old boy. That sounds very wrong."

"Anyway, not to worry, Leo," Emma says. "I'm sure we'll find you something. First thing tomorrow, I'll call Libby and see if she has anything open."

Excellent. Libby's her brother's wife and we get along famously. She'll definitely find a spot for me. "Thank you, Emma. I really appreciate it, and I won't let you down."

"You better not, or you'll be answering to me, you little wanker," Pierce says.

"Oh, like that's so terrifying coming from a man who was taken down by a gecko."

"It was a giant Komodo dragon, thank you very much."

Emma cups her hand over her mouth and whispers, "Medium-size iguana."

"I heard that."

6

Mum of the Year Nominations and No-no Words

Brianna

OKAY, so let me bring you up to speed on my terrible day (which won't end for another nine hours). Izzy ate too many sweets at the barbeque and threw up all over the backseat of my car, not to mention on her faux-fur vest, her moustache, and eventually in her wig in her attempt to 'keep it all in one place.' So instead of studying, I spent the better part of my afternoon cleaning vomit out of the upholstery and carpet of my Corolla in the blistering heat of the late afternoon sun, which, if you've never done it, is quite the fun time, and not disgusting enough to make you gag repeatedly *at all*. At least I had Jerry to keep me company while I cleaned. He smoked weed and pointed out when I missed a spot.

After my two-minute get-the-puke-off shower, I opened a can of chicken noodle soup for dinner. While it was heating up, I tried to log on to the school's law library, only to find I've been barred access because I have overdue fees I didn't know about. This led me to a frantic sorting of my unopened mail, which proved fruitless. What did help, however, was going through Isabelle's play desk where she pretends to be a law student like Mummy. Adorable on so many levels but seriously problematic because, as it turns out, she's been opening all the mail with the symbol from the university on the envelope, changing the name at the top to hers, then filing them in her to-do folder.

After I found them, I scolded Isabelle—gently, since she was still lying on the couch looking rather pale—and discovered I'm behind on the library access fee of $250, and that the rates for resitting the bar exams have been raised by $100 each, which is already due. By this time, the soup had boiled over and made a huge mess on the stove.

Fast forward to me pulling into a parking stall at the resort and sprinting to the lobby in my heels, an absolutely unacceptable fifteen minutes late for my shift.

"I'm so sorry I'm late!" I say as I rush across the busy open-air lobby to the concierge desk where Toni is waiting. She's the head concierge I'm replacing tonight.

She gives me a sympathetic smile. "Everything okay?"

Toni is a total godsend. She and I have been working together long enough that she knows I'm not one to slack off or show up late without a bloody good reason. "Isabelle got sick. She overdid it on the sweets at the engagement party from hell and vomited all over the backseat of my car. Then I ruined dinner because I got distracted by some bad financial news, so I ended up making peanut butter and jelly sandwiches and eating mine on the way here."

"Whoa, that doesn't sound good. Anything I can do to help?" Toni's five years older than me and gets by nicely on our salary because she and her boyfriend—also named Tony—are DINKs. I'm not being rude. It stands for Double Income No Kids. Instead of children, they're plant parents, which honestly sounds delightfully stress-free.

"No, thanks though. I'll sort it out. I just have to be creative," I say, noticing that pain in my gut that reappears when I think of my bank account. "Did Rosy notice I'm late?"

Rosy is pretty much the mama bear of the resort. She's been here for about a hundred years, and she's tough as nails when it comes to the staff, but a total marshmallow when it comes to children. Whenever I bring Isabelle in, she melts and dotes on her the entire time.

"She did, but I told her you were already here, and that you had gone to deliver a package to one of the rooms in building E." Building E is the farthest from the lobby.

I let my shoulders drop with relief. "Thanks, Toni. You're the best."

"I know you'd do it for me, sweetie," she answers, unlocking the cabinet under our wooden desk and getting her purse out.

"Yes, I would. Has it been busy today?" I'm badly in need of a quiet night so I can figure out where the hell I'm going to come up with the money I apparently needed last week in order to get back in good standing with the university. I'd also love to crack open my Probate and Succession textbook. Well, perhaps love isn't the best word. Must is more accurate.

"Not horrible, but we did have an RHM couple check into to A-355, so I'd expect to hear from them a few times before the night is over."

"Brilliant," I say, completely devoid of enthusiasm. RHM is our code for the worst kind of guest. They are both rude and high maintenance. They typically start out their stay by scouring the room to find deficiencies so they can demand a free upgrade. Then, once they get the upgrade, they whine about how long it took the bellboy to get there to move their luggage, and that the upgraded room has something wrong with it too, and don't we have anything better because this isn't at all what they've come to expect from a five-star all-inclusive resort? I will *not* miss dealing with them when I finally quit.

"All right, I'll leave you to it, Bree. Good luck tonight."

"Thanks."

I lock my purse in the cabinet and take a second to straighten myself up, preparing for the night ahead.

"Bree, there you are," Rosy's voice rises above the sounds of the whirring fans and the chatter of the guests.

I smile at her as she crosses the floor, but she doesn't smile back. She gives me *the look*, which says she knows damn well I was not delivering a package just now. She raises one eyebrow. "How'd the package delivery go?"

"So quick it was almost like it didn't happen," I answer, guilt written all over my face.

"Thought so," she says with a hint of a reluctant grin. "Just get here on time from now on. You're my best concierge, and I don't want to have to write you up."

"Thanks, it won't happen again." I hope.

"It better not. Things are going to get a little hectic around here. The IT department is finally rolling out that new computer system tomorrow, so I need you to be ready. You'll have to find time to do the tutorial during your shift, and maybe during your lunch break. It took most of the staff about three hours to complete."

Terrific. Instead of studying probate, I'm going to be studying a new computer system that won't help Future Bree in the least. "I'll get right on it."

She hands me a piece of paper with my username and login ID. "Oh, and Jeremy called to say that he can't make it in again, so I fired him. The concierge desk is going to have to pick up the slack until I find someone to replace him."

Perfect. Bellboy duties are the worst. I give her a bright grin. "Absolutely."

"How are your studies coming?"

"Couldn't be better," I say with a confident nod.

"Good for you. I honestly don't know how you manage it all, girl."

Me, either.

***

It's almost eleven p.m., and I can barely keep my eyes open. I have finally finished the tutorial on what may be the least user-friendly hotel management system someone could dream up. We're all going to be given swipe cards that have to be used pretty much every time we do *anything* on our computers, so every decision we make or website we visit can be monitored. Based on the track record of Kevin, our IT guy, I'd give it about a 10% chance that this roll-out will actually work, and a 90% chance that we end up with absolutely no computers from launch date until high season ends.

But at least it's quiet for now. We're down to a skeleton crew—Mario and Todd, the security guys, and Donalda and Onika at the reception desk. The breeze is cool this evening, and the pair of troupials nested on one of the cross braces of the sloped thatched roof have gone to sleep.

I log onto my bank account and open my Google Doc budget spreadsheet to see where I can possibly squeak out the money to at least pay my library access fee. Sadly, a large influx of cash hasn't appeared in my account since I last looked, meaning I'll have twelve dollars to play with until my next cheque comes, and that's without even taking into account the wedding expenses. I sign out of my bank account, trying to dislodge the lump in my throat. *Do not cry, Bree. Don't even think about it. This is a temporary problem, and you are smart enough to come up with a solution.*

I'm going to channel my inner Scarlett O'Hara and save this for tomorrow, because after all, tomorrow is another day. Not that Scarlett O'Hara is my role model or something, because she's obviously a deeply flawed character. But she *is* tenacious, which I'm going to need to be to survive the next few months. I'll finish my shift, get a good night's sleep, and find the answer first thing tomorrow morning.

***

The Next Morning

"Shit," I mutter, glad that Izzy's not up yet so I don't have to dial back my language to child-safe swears like shitake mushrooms or fudge doodles. I should be catching up on my sleep, too, but I woke at five, worried about…oh, a million things…money being the biggest problem at the moment. I've just finished a budget for Amber's wedding that has led me to the inescapable conclusion that I'm totally screwed.

. . .

SAVINGS: $720
   NET MONTHLY EARNINGS: $2, 500
   MONTHLY EXPENSES:
   Natural Gas: $126
   Food: $750
   Insurance (Vehicle/home): $124
   Gas for Car: $50
   Electricity: $189
   Rent: $1500
   Saving for Isabelle's Education: $100
   TV/Internet: $100
   Mobile Phone: $85
   VISA Minimum Payment: $100 (Total Owing $5000 –
MAXED!!)
   TOTAL: $3024
   Left at E.O.M. $ 196

UPCOMING EXPENSES:
   Bar Exam Fees: $800 (Due next month)
   Law Library Fees: $250 (overdue)
   Oil Change/Repair Oil Leak on Car: Quoted $650

ESTIMATED WEDDING EXPENSES:
   Dress: $300
   Shoes: $100
   Hair/Makeup: $150
   Bridal Shower Gift: $100
   Engagement Gift: $75
   Hen's Weekend: $1000
   Flower Girl Dress: $100
   Shoes for Izzy: $25
   Izzy's Hair: Free. Do it myself
   Wedding gift: $200
   TOTAL: $3750

. . .

Getting up from the table, I pour myself a second cup of coffee and stare out the window into the small back garden while I brainstorm easy ways to come up with a few grand in cash in the next few weeks. The stairs creak, and when I turn, I see Aunt Dolores looking every bit the crazy cat lady in her ratty bathrobe that I'm pretty sure is from the Cold War era. Her hair is in pink sponge rollers, and Milo, Puddy Tat, and Knickers are snaking their way through her feet at she patters her way to the fridge in search of her morning bacon fix.

"Morning. How's my favourite niece?"

"Meh. How are you?" I ask, having another sip of coffee.

"I slept funny, now my elbow hurts," she says, opening the fridge door and taking out a bag of bacon. She opens it, takes out one slice, and nibbles on it. "Getting old isn't as fun as they pretend it is on Viagra commercials."

"I bet," I answer, sitting down in front of my laptop and googling "quick easy ways to make money on the side."

I open the first page that pops up, hoping to find the answer to my problems.

"What's a side hustle?" Dolores asks, peering over my shoulder at the screen. "Is that some sort of new dance move?"

"No, it means getting a second job on the side. Like tutoring or babysitting," I say distractedly.

She stands right behind me chewing bacon in my ear while Puddy hops up on the table and lifts one paw up toward her, which is Persian for, "Give me some bacon before I claw your eyes out." Dolores does what she's told, breaking off a tiny piece for each of her furry companions. "Well, you don't have time for a side hustle. In case you haven't noticed, you're too busy to sleep, so I don't know how you'd manage dog walking. And there's no way I want you to turn this place into a daycare. As much as I love Izzy, she makes as much noise as I can handle."

"Yeah, agreed," I say, scrolling down, passing by the rent-a-room bit since I'm already on the couch and would prefer not to sleep on the floor, thank you very much. "Huh, find things to sell that you don't use." I smile up at Dolores, who totally misreads my intention.

"I don't think you'd get much for me. I've got more wrinkles than one of those wrinkly Chinese dogs."

"A Shar-Pei?"

"Yeah, that's the one."

I roll my eyes. "Glad we cleared that up, but I didn't mean you. I meant things like Izzy's baby stuff. I wonder if there are other things out in the shed that we could make some money on." I snap my fingers, "I could sell my bike. When's the last time I rode my bike?"

"You have a bike?" she asks, licking bacon grease off her top lip.

"Exactly."

***

An hour later, I've fed Isabelle some breakfast, and I found the key to the shed that Dolores insisted was not on her keychain but in a box somewhere in her closet for safekeeping. Guess where we found it after emptying every box in her closet? Yup, her keychain in her purse. By the time I get out into the yard, the morning sun has grown hot. I unlock the shed while Isabelle, who is excited to see what treasures await us, hops up and down next to me.

The hinges groan loudly as I open the door, allowing a cloud of dust to float out toward us. I stare into the dark, muggy space, filled with apprehension at the possibility of what could be living in there.

"Come on, Mum! Let's go," Izzy says, tugging my hand impatiently.

"You go first." Oh, yes, Mum of the Year is sending her four-year-old into the scary shed ahead of her.

Izzy tips her head back and stares at me, "Not by my own self. It's dark in there."

"Yes. Yes, it is." I prop the door open with a brick, take a deep breath, and step inside the dingy little building. It's so packed there's barely enough room for me to stand inside, let alone Izzy, who sneaks around from behind me so she can examine the piles of boxes, old furniture, and other odds and ends that have been crammed in over the years. Isabelle's crib, which has been taken apart and wrapped in a blanket, sits to my left, along with the jolly jumper and high chair my parents bought her.

"Was that mine?" she asks.

"Umm-hmm," I say, picking up the jolly jumper and carrying it out into the bright sunlight. Setting it down, I say, "That's one thing out. About a thousand more to go…"

By the time the shed is almost empty, Isabelle is riding around the patio on her tricycle pretending she's in a parade. She waves to the stuffed animals and dolls she's brought outside to watch the festivities. Mr. Bananas sits in the dusty plastic high chair looking pleased even though things didn't work out between us. My arms are tired and my back aches, but I have three big-ticket items to sell—my mountain bike, the crib, and an armchair that I'm pretty sure I can advertise as vintage once it's been thoroughly vacuumed and the wood accents polished. It belongs to Dolores though, so that money will go to her.

She comes out with a tray of waters and a plate of cookies with little bits of bacon sprinkled on top. "Snack time!"

I wipe my forehead with my arm, take a glass of water from her, and drink it down in long gulps. "Ahh, thanks. I needed that."

Gesturing to the pile, I say, "Good progress so far."

Dolores shakes her head. "What progress? All I see is a huge mess in the yard."

"I'm going to turn this mess into money," I answer, watching Isabelle as she cycles into the nearly empty shed.

"Be careful, Izzy. There are a few things I need to clear out of there."

"I will, Mummy," she answers, sounding annoyed at my reminder.

This is followed by a loud crashing sound and a tiny, "Uh oh."

My shoulders drop and I get up to investigate, only to find Isabelle sitting on her tricycle next to a floor lamp that is now sideways on the plywood floor. "Come on out of there, silly beans."

She cycles past me and out into the yard. A second later, I hear Dolores say, "Come have a bacon chocolate chip cookie, love."

"Yum!"

I pick up the floor lamp, move it to the side, and struggle with a twin mattress that someone has managed to lodge in here. Once I've lugged it outside, I let out a big breath. "That's the last of it."

"You won't get much for that mattress. It's got a big yellow stain on it," Dolores says.

"What does that mean?" Isabelle asks.

"It means someone peed the bed," Dolores answers, wrinkling up her nose.

Isabelle's eyes grow wide, and she starts giggling. Shaking my head, I go back inside to see what the mattress was hiding. Huh, an old porcelain sink that looks like it's actually been installed. "Dolores, did you know there's a sink in here?"

"Yup."

"Does it work?" I call over my shoulder.

"Why? You want to wash up after touching the pee mattress?" Her voice grows louder, and her shadow fills the entrance. "As far as I know it works."

I make a slow turn around the shed, which seems much larger now that it's empty. It's dark and dingy, but there are two picture windows that have been covered with cardboard sheets Dolores put up so that no one would be able to see all her *treasures*. "You know, we could probably rent this out."

"Rent it out? Like for someone to store their stuff in it?"

"No. For someone to live in."

"Nobody's going to want to live in an old shed in our yard," Dolores says, popping a large chunk of cookie into her mouth.

"Not right now, but if I scrub it up, put down an area rug, add a small table and chairs, maybe a hot plate…" My mind spins with possibilities.

"There's no biffy. Where will they shower?"

"They can come inside to shower and use the toilet on the main floor."

"You seriously think you'll find someone desperate enough to rent out a shed?"

"Yup. And if I make it cute enough, we could get a few hundred a month even," I say with a big grin.

Dolores opens her mouth to protest, but I silence her with a shake of my head. "This is going to work. They manage this type of reno in a few hours on those HGTV shows. I bet I can have it done by the time I go back to work on Tuesday."

I beam, excitement flowing through me for the first time in a long time.

"Sounds like a lot of work," Dolores says.

"Nah, this'll be easy!"

***

So, 'easy' may have been the wrong word. I should have gone with "worth the massive amount of trouble" or "possible for people with a base knowledge of building and proper power tools." It took me almost five hours of scrubbing to find out that the floors are indeed rotted plywood, and the windowsills need to be scraped, sanded, and repainted. Also, there's something wrong with the sink, because when I finally managed to get the water turned on, it sprayed everywhere—mostly on my shirt and face.

But no problem. I can and will do this. I have exactly twenty-eight hours to get this done before my next shift. It's not leaving me any time to study, which means I'll be two full days behind in my plan, but if I can't pay for the bloody exams, all the studying in the world will be for naught.

I'm almost finished mopping up the water when I hear my dad's voice greeting Isabelle. "Hey, Sonny, did you shave off your moustache?"

"Grandpa!" she shouts.

I make it out of the shed in time to see her hop up into his arms for a big squeezy hug. "Hello, peanut," he says, giving her a kiss on the cheek.

"Do you want to watch my bike show? I been practicing for two weeks," Isabelle says, demonstrating her budding concept of time.

"Absolutely I do. You know, when I was driving over here, I was hoping I'd see a big bike show today," my dad says, setting her down on the patio and ruffling her hair.

"Okay. I'm going to make the tickets." This is Isabelle's favourite game—charging admission for her shows to senior citizens who can't resist her chubby little face. Smart girl.

"Hey, Dad," I say, walking over and giving him a quick kiss on the cheek.

"Hey, Breenut, I see you're using your day off to rest and relax," he says with a little wink.

"Learned my relaxation skills from you," I say, holding my T-shirt away from me and wringing out the water.

"What's this all about?" he asks, gesturing with his head to the pile of things I've removed from the shed.

"I'm turning the shed into a rental suite."

He blinks in surprise. "Really?"

I nod firmly. "Turns out it has electricity and plumbing. The renter will have to come into the house for the toilet and shower, but otherwise, he or she can be self-sufficient."

Walking to the door of the shed, he pokes his head in, then turns back to me. "I don't know. Do you really think you'll get anyone to rent it?"

"I had a look online, and there aren't many places to rent on the island at the moment," I say, hoping I sound confident. "If I can make it clean, cozy, and cute, I'll find the right person."

Dad gives me a big smile. "Well, let's get to it then."

"Really? You want to help?"

"Of course I do. If there's one thing parents never get sick of, it's helping their children," he says, with a smile. "Besides, I needed to get out of wedding-planning central. Things were getting ugly between your mum and Amber this morning."

"So you figured you'd hide out here for a while?"

"I'm no dummy. Maybe I'll rent this out until after the big event."

I chuckle and put my arm around his shoulder. "For you, I'll lower the rent to $550 a month."

***

After one trip to my parents' place to pick up tools, three trips to the hardware store, two thrift-store stops, and a late night of working, the garden suite—as I've started to call it—is almost ready. It's now eleven a.m., so I have five hours until I need to be at work. I sigh happily as I put the final coat of white paint on the windowsill.

My dad is using his truck to pick up a wrought-iron bed frame I managed to buy on Craigslist this morning. He and my mum had an extra double mattress they aren't using, so he's bringing that over as well. I hum to myself while I paint, feeling hopeful for the first time in a long while.

Dolores, who has been blowing bubbles for Izzy to chase around the yard, walks in. "Well, I'll be damned. Look at this place."

"Nice, right? Would you rent it?"

"God, no. It's a shed. But it's still hard to believe how it looked yesterday morning." She walks around the new plywood floor.

"I found an area rug at the secondhand store. It's a little worn, but it'll make this feel a lot less like a toolshed and more like a cozy cottage."

"You are one resourceful young lady."

"Thanks," I say over my shoulder.

"Resourcefulness is genetic, you know. They discovered the gene for it last year. It runs on our side of the family," she says, walking over to inspect my paint job. She points to one of the cross-braces of the window. "You missed a spot."

"Thanks."

"Yup. Resourcefulness, amazing eyesight, and great tits. All of us Lewis women have all three."

Isabelle, who apparently has been listening from the doorway, asks, "What are great tits?"

I grimace at Dolores. "You want to take that one, Auntie?"

"If I wanted to answer difficult questions, I would've had children of my own."

With that, she walks out, leaving me to explain that tits is another one in the long list of no-no words Auntie Dolores uses.

7

Working Man Blues

Leopold

So THIS IS what a job interview feels like.

It's actually much more nerve-racking than I would've imagined. I'm currently sitting in a rickety metal chair across from a woman named Rosy, who is some sort of manager here. Turns out she was away for a few days, so my interview was postponed, which gave me the chance to savour the good life for an extra seventy-two hours. But now that I'm here, this is all starting to feel all too real.

After spending a total of five minutes filling in the application form—it's a surprisingly quick process when you don't have anything to write under job experience—I was ushered into her office to discuss job opportunities. At least that's what I thought before she pulled out a questionnaire from her desk drawer, clicked open her pen, and suggested we get started.

At the moment, she's writing down my latest answer, which I don't think she found very pleasing. She asked me if I consider myself successful, and if so, why, to which I answered, "Yes, because I've had a life full of adventure and fun, and I've never had to pay for any of it."

Rosy examines me over the top of her bright-purple glasses. "I don't suppose you can describe your work style since you've never had a job."

"Why don't I take a stab at it anyway?" I ask with a bright smile. "I'm a people person, Rosy. I'm friendly, and I love a good chinwag, so I suppose you could say I'm just the sort of fellow you want in a job, such as... Oh, I don't know...bartending, maybe?"

She narrows her eyes at me. "Yes, I see that you seem to be rather fixated on that idea based on your lengthy description of your experience mixing cocktails for your nanny."

"Oh, you noticed that, did you? I've even mastered the toss-behind-the-back thing with the martini shaker. It's a definite crowd-pleaser." I know Emma said it's hard to get a position tending bar, but I still had to try...

"Do you have any medical conditions that would preclude you from heavy lifting?"

Heavy lifting? Oh, I get it. Because of the cases of wine and such. "No physical problems whatsoever. I'm fit as a fiddle."

"It says here you have a degree from the University of Valcourt with a major in Anglo-Saxon, Norse, and Celtic, and a minor in Alchemy."

She puts down her pen and stares at me, clearly waiting for an explanation.

"Yes, can you believe they still have alchemy there? If there's one thing about UVal, it's their inability to let go of tradition."

"Just out of curiosity, what exactly do you learn in alchemy?"

"It's quite interesting actually. It's both medieval chemical science and speculative philosophy aiming to achieve the transformation of base metals into gold, discovering the universal cure for disease, and, for lack of better words, the search for the fountain of youth."

She pushes her glasses up onto her head. "And you believe in that?"

"No, it's total bollocks. If there were even a shred of truth to it, someone would have figured it out by now, and we'd all be immortal with bags of gold lying about everywhere," I answer. "Mind you, if we all had unlimited amounts of gold, it wouldn't be worth anything, would it?"

"So how did you decide to make that your minor?"

"To piss off my father."

Based on the expression on her face, I'm relatively certain that was not the right answer. Bugger.

Rosy sits back in her chair and taps her pen on her desk. "Do you generally have trouble with authority, Mr. Davenport?"

"No, madam, I do not. My father is the exception to the rule. I'm otherwise very good at following orders." Everybody lies in these things, yes?

Rosy gives me a long, hard look. "I know you're Pierce's brother, but that doesn't mean I'm going to stand for any funny business. It's an important job. In fact, it's one of the key positions here at the hotel, because you have direct contact with our guests. If you're too slow, or aren't friendly enough, or you have the tendency to drop things, we'll end up getting a lot of complaints, and even worse, poor reviews on TripAdvisor. And believe me, in the hotel industry, every bad review you get is the equivalent of having a thousand people cancel their rooms."

I give her a confident smile. "Well, then I'll be perfect for this job. As you can see, I'm very friendly. I'm also highly coordinated, have an exceptional amount of stamina, and lightning-fast reflexes." Ha! Maybe getting a job isn't going to be so hard after all.

"How long are you planning to live on the island?"

Best to be vague about this one. "I'm here indefinitely, but no less than six months, and I can assure you that should you hire me, I will show up every shift on time wearing a smile."

***

A bellboy. It turned out the entire interview was to determine whether or not I'm qualified to be a lowly bellboy. Even the title lacks dignity. It's really the worst of all the boy jobs. Cabana boy wouldn't be so bad, because of being outside in a cabana working exclusively with a few super relaxed, most likely tipsy clients. Pool boy is always a big hit with the ladies since it's one of the very few jobs you can do shirtless. But bellboy isn't exactly one of those vocations that has women swooning. Although I suppose since women are off-limits, it's probably better if I'm employed in an invisible position.

Turns out I can start immediately because one of their late-shift bellboys quit yesterday. Yay, what a timely coincidence. Read that with absolutely no enthusiasm whatsoever.

I change into the uniform—a white golf shirt with the Paradise Bay logo on it and a pair of khaki shorts that looks obviously very goofy with my black patent leather dress shoes and black socks. I texted Pierce to see if he could bring me a pair of Keds, but he hasn't gotten back to me yet, which likely means he's either locked away in his writing cave or too busy laughing hysterically to bother texting back. Balls. Why couldn't *I* have written some dumb fantasy books? It can't be that hard, can it?

I sigh as I stare at myself in the bathroom mirror. This is really happening. As of a few minutes ago, I am among the working class. Better get to it.

I open the door to the hallway to find Rosy waiting for me. She glances down at my shoes. "You may want to wear something more casual and more comfortable tomorrow. You'll be on your feet for eight hours every shift."

"Good tip. Thanks."

Gesturing for me to follow her, Rosy leads me down the hallway to the lobby area.

Feeling like a complete fool in my dress shoes, I can't help but notice all the other staff are wearing boat shoes or casual Sketchers. There's even one guy with a pair of Adidas Ultra Boosts. He must be the alpha of the pack. We walk past the reception desk that lines the entire back wall of the open-air lobby, and over to a smaller desk to the right of it. A woman who appears to be about my age stands behind the polished wood desk, concentrating very hard on some papers in front of her. She must be a supervisor or something because instead of wearing a golf shirt and shorts, she's in a rather unflattering white dress shirt and beige suit jacket. Her dark hair is in a low pony-tail, and there's something severe about her expression, as though she has the weight of the world on her shoulders. When Rosy approaches and she looks up, I see that she has beautiful, big brown eyes and high cheekbones my mother would pay a lot of money for.

As I hurry to catch up with Rosy, something tiny and bright-green swoops down from the thatched roof and does a buzz-by of my head. Immediately fearing it's nature's most terrifying of fauna—the butterfly—I duck and yelp, "Jesus!" in a high-pitched voice. The tiled floors and high ceiling cause my voice to echo in the otherwise quiet lobby, and soon the rest of the staff have stopped what they're doing to stare.

"It's just a bird, mate. She won't hurt you," the Adidas-sporting alpha says with a smirk.

Great, now I'm the loser in the black dress shoes who's frightened of birds. "Righto, I know," I say, giving him a confident nod. "Just took me by surprise, is all."

I continue walking, thanking my lucky stars that the lobby isn't infested with butterflies or moths. Birds I can handle—almost—but not insects with wings. I'm not scared of them, but I do have what I consider a very normal amount of anxiety around them. Who *isn't* scared of the creepy, furry, flying little buggers? The way they land on a window at night and stare at you with their enormous eyes like they want to nibble on your skin when you fall asleep. Gives me the spine-tingles just thinking about it.

I hurry to catch up with Rosy, glancing at the woman I assume I'll be reporting to directly. I can tell she's talking about me because of the quick glance in my direction. She gives me the once-over, her eyes focusing on my shoes and socks for a moment before she turns back to Rosy.

Turning to me, Rosy says, "You're going to have to move faster than that, hotshot if you're gonna make it in this business. You just let a fat little old lady beat you across the lobby."

"Yes, of course. I shall speed it up." For some reason, I pop my P on the word up, sounding like a complete dork. The young woman gives me a look of dread.

Rosy points to her. "This is Brianna Lewis. She's the head concierge on the four-to-midnight shift. You answer to her directly, but if there's any trouble, she reports you to me. And trust me, you do not want to be reported to me."

I stare a moment too long at my new supervisor, struck by how lovely she is.

Rosy taps me on the shoulder. "Hello? Leopold? Did we lose you already?"

Looking back at Rosy, I feel myself blush. "Not at all. Ms. Lewis will be my supervisor, and if I mess up, she'll be forced to rat me out to you." I smile at Brianna. "Even though I'm certain it would cause her great distress to do so."

Ms. Lewis raises an eyebrow at Rosy and folds her arms. "Seriously?"

Leaning in, Rosy says something under her breath that I can't hear, but it clearly doesn't please my new supervisor, because she closes her eyes for a second and sighs before opening them again.

Rosy pats me on the shoulder, then turns to walk away, calling back, "Brianna is going to take you on a quick tour of the property to get you started. I'll have the concierge desk covered for the next thirty minutes while you show Leo here the ropes." She glances at me again. "Good luck, Leo. You're going to need it."

As she walks away, I swear I hear her laughing.

Extending my right hand, I say, "Hello, milady. I'm Leo, your faithful servant." I give her a flirty smile, which she does not return. "I vow to do whatever it takes to make your life better."

When she shakes my hand, she's quick about it—reminding me more of a hardened businessperson than a young woman in an ill-fitting skirt suit.

"Rosy says you don't have any work experience."

"You say that as if it's a bad thing," I raise and lower my eyebrows in hopes of a laugh.

Nope. Not even a hint of a smile. She lets out an irritated sigh. "I'm an extremely busy person. I don't have the time or patience to play around. This job may be a joke to you, but I *need* it, and I won't have anyone messing this up for me. So save the charm for the guests, straighten up, and pay attention, because I don't repeat myself."

Yikes. Lovely Brianna is also a little bit scary.

Taking out a foolscap-size map of the resort, she hands it to me along with a pen and a pad of paper.

"Come on," she says, turning unceremoniously and hurrying down the steps to the side of the building where a dozen golf carts are parked. She gets in the driver's seat and starts it up as I get in. As soon as I'm beside her, I catch a whiff of a delightful scent. "That is a lovely perfume you're wearing."

She scowls as she pulls out of the stall. "It's Vicks VapoRub. My daughter is sick."

So *that's* why she's miserable. She's married with children. That would do it.

We head down the palm-tree-lined paved path. "As you can see on the map, the buildings are called A through F, the closer they are to the beach, the more luxurious the building. This one here, building A," she says, pointing to a four-story white hotel building, "has a lovely jungle view on the opposite side, and it has its own pool and an open-air Japanese restaurant at night that doubles as a buffet for breakfast and lunch.

The trees clear, and a large, very refreshing-looking pool comes into view. Couples in swimwear lounge around while a few children splash each other. I should be one of those adults. Or one of the ones splashing, really.

We make a sharp left and soon stop in front of a large restaurant bar with an outdoor amphitheater. "This is the hub of the evening activities—it's a night club with live shows every night."

Brianna waits for a small crowd of people to move off the path, then takes off again, the battery whining under the strain as we pass through a lush jungle area. "You'll need to learn the quickest route to get from the lobby to each of the buildings should a guest need anything and a porter not be available." She points to the left. "Building B and C are attached with a walkway. That pool is adults only."

"Nice," I say, craning my neck to see if I can spot any bathing beauties.

I swear my supervisor must know what I'm doing because she swerves quickly, causing me to lose my balance. I grip the arm of the seat with one hand so I don't fall out.

We quickly pass by several other restaurants, two enormous swimming pools that line the beach, as well as the beach bar at which I should be working. It looks like an absolute blast, with Bob Marley playing from the speakers, and even some swings on one side for patrons. The bartender, a woman in her thirties, doesn't appear to be having any fun at all really. That bar *needs* me.

The path runs along a long, pristine stretch of beach leading to the crystal-clear-blue water that laps gently against the shore. A large dock waits for the catamarans that I know are out to sea. In the distance, I see a speedboat pulling someone who's enjoying the view from a parasail. I watch, wishing I was the one floating in the air right now. I suddenly realize Brianna has been talking this entire time, and I haven't heard a word.

"…Take orders from me as well as the reception desk because most people phone them if they've forgotten a toothbrush or other toiletries, etc. As a bellboy, your main job is to help with their luggage, of course." She pauses and gives me the once-over. "You look like you've stayed in your fair share of hotels."

What exactly does that mean? "Yes, I suppose you could say that."

"Excellent, so you should understand the concept. When the guests arrive, they line up at the reception desk to check in. They usually arrive in big groups, having all taken the same shuttle bus from the airport. They're almost always tired after having had a long trip." She takes a sharp turn, and we're headed away from the sea and toward the other guest buildings. I see the Brazilian Steakhouse where Emma works, and I find myself wondering if she may have a job as a host or some such. Anything but a bellboy.

Brianna continues pointing while she weaves in and out of throngs of meandering tourists. "Building C. The main buffet is attached to it, right there. We normally stick young couples and groups of singletons in C, so that's where you're going to get calls for condoms and such.

We have them in the back closet behind the concierge desk. They are to be brought in a small paper bag. You knock gently at the door and leave before they open it so as to avoid any embarrassment."

"Duly noted." Or I could hang around and see if maybe there's a third wheel in the form of a cute female in need of some company. Or not, since I've signed a contract that states no one may ride the Leopole for half a freaking year.

Before I know it, we've passed by a mini-golf course, some lovely tropical gardens, and some tennis courts, and we're making our way around to the parking stalls next to the lobby again.

I follow Brianna as she hurries up the steps much faster than someone of her height should be able to move. Especially someone in heels and a skirt. I rush to catch up, trying very hard not to focus on her curvy legs. They look smooth and highly touchable, not that I should notice.

She spins around when she reaches the top of the five steps into the lobby, her cheeks red, her skin glowing. I'm temporarily struck by how lovely those deep-brown eyes are of hers. She has lashes for days. And they look real.

"Your job is to notice if anyone is struggling with their baggage and to offer to put it on one of these luggage carts," she says, pointing to the carts that are lined up against the wall behind us. "When they've checked in, you help them get outside and load their things on a golf cart for the ride to their building. The quicker we clear the lobby, the better. When it gets too full of luggage and people, it makes us seem as though we're not very efficient. Because we're the first impression guests have of the resort, we need to be spot-on every time to avoid bad reviews on TripAdvisor."

She continues on quickly, while I watch her full lips and try to concentrate on what she's saying, because I know it's probably key to my success, but dear Lord, she's mesmerizing. "Most guests don't want to think about the fact that there are other people on their vacation, so they're happiest when they walk into a completely empty lobby. Obviously, this is not possible if a shuttle has just arrived, but our goal is to clear the lobby within fifteen minutes of each bus arriving. Anything more than that is too long for the guests. Watch for anything that will interrupt the flow of traffic through the lobby and fix it as quickly as possible. Understand so far?"

Not really. "Absolutely." As in I'm absolutely attracted to my boss.

"We separate the guests into priority levels. The first category of priority guests are families with young children. They typically need the most help because they'll have so much stuff with them—car seats that they needed on the shuttle, bags with life jackets and other flotation devices, toys, special blankets, that sort of thing. They typically look like they brought their entire house with them, and both parents are normally quite stressed upon arrival, and the typical state for a child after a lengthy day in an airplane is cranky and wired at the same time. The parents tend to unwittingly leave all of their luggage scattered about, so as soon as they walk in, grab a cart and go help them before they spread out and block all the exits.

"The second category of priority-one guests are senior citizens travelling alone. If they're with younger family members, you can move them down to a priority-level two, especially if they're travelling with hovering middle-age adults, because that age bracket is most likely to A) keep their luggage nice and tight in one spot, and B) instruct their parents to go sit down and relax for a few minutes while they're at the desk. They're very self-sufficient, so if you see middle-aged people, you can breathe easy, because they are low maintenance for the most part. So far, so clear?"

"One question. What if you have a senior citizen travelling alone that walks in at the same time as a family with say, three toddlers? Who do I go to first?"

"The senior. Always the senior first. They'll have less baggage, higher expectations, and you can deal with them much more quickly."

"Got it. So then once they're done checking in, I load up their things in a golf cart and take them over to their building?"

"The only time you get to drive a golf cart is when you have to deliver an item urgently. As a bellboy, you simply take the luggage cart down this ramp over here to the side and load their things onto a cart where one of the porters will be waiting. Then you hurry back here to help with whatever else is needed."

Nuts. That sounds considerably less fun than driving around the resort. "Okay, gotcha."

"This is an all-inclusive resort, so whatever you do, don't hold your hand out for tips because you're not getting any." Brianna continues rattling off instructions at a furious pace while she simultaneously sorts through some forms on the desk. Good God, she's intimidating—gorgeous, whip-smart, and in command. "On the far side, you'll see the table with trays of juices and glasses of water. The catering department takes care of that, but should you notice that we're missing any one of those three types of juices or water, it's your job to call catering for refills. Pick up the phone, press nine, then press 551 to reach the catering manager. The yellow juice is actually orange juice, the orange is passionfruit-mango blend, and the pinkish-red is a sickeningly sweet fruit punch that is very popular with children and hungover adults. Got that?"

"I think so. But if I get confused, I'll just ask."

"Sure. Just don't ask me."

"Because you don't repeat yourself."

"Exactly. We have a bus arriving in exactly three minutes containing sixty-two guests that will be spending the next week here at Paradise Bay. We're a family-friendly resort, and we also get a lot of *Clash of Crowns* fans as well, because Pierce Davenport stayed here while he was finishing the last in the series, so it can be an odd mix of people. We also have a private island that is part of the resort called Eden. You likely won't ever see one of those guests, because they get picked up at the airport and bypass the lobby altogether. If for some reason they end up here, they become our priority-one guests. Give them anything they need or want immediately, no matter how ridiculous the request. Now, before the bus arrives, do you have any questions?"

Oh, about a thousand, such as what was that catering number again, and if the orange juice isn't orange, then what is the orange juice again? And how serious are things between you and your husband? Dammit, I probably should have paid more attention. "Just one. When I was signing my employment form. It said that the rate of pay was 11.75. It is that a per-minute rate?"

Brianna narrows her eyes. "Oh, I get it. You think you're a comedian, don't you? Look, Leo—" The way she says *Leo* is as though it's a dirty word, "—it's obvious you come from money. I'm not sure why you applied for this job—maybe you lost a bet, or you thought it would be a lark to be a bellboy—but this is how I feed my family. So if you're going to screw things up for me, I'll go straight into Rosy's office right now and tell her this won't work out."

So it's per-hour then. Shit. I have never felt so stupid in my entire life. "I can honestly say that nothing in my life up to this point has been as important as me keeping this job. And that is the God's honest truth."

"Sure." She says, oozing sarcasm.

The sound of a diesel bus grows louder. I'm about to be initiated into the working class, and something tells me this isn't going to be all shits and giggles...

8

Beggars Can't Be Choosers; If You Don't Have Anything Nice to Say, Don't Say Anything At All; and Other Annoying But True Sayings...

Brianna

The Next Day

I'M A WOMAN ON A MISSION. And trust me, when this particular woman is on a mission, you better clear the hell out of her way or expect to get mowed down by her size-sevens. *Especially* if you're a certain ludicrously handsome guy who's all sculpted from spending too much time in the gym instead of learning practical skills like following orders.

I mean, can the guy lift heavy things? You bet your sweet buns he can. But does he know what to do with them once they're in his muscly arms? No. No, he does not.

Because of that, there is absolutely no way in hell I'm going to work another shift with one Mr. Leopold Doesn't Know His Arse from a Hole in the Ground. Last night was a *complete* disaster. Not only did he *not* help in any way, he *actually caused* several major catastrophes singlehandedly, including, but not limited to, calling Room A-551 repeatedly to order juice for the lobby. The guests were nice about it the first four times, but by the fifth, they took a golf cart all the way over here to yell at his supervisor. Lucky me.

He also started a huge row between a couple of newlyweds by hitting on the bride, who enjoyed his attention a little too much for her groom's liking. The bride, who apparently, doesn't like being told who she "can and cannot flirt with just because she's married now" pulled the tablecloth out from under all the passionfruit-mango juice, breaking two dozen glasses and making a massive, not to mention dangerous, mess on the tile floor. So that was awesome.

And guess what? By the time security escorted the unhappy couple out of the lobby, I got back to the concierge desk in time to see Leo, who promised he could handle the juice order from now on, hanging up the phone with wide eyes. "I did it again, and they are *really* pissed this time."

And those are just the lowlights. Truth be told, I'm not even sure if he knows how to use a *coat hanger*, let alone a luggage cart. He certainly doesn't seem to understand the concept of hurrying, instead seeming to believe his job is to chitchat with all the guests upon arrival.

So today, I've arrived fifteen minutes early for my shift. I'm going to march straight into Rosy's office and *demand* that they fire him. I know someone useless when I see them, and he is *by far* the most useless one of the bunch. I stalk into the lobby, barely noticing Mario, who says something along the lines of, "Uh oh, Brianna's mad."

One of the other security guards chuckles and says, "I hope she's not mad at me. I don't think I could handle her wrath."

That's right, boys. Stay the hell out of my way, because Brianna Lewis is kicking arse and taking names today.

Ignoring them, I spot Rosy behind the front desk on the phone. Perfect. I don't have to storm as far. Kevin, our IT guy, is standing beside her, scratching his mess of red hair as they both stare at the computer screen. Onika and Donalda, the receptionists on duty, stand at another computer terminal, looking equally confused. Not caring what the problem is, I walk up to Rosy. "I need to talk to you right away. "

She holds up one hand without looking at me. "Not right now. This bloody new computer system isn't lighting up properly."

Kevin barks out a laugh. "Loading up. Not lighting up."

Rosy levels him with a sharp glare. "Whatever it is, it's your job to make it work. We've got a busload of people showing up in less than half an hour and no way to check them in."

"I'll have it up and running. Don't worry." He rolls his eyes at me and shakes his head as though the idea of a new computer system not working perfectly moments after installation is absolutely absurd. "Just give me five minutes."

Rosy sighs. "I know what you're going to say, and I don't want to hear it. We have to give him a chance, Brianna."

"Why? He is *literally* the *worst* bellboy I've ever seen. He doesn't even understand the concept of loading the big items on the bottom and the small things on the top. Who doesn't get that, Rosy?" I ask, my voice rising in desperation. "I mean, seriously? Who!? My four-year-old daughter understands the concept because when she builds a sandcastle, she doesn't start with the little cups. She starts with the big bucket, and she hasn't even gone to *kindergarten* yet. Do you know what I'm saying? He doesn't start with the big bucket, Rosy."

Rosy seems unconcerned. "Well, you'll have to do a better job training him, won't you?"

Oh, *no frigging way* is she going to pin Mr. Incompetent's incompetence on me. "He's a lost cause. Trust me. It's one thing to have somebody with no experience, but I really can't do anything with a guy who has zero common sense."

Kevin cuts in with, "In actual fact, common sense is exceedingly rare. I can count all of the people alive with common sense on one hand." He holds up his right hand and starts naming them. "Bill Gates, Tim Cook, Warren Buffet, famed mathematician Ruth Lawrence, and Jay-Z."

Rosy turns to him and puts her hands on her hips. "What about Stephen Hawking?"

"I said living."

"He passed away?" Rosy asks, her face falling.

"Uh, *yeah*," Kevin says sarcastically.

Turning to me, Rosy says, "Really? How did I not hear about this?"

Rubbing the bridge of my nose, I say, "I don't...I don't know, it was a very big news story, but can we please get back to the topic of firing the new guy, who by the way, thought he was going to get paid $11.75 *per minute?*"

Kevin busts out laughing. "Per minute. That would be $705 per hour. Bahahaha."

I give Rosy, an I-told-you-so expression. "See? Kevin gets it. Now, Leo's going to be here any second, so we need to figure out how to get rid of him."

Rosy purses her lips. "Did you happen to catch Leo's last name?"

"What does that have to do with anything?"

Taking off her glasses, Rosy lets them hang from the chain around her neck and stares at me. "Davenport. As in Pierce Davenport's little brother..."

A sharp stab of envy followed by crushing anger hits. "He's *Pierce Davenport's* brother? All the more reason to fire his arse and give the job to someone who needs it."

Rosy shrugs. "No can do. Emma brought him in on her way to the restaurant yesterday, told me he's desperately in need of employment and asked me to find a suitable position."

Nepotism strikes again. "Well then, you're going to need to find something more suitable. Like maybe he could handle a job in janitorial or groundskeeping. Something that doesn't require efficiency or a functioning brain, neither of which he has."

"I don't have openings in any other areas right now, but I *do* need a bellboy. Quite frankly, I expect more from you, Brianna. You're normally very good at training newbies. That young man may be useless right now, but someone of your intelligence should be able to bring him up to speed quickly. He's obviously capable of learning because he has a degree from the University of Valcourt."

Seriously? How? "In what?!"

"I don't know, something to do with chemistry."

"Well, I doubt he actually did any of the coursework himself. His rich parents probably paid off the dean like those Hollywood celebrities, because there is *no way* someone *that useless* could have gotten a degree in anything from anywhere."

Kevin, who has been watching our exchange, glances past my left shoulder and snorts out a laugh. "She's talking about you, in case you weren't sure."

From behind me, I hear Leo's voice. "I gathered that. Thank you."

I close my eyes for a second and slowly turn to see Leo standing there with a small smile, even though his eyes are filled with hurt. My heart sinks to my ankles, and my face burns with shame.

Kevin bursts out with a loud giggle. "Oh, man, this is so awkward."

"Quite," Leo says in a soft voice. He gives me a slight nod. "Hello, Ms. Lewis. Useless bellboy reporting for duty."

I suddenly become aware that the lobby is completely silent. Everyone has stopped what they were doing to see how this is going to play out. Rosy is the only one distracted by the computer screen. She claps her hands together and says, "I'll be damned. You got it to work."

Kevin rolls his eyes, even though it's clear he's trying to hide his own sense of relief. "Obviously."

With the computer crisis averted, Rosy glances back and forth between Leo and I. Pointing her finger at him, she says, "I know you heard what she had to say about you, so you better pick up your socks today, or this isn't going to work out."

"Of course," he says. "I shall do my best to turn things around."

"Good," she says. "I gotta go. You two kids play nice in the sandbox."

9

Too Many Alphas in the Pack

Leopold

I FINALLY UNDERSTAND why people use the phrase "a fish out of water" to describe moments when you are out of your element. It's my second shift as a bellboy, and I feel like I'm flopping around on the floor, making a big mess of everything.

My supervisor has a chip on her shoulder that must weigh twenty pounds because she is the most surly, snappy woman I've ever met. I have no idea why I found her so attractive when I first met her. Well, actually, I *do*. It's because she's empirically attractive—smart, pretty, delightfully curvy. But no matter how good-looking or smart a person is, how could anyone marry someone like her? Her husband must be either a saint or a masochist because otherwise, there's no way anyone could live with her. And her poor daughter, having to grow up with someone so devoid of joy.

Actually, that's not true. She's nice to everyone *but* me. Right now, she's having a warm and cozy chat with one of the receptionists over at their desk. She's even laughing—and come to think of it, it's the kind of laugh that could fool you into believing she's a nice person.

Huh. So I guess it *is* personal. But honestly, what have I done that is so horribly offensive to her? The only thing I can think of is that she's perturbed at my very existence. Maybe she hates men. Or rich people. Or rich men. Or just me.

And to be honest, I'm no longer a fan of hers either, not after witnessing her efforts to get me fired for simply being new at my job. I'm currently at the concierge desk going over the list of instructions Brianna wrote out for me a few minutes ago. This would have been rather helpful yesterday, don't you think?

Vital Phone Numbers:

Catering Manager: Dial 9, then 551

Janitorial Manager: Dial 9, then 244

Security: Guards are posted here but should they be away, Dial 9, then 322

Luggage Cart: Largest items go on first. Ensure they are stable before stacking bags on them. Use hooks for carry-on bags that have straps. Ensure your view won't be obstructed by items while pushing the cart.

Conduct: Do not flirt with female guests (or male guests, for that matter). Do not flirt with staff members. Do not flirt, full stop. Do not hold your hand out for a tip and say, "Sharing is caring."

ABW: Always Be Watching for work that needs doing. Has something been spilled on the floor? Wipe it up or call janitorial for larger spills and put cones around the wet area. Cones are located in the closet (first door to your right in the hall where the offices are located). Are we low on juice/water? Are the luggage carts lined up like soldiers? Is your shirt tucked in properly?

So this is a little obnoxious, no? No flirting, full stop? That's a rather vague concept. One person's flirting is another person's friend-liness. Not to mention the fact that she's basically ordering me not to have any fun whatsoever. And when did having some fun hurt anything?

Well, I suppose one could say there are countless examples of fun doing a great deal of harm. Like any time any teenager has unpro-tected sex, or anytime anyone brings a handgun to a house party to show it off, but still. Flirting is not in the same category at all. It liter-ally is harmless. Unless someone harms you for doing it, like that married guy last night who wanted to fight me in the parking lot.

But never mind any of this. I should just forget about it because I have bigger fish to fry. I need to figure out where the hell I'm going to live by the end of this week, and I don't have the first clue how to do it. This morning, I asked Pierce if he knew where I could rent something cheap, but he was no help at all. He said, "Define cheap."

So I told him what my hourly wage is, at which point he laughed uncontrollably until tears were streaming down his face. Then he said, "You're so fucked" as he walked down the hall to his office. As soon as he closed the door, he began laughing again. Arsehole.

The entire exchange did make me realize that I need to find a higher paying job—possibly something without the word "boy" at the end of it. I glance around, spotting the security guards standing at the front. They're the alpha dogs around here. They've got those wicked security earpieces in and dark-blue baseball caps on that say "Paradise Bay Security." Guard has a much better ring to it than boy. Security guard. Bodyguard. Women love anyone that can guard them. Plus, I bet they get paid *a lot* more than me. Probably a cool million a year or some such. I could score a pretty sweet pad with that kind of cash. Maybe oceanfront with a maid. I wonder if they might have an opening?

Checking the schedule on the wall, I can see we've got another ten minutes until the next busload of guests arrive, so I decide to go introduce myself. Can't hurt to let them know there's another alpha in the house, right?

"Hello, fellas," I say, smiling at the two men who were deep in a conversation that I realize I've just interrupted. Suddenly, I'm unusually nervous. They're much bigger up close, and to them, I'm just a lowly bellboy.

Mario gives me a little nod. "Hey, man."

"Whatcha talking about?" *Whatcha talking about?* Really? Have I suddenly turned into an eight-year-old girl at recess?

The tall one whose name tag reads "Todd" says, "The Cricket World Cup."

"Oh, I must have missed it. I was here until midnight. That's my shift. Four to midnight, five days a week," I answer, nodding way too much. "How about you? What's your shift, Mario, my man?" *Fuck, Leo, just shut the hell up.*

"Ten to six," he answers before turning back to Todd. "I can't see India taking it this year. Not without Singh."

"Nah, you're wrong. They're still the number-one team in the world even without him. I know everybody gives him credit, but that bench is stacked with talent."

"So I haven't missed the match then," I say for some stupid reason.

They both stare at me for a second, then Mario says, "No, it starts next month."

"Cool. Cool, cool, cool, cool, cool," I answer, still nodding. *Okay, Leo, stop nodding and never say cool again.*

"Are you a big cricket fan?" Todd asks.

"Not so much. I do follow football though. Go Valcourt United!" I say, pumping one fist in the air with a little chuckle.

"Great," Todd says.

"Yes, it's quite exciting. Cricket, too," I add, pointing at Todd as though he invented the sport. "Have you two worked here long?"

He nods. "Five years."

Mario says, "Seven for me."

"Awesome, Mario. So you must be next in line for bartending."

He screws up his face in confusion. "Um. No, I'm head of security."

"Ah! So you've already worked your way up already. Good for you, mate," I say, hoping I don't sound condescending. "Say, you wouldn't happen to need another body in security, would you? This whole bellboy thing isn't really my gig. I fancy myself more of a man's man than a man's boy if you know what I mean…"

Fuck. Did I just say a man's boy? I don't even know what that means, but it sounds very wrong. My mouth continues on without direction from my brain. "I've actually done extensive martial arts training, so I'd be a great fit in protection services." Well, that's not strictly accurate, but I *did* practice the crane kick a ton after I saw *Karate Kid* when I was eight. I even gave Pierce a bloody nose once.

"Oh, really? Well, that's good to know," Mario answers, scratching his neck. "At the moment we're fully staffed, but if something pops up, you'll have to put your name in for it."

"Cool, cool, cool." Managing to stop myself at three cools this time, I cup one hand over my mouth and speak out of the side of my mouth. "Because between you and me, I don't think Brianna is my biggest fan."

Todd gives me a mock-sceptical look. "You think?"

Both men bust out laughing, and I stand like an idiot, waiting for them to stop. Why did I come over here again? Oh, yes, to prove I'm an alpha like them. Mission accomplished. Todd's keen awareness of Brianna's hatred of me pops into mind. "So it's obvious to everyone, then. Any idea what I've done to offend her, because I'd love to fix it."

"I'm afraid it's just your general existence," Todd says, without a hint of apology.

Mario smacks him on the chest, then says, "Don't listen to him. Bree's been under a lot of pressure lately. She's actually a really sweet person."

"I'm sure she is. Any idea as to how I can make her not hate me quite so much?"

"Brain transplant maybe?"

Mario cuts off Todd with a sharp glare. "Work hard. Help her out. She'll come around."

"Thanks for the tip. I'll do that."

***

"How did it go today?" Emma asks, pouring me a glass of sparkling water as soon as I walk through the door.

I flop down onto the couch with a big sigh. "Horrible. I'm not sure I'm cut out to be part of the workforce."

"You're being too hard on yourself." She hands me the glass, then curls up on the enormous beanbag chair with Pierce. "Just because you're new at it, doesn't mean you're bad at it. There is bound to be a pretty steep learning curve."

"For being a bellboy? It's not rocket science."

Pierce gives me a wry expression. "Might as well be for you, though. You're about as out of your element as the average person would be at NASA."

"Thanks for that." I roll my eyes and take a big gulp of water, wishing Jesus would show up and turn it into vino. That wouldn't count, would it? If the booze came from a divine source?

"I'm not having a go," Pierce says. "I'm serious. You've never even had to do so much as pick up your own socks off the floor your entire life. You can't expect to go from never having had to be responsible for anything to holding down a job and not expect to have some challenges."

"I suppose. If I could go back in time, I would never have shagged Sonia. If I hadn't done that, everything would be fine."

Emma wrinkles up her nose. "Do you really believe that everything was fine the way it was, Leo?"

"Yes. I did whatever I wanted, whenever I wanted. I *literally* had the perfect life until I messed it all up by messing around with the third in line to Sweden's throne."

"Leo, as much as it pains me to admit, I think Father's right this time. You do need to grow up. Take it from me, there's no better feeling in the world than accomplishment."

Emma smiles. "He's right, you know. When I finished culinary school, it was one of the happiest days of my life."

Nodding, Pierce adds, "You've never allowed yourself to have that sort of sense of pride."

"I thought pride was one of the seven deadly sins," I say. "Besides, carrying people's bags around isn't exactly writing the world's most popular fantasy series or becoming a famous chef."

Reaching over, Emma pats me on the knee. "Everybody has to start somewhere, Leo."

"But surely everyone doesn't have to start out as a glorified donkey."

Brianna's words come surging through my mind again, reminding me how useless I am. A sense of desperation takes over, and I turn to Emma. "You don't happen to have an opening at the restaurant, do you? I'll do anything. Scrub pots or...scrub other things that need scrubbing."

Emma shakes her head, her expression full of sympathy. "I'm sorry, I don't. Besides, I imagine your father'd have something to say about it if you worked directly for me."

"The cards have been dealt, Leo," Pierce says, trying to hide his smile. "I'm afraid you're going to have to play the hand you got this time around."

I glare at him. "Would it be too much to ask you not to enjoy this so much?"

"Yes. Yes, it would."

10

Guilt, Hope, and Bad Decisions...

Brianna

KANDI: *I've booked the house for the hen's weekend and put down the deposit. No going back now! Whoohooo!!!*

    VALERIE: *Nice! What about this? Matching tats to commemorate the trip?*

    QUINN: *YESSSSS PLEASE!!!! Butterflies on our ankles?*

    KANDI: *Or shot glasses on our hips?*

    VALERIE: *I'll book it.*

    Me: *Sounds super fun, but I'll bow out of the tattoos. #needlewimp*

    KANDI: *You're SO getting a tat, Bree! We'll get you pissed first so you won't feel it.*

***

Have you ever been so wrapped up in your own anger that you've done something impulsive and shitty, only to be immediately filled with an all-consuming sense of regret? That's how I feel about Leo overhearing my conversation with Rosy yesterday. I honestly cannot get it off my mind. I mean, *really*, that kind of nastiness is just plain… nasty. I called him useless, completely devoid of common sense, and a burden to society. It's all true, but I should have asked to speak with Rosy privately, *then* said it.

Urgh. There is literally no coming back from that, is there? He will forever think I am the most awful woman to walk the earth. I didn't even give him a chance. I just saw his expensive shoes, his one-hundred-dollar haircut, and the way he carries himself like a trust-fund baby, and I decided to hate him.

I'm going to be really honest here, which isn't always easy. If he'd been wearing old, cheap shoes and looked like he'd cut his own hair, I would have had all the patience in the world to teach him how to do his job. What does that say about me as a person? Don't answer that.

I add two heaping spoonfuls of sugar to my coffee and stir it, glad to have a few minutes to myself. I'm in the staffroom, and it's 7:47 p.m., my dinner time, which means I have exactly thirty minutes—well, twenty-eight now—to eat, suck back enough caffeine to get me through the remainder of my shift, and sneak in some reading.

The only problem is I can't concentrate because Leopold's sad green eyes keep popping into my mind, and I end up feeling like some horrible person who kicked a puppy for no reason at all. Not that there's ever a reason to kick a puppy, obviously, but it would be *especially* bad to do if the puppy hadn't, say, bitten your nose, or torn up your favourite heels. Leo *tried* to do a good job, but the truth is, I'd made it extra difficult for him to be competent, then blamed him when he messed up.

It's become obvious that he is, in fact, intelligent and can most definitely follow orders if the orders are given clearly. Once I wrote everything down for him, he has done a better-than-average job, except for the flirting. He still needs some work to tone that down, not that I'm going to harp on it. I'm not going to harp on anything because for the most part, we aren't speaking unless absolutely necessary, which is rather awkward. I don't even know what to say to make it better, either. "Sorry you overheard me saying awful and unfair things about you yesterday. Oh, and for trying to get you fired. We good?"

Oh, whatever, Brianna. You can't fix it now, so just eat and study already. I open my lunch kit and my laptop, then pull out my stale bagel with cream cheese, but instead of opening my online Caribbean Tax Law textbook as I should, I open my Craigslist account to see if anyone has answered my ad.

Huh. Not one view yet. Bugger. Sitting back in my chair, I lick my fingers just in time for Leo to walk in and see me with my ring finger jammed into my mouth. Perfect.

We exchange uncomfortable nods, then I glance back down at my screen, my face hot with shame. Without saying anything, he strolls over to the fridge and gets out a takeaway container that I recognize as coming from our resort—likely the Brazilian restaurant. He dumps the contents onto a plate and pops it in the microwave. I bet his brother's girlfriend brought that home for him. Lucky bastard. What I wouldn't give for a meal from the steakhouse right now. Plucking my baggie of carrots out of my lunch kit, I take one out and chomp down on it, wishing it were a juicy piece of Brazilian-spiced meat.

I stare at my ad, trying to think of ways to punch it up a bit.

For Rent: Lovely, affordable garden suite. Newly refurbished with a cozy area rug, super comfortable double bed with never-before-used bedding, kitchenette, and large picture windows. Quiet neighbourhood, private setting in back garden.

$400/month

Immediate possession available. First and last month's rent required up front.

"What's that?" Leo asks.

I jump a little, realizing he's sidled up behind me and is standing over my right shoulder, smelling way too good to be a bellboy, I might add.

I quickly close the tab. "Nothing. Just…a thing." My face glows hot as I turn to him and stare into those stupidly mesmerizing eyes.

"A thing that's also nothing?" he asks, looking amused. "Now all I want to do is find out more…"

"It's more nothing than something," I say with a nod.

"Are you renting that out?"

I nod. "I've repurposed a shed into a little suite."

"Is it still available?"

"Unfortunately."

"I'll take it," he says.

Glancing up at him, I wrinkle my nose. "No, you don't want to live there."

"Why not?"

"It's not exactly a luxury penthouse. It's tiny, just basically a bed and four walls."

"That's fine. I don't need much. Besides, I did the math, and it turns out I can't afford the fully staffed, beachfront villa I had my eye on."

I honestly can't tell if he's joking or not. "I thought you were living with your brother?"

"It's time I strike out on my own. You know, stand on my own two feet." He stands and walks over to the microwave. When he opens the door, the heavenly smell of his dinner fills the room. Oh God, that is so much better than this stupid rubbery carrot that's been sitting in my fridge for weeks.

I shake my head. "You'd hate it. Trust me."

Nodding, he says, "Righto. You'd probably prefer someone else to let it, anyway. Someone who's…not me."

I close my eyes for a second. "Leo, I owe you an apology about what I said yesterday. I'm not normally so mean."

"That's okay. I know I did a crap job of things my first shift. I'd want to get rid of me, too."

"It's not… You didn't…"

"Oh, I *did*. I can see calling room 551 once. *Maybe* twice, but *five* times?" he says, sitting down across from me.

We wince at each other for a second, then both laugh a bit. "That was particularly awful, wasn't it?"

Leo nods. "When she came storming in wearing that negligée under a jacket? I very clearly interrupted what was likely a much-needed intimate moment."

The thought of an intimate moment with Leo pops into my mind, and I whisk it away as quickly as possible. "I think you may have done, yes."

"The entire shift was bad. I've honestly never been so flustered in my life. I couldn't even figure out how to use the carts properly."

"I should have written down the instructions instead of making things harder for you."

"They've proven most useful. Thank you."

"You're welcome," I say, smiling at him for a second. I quickly turn my gaze to my laptop screen, afraid to stare at his gorgeous face too long. "And again, I really am sorry about earlier."

"Apology accepted. Now tell me about this garden suite."

"I can't see you there. There isn't even a washroom, so you'd have to come into our house to use the loo and shower." An image of this preposterously gorgeous man showering pops to mind. Naked. And wet. And soapy. And... oh God, can he read my mind? Because he is giving me this lopsided grin that seems to say he can read my dirty, dirty thoughts.

"I'd be the perfect renter, I promise. You won't even know I'm there," he says. "Except for the monthly cheque."

Do not say yes. Find anyone but him to let the suite, Bree. You'd be better off trying your hand at pole dancing than having him live with you. "I'd prefer cash."

11

Booze and Ice Cream—the
Answer to All of Life's Problems

Leo

WELL, this is nothing short of a disaster. The lobby is filled with hot, angry, exhausted guests, and we've got no way to check them in. Even if we could check them in, we're unable to program the keycards, so they couldn't get into their rooms. To make matters worse, it appears all of our new arrivals are either elderly people travelling alone or families with dozens of toddlers, so I honestly don't know who to help first.

Libby is barking orders at all of us simultaneously while Bree is desperately trying to locate that sarcastic IT guy who, it seems, has disappeared at exactly the worst moment.

"Hello everyone," Libby yells. "Welcome to Paradise Bay."

"You mean Paradise Delay," a man answers, setting off a chorus of "yeahs" and "no doubts."

"We are very sorry about the long wait. We'll have you out of here and onto your vacation as soon as humanly possible. In the meantime, please help yourself to some juice, water, or coffee."

Grumbling comes from around the room as a few of the guests

walk over to help themselves to a drink, and the rest hold their places in line.

"Leo," Libby yells at me, snapping her fingers. "Get moving with the carts. Start stacking luggage."

"Righto," I say, hopping to it. Maneuvering my way around the lobby proves both dangerous and difficult with tiny humans running everywhere. I stop at the nearest family and smile at the weary parents. "Hello and welcome."

The blond woman scowls at me while the baby she's holding pulls at her earring, stretching her earlobe in a way that makes my stomach turn. "How much longer is this going to take?" she asks while a boy who looks to be about six pulls on her other arm and shouts, "I want to go swimming, Mummy! You said we could swim as soon as we got to the Caribbean!"

Turning to him, she says, "I know, baby, but these people won't let us until we check into our room."

The pint-sized tyrant glares at me. "You're a nasty man to keep us here. I want to go swimming NOW!"

Chuckling, I say, "Yes, and *I* also want you to go swimming as soon as possible, my young friend." Preferably into a riptide. "How about you help me get your bags onto this cart so we can get you on your way quicker?"

"No way! That's *your* job."

He's got a point, doesn't he? The little bastard. I quickly start stacking their belongings onto the cart. "Where are you folks from?"

Worn-out dad, who is wrangling his daughter—a gifted climber who has shimmied up the pole of the cart—turns to me. "London, which means we were up at three a.m. to get to the airport."

"Oh, dear, so you must be at your wit's end."

"You think?" he says, sarcastically.

I need this job. I need this job. I will lose my inheritance if I quit or get fired. "Would you care for a refreshment?" I ask, pointing to the table on the far side and suddenly noticing there are only a few glasses of the awful passionfruit-mango drink left.

"Does it have booze in it?" the woman asks with an expression that says the answer to that question will determine whether or not she bursts into tears. I glance at her son, who is clinging to her arm and lifting his feet off the ground as though his mum is a jungle gym instead of a human being.

"I want to swim *now!*" he says again.

I smile broadly at her. "If it's booze you need, it's booze you shall have, milady. Let me tidy up the mess of luggage, and I'll get this party started."

Her eyes fill with hope, and she nods gratefully. I can't help but pity her. She must need copious amounts of alcohol every damn day to get through her life. I need to fix this for her.

Five minutes later, the carts are full, I've placed the juice order and begged the catering manager for as many appetizers as they can bring. I'm now in a golf cart on my way to the nearest bar. When Bree saw me leaving, she gave me a what-the-hell look, but since she was on the phone, she couldn't stop me. I mouthed, "Trust me," to her and took off like Pierce when he sees a lizard.

I hit the brakes and all but run to the open-air bar that sits poolside. Giving the bartender a quick nod, I say, "I need a package of solo cups, two bags of ice, two bottles of vodka, two rum, two bottles of tequila."

"For what?"

"Emergency lobby party. Libby's orders. Chop-chop."

Apparently, dropping Libby's name is the equivalent of "open sesame," because he starts moving at lightning speed. "I'm going to take some of your lime and lemon slices as well," I say, stepping behind the bar and finding a clean stainless-steel bowl. I spot an empty cardboard box on the tile floor and set it between us, and the two of us fill it with the supplies I need.

The sound of the resort's reggae band comes floating across the water. "Can I have them, too?" I ask, pointing to the four musicians.

"You can have them. If I never hear "Stir It Up" again, it'll be too soon."

Moments later, I'm off again toward the ice cream bar that sits along the path toward the beach. I load up with boxes of ice cream bars, popsicles, and drumsticks, get back in and head toward the lobby, only to have another brainwave while I drive past one of the pools. "If it's swimming he wants, it's swimming the little bastard will get."

I make one last stop at the pool, filling up the backseat with towels and commandeering a lifeguard named Monica from the deck. Can you commandeer a person? I'm not sure if that's a thing, but I'm doing it anyway.

I pull up to the lobby with a screech, the band in a golf cart behind me. Turning to Monica, I say, "Grab the towels and head to that fountain. I'll have some customers for you momentarily."

I like Monica. She doesn't ask a lot of questions and instead shrugs and does what I've asked. I point the band in the direction of the front steps. "If you can set up under that large palm tree, that would be perfect."

Bree spots me immediately and hurries down the steps. "You can't just take off like that. Especially when we're in the middle of a crisis."

"Sorry, but in a few short moments, the crisis will be averted, and you will love me."

She follows me as I walk around to the other side of the cart. "Unless you left and came back a computer genius, we're screwed."

I lift the boxes of ice cream out and hand them to her. "Computers aren't my particular strong suit, but you could say I'm a bit of a party savant."

"Oh, well, that's something to be proud of..." She watches me as I lift the box of bottles out of the trunk, her expression the epitome of skepticism.

"Give me five minutes. I'll have these people so happy they won't care if they *ever* get to their rooms," I say. "In the meantime, I need you to give each of the people in the queue a number to hold their place in line."

Hurrying up the stairs, I make my way behind the refreshment table and quickly set up a makeshift bar. A room-service cart pulls up to the steps, and two servers get out.

Two minutes later, there's a wonderful spread of appetizers, complete with plates and napkins ready. Next to them sit the boxes of ice cream treats, and I'm standing on the other side, ready to make cocktails.

I cup my hand over my mouth and call, "Hello everyone! If the lovely Brianna has already given you a number, come on over to have a bite and a drink. We've got ice cream for the kiddies—or grown-ups who like that sort of thing—and for the swimmers among us, we've arranged for a very special, never-before-done Paradise Bay wading pool and fountain experience right outside! Don't worry, mums and dads, we've got towels there and one of our top-drawer lifeguards, Monica, will be happy to keep an eye on your children while they splash around. Let's not let some silly computer business stop you from starting your vacation."

The children are the only ones who seem to share my enthusiasm, making a beeline for the fountain fully clothed while their parents call to them to remove their shoes. The other adults grumble but make their way over to the table, anyway. Bree comes to stand next to me and hands out ice cream treats and napkins while I take drink orders.

Worn-out, sweaty British mum is first in line for a boozy drink, her baby now passed out on her shoulder.

"What can I get you?" I ask.

"Just so long as I can't feel my teeth by the time I get to the bottom of it, I really don't care what's in it."

Oh, dear. That doesn't sound good at all. "One double tequila sunrise coming up."

Twenty minutes later, the lobby party is in full swing. The kids aren't the only ones splashing around in their clothes. Several of the tipsy seniors are in there as well now, laughing it up as the band plays on. IT guy finally pulls up and saunters casually into the lobby as though there isn't a major computer fuck-up. Libby gives him a look that gets him moving and then makes her way over to me. "Rum punch, please."

"Yes, ma'am," I say, lifting a red cup off the stack and twirling it before scooping some ice into it.

"You showed a lot of initiative today, Leo," she says. "Thank you."

"Thanks, Libby." My chest swells a bit with pride, which I know is silly under the circumstances. It's not like I discovered a way to remove microscopic plastics from ocean water or something. But still. I've never been told I have initiative before.

She sucks back the entire drink and then tosses the cup in the garbage. "This never happened."

"Okay, everyone! Crisis is over," IT guy calls out, "The computers are back up!"

Most of the guests glance at him, shrug, and carry on with the party, while a few make their way to the desk. Bree, who is still standing beside me, laughs in spite of herself. "Not bad, rich boy. Not bad at all. You do realize I'll have to rescind my offer to let you rent my suite though."

"And why exactly would that be?"

Amusement crosses her face and makes her look absolutely lovely. "I've seen what kind of party you can throw in under fifteen minutes."

I hold up one hand. "What if I swear on a stack of bibles that I won't throw a party? Not even a small one. Not even one sip of wine, not one woman will be brought back, no fun of any sort."

Raising one eyebrow, Bree says, "That sounds a little unrealistic. No fun of any sort?"

"Okay, I might laugh if I see something amusing on the telly, but I promise not to laugh so hard I cry," I say. "I swear on my mother to be a very good, very quiet tenant. Clean, too."

"Fine. We can give it a trial run, but no second chances. If you can't follow the house rules, you'll be out on your arse." She bites her lip a little after she finishes laying down the law, and I wonder who she's trying to convince about the no-second-chances thing. If I had to guess, I'd say it's her.

12

Full Bummed

Brianna

"WHO'S *THAT*, and why is he naked?" Aunt Dolores asks, leaning over my shoulder to get a better look at my computer screen.

Nuts. I thought I was the only one up, so I've Googled Leo Davenport to get the whole story. And not because he's so hot that I need to see pictures of him, but because if he's going to live in my yard (and use my shower), I need to know more about him. For safety purposes.

"Is that the Queen of England?" Dolores asks.

"Yes," I say, quickly trying to close the article but failing because my laptop has chosen this exact moment to freeze.

A giggling sound comes from my left, and I turn to see that Isabelle has also gotten up early today. "That man is full-bummed," she says, covering her mouth with both hands as she laughs hysterically. "Mum is looking at a full-bummed man!"

I slam my laptop shut, my face heating up. "I didn't mean to see that! I was just…doing research on a person I work with. What do you want for breakfast, sweetie?"

"Why was he naked?" she whispers, her eyes wide.

I stand and move in the direction of the cupboard to get a bowl down (and to avoid eye contact with my child). "He's a very silly man who thought it would be funny to go streaking at the Queen of England's birthday party."

"That *is* funny. What did the Queen say?" Isabelle says, giggling some more.

So now we have an accurate assessment of my new renter's maturity level. Perfect. "She told him his behaviour was inappropriate for a garden party and asked him to put his clothes on and go home before she had the police come and collect him. Now, do you want oatmeal?"

"Can I have chocolate chips and bacon in it?" Isabelle asks.

Relieved that she's moved on from discussing the full-bummed, built man I was just staring at, I say, "Ten chocolate chips, but only if you eat your banana slices."

13

The Glamours of Shed-Living

Leo

I HAVE HONESTLY NEVER FELT as ridiculous as I do at this moment. I'm in the passenger seat of Jolene-My-Parole-Officer's car, as she drives me, along with my luggage, over to Bree's house. As per my stupid contract, she has to approve of the accommodations before she hands over the $500 for my deposit.

Since I don't have my first paycheck yet, I've had to beg Pierce for some seed money—$300 to cover the rest of the first and last month's rent, as well as enough cash for some groceries. He lent me $400 but made me sign an I.O.U. that states I'll pay him back with 5% interest. Prick.

Jolene, who I've discovered isn't big on small talk, is, however, big on American country music from the nineties. We're currently listening to a fellow named Garth Brooks, who apparently has many friends in low places. To be honest, it's sort of catchy, even if it does make me desperate for whiskey and beer to chase all my troubles away. Jolene being problem numero uno.

As we turn into a residential area called Old Fort Bay, the houses shrink in size. Each one is painted a different primary or pastel colour, making the neighbourhood appear as though it was decorated by the Easter Bunny. Palm trees hover over the streets as though waving you in to a more relaxed life.

I glance at Jolene, who is tapping her fingers on the steering wheel to the beat. "So, Jolene, I was wondering if I can ask you a favour."

"You can ask, but the answer is most likely a hard no."

"What are the chances I could hold the money so as to avoid the embarrassment of needing you to pay my landlady?"

"Zero to none," she says.

"Brilliant," I mutter, staring out the window as we slow in front of my home for the next six months—a baby-blue house with an ancient rust-coloured Toyota parked out front. An elderly woman sits on the front steps eating from a baggie while she watches a young girl, who I can only presume to be Bree's daughter, ride around the driveway on her tricycle. A man who very much resembles Jerry Garcia in a shorty robe stands on the grass watching the girl. Christ, that must be Bree's husband which means I'm going to have to see that when I wake up each morning.

Jolene pulls to a stop and takes the key out of the ignition. Leaning forward, she peers past me out the window and snorts. "You're certainly moving down in life, hey?"

Before I can answer, she snorts again, which turns into a cackle as she gets out of the car. Suddenly, none of this seems like a good idea. Why would I rent a place from my surly boss who clearly doesn't want me here? I close my eyes, reminding myself this will all be worth it. In six months, I'll have earned my way back into the luxurious world of the Davenport clan. Six *long*, horrible, soul-sucking, humiliating months.

I get out of the car and give the woman on the step and the man a quick wave. "Hello, I'm Leo, and this is my…Jolene," I say, pointing to my parole officer, who is now leaning on the front corner of her car lighting a cigarette.

I open the trunk and remove my suitcases, feeling very much like I'm on the clock.

The little girl cycles over and tilts her head back so she can study me. "I'm Isabelle. You is tall."

"Thanks. And you is a terrific cyclist."

"I know," she says with a shrug before she executes a wide turn and peddles away toward the bearded man. She points a thumb over her shoulder and tells him, "He's our new renter man. That's him's friend."

I smile at the man and take two steps up the driveway, putting down one of my bags to shake his hand. "I'm Leo. You must be Bree's husband."

He holds out his hand. "Jerry. I live next door actually."

Jerry. For real? "Good to meet you."

"My mummy doesn't have a husband. She says men are pointless."

"Now, Izzy, that's girl talk." The older woman stands and walks over to meet me, her steps much livelier than I had expected. "It's true, but it's also not something men generally like to know. I'm Dolores. Bacon?"

She holds out the soggy baggy filled with greasy brown strips.

"Thank you, no. I just had breakfast."

"So? Bacon is just for fun." She turns to Jolene and gestures toward her. "Bacon?"

Jolene nods and reaches for the baggy. "Sure, thanks."

Isabelle, who has been demonstrating her ability to bike in tight circles as quickly as possible, stops a hair away from my left foot. "Did you ever eat a bacon ice cream cone?"

I stare down at her cute little face. "I can't say I have."

"Lucky you," Jerry says.

"Don't mind him. He's one of those irritating vegans. He also has an irritating habit of playing bass at all hours of the day and night," Dolores says, rolling her eyes. Turning to him, she says, "Jerry, go put some damn clothes on. You're going to scare away our new tenant with those hairy legs."

My eyes grow wide as I wait to see how Jerry will react. To my surprise, he bursts out laughing and shakes his head at Dolores. "You old flirt."

"Who you calling a flirt?" she says.

The front door opens, and Bree comes hurrying down the steps with a dishtowel in her hands. "Leo, hi."

Her hair is dripping wet, and she looks much lovelier in her house clothes—a navy-blue V-neck T-shirt and a long, colourful skirt that fits her curves much better than that dull beige suit. She glances at Jolene, her face screws up in confusion. "Did you take an Uber here?"

"Yes, yes, I did." This was a terrible idea, wasn't it? There is literally no way Brianna won't figure out Jolene isn't my Uber driver, especially when she sees her hand over a wad of cash in a few minutes.

"Oh, that's nice," Brianna says, waving to Jolene. Peering up at me, she says, "Shall we go back and have a peek at the suite?"

"Let's do this."

We start up the driveway, and Jerry holds up one hand for a high five as we pass. "Welcome to the neighbourhood."

"Thanks, mate."

"Come on by if you ever want to jam." Pulling a rolled-up cigarette containing what I can only assume is weed, Jerry starts for his house.

Isabelle zips past us on her tricycle, clearly thrilled to be in the lead. "The big house is mine," she says pointing to the two-storey building. "And the little one is yours. It used to be where I kept my trike, but you can sleep there now."

"Thanks." I chuckle a little as Bree and I exchange a look.

"You're welcome," Isabelle says, coming to a sudden stop in front of the garden shed. She parks her tricycle next to the wooden porch and steps up onto it, obviously feeling very important at her first foray into being a landlord. She gives me a very serious expression, tilting her little head at me. "Hey, you is the full-bummed man my mum was staring at on her 'puter."

Full-bummed? "What's that?"

"Nothing!" Bree says urgently, her entire face and neck turning bright pink. "Isabelle, why don't you go inside with Auntie for a drink?"

"I'm not thirsty," she answers without taking her eyes off me. "Were you really sad when the Queen told you to go home?"

Bree rushes over to her daughter, takes her by the shoulders, and turns her toward the house. "I think *Dora the Explorer* might be on. Why don't you go see?"

"No, thanks," Isabelle answers, shaking her head. "I think I'll stay out here. Him is funny." Turning to me, she says, "You can't be full-bummed if you're going to live here, because the police will come collect you and put you in jail."

I'm left speechless for the first time in, well, in longer than I can remember, actually. My mind races to catch up while Jolene, who has followed us, glares at me as she takes a bite of baggie bacon. A completely mortified Bree gives her aunt a pleading expression.

"Come on, Izzy," Dolores says, holding out her hand. "Your mum clearly wants you to keep me busy so I don't embarrass her. Let's go feed the cats."

I can't help but grin as they walk up the three steps into the house.

"Sorry about that. I wasn't staring at you. I Googled you—for safety reasons—and that picture popped up, but I wasn't gawking at your full-bum—nakedness... You. My computer froze and..." Bree's voice trails off, and she turns to unlock the ocean-blue door. "You can't be too careful when you're renting out a flat to someone you don't know very well. Especially because you'll have to come in to use the loo."

She risks a quick glance in my direction, and I do my best to stifle a grin. "Absolutely," I say with a firm nod. "Safety first."

She closes her eyes for a second, then opens them, wearing a guilty expression. "Exactly. So like I said yesterday, it's really small." She steps aside and lets me go in.

I walk into the bright space that smells of fresh paint and look around at my new home, my stomach dropping with a thud as I set my bags down. I'm no longer going to be living in a beachfront mansion, complete with a steam shower, hot tub, and a king-size bed. I'll be here, in a garden shed, sleeping with my feet hanging off the end of this small mattress. But beggars can't be choosers, can we?

Pasting a smile on my face, I say, "It's perfect. Thank you."

Jolene snorts as she pokes her head in. "Not exactly a suite at the Marriott, is it?"

Bree sets her gaze down at the floor, obviously hurt by Jolene's insult. She's clearly put a lot of work into making this a cozy home for someone—for me, as it turns out.

I give Jolene a sharp glare. "I think it's terrific. Please give Ms. Lewis the cash, then you may leave."

Jolene reaches into the pocket of her cargo shorts and pulls out the wad of money, then hands it to Brianna, who glances back and forth between us expectantly.

"We made a bet earlier. She lost," I say.

Jolene raises one eyebrow and my stomach tightens automatically at the thought of her spilling the beans. But Brianna saves me, "None of my business."

As she counts the cash, Jolene turns and starts toward the gate. She gives a little wave over her shoulder as she calls back, "Nice to meet you, Ms. Lewis. I'll see you later, Leo."

"I look forward to it." I take out three hundred from my wallet and hand it to my new landlady. "Here's the rest."

"Perfect," she says with a smile that I can only describe as extremely relieved. "Well, I'll leave you to get settled then."

As soon as Brianna leaves, I flop down onto the bed and let out a long sigh. It's no pillow-top with thousand thread count Egyptian sheets, but it's not awful. Oh, that's not exactly true. It's pretty awful.

It's a shed.

I live in a shed with a tiny, uncomfortable bed.

How the hell did I end up here? Working as a bellboy and living in a shed? Oh, yeah, I shagged that Swedish princess, then took off before she woke up without so much as leaving a note. I stare up at the white ceiling and remind myself this is only temporary. Six month's penance, then I'll be free to go back to my real life.

But for now, I have to figure out the whole feeding-myself bit. And I need to go fess up to my landlady.

***

"Come in," Brianna calls in response to my knocking.

I pull open the screen door and walk into the small but bright kitchen. Bree is standing at the counter looking very much as serious as she does at work. She's got a list in front of her, a pen in her hand, and her face is scrunched up in that I've-got-the-weight-of-the-world-on-my-shoulders sort of way she has.

In the other room, I hear a children's show coming from the telly. I glance over and see Dolores dozing on the couch while Isabelle hums along to the song and colours from her position kneeling in front of the coffee table.

Brianna gives me the same patient smile she gives guests at the hotel. "What can I do for you?"

"You know what? I can figure it out. I can see you're busy."

She sets down her pen and sits back. "Not at all. What do you need?"

"I was just going to ask where the nearest grocery store is," I say, feeling foolish for bothering her. But her expression doesn't say she's annoyed. It's sort of a gaze-into-my-eyes type look.

She swallows hard and shakes her head a little. "There's a Goody Mart five blocks south, but it's overpriced. I'm going to Superstore in a bit, if you want a ride."

"Are you sure you don't mind?" I ask, unable to stop staring at her.

"Not at all. I'll come out and get you when I'm ready."

A large calico cat appears from under the table and trots over to me, then proceeds to rub against my leg.

"That's Knickers. She loves everyone," Bree says.

"Hello, Knickers." I crouch down to scratch behind her ears, causing a loud purring sound to start up. A second later, drool seeps from her mouth. Well, that's a little gross, no? "Oh, dear. I'm afraid she's leaking."

Bree stands and takes a couple of tissues from a box on the counter. She hands me one, then wipes the cat's chin. "Sorry about that. She's a joy-drooler."

"That's all right. So am I." I wipe my fingers and straighten up as two more cats appear. These two are much smaller Siamese cats. One of them hisses at me, jumping sideways across the room with his back arched and tail straight up. I flinch and hold my arms tight to my chest.

"That's Milo," Bree says, picking up the angry cat and rubbing his neck. "He's not a fan of men in general, so probably don't try to touch him."

"Good tip. Thanks."

The other cat, who looks exactly like the angry one, rubs against my leg.

"That's Puddy Tat. She's the friendly one of the two. But if you don't give her attention right away, she'll claw her way up your body which hurts so much more than you'd think."

"Brilliant. Exactly how many cats do you have?"

"Zero. My aunt has three cats."

I nod. "One joy-drooler, one man-hater, and one clone to the cat I shouldn't touch who will claw at me if I don't try to touch her immediately. Got it."

"Yup," she says with an apologetic smile.

"This is going to be an adventure, isn't it?"

14

Life Lessons from Scully and Mulder

Brianna

WEDDING Dress Shopping WhatsApp Thread

AMBER: Hey peeps! Today's the big day! We're meeting at Valencia's at 1 p.m. sharp. With any luck, we can find the perfect bridesmaid's dresses before Bree has to leave for work.

KANDI: One word: backless.

VALERIE: Ooh! Sexy!! YES!

QUINN: I'm in. I've been working on getting rid of my tan lines.

ME: See you at one!

Wednesday To-Do's

Quality Time with Izzy!

Scrub disgusting toilets, tubs, sinks

Hopefully figure out WTF is wrong with mower, fix it, and mow grass

Laundry (whites, darks, colours)

Dress Shopping with the stick women/find graceful way to get out of having to humiliate self by wearing backless dress in front of everyone I know

Study Torts—chapters 11-15

Make healthy supper
Lose twenty pounds by July

"Okay, Bree, you've got this. You may have thirty hours of stuff and only six hours to do it in, but you'll get it all done because you are Superwoman." I stare at my reflection in the mirror, but the woman staring back doesn't seem convinced. She looks like she wants to crawl back into bed for a few days of blissful sleep. "Nope. Not an option. Don't even let yourself think about it."

Tying my hair back into a ponytail, I hurry to the kitchen with that sense of dread filling my belly again. Urgh. Backless dresses and big boobs are not exactly compatible. Double D's with no bra is no bueno. They'll be sitting somewhere south of my rib cage the entire day. I'll just have to put my foot down. Either that or I'll have to put my boobs down. If the rest of the bridesmaids want to show off their backs, they can do it at the rehearsal dinner.

I pour myself a cup of coffee, slap some strawberry jam on two pieces of bread, and open Torts: Cases and Context. I flip to page 342 while I wonder if there's any way to clone myself by this afternoon. Since that's not likely, I might as well make use of the few quiet moments I have right now.

The backdoor opens, and a second later, the bathroom door closes. Great. Leo's inside, which means I won't be able to concentrate on account of proximity. To be honest, I had a bit of trouble falling asleep last night. Yesterday's shopping trip was crazy awkward. It started out fine enough. We decided to share a buggy, but somewhere around the cereal aisle, we both seemed to realize that everyone there assumed we're *together* together, not just a landlady/supervisor and a tenant/bellboy. Somehow the thought of other people thinking we're a couple made the whole concept a weird possibility, even though it's totally not a possibility. Seriously, it's not.

Even though it was kind of nice to have a man load all the groceries in the trunk and put the buggy away. And I told him not to bother buying coffee because he's welcome to come inside and have some of mine. Except when I said it, I sounded like some hot-to-trot character in a 1950's movie. "Why don't you come up and see me sometime?"

"Morning, Bree," Leo says, snapping me back to reality. He glances at my open textbook. "Oh, sorry. Don't let me interrupt you."

"No, it's no trouble," I say, suddenly self-conscious about my no makeup/boring low pony/mowing-the-lawn outfit of oversize T-shirt and cut-off jeans. How the hell can he look so good at this hour? "Mugs are in the cupboard above the coffeepot. Help yourself."

"Thanks. I think I will."

I watch him for a second, taking in the way he moves his long, lean body with such confidence. He has a regal air even though he's just in a pair of board shorts and a fitted green T-shirt. I set my gaze back to the page in front of me, but the words are all jumbled together. What is it about this guy that turns me to mush? Oh, right. He's insanely hot.

"God, that's your to-do list for the day?" he asks, sitting down across from me.

"Uh-huh." I don't dare let my eyes move in his direction because my expression will give me away, and I'm trying to pretend to be too busy to notice him.

"I think you'd look really lovely in a backless dress."

Oh, crap. Why did I put that in writing?! My entire body flames with embarrassment. "Certain looks don't flatter curvy girls," I say, snatching my list and tucking it under my book.

"Agree to disagree," he says, grinning at me over his mug. "Who's getting married?"

"My little sister."

"Bridezilla?"

"I prefer to think of her as highly anxious."

"Bridezilla." He nods before giving me a hard stare. "You need help."

Raising one eyebrow, I say, "Like a personal trainer?"

"God, no," he says, narrowing his eyes in confusion. "With your to-do list."

"Oh, right. That's okay. I've got it covered."

"Ah, I see. And just how are you going to manage everything on that list before our shift?"

"Easy. I've already put in the first load of laundry. Once Izzy's up, we can play maids while I clean the bathrooms and fold the clothes. It's not the *best* quality time we could have, but she's used to me being busy. Besides, helping out won't kill her, and she likes playing pretend. We'll have fun," I ramble on, my working-mum-induced guilt flowing out. "I'll make a pasta salad for dinner while I study, then zip outside and mow the grass, shower and run to the dress store, then pop to work."

Leo stares at me for a moment. "Where you'll be on your feet until midnight."

"I'm used to it. That's the life of a student-slash-single mum-slash-concierge," I say with a shrug. "But if I play my cards right—and I'm pretty sure I am with this whole law-school thing—sometime in the not-so-distant future, I'll be able to *pay* someone to do the cleaning and yard work."

"And that thought keeps you going."

"That, caffeine, and chocolate," I say, licking the jam off my fingertip. "Which is why I shouldn't be in a backless anything."

He leans toward me and lowers his voice. "You should stop putting that image in my mind, Ms. Lewis, or I'm going to have trouble keeping things strictly business with you."

I roll my eyes even though my bones have turned to liquid goo. Doing my best to pretend I'm not affected, I lean in and match his tone. "Your empty flattery will get you nowhere, Mr. Davenport."

"There's absolutely nothing insincere in what I've said. You're stunning. Deal with it." With that, he stands and walks out the door, coffee mug in hand, as I stare after him and try to tell my stupid heart to slow down because he is trouble personified. He's the dangerously handsome heartbreaker type who will leave you knocked up and shattered.

"Is he gone?" Aunt Dolores asks, peering around the corner from the staircase.

"He just left."

"Good. I can't handle anything with a penis before ten a.m." She walks straight to the fridge to retrieve her pre-breakfast bacon.

"I know the feeling."

I get up and go to the laundry closet to change the load. When I come back to the kitchen, Dolores is staring out the window. I walk over to see what's got her attention. Turns out it's Leo crouched down in front of the mower with my toolkit open beside him.

"Oh, this isn't good," I mutter.

"Why not?"

"As if he knows the first thing about lawnmowers," I say, watching him as he unscrews the gas cap. "And even if he does, I certainly don't need some man to think I owe him."

Dolores wrinkles her nose up. "He's trying to help. 'Don't look a gift horse in the mouth.' John Heywood."

"'Trust no one.' *X-Files*." I hurry outside to put a stop to whatever Leo thinks he's doing before I end up needing a new mower.

I get outside just in time to hear it start up. Huh. He got it working. And now he's actually using the machine. Properly. Watching him, I find myself torn between letting him finish the job and taking over so I can do it myself. He turns when he reaches the fence, and when he sees me, he smiles and shuts off the machine. "It was just a loose spark plug."

"Thanks," I answer. "Where'd you learn to fix lawnmowers?"

"We had a nice gardener when I was growing up," he says with a shrug. "He used to let me help out."

Coming from anyone else, I would assume this was a joke, but not from Leo. He gestures toward the house with his head. "Go enjoy your quality time."

I open my mouth to protest, but he says, "Relax, you don't owe me for this. I'm practicing my landscaping skills. I need something to fall back on in case my supervisor tries to get me fired again. Now, if you'll excuse me, I'm very busy today."

***

. . .

I hurry down the shaded sidewalk toward Valencia's, which is the place for all things wedding attire on the island. It's on the swankiest street in San Felipe, which runs along the beach and is lined with cafes, clothing stores, and jewelry shops that cater to the tourists. I'm running ten minutes late, and my hair is wet, but at least I'm clean and I'm here. I managed to get through almost everything on my list, and what's left—three chapters to study—can be done on my breaks at work.

There's an extra spring in my step, and as much as I hate to admit it, it's because of Mr. Tall, Built, and Helpful. I don't know how much time, not to mention money, he saved me by fixing the mower, and he did a surprisingly nice job of the grass. I am seriously grateful.

Okay, full disclosure: His use of the word stunning may have something to do with my mood. It keeps popping into my mind as I weave through the meandering crowd of middle-aged people who look like they're fresh off a cruise ship.

You're stunning. Deal with it. Oh, that sets off a flock of butterflies in my stomach. Hmm…do butterflies fly in flocks, or is that just birds?

Anyway, whatever. He's just buttering me up. And even if he's not, I definitely need to forget about that whole moment in the kitchen this morning because… Well, because I'm his boss, number one, and number two, I'm his landlady, and number three, he's a rich guy, and I hate rich guys. He's a generous, fun, sexy, rich guy who knew exactly what I needed to make my day so much better. But he's also a heart-breaking bastard, I'm quite sure of it.

Skidding to a stop in front of the dress shop, I spot my sister and her friends inside. Valerie is modeling an emerald-green dress with a midi skirt and a tasteful V-neck. Not my favourite colour, but I wouldn't hate wearing that. I yank open the door, take a deep breath and hope we can all agree on that dress and get out of here.

"She made it," Quinn says, tossing a thumb over her shoulder.

There's a visible deflation in the group's excitement level that doesn't go unnoticed by me. I cement a smile on my face and remind myself this is all for Amber, who I love very dearly. "Sorry I'm late. That's a lovely dress."

Kandi shrugs. "I don't know. It's a little plain."

"Plain? I think it's perfect," I say. "Very flattering." Not to mention nicely modest and would suit a variety of body types—including curvy.

Quinn shakes her head. "No cleavage. No sex appeal. It's a no."

Valerie nods. "Agreed. It's a big old no for me, too."

Brilliant.

***

"So? How was dress shopping with the stick women?" Leo asks as he gets in the car. We've agreed to carpool to save money on gas and save him an hour on the bus to and from the resort.

I pull out of the driveway and start slowly up our street to the main road. "It was as fun as I expected."

"So absolute torture culminating in a dress choice that you shall have nightmares about for the rest of your life?"

I chuckle a little, surprised he could so succinctly sum up my afternoon. "The nightmares will fade after the wedding—I hope. And perhaps after several years in therapy."

"Oh, if that's all, then there really was no need for you to have been filled with such dread earlier," he says tongue-in-cheek.

Turning onto the highway that runs along the south shore, I start to relax a little. "All the other bridesmaids went on and on about how they can totally wear the dress again, but not me. I just dropped three-hundred dollars on a dress so low-cut I'll have to ladyscape to wear it."

Leo bursts out laughing, and I join in, glad to have someone to laugh with about all this silliness. When he's done, he leans toward me and says, "Is there any way I could score an invite to the big event?"

"Oh, yeah, because that's what I need, another person trying to unsee what I've got going on."

His smile fades. "Why are you so hard on yourself?"

"Because I have a mirror, and excellent vision. I also know what men like, and it sure isn't this."

He pauses for a second, then says, "Brianna, I'm going to ask you a strange question, but bear with me, because there is a point to it, I promise. Have you ever looked up porn online?"

My head snaps back, but before I can protest, Leo says, "You don't have to answer that. If you had, you would see all kinds of videos from big-breasted to MILFs to mature ladies to huge booties."

"Okay…maybe we should change the subject."

"My point is, there's not one way for a woman to be desirable, regardless of what the diet industry and cosmetic companies want you to think. For every different female body, age, face, and race, there's a man or a woman who will be into what she's got going on."

"Ah, so there's a pot for every lid. Thanks, Leo," I say, feigning delighted surprise.

"Believe me, there are a lot of lids for your pot."

We pull onto the long, palm-lined road leading to the resort, and I slow down, not quite ready to end this conversation. "Well, thank you, Leo. It's very kind of you to try to make me feel better. The truth is, I'm happy being a pot with no lid."

"In that case, there are going to be a lot of horribly disappointed lids out there."

15

Shy Bladder Meets Snarky Parole Officer

Leo

"Leo, you old duffer, where the hell have you been?" It's my friend, Alexander Billingsworth the fourth, on the phone. He's fifteenth in line for the throne of Avonia, which is to say, he's never getting his skinny arse on that thing. He and I went to Eton together and have run in the same circles ever since. Tremendously fun bloke, but don't leave him alone with your girlfriend.

"I'm in the Benaventes for a while." I look around at the walls of my shed. "Thought it was time for a change of scenery."

"Crikey! You're all the way down there? I heard Alistair kicked you out of the kingdom for shagging that Swede, but I figured you'd just gone to England."

"Yes, well, I decided to get some sun while I let the old man cool off."

"Sounds delightful. An island of women who don't know better than to get involved with the likes of you." Alexander laughs, and I hold the phone away from my ear to avoid the painfully loud, donkey-like sound. "Listen, any chance you could make your way to Cannes? Cuddy's rented a twelve-bedroom villa just off Gazagnaire Beach. It's going to be four spectacular weeks of partying and topless women sunbathing."

Oh, that does sound spectacular. *So* much better than what I'm doing at the moment—scraping burnt egg from my one and only pan. "As much as I'd love to, I better take a pass this time."

"Who is she? And is it serious?" Alexander asks.

"No one. I'm working on a bit of a venture here that has some definite potential." As in, I could potentially lose everything if I don't go through with it.

"Really? You? A business venture?" he asks as though it's so shocking for him to think *I* might try to do something with my life. He's one to talk. It's not exactly like he just missed being on the Forbes 30 under 30 list by a narrow margin.

"Yup. Nothing big yet, but it could be if I stick it out." If you consider having your parents finance your life *big*.

"Don't tell me you're getting all responsible on me," Alexander says with a snort.

"Christ, no. It's more of a get-in-and-get-out thing. I'll be back to my loafing ways as soon as humanly possible." Or as soon as this pan is egg-free so I can relax a bit before my appointment at Jolene's office.

"I'd recommend you get out by the end of the month so you won't miss out on Cannes."

"Duly noted. Listen, I better run. Say hello to everyone for me."

"I probably won't."

That's because as soon as he hangs up, he's probably going to take a few hits from his glow-in-the-dark bong, and about thirty minutes from now, he'll have forgotten where I am.

***

"Oh, good. You're here," Jolene says, appearing about as excited as I imagine she'd be if I were her gastroenterologist and it was time for her colonoscopy. She steps aside to let me through the door to her office, which is really just a tiny room at the back of her house with a desk and a couple of chairs.

"You look lovely this morning," I say, giving her a bright smile.

Tilting her head, she says, "Let's dispense with the flattery." She thrusts a small clear plastic cup in my direction. "I'll need some urine."

"Righto. Where's the little boys' room?"

"It's down the hall, but you might as well do it here since I have to be in attendance anyway."

No fucking way. "That hardly seems necessary, Jolene."

"Not only is it completely necessary, but it's also part of your contract." She pushes the container toward me, but I don't take it. Instead, I stare at her, slack-jawed at the thought of unzipping my pants in front of a middle-aged woman in a Hawaiian shirt and cargo shorts.

"Relax. I promise not to peek at your naughty bits. Now, turn around and let's get this over with."

"You really think I would go to the trouble of purchasing urine from someone?"

"Yes, I do. There's a fortune at stake, Mr. Davenport."

"Excellent point." I take the cup and turn around, silently repeating, 'It'll all be worth it. It'll all be worth it.'

Quickly unzipping, I do my best to put the cup inside my pants rather than exposing Leopole. I wait, but nothing happens. *Oh, come on. This is not the time for a shy bladder. Just do it, Leo.*

Go.

Now.

Seriously, go already.

"Huh, most men don't have this problem until they're much older."

"I don't have a problem," I snap. "I'm just not used to…doing this in front of a woman."

"Think of me as a man with ovaries."

Oh, well that ought to help. Come on, mate. Relax and pee. But not too much. Just enough to fill this cup.

"Would you like a beer?"

"I'm not falling for that one," I say. "I may be lazy, but I'm not stupid."

"Had to try."

"Did you?" I ask, looking over my shoulder.

"No, but I wanted to," she says, smirking a little.

"That's the closest thing to a smile I've seen from you."

"That's because I'm enjoying the awkwardness of this situation."

***

Okay, so fast-forward through me eventually managing to provide a pee sample, showing her my first paystub so she could make a copy, and answering approximately thirty questions about my relationship with my landlady. Apparently, Jolene noticed a "spark" between us when she met Brianna. I tried to explain the only thing that excites me about Brianna is that she's providing me a means to meeting my goal, but Jolene isn't buying it. When I leave, she waits until I reach the sidewalk before calling to me, "Don't forget to keep it in your pants, Davenport. That is until you're back here to give your next sample."

That's nice of her, isn't it? To make it sound like I'm some sort of sperm donor, or that she's dabbling in switching teams and I'm the guy she's dabbling. I set off down the street, checking the time on my phone, and trying to forget about the last hour of my life.

The good news is the rest of my day is set to be an incredible combination of learning how to do laundry, figuring out what to pack for my dinner, buying a used bicycle on Craigslist, and going off to the resort, where instead of sipping cocktails by the pool like I would in my real life, I'll play a glorified mule to a bunch of surly guests.

To be honest, my I-can-make-anything-fun attitude is most definitely being sucked out of me with the power of a new Dyson. Oh, and in case you're surprised that I know that's a brand of vacuum, bear in mind, I do watch television, and that Dyson fellow seems to adore starring in commercials that run every ten minutes on every channel. Anyway, my point is, I've only been working for a month, and I can already understand why so many people on this planet have absolutely no will to live. Get up, complete all kinds of tedious tasks, do meaningless work all day or night, go to bed only to get up and do it all again. How do people do this for forty or so years without going completely insane?

Okay, Leo, that's enough self-pity for one lifetime. You only have to do this for six months, then everything will go back to normal. And by normal, I mean I can get the hell out of Paradise Bay and back to paradise.

16

Pampered Men, Mom Guilt, and Truth Lassos

Leo

"Pierce, what are you doing right now? And more importantly, what is your maid doing right now?" I ask.

"Writing, and I don't think your feelings for Mrs. Bailey are mutual," Pierce says.

"Ha ha. I'm not looking for a shag," I say, staring at the pile of laundry in front of me. "I thought maybe I could swing by to visit my favourite brother and have my laundry done."

"As much as I love being used by you, I refuse to do anything to jeopardize your future. What if your parole officer caught Mrs. Bailey with her hands on your dirty knickers?"

I hear the caw of a seagull, which means Pierce must be sitting outside on one of his expensive lounge chairs while he works. Prick. "Don't tell me you're going to rat me out for getting my tighty-whities washed, dried, and folded?" I ask, a sense of righteous indignation building in my chest. "Are you suddenly switching allegiances?"

"On the contrary. I'm as solidly on your side today as I ever have been, which is exactly why I won't allow you to take the easy way out," Pierce says.

In the background, I hear the familiar voice of Mrs. Bailey. "Your morning smoothie, Mr. Davenport. I've added some pre-soaked chia seeds. Do let me know if it's to your liking, sir."

"Brilliant, I'm sure it will be extra healthy. Thank you, Mrs. Bailey."

A moment later, I have Pierce's full attention again. "Sorry, Leo, where were we?"

"You were telling me how soft I am right before you were served your fruity chia-seed smoothie by your housekeeper."

"Ah, yes. You seem to be forgetting the many years of head-down, arse-up, non-stop work I did to land where I have."

"I didn't call to be lectured or to listen to you gloat about how rich you are."

"No, you called because you don't know how to use a washing machine, and now you're pouting because you have to figure it out for yourself," Pierce says before loudly sipping his smoothie.

Well, he's got a point there, not that I'm going to admit it. I stew silently for a moment.

Pierce clears his throat. "Leo, have you considered the alternative to this ridiculous contract?"

"You mean living in poverty for the rest of my life?"

"Well, there's certainly the risk of that, obviously, but I have a feeling that if you didn't have the Bunny and Alistair safety net, you'd find yourself to be quite capable of earning a good living."

"That's kind of you, but I'll take a hard pass. After a month of living the life of a working stiff, I think I'll go back to being happy, thank you very much."

"You weren't happy. You were rudderless and bored every day of your life."

"On the contrary, I was never bored, because unlike other people, I'm fully capable of finding inventive and exciting ways to amuse myself. Unfortunately, on my current budget and time constraints, none of that is possible," I say. "Now, since you refuse to help me, I should ring off and try to figure out how to work the bleeding washing machine. I've been free-balling it for two days now, and I kind of miss my boxer briefs."

"All right. Good luck with your domestic chores. Just know that you can count on me for assistance should you choose to be an adult human being rather than our mother's pet."

"I won't say what I'm thinking at the moment, Pierce, because I'm far too much of a gentleman."

"No, you're not. You just can't think of anything clever."

Bastard. I wish he didn't know me so well. "Good day, Pierce. Don't choke on your chia seeds."

***

"What the hell does permanent press mean?" I mutter, staring at the dials while the pile of dirty clothes tips precariously at my feet, threatening to spill all over the hallway.

I really need to sort this out fast because Milo the man-hater is currently practicing the not-so-subtle art of murdering one of my socks, and I'm pretty sure once he shreds this one, he'll move onto the rest of them. I originally mistook him for Puddy Tat (who adores yours truly) and attempted to take the sock away in exchange for some scratches behind the ear. Turns out, I'm the one who got scratched—all over my left hand. Then he hissed in my face and tore off down the hall with it. My goal is to get these clothes safely into the wash before he returns for seconds.

What kind of sadist invented these stupid machines? I can't even find the button that pops open the round hatch on the front. I briefly consider asking Brianna for help but decide against it. When I walked in the house, I saw her sitting at the kitchen table with her books spread in front of her, which means her current pursuit has a good deal more long-term value than mine. A movement down the hall catches my eye, and I look up to see little Isabelle, who is dressed as Wonder Woman, but for some reason with the addition of enormous blue furry gloves.

"Good morning, my young friend."

"Do you know my name?" she asks, squinting her eyes at me.

"Of course I do. Your name is Isabelle Lewis."

Shaking her head vigorously, she shouts, "I'm Wonder Woman!"

She charges in my direction and skids to a stop just short of my dirty clothes.

"Yes, well, obviously I know that's your *true* identity. I didn't want to say it out loud in case Lex Luthor happened to be listening."

"Him isn't here, silly. Superman killeded him."

"Right. How did I forget?" I turn back to the washing machine, tapping my finger on my cheekbone while I try to discern the proper way to open the door. I start randomly turning the dials and pushing buttons, but *nada*.

"What are you doing?" Isabelle asks, giving me a sceptical look.

"It's a secret, but I suppose if I don't tell you, you'll use your lasso of truth on me."

She nods excitedly at the thought.

I glance from side to side as though making sure no one else will hear me, then lean down and whisper, "Laundry."

Her face falls at my boring, grown-up response. *I know the feeling, kid.*

"Say, you don't happen to know which one of these buttons opens the hatch, do you?"

"Hatch?"

"The round thing there. The hatch."

"That's a door, silly." Isabelle wrinkles her nose at me with an expression I can only describe as disgust. "Here," she says, yanking it open.

"Well, that was deceptively simple," I say, feeling more than a little bit foolish. "Thank you, Wonder Woman."

I pick up as much of the clothes as I can and start shoving them unceremoniously into the machine.

"You're doing it wrong," Isabelle says, shaking her head. She waves me away, sticks her entire torso into the machine, and emerges with my clothing. "You gotta sort them first."

I watch as she deftly sorts the clothes into three piles. Things that are white or very light, dark clothing, and colourful things.

"Why are you doing that?"

"Because the black clothes will make the white clothes all grey, and the red shirt will make your white socks all pink. I like pink socks, but you is a man."

"That's a little sexist, don't you think?" I ask. "Just because 'I is a man,' doesn't mean I can't wear pink socks."

Putting her furry blue hands on her hips, she gives me a hard look. "Do you want pink socks?"

"Well, no, but—"

"Then you better sort them."

A moment later, she's got the sorting done and starts stuffing my pile of whites into the machine. I crouch down to help, feeling rather sheepish. When we finish, I hold my hand up for a high five. "Thank you, you really are a superhero. Do you know where the powder goes?"

"I'm four. I'm not stupid."

From the kitchen, Brianna calls, "Isabelle Naomi Lewis, we don't use that word in this house."

"Which word?" I whisper to my small friend.

Cupping her little hand over her mouth, she whispers, "*Stupid.* It's a bad swear word people say when they make fun of someone whose brain can't work good."

"Ah, I see." Wait a minute. She just implied that *I'm* stupid because I didn't know where the powder goes, which means she thinks my brain doesn't "work good."

I wonder if this day could get more humiliating?

Isabelle slides open a small tray near the top of the machine and points a blue finger. "Put the powder in here. Then you close it and turn it on."

Her eyes light up. "Gotta go! *Paw Patrol* is on."

I watch as she thunders down the hall, taking a sharp left into the living room.

"Here, let me show you the rest," Brianna, who has snuck up behind me, says.

She takes hold of the large dial. "Pull out, turn to here, push it back in, and you're done. Give it about thirty-five minutes, then come back and you can hang this on the line outside and pop in the next load. You're welcome to borrow my laundry basket."

She waits while I follow her instructions. When the sound of pouring water starts up, I feel a surge of excitement. Clean undies at last! Oh, Lord, my life truly is pathetic, no? I smile down at Brianna. "Thank you."

I follow her into the kitchen to pour myself a coffee while she sits back down in front of half a dozen open textbooks.

"I see you've been busy today."

"Yes, and unfortunately, my aunt went to the north side of the island with some friends for the day, so Isabelle has been stuck in front of the TV all morning."

"In that case, she must be very happy," I say, thinking of how much I would enjoy a full day on the couch right now.

"Not really. She's quite bored. I'm not exactly up for a mum-of-the-year award with the amount I've had to study these past few months."

"You're awfully hard on yourself," I say, sitting down at the table.

"Well, that's what happens when you read a bunch of books on childhood development that tell you how TV is junk food for the brain. So while I'm pursuing my dream, I can't help but feel a sense of panic that I'm permanently stunting her potential."

"Christ, you're putting high stakes on one day of her watching television."

"Welcome to mum guilt."

"So you're working your arse off to give her a better life, and somehow you're viewing that as a failure on your behalf?"

"Got it in one," she says, picking up her pencil.

I watch her for a moment, wanting very much to talk her out of feeling guilty for trying to give her daughter a better life. Deciding that it's not my place, I say, "Well, why don't I play with Isabelle for a while?"

Brianna shakes her head. "That's okay, really."

There's something about the way she says it that I find slightly offensive. "Surely I'm qualified to play some games with a four-year-old. After all, according to you, I am an overgrown man-child."

"I didn't mean it like that," Brianna says. "It's *my* problem, not yours. And I'm sure you've got better things to do than play with Isabelle."

"One would think, but I *literally* have nothing else to do while I wait for that machine over there to clean my clothes."

I feel a tap on my shoulder and turn to see a furry blue hand is doing the tapping. "Is you going to play with me?" Isabelle asks excitedly.

"*Are* you going to play with me? *Are you*, not is you," Brianna says while Isabelle grins up at me hopefully.

"Are he going to play with me, Mum?"

Brianna fights a smile, looks at me, and murmurs, "You don't have to do this."

"I know." Giving Isabelle a big smile, I say, "Do I get to be Spider-Man?"

17

Lies, Ice Cream Men, and Other Things That Should Be Banned

Brianna

THIS IS WEIRD. I've had nearly an entire hour of uninterrupted study time. I can't remember this happening since Izzy was born. Apparently, overgrown men-children are not only qualified to amuse children, but they're pretty damn good at it. The two of them are playing in the garden, and I can hear her giggling away through the open window. Is this weird? What if he's some sort of weirdo? I should probably check on them. I walk over to the sink and peer out the window, my heart tugging. Well, as if that isn't adorable? Isabelle is perched on her tricycle, peddling as quickly as her legs can take her, chasing Leo around the driveway in large circles. Somehow, she's managed to talk him into wearing her red cape, and he's doing a most convincing job of pretending to be terrified of Wonder Woman. A laugh escapes me as I watch. Although the logical side of me is insisting I get back to work, there's another part of me riding a wave of grief for what my daughter has missed out on by not having a dad.

Did I just suggest mums can't be fun? Blech. I shake my head, trying to clear the thought from my brain and reminding myself that Isabelle is fine. Annoyed at myself for allowing my mother's antiquated opinions to seep into my psyche, I sit down and get back to studying. Within a few sentences, I'm lost in the world of civil disputes regarding property matters.

A couple of pages later, the back-door bursts open, and Isabelle comes running in. "Mum, Mum! The ice cream man is coming!" She hollers, hopping around like she has to go pee really badly.

Bugger. I hate that guy with his Pied Piper music blaring out of the speakers on his little van, enticing children everywhere to beg their parents mercilessly for delicious ice cream treats. Glancing at the clock, I quickly calculate the amount of time until supper. This ice cream *would* buy me another hour before I'd have to cook. Oh, wow, I'm a bad mum today, aren't I?

But seriously, will eating dessert before supper *just the one time* really harm her?

Leo appears beside her, his face damp with sweat from running around in the heat, and his expression full of excitement. "Did she say yes?" he asks Isabelle.

Sighing, I say, "I don't know, Isabelle. It's getting close to supper time. What if we save it for dessert?"

Her shoulders fall, and her bottom lip pulls away from her face. "I promise I will eat every bite of my vegetables."

"Me, too," Leo says with a firm nod.

Unable to help myself, I chuckle as I stand up and cross the room to get my purse.

"Yay! If my mum gets her purse, it means we can have ice cream!" She holds her hand up for a high five, which Leo gives her.

"Yes!" he says.

Pulling a twenty out of my wallet, I hand it to Isabelle. "Pick out one thing. *One.* And make it small. You don't want to spoil your appetite. And can you grab me a fudgsicle please?"

Leo grins. "My treat. I'll go get my wallet."

"My treat. You've been a huge help today."

"Oh, but it's been terrific fun for me, too, and I'd love to treat you."

Tipping my chin down, I give him an I'm-serious-so-stop-arguing face. It seems to work, because he says, "Thank you."

"Thank *you*," I say to him as I hold the bill out.

Snatching the cash from me, Isabelle zips out of the room and toward the back door, grabbing Leo's hand as she rushes out. "Hurry, before he disappears!"

"I want the change back, Miss Flutter Pants!" I call as the door slams shut.

Huh, perhaps this day is going to be a nice one after all?

***

"What happened to 'Mum, I promise to eat all my vegetables if I can have ice cream?'" I ask, raising an eyebrow at Isabelle and watching as she pushes the cooked carrots around on her plate. She's sitting slumped to the side with her hand on the crook of her elbow, looking very much like she might fall asleep right there. I guess all that sun and fresh air tuckered her out, which could seriously work in my favour. If she falls asleep nice and early, I might actually get caught up to my planned study schedule.

"I don't feel good," Isabelle says, "My tummy hurts."

"Nice try, kiddo, but I wasn't born yesterday. Now, eat your car—"

A heaving sound erupts from Isabelle's chest, followed by a splash as a tremendous amount of liquid hits the floor. Puddy Tat and Knickers bolt from under the table and take off as though they're being chased by Cujo.

Oh, bollocks.

"Mum, I barfed," she cries, gasping for air before belching and vomiting again.

I bolt out of my chair, knocking it over, then take hold of Izzy's long hair and pull it back away from her face while she continues to get sick. I rub her back with one hand and say soothing things about how she'll be okay, and I'm sorry I made her eat the carrots, and I'm sorry I just said that thing about the carrots because probably she doesn't want to think about that right now…

The entire time, I keep one eye closed, only peering through the other one as though that will help me not smell it. I try very hard not to breathe through my nose, because, like many people, the smell of vomit often makes me vomit. As a mum, that renders me somewhat useless in these situations.

The back door opens. Oh, nuts. You know who else is not good with vomit? Aunt Dolores. She used to gag even when Izzy spit up milk as a baby. "Auntie Dolores! Don't come in here. Isabelle is throwing up!"

Rubbing Isabelle's back, I shush her. "Try to calm down, honey. You'll be okay." My words are wasted because trying to tell a four-year-old that they're not going to die in the middle of vomiting is about as useful as trying to explain the theory of relativity to a gerbil.

"Oh, that is *a lot* of vomit," Leo says from his position in the entrance to the kitchen.

I glance up at him for a moment and see he's holding his towel and a change of clothes, which explains why he's come inside. For some reason, the sight of him makes me angry. I knew I should never trust a man. "How much ice cream did you let her have?"

"Obviously too much," he says, surveying the mess.

"Did you not hear me tell her she could have *one small thing?*"

"Well, yes, but she said she normally gets a Drumstick and Revello when she's with your aunt."

"And you *believed that?*" I snap, turning back to Isabelle, who seems to be done for now. Her eyes are closed, and she's leaning her clammy cheek on my arm.

"I thought children were unfailingly honest."

"That's only when it comes to *insulting people*. When it comes to sweets and bedtimes, they're pathological liars."

"Oh, God. I'm so sorry," he says. "Let me help."

"Nope," I snap. Picking Isabelle up under her armpits, I stand her on the chair and strip off her puke-covered pants, gagging as I work. "You've done enough, thank you. Come on, Izzy. Let's get you in the bath."

She looks at me, her face green. "It's not him's fault, Mummy. I told him it was okay."

"Well, he's supposed to be a grown-up. He should know better." I carefully take her shirt off over her head and set it on the floor next to her pants, then pick her up and hold her close as I make my way down the hall and up the stairs to the bathroom.

Thirty minutes later, Isabelle is tucked in bed with a bucket propped up next to her pillow in case there is another round of 'I ate too much ice cream because my mum's an idiot and she allowed me to play with an irresponsible man all afternoon.' The colour is returning to her cheeks as I place a cool, wet face cloth on her forehead. "Will you be okay here for a little while? Mummy needs to go clean up the kitchen."

She nods bravely. "I'll be okay, Mummy."

"That's my girl. You rest up. I'll be back to check on you soon." I give her a kiss on the cheek, then hurry down the stairs filled with dread at what I'm about to face. *Just get it over with, Brianna.*

When I reach the kitchen, I stop, shocked to see that not only is the entire floor clean, but the dishes have been done, the table's been cleared, and I can hear the washing machine running. Huh. Well, that's a surprise. My righteous indignation fades out, replaced by guilt at how mean I was to Leo.

I grab two bottles of ginger beer from the fridge and head outside, finding him on the tiny front porch of the suite with his feet propped up on an overturned bucket, looking at his mobile phone. Swallowing hard, I walk over and hold out one of the beers. "This comes with both my deepest gratitude and regret."

He glances up at me and gives me a small smile, then looks at the beer and shakes his head. "While I appreciate the gesture, I really can't take that."

"What are you talking about? You've more than earned it after cleaning up that hideous mess. You did an amazing job, by the way. It's like it never even happened."

"Oh, it most certainly happened," he says, wrinkling his nose up, then chuckling. "But I can't drink that. I made a promise I will take a break from drinking, and I intend to live up to it."

"Oh, sorry, I didn't realize you had a problem."

He seems taken aback. "I don't. Not that kind of problem anyway.

Lots of other ones though. Not drugs or anything, just a general lack of responsibility."

"Well, you seem to be getting over that." I stare at his attractive face and am reminded of the fact that he is not for me, no matter how amazing it would be to have someone with whom to share puke duty and all the other less disgusting things in life. But that's not what this is about.

He's a rich, privileged tourist in my life, and getting attached to him in any way, shape, or form would be beyond stupid. "You didn't have to do that. I could've handled it."

"I didn't clean up because I believe you incompetent. I cleaned up because you were right. It was my fault that Isabelle got sick, and I wanted to do what I could to make things better."

"Well, thank you. It's not your fault, though. I should have told you she's a lying puker," I say, staring down at my bare feet to avoid the pain of memorizing his face. Unable to help myself, I glance back up at him, feeling that melty, soft happiness in my belly that shouldn't be there. "Anyway, I should go back inside in case Isabelle needs me."

"How's she doing?" Leo asks, sounding like the most sincere person on the planet.

"She's fine. All clean and tucked into bed."

Nodding, he says, "Good. I'm glad to hear that. Can you tell her I'm sorry that I let her indulge?"

I shake my head. "How about instead, I tell her you said you hope she's feeling better?"

"That works, too," Leo says, holding my gaze for long enough to make me wonder what he sees when he looks at me.

"Goodnight, Leo. And thank you for everything today."

"You're most welcome."

18

Tattoos, Booze, and Other Ways to Ruin a Perfectly Good Weekend

Brianna

I AM IN HELL, and I will remain there for the next fifty-four hours and twenty-one minutes, at which point I will climb into my Corolla, which is waiting for me in the airport parking lot, shut the door, and breathe the biggest sigh of relief of all time. Until that moment, however, I shall: A) channel my inner Emmett, the construction worker from the Lego Movie, and pretend everything is awesome, B) act like I don't despise my sister's plastic, ridiculous friends, C) refrain from speaking ill of my sister's stupid fiancé, and, D) smile and laugh and pretend to care about anything that matters to them, including but not limited to: whatever the Kardashians are up to, the latest hair and makeup trends, who Rhianna is dating now, and which of the contestants on *The Bachelorette* really should have been sent packing by now.

So basically, I'm going to play a lot of make-believe while we drink cocktails by the pool. I'll be in my stretchmark-hiding mumkini— a tank-top-style two-piece with a skirt that goes over my bikini bottoms to hide my thighs and extra ruching on the top to hide my muffin top. Then I'll pretend I'm super thrilled to get our drink on at supper so we can hit the clubs hard all night. The important thing is for Amber to have a wonderful, memorable experience that she can look back on fondly when she's knee-deep in laundry after she and Zidane have the three strapping boys and one little ballerina they have planned.

It is Friday at three p.m., and we are midway through our one-hour flight to Isla del Sol for the 'World's Most Epic Hen's Party!' Yay. The rest of the bridal party is knocking back Alabama Slammers like they're in a race to see who can throw up first. My money's on Quinn, who weighs about ninety pounds, even under the weight of those fake eyelashes—which honestly make her look as though she keeps her two pet tarantulas fastened to her eyelids for safekeeping. *Oh, that wasn't nice. Bad Bree.*

I was already in a shit mood because last night at work, Rosy caught me studying when I was at the desk. I was so caught up in Torts that I completely forgot to call a cab for a couple who needed to get to the airport. By the time I called, it was too late, and they ended up missing their flight, which is as big a screw up as they come as far as concierges go. I got chewed out for twenty minutes and she threatened to dock my pay for the airfare (two tickets all the way back to Avonia, which is not something I'll be able to afford anytime soon). Lucky for me, Harrison showed up when he heard all the yelling and he smoothed things over for me. I won't have to pay the resort back, but I am on 'probation' which sucks big time. I've never been on probation in my life. Never even had a note sent home when I was in school. So being in this kind of trouble has made me even more cross than I would normally have been on a stupid hen's weekend with my sister's stupid friends.

I have somehow ended up sitting in the middle seat. To my left is Kandi, who *absolutely must* be by the window so she can get as many sweet pics of the scenery as possible for her IG followers. To my right is Amber, who has the aisle seat so she can talk to Quinn and Valerie as well as us. The four of us bridesmaids are wearing customized pink V-neck T-shirts that say, "Amber's Bitches" except, instead of an 'I,' there's a sparkly gold penis, so that's rather classy, wouldn't you say? Not the least bit humiliating for someone who's both a mum *and* a future barrister. I sure hope I'll be tagged in dozens of shots wearing this shirt that's about as undersized on me as the Grinch's heart. You know, *before* that little Cindy Loo Who guilted him into returning everyone's stuff and singing songs while he held everyone's hands.

Kandi leans across me to talk to Valerie, who is four seats plus one aisle over from her. "Val! Val! Val!"

Nope. Valerie didn't hear her on account of the insane noise of this humid, cramped Island Hopper propeller plane. It's not only the engines that are noisy but the people aboard this Friday afternoon's 'party flight.' And that's not my name for it. That's what the captain called it when he was giving his welcome-aboard speech over the speaker.

Kandi is clearly not a quitter. "Val! Val Valerie! Val!"

Glancing at me, Kandi laughs. "Oh my God, is she deaf, or what?"

"Right?" I ask, hoping she'll give up now that shouting has yielded no results.

"Val! Val! Valerie!"

Nope. Not giving up. Instead, Kandi is screeching loud enough to burst my left eardrum.

I tap Amber's hand, who then nudges Quinn on the shoulder and tells her Kandi has something she wants to tell Valerie. Oh, thank God.

When Valerie finally makes eye contact with Kandi, Kandi says, "These Alabama Slammers are *delish*, no?"

Valerie nods and shouts, "Oh, yeah, baby! It's party time!"

Well, at least she had something really important to say. It would have been super annoying if Kandi put us all through that just to say something inconsequential…

Quinn leans across Amber and stares at my breasts. "You're hot, Bree. Fitted T's are your thing. You'd totally find a man if you wore them more often."

"Do you think?" I ask, feigning delight.

"Oh, yeah, totes," Quinn says with a firm nod. "I wish I had huge cans like yours."

"Me, too!" Kandi adds. "Yours aren't even all droopy."

"Yeah, they're like not even mum boobs at all," Quinn says.

"Hashtag blessed," I say, holding up my drink.

The other girls laugh, and I go along, but on the inside, I imagine kicking open the window and squeezing myself out of it—huge, perky boobs and all—and plummeting to my death.

"We're rocking these T's," Valerie says. "Where did you get them, Quinny?"

Quinn shrugs, even though she's delighted someone finally asked. "Oh, just this online store from China that my brother's girlfriend told me about. I had to order them *ages* ago so we'd have them on time, but totally worth it, no?"

I nod out of obligation. "Totally." As in, I'm totally going to lose this accidentally on purpose as soon as humanly possible. "What do I owe you for this?"

"Oh, don't worry about that, I was happy to get them for everyone," Quinn says. "They were like twenty-two fifty because of all the custom printing on them. Plus, I had to pay five dollars extra for the sparkly penises, so it was more like $27.50 plus shipping, which worked out to like $4 per shirt, but seriously, you do not have to pay me back if it's out of your budget. I know money is tight for you, so just buy me a drink or something when we get there."

"Oh, no, that's fine. I want to pay you back." $31.50 for this rag that's so thin you could spit through it? My God, I haven't spent that much on an article of clothing for myself in *years*, if you don't count the backless bridesmaid dress, that is.

Kandi grabs my arm. "The best part is, we can wear these *all* weekend because the villa has a washer and dryer."

Quinn leans over and says, "So even if we wear them like, three times, it'll bring the cost down to like, ten dollars per wear, so that's practically free."

"Good point," says Amber, who is wearing a tight white T-shirt that bears the words, "These are my bitches" on the back of her T-shirt. On the front, it says, "Zidane's Ho," which offends me on so many levels that in the words of Kandi, *I can't even.* Taking a big gulp of my drink, I decide my best strategy *might be* to stay slightly drunk all weekend to get through this. Not so drunk that I tell Amber she's making a huge mistake, but drunk enough that I won't want to throat punch my sister's horrible friends.

Amber watches me suck back my drink, then leans in and lowers her voice. "Is that a celebratory drink or an I'm-going-to-numb-myself-out-because-I-can't- stand-any-of-this drink?"

Oh, she knows me so well. I smile brightly and squeeze her hand. "Celebratory, obviously! This is going to be *so* fun."

"No, it won't. You're going to hate every minute of this," Amber says, raising one eyebrow.

"But I promise I'm gonna try really hard not to."

"And that's why you're the best sister ever." Amber gives me a big wet kiss on my cheek, then turns to talk to Quinn. According to my watch an entire four minutes have gone by already, so at least there's that...

***

"Hello, Lamb, it's Mum," I say into the phone.

I'm currently hiding in the restaurant bathroom so I can say good-night to Izzy, whom I miss so much it hurts. She's staying at my parents' place until Sunday night to give Aunt Dolores a break and to give my parents some Izzy time, as they call it.

"Hi, Mummy!" Her sweet little voice comes across the line, tugging at my heart. "We went fishing this afternoon, and Grandpa let me drive the boat."

I smile at the image of it, remembering doing the exact same thing at her age. "Well, that is just wonderful, sweetie. Sounds like you're having a great time."

"I am. I been in the new pool all day 'cept when we went fishing. Grandpa says I'm part mermaid. Grandma says I can stay up until 9 o'clock and I'm allowed to eat ice cream before bed."

How is she back on ice cream again after vomiting up so much of it only a few days ago? Kids really do bounce back faster than adults. I stare at myself in the mirror above the sink, trying to discern if I look as tipsy as I feel.

My eyes are drawn to my chest by the glittery penis. Huh. Perhaps this T-shirt doesn't look so bad on me after all. I cover-up the penis with my hand and wonder if it would be possible to lose 15 pounds, then get these stupid letters and the dick off of it.

"Grandma wants to talk to you."

Awesome. "Okay, Honey Bunny. I love you so, so, so much. You have a terrific sleep, and I will call you again tomorrow."

"Sounds good, chicky!"

"Brianna?" My mum says.

"In the flesh. Well, I mean, on the phone." I chuckle at my own joke.

"How are things going?"

"Good, yeah, everyone's having a great time," I say, carefully pronouncing my words so I don't sound drunk. "The villa is very nice. We're finishing up supper."

"Good," my mum says, her tone conveying concern. "I just wanted to make sure everything is going all right between you and the rest of the girls. Sometimes these things get a little out of hand, and I don't want you to ruin it for Amber."

"Oh, well, thanks for your faith in me."

"That didn't come out right. It's just that…you know how you have a bit of an edge? Maybe you could tuck that away for the next couple days and make sure everybody has a really nice time…for Amber?"

Rolling my eyes, I make a face in the mirror. "Yeah, don't worry. I left all my sharp edges at home so no one would get hurt."

"See? There's that sarcasm. I don't think you left all your edges at home, young lady."

"Mum, I scrounged up a thousand dollars to be on this trip so I can make my little sister happy. Do you *really think* I'd do that if I was planning to ruin everything?"

"Well, no." She sniffs. "Not on purpose, obviously."

"Don't worry about it. I know how to behave, Mother," I say with a sigh. "Now, I better go. I don't want them to have to wait for me.

They're all eager to get to the first strip club. Apparently, it's ladies' night, and drinks are only a dollar until ten p.m."

That's not true, we're not going to a strip club, but why not horrify my mother if I get the chance? I hang up the phone before she can protest, then pull the door open and walk very deliberately back toward our table, hoping I appear respectably sober-ish. A greasy-looking guy, who's incidentally sitting at a table with either his wife or girlfriend, gives me the once-over and a knowing grin directly at my penis-clad chest. Gross.

Valerie screams when she sees me as though I'm her long-lost twin. "There's Bitch One!"

Oh, yeah, I forgot to tell you, we've all been numbered now, like Thing One and Thing Two from Dr. Seuss, only in our case, there are Bitches One through Four. But that's okay, at least it's better than what they're calling Amber. Instead of the Cat in the Hat she's the C*nt on the Hunt.

I think I'll have another drink…

***

"I'm not saying nobody else should get tattoos. I'm saying *I'm not* doing it." We're now standing in the lobby of Randy Andy's Tattoos & Piercing Emporium, which, if you ask me, should be renamed Randy Andy's Dungeon of Dirty Needles and STI's. Other than Randy Andy, there's a super-high-looking blond surfer dude already sporting sleeves of tattoos. He's sitting on one of the metal chairs in the waiting area sipping a massive can of Red Bull as he pours over the sample binders.

It's ten p.m., and for some reason, Quinn booked us for tattoos at this hour. I'm ready to go back to the villa, put on my jammies, and curl up with a book. Instead, we're getting tattoos followed by barhopping until six a.m.

Quinn smiles at Andy. "Sorry about this. We'll just be a second." Turning to me, she lowers her voice. "I put a lot of work into finding the best place. According to Google reviews, this place has a 4.1-star rating, which is the best on the island."

So for Quinn, "a lot of work" is googling something on her phone. Perfect. "Yeah, 4.1 out of five feels like a miss to me when it comes to *permanently altering* your body. That means, mathematically speaking, almost one out of every five people who walks in here excited leaves not-so-happy *for the rest of their lives*." I point around the circle, counting, "One, two, three, four, five. One of us is going to leave really upset. Possibly forever." Glancing over my shoulder, I say, "No offense, Randy."

"It's Andy. None taken," he says with a quick nod.

"But, Bree, we're all doing this for Amber, remember?" Valerie says, using a tone one would reserve for toddlers or people with advanced dementia. "So we'll *all have* the same tattoo on the back of our left shoulders, and everyone will see it when we stand at the front of the church?"

"Except under the heart everyone will have a different number," Valerie adds.

"You get to be Bitch One, Bree. Bitch One is the best bitch," Kandi says, tilting her head.

"We'll be a united front," Kandi says. "The tattoos show our undying faith in Amber and Dane's love."

"Gnarly idea, ladies," surfer guy says, smiling up at us. "Matching tats on classy ladies like yourselves would be immeasurably hot."

I level him with the same look I gave Isabelle when she used an entire tube of Vaseline to "wet her hair." Surfer guy lowers his gaze back to the binders. One down, four idiots to go.

Quinn puts her hand on my arm. "Brianna, don't you *believe* in their love?"

No. No, I don't. "Of course I believe in their love. In fact, I believe in it so much I know for sure the success of their marriage in no way hinges on me having a heart with a Celtic sisterhood knot in the centre on my shoulder. As lovely as it is, it's a lot of money…and I'm a mum, so…"

"We'll pitch in for yours," Amber says, her face lighting up.

The rest of the girls nod enthusiastically, even though I can see on their faces that not one of them is actually excited about the thought of paying for my tattoo. Not that I blame them. I don't want to pay for it, either.

"Sweetie, I'm *really* not a needle person, okay?"

Kandi grabs my forearm and sways. "That's why you should have had more drinks at the restaurant. *Nobody's* a needle person."

"Well, actually I am," Andy mutters.

Turning to the other girls, Kandi says, "I got this. You guys get started, I'll take her somewhere and get her wasted. By the time we come back, it'll be our turn."

"No, thank you, Kandi," I say, plucking her clammy fingers off my arm. "I will not get one here or there, I will not get one anywhere. Not on my arm. Not on my hip. Not in this place, not on a ship. I will not get a heart tattoo. I will not get one," Running out of rhymes, I say, "But you ladies go ahead."

Amber steps up directly in my face, tears filling her eyes. "Why can't you do this *one thing* for me? You're my sister. These tattoos are like saying you're part of my tribe. You, of all people, should be proud to be in my tribe!"

Quinn leans over her shoulder and nods. "It's the sisterhood of Amber."

"You *have to do this,*" Kandi says. "I'm gonna make you do this because otherwise, you're going to regret it for the rest of your life."

Seriously? "Yeah, I'm really not. I've actually never met *anyone* who said they regretted *not* getting a tattoo."

Randy Andy, who's been staring silently from behind the counter this whole time, nods at me. "I shouldn't say this, but I think she might be right there."

I glance at him while my mind spins. I could either do the decent thing—thank him for helping me make my point, and hope the rest of the bridal party is swayed. Or I can do what any good attorney would do, and go for the jugular. I pick the second option. Holding up one finger, I begin my cross-examination. "Would you agree, sir, that you've occasionally had customers who come back in to ask how to get rid of their tattoo?"

"You mean because they didn't like the artwork?"

"It's a yes or a no, sir. Have you ever had a customer come back in because they wanted to get rid of a tattoo you gave them?"

"Yes, but—"

"Thank you for answering the question," I say firmly. "You do have dissatisfied customers, don't you, Andy? And not just once in a while. According to your rating on Google, nearly one in five people who come here leaves unhappy. Isn't that right?"

"It's not like that because—" he starts.

"Are you saying if I do a Google search of this establishment, I'll find a higher rating?"

"No, but—"

I hold up one hand. "No further explanation needed. We get the point, sir."

Surfer dude chimes in with, "You're a hardass, lady."

Amber glares at me. "Those reviews aren't accurate because people are more likely to complain than leave a compliment."

"She's right, you know," Andy says in an urgent tone. "People love to complain, especially online instead of to your face. Most of the time when someone changes their mind, it's because they were either drunk or super high, and when they sobered up, they realize they don't want a dragon on their forehead or neck or whatever. It's not because I screwed up."

"Ha! *We're* not getting forehead tattoos!" Quinn says, as though she's just proven her case.

Ignoring her, I continue questioning the witness. "Thank you, Andy. I have one last question for you, and then I'll let you get on with your evening. To the best of your knowledge, have you ever had anyone return to your…emporium, crying or in a rage because they wish they'd already had their tattoo done?"

"No," he says, scratching his scruffy chin. "Never."

"Thank you." I turn back to the group, triumphant. How can they possibly want to go through with it now? "You see? We will not regret *not* getting tattoos, but there's a 20% chance we will have serious regrets about getting them."

Amber makes a loud growling sound that comes from deep in her chest. "Arg! Why do you have to go all lawyer-mum on us? I *hate it* when you do this!"

"How to ruin your sister's weekend," Valerie mutters.

"Yeah, nice," Quinn adds, shaking her head at me.

"I will *never regret* having a sisterhood tattoo," Valerie says, crossing her arms across her chest. "Ever. I will want to remember this weekend and their wedding *for the rest of my life.*"

She stretches out one arm in front of her, palm down, peering around the group dramatically. "Who's with me?"

"I am," Kandi says through gritted teeth, putting her hand on top of Valerie's, as though this is the uniting of a group of warriors about to unleash hell on the evils of the world.

"Me, too," Quinn says with a firm nod, covering Kandi's hand with hers. "I choose to join the Sisterhood of Amber."

Well, she booked the appointments, so…

Amber puts her hand in and gives me a pleading look. "It would mean so much to me if you were part of the Sisterhood."

"We're not even Celtic." I let the words slip out before I can think to stop them. Amber sniffs, fighting back tears that cause my heart to sink. "I'm sorry. It's just…is it really so awful if I don't participate in this *one* activity? I promise I'll do everything else this weekend."

She tries to fan her tears away quickly with her perfectly manicured hands. "Why can't you just be fun for one weekend?"

"I'm trying, Amber. I really am. What if we all got matching necklaces to wear to the wedding?" I suggest.

"Don't be such a puss," Valerie says. "You gave birth to a baby, for God's sake. This won't be nearly as painful."

"You know what? That's enough," I say, holding up one hand. "I'm not going to be bullied into getting a tattoo, all right? So forget it, already. I've tried to be nice about it, but it's an idiotic idea. Nobody needs a tattoo commemorating a hen's weekend, or to depict their faith in someone else's stupid marriage, which statistically speaking, has a fifty percent chance of ending in divorce, which means there's a pretty big chance you'll have a symbol of their love long after it ends. No offence, Amber. I'm not implying you and Dane won't make it but it's a statistical fact."

"One that didn't need to be mentioned," Quinn mutters.

Amber bites her bottom lip, clearly trying not to burst into tears, and I realize I'm doing precisely what my mother said I would—which is ruin her special weekend. Guilt overcomes me, and I close my eyes for a second. "You're right, Quinn. I'm sorry, Amber. I'm just scared of needles." And hepatitis. And I'm broke. And have no desire to commemorate this crap weekend permanently. "I have no right to ruin your fun time. Let's start over, okay? You go ahead, and I'll…take photos of you all getting your tattoos."

Amber stares at me for a second, hope filling her eyes. "So you'll stop trying to talk us out of it?"

Nodding, I say, "Get as many tattoos as you want. Put Dane's name across your face in some swirly font for all I care. I just want you to be happy."

"Thanks, Bree," she says, hugging me tightly. "I'm sorry I tried to talk you into getting a tattoo. I sometimes forget how hard your life must be."

"That's okay. You're trying to make me part of your tribe which is really sweet," I say. "Most brides would probably leave their boring old sister at home, but you invited me along."

Randy Andy takes this as his cue and says, "Who's up first?"

***

Four bars and too many shots later, my head is spinning as I sit on a stool and hold the table for the rest of the bridal party while they gyrate dangerously close to one another on the dance floor for that imagine-us-kissing attention. It totally works, and as the pounding beat of a remix of "Thing for You" by Martin Solveig thunders through the stuffy, crowded club, a group of guys who've been eyeing Amber and her friends dance their way over to them, overbites already on full display. Within seconds, they're all paired up. Let the dirty dancing begin.

Urgh. I don't think Dane would love to see that guy's hands

clutching his fiancée's hips like that. Or that grinding. I watch as I sip my vodka slime, wondering if I should put a stop to it. Somehow, my brain is unable to come up with the right answer, so I stay put. The truth is, Dane is very likely tied to a chair centre-stage at a strip club with someone named Cherry Rain rubbing up against him at this very moment.

Ha! Cherry Rain. That's a funny stripper name. I laugh so hard that I flail, accidentally knocking Valerie's purse off the table. "Bugger." I slowly slide off my chair and grope around the dark, sticky floor for it. Even in this drunken state, I'm fully aware of how disgusting this is. When I finally find it and pop back up, I stumble a bit as I seat myself again.

Okay, no more drinks for you, Brianna. Well, after I finish this one, that is. I don't want to be wasteful…

Now, where's my baby sister? I scan the bobbing crowd, trying to focus, then spot Amber, who is now being held up by Mr. Sleazy Dancing Man. She has her legs wrapped around his waist, and they're simulating sex. Oh, dear. That's my cue.

I push my way through the club in my mission to get Amber away from the dirtbag. When I get on the dance floor, Quinn pokes my arm and points to the bride. "Oh my God! She's having so much fun!"

Not bothering to answer, I cut across the dance floor and tug on Amber's arm. "Get down from there."

Turning to Mr. Sleaze Bag, I bark, "Put her down, now!"

He does what I say, which only emboldens me. Wagging a finger in his face, I say, "Look, pal, she's practically married. Go find someone single to grind."

"She's not married yet," the guy says, wrapping his arms around Amber's back and pulling her to him.

I slap his arm. "Off! NOW!"

I must sound scarier than I think because he listens and lets go of her. Grabbing Amber's hand, I pull her as I walk toward our table. "You come with me."

"But I'm having fun," she whines.

Turning back to her, I stop in the middle of the dance floor. "Is this the type of fun Dane would like to see you having?"

Her shoulders slump, and her face crumples. She shakes her head and wails, "I don't deserve him!"

Oh, for God's sake.

Amber sobs and clings to me, nearly pulling me down in my unsteady state. "I'm a terrible person. He shouldn't marry me!"

"You're not a terrible person. You're just drunk."

Pulling back from me, she shakes her head vigorously. "No, I'm awful. Dane could do so much better."

"*Dane* could do better? Not fucking likely," I slur. "Dane's an idiot. If anything, you're too good for him. Except just now when I had to stop you from humping that stranger on the dance floor."

Wait. Did I just say that out loud?

Amber stares at me, her bottom lip quivering like it did when she was about to have a tantrum as a child.

Screwing up her face, she screams, "You hate my fiancé! I knew it!"

She storms past me, weaving in and out of the club-goers with surprising speed given how drunk she is. I follow her, trying to grab her arm and begging her to wait. "Wait, Amber. I don't hate him. I'm sorry. I never should have said that."

She stalks past the bouncers, and soon we find ourselves on the quiet, dark sidewalk. A smattering of people stand around smoking and chatting. Managing to grab her hand, I turn her to me. "I'm sorry, okay? Dane's a great guy. I only said that so you won't think you're a bad person."

"No, you didn't. You've never liked him because he's not some boring book-smart guy. But I love him, Bree! I *love him*, and he loves me!" Her raised voice is now attracting the attention of anyone within a block, but we're both too drunk to care. "I just wish you could be happy for me instead of jealous! I know you're pushing thirty and you're single, but can't you just support me?"

Jealous? Pushing thirty? Oh, it is on now. "You think I'm jealous that you're about to marry some meathead?" I shake my head so hard my entire body sways. "I wouldn't marry a guy like him if someone had a gun to my head. He's a moron, and he's going to drag you down with him. You could be so much more than this, Amber!" I yell, gesturing to her T-shirt. "You're smart and funny and beautiful, and you're settling for the first guy who came along, instead of waiting for the right guy. Or no guy! No guy would be a much, much better option. Be on your own. Make something of yourself. Don't just settle for being Mrs. Hammer, mother of four, pretty, vapid housewife."

Amber's head snaps back like I just slapped her face, and I might as well have. "So that's how you really feel," she sobs. "I knew it deep down, but I hoped you could accept me for who I am."

"How can I accept you wanting to throw away every ounce of potential you've got? You could be so much more than you are."

A gasping sound comes from behind me, and I turn to see Bitches Two through Four glaring at me. They surround her, forming a tight circle meant to cut me out, while they say soothing things like, "Don't listen to her. She's only upset because you're getting married before her. No one would ever be good enough for Bree. Let's go back inside and forget about this. We're your real sisters."

Quinn glares over her shoulder at me. "Just because Roderick took off on you and you're stuck raising Isabelle alone, doesn't mean other people can't find true love."

"Yeah," Kandi adds. "So you're older than her and still single. You don't have to be such a bitch to your little sister for being happier than you."

My head snaps back. "So according to you, because I don't want her to settle, I'm suddenly a bitter old spinster who's trying to ruin my sister's life?"

Shrugging, Kandi says, "If the orthopedic shoe fits..."

"Okay, I can't," I say, throwing up my hands. "Sorry, Amber. I tried. I'm going back to the villa. Maybe things will work out better tomorrow."

"I think you should go home," Amber says quietly, dabbing at the skin under her eyes.

My shoulders drop, and I stare at her for a second, not sure if I should be hurt or angry or what. "Really?"

Nodding, she looks me in the eye. "Really. I tried to include you, but you just don't want to be part of my special time." She shakes her head. "It's my fault, I shouldn't have forced it."

Kandi puts a protective arm around Amber. "Don't you dare blame yourself."

Quinn rubs Amber's upper arm and simultaneously scowls at me. "Yeah, Ambs, this is *so* not your fault."

"This is supposed to be a happy occasion," Valerie sniffs, trying to make herself cry so she can win the Most Sensitive Friend Award at the end of the weekend.

"Come on, sweetie," Kandi says, moving Amber away from me. "Let's go find a place that serves all-night breakfast. We'll get you some pancakes."

"That's what you need right now," Valerie says, scrambling to take the other side of Amber. "Your posse and some pancakes."

"Okay, well, I guess I'll find a flight home, then," I say quietly.

Amber turns over her shoulder and nods. "That would be for the best."

"Oh, and make sure you leave the money you owe me for the T-shirt," Quinn says. "It's $31.50."

19

The Otis Redding of Bellboys

Leo

IT'S LATE SATURDAY MORNING, and I have to say, for once in my life, I'm bored out of my mind. Like, completely and utterly bored. I made lunch plans for tomorrow with Pierce and Emma because I thought it would take me all day to finish my domestic chores, but it turns out I got through them much faster than anticipated. I've already gotten through my shopping, laundry, and sweeping out my little house. I even stripped the bed and washed the sheets, which are now providing the only movement in the yard as they flap in the gentle breeze on the line. I find myself wishing a certain little preschooler was here cycling around in a cape.

The sound of the bass guitar next door causes me to perk up my ears and reminds me of Jerry Not Garcia's offer to go "jam" with him. I don't play any instruments but perhaps he's got a set of bongos or a triangle I could try. Any idiot can play the triangle, right?

Getting up from my lawn chair, I stretch, feeling an odd pang of loneliness that I doubt Jerry can cure. Only twenty-eight hours until Bree and Izzy are home, not that I'm counting or anything...

A car pulls up onto the driveway as I reach the gate. It's Brianna's little Corolla, which sparks joy for me like that Marie Kondo woman seeing an organized sock drawer. I open the gate and walk out to greet her. She's sitting perfectly still in the driver's seat, the expression on her face indicating something is most certainly wrong. She closes her eyes and leans her head against the back of her seat.

I stop short and consider sneaking away before she opens her eyes. Would she even want me to see her so upset? I should walk away. Oh, bollocks… She's crying now, and her face is all twisted up. What kind of man would I be if I didn't at least try to help? The kind my father thinks I am.

Walking over to the driver's side, I tap on the window with one knuckle, startling her. She quickly wipes her tears away before opening the door.

"Hey, Leo, what do you need?" she asks, doing her best to sound like Concierge Brianna. She plucks her handbag off the passenger seat and tries to get up, except she's forgotten to unbuckle her seatbelt, so her attempt is thwarted. It snaps tight, and she's jarred back into place. "Of course," she mutters, unbuckling the seatbelt.

"Want to talk about it?" I ask.

She shakes her head as she stands. "Thanks, but I think I need to have a long bath and lie down for a while."

"All right, well, I'm here if you need a friend."

"Great," she says, shutting the door to her car and walking to the trunk to open it.

I follow her and take her suitcase before she can get to it. "Better let me do this. I am a professional, after all."

That earns me the tiniest flicker of a smile, sparking a need to get a really big one out of her—a laugh, too. I spot a small blue teddy bear poking out of her purse. "Cute bear. Izzy will love that."

"It's just a stupid airport bear. I was going to get her an amber necklace, but I didn't make it to the shop where they sell them, so instead of bringing back something truly special for her, I have this cheap, crappy stuffed animal." Her voice cracks, and she takes a deep breath, blinking quickly.

"What happened, Bree?"

"Nothing. I don't want to talk about it," she says, shaking her head

146

at me. "It turns out I'm completely incapable of fun. In fact, I'm so shitty at it, my sister actually asked me to leave. I ended up getting a cab to the airport around 1 a.m. and slept on a bench until the ticket counter opened, like one of those Amazing Race contestants, only a drunk, pathetic one who would definitely never do the bungee jumping, not even for a million dollars."

Oh, dear. It's worse than I thought. "Sounds horrible, Bree."

"No, it's fine. I don't even care." Her voice does that thing where it goes up by three octaves. "In fact, it's a good thing, because I need to study, so I could use an extra day at home," she says, trying to be brave even though tears are pouring down her cheeks. "Now I'll have tonight and all day tomorrow to get caught up, because when I called Izzy to tell her I was home a day early, she didn't want to come home." Her face crumples. "I guess my parents are more fun than me, too."

"Oh, dear. I'm so sorry, Bree. If you don't object, I'm going to give you a hug and you can cry on my shoulder for as long as you need." I set the suitcase on the driveway and wait a second.

Swallowing hard, she says, "You don't have to. I'm fine." Except she's clearly not fine because her voice shakes, and big sobs erupt from her chest as she buries her face in my shirt.

I wrap my arms around her and hold her while she cries, my heart breaking for her. She needs someone to take care of her for once, even if it turns out to be me. Taking a deep breath, I catch a whiff of her shampoo. It's a soft floral scent that suits her perfectly. I rub her back with one hand and make little shushing noises, telling her it'll be okay. Inside, I'm overwhelmed by the need to take care of her and to hold her until she's happy again, which is an entirely new experience for me. I'm struck by the fact that having her in my arms like this feels exactly perfect, even if she is crying. *Huh.*

After a few moments, she lifts her head. "And now I'm being completely unprofessional. Shit fuck."

"Shit fuck?" I ask, trying hard not to smile.

"And I'm out of practice at cursing," she says, listing another major flaw in her personality.

"Is that a bad thing?" I ask, putting both hands on her shoulders.

"Yes, I sound like an old woman. I'm the only twenty-six-year-old in the world who's skipping the rest of her twenties, thirties, and forties and going straight to being a senior citizen. I should just buy some Blue Blockers and get it over with." She sniffs.

"Blue Blockers?"

"They're these really ugly sunglasses that block the sun from the sides as well as the front," she says. "They're actually quite practical. Dolores has some, and I borrow them sometimes when I'm driving and the sun is in my eyes." Lifting one hand to her forehead, she says, "Oh, God, I actually *like* Blue Blockers."

She leans her head on my chest again and sobs while I hold her. So this is what happens when Brianna Lewis, the world's most on-top-of-everything woman, falls apart.

"I should have gotten the stupid tattoo."

Tattoo? And suddenly it all comes clear. Wild weekend away. Mean girls pressuring her into doing something she doesn't want to do and probably can't afford. A wave of anger comes over me, even though I don't even know these women. "No, you absolutely shouldn't have."

She pulls back and looks up at me, her eyes red and swollen. "You would've gotten the tattoo, wouldn't you?"

"What I would have done is irrelevant," I say. "Besides, don't go by me. I'm not known for my stellar decision-making."

"I suppose that's true."

"It is. That's why no one uses 'what would Leo do' as a guidepost for living."

Bree chuckles through her tears, and I grin down at her, feeling victorious for managing to make her laugh. Her face grows serious and she says, "You're good at everything."

"Am not."

"No, it's true. You may not have a fully developed sense of ambition but otherwise, you're good at everything you try. Like winning people over and whipping up parties in the blink of an eye, whereas I'm basically a no-fun grouchy pants."

"Believe me, I have a plethora of faults."

"Nothing that makes you unlikable."

"True, I am highly likeable, but I do have some flaws that might surprise you," I say.

"Name one."

"I'm terrified of butterflies. And other flying things, actually, like birds, bats, and moths. Butterflies are the worst though."

Scrunching up her face, she says, "But they're harmless. They turn to dust if you touch them."

"I know, and yet, still scared," I answer with a shrug. "In fact, if one gets too close to me, I gag."

Bree hides her mouth, trying not to laugh. "Sorry. I know I shouldn't find that funny."

"No, go ahead. I know it's hilarious."

"Did something happen to you as a boy?"

I give her a quick nod. "Two older brothers and a grandmother with a butterfly-filled solarium."

A look of understanding crosses her face. "They locked you in?"

"Overnight, yes. When I was four. Our nanny thought I'd gone to bed on my own."

"That's not funny at all, really," she says, her face filled with concern.

"It's fine. I got them back. I found two garter snakes in the garden and put them in each of their sock drawers."

Bree laughs. "So, let me get this straight. Snakes, no problem. Butterflies…"

"I scream like a girl, yes. So you see? Not perfect at all." Picking up her suitcase, I say, "Now, milady, why don't I show you to your suite so you can have that bath and nap you were talking about?"

Nodding, she turns and walks to the front door. "Thanks. I should rest a bit, or I won't have the brainpower to study."

I follow her into the house, put the suitcase down at the bottom of the stairs, and stare at her for a moment, taking in her lovely face. She seems so worn out and lonely, it breaks my heart. "I don't really want to leave you alone like this."

"I'll be fine." She shrugs. "I should work."

"What if…instead of sitting in here by yourself for the rest of the weekend trying to focus on those awful textbooks—which will be rather a waste of time because you're too upset to concentrate—you let me take you out and show you how to have a spectacularly wonderful time?" My heartbeat picks up as the words tumble out of my mouth, and I find myself praying she'll say yes because somehow the answer to that question matters so very much.

Sighing, she says, "I shouldn't."

"Why not? You had the entire weekend booked off anyway. Give yourself one perfect day. Just one, then you can get back to your real life with a renewed vigor," I say, giving her my most charming smile.

"I shouldn't spend any more money this weekend…"

"Me, either, but that doesn't mean we can't have an amazing time. You go relax in the tub. I'll sort out a day you'll never forget. Meet you back here in an hour and a half?"

A painfully long moment passes as I wait for an answer. When it comes, it's in the form of a tiny grin and a nod.

20

One Fine Day

Bree

WELL, I have to say, a bath and a nap was exactly the thing I needed. I'm not nearly as pathetic and weepy as I was earlier. I no longer have the irresistible urge to buy Blue Blockers, and I'm at peace with the fact that I'm not as fun as A) my sister's idiot friends, and B) the above-ground pool my parents put in their backyard to bribe Izzy to stay over.

What I am, however, is embarrassed for crying in front of Leo. Also, I'm completely discombobulated, because it almost feels like he was asking me on a date, which he probably wasn't, because come on, he's *him*, and I'm me, and there's no way a guy like him would want to date a girl like me. And as ridiculous as this sounds, and as much as I hate—repeat *hate*—to admit it, I very badly want to date him. Hard. Several times in a row, to be honest. And between you and I, I haven't wanted to date anyone since I found out I was pregnant with Isabelle. Certainly not several times in a row.

Not that I can date him. He is both my employee and my renter. Plus, the logical, reasonable, smart side of me knows exactly who he is and dislikes him for it. He's the rich playboy who, when done slumming it here, will be on his way back to Avonia, never to return. Period. So shut up, lady bits, because as much as you want to, you cannot, will not, and won't have him. Oh, I guess will not and won't are really the same thing, but just to drive the point home to my lady bits. No. Nada. No sweaty, hot, hard dating. None.

But he is awfully cute. And sexy. And charming. Oh, and thoughtful. Sigh…

I reread the note he left on the kitchen table:

Bree,

Get ready for the greatest afternoon/evening of your entire life. Only one rule —we both have to say "yes" to everything (like they do at improv theatres). Don't worry, strictly plutonic activities planned and no permanent ink of any kind. If you can agree to that one rule, I promise you will have the best time you can remember. I'll be back ASAP with our mode of transportation. Dress is very casual, but make sure you have swimwear. I've got the towels packed, and dinner is sorted.

Cheers,

Leo

P.S. Let yourself have this. You deserve it more than anyone I've ever met.

Well, that's so sweet, isn't it? Sweet and terrifying in a way that has my stomach flipping and flopping like a tilapia that's been tossed onto a boat deck. It's the word "swimsuit." Oh! I could pretend I forgot it, or I couldn't read his writing, or tell him I'm on my period. I cringe as I imagine myself saying, "Sorry, but it's my time of the month" to his gorgeous face. Embarrassing to be sure, but no less so than letting that hunk of manly perfection see me in my mumkini.

Improv rules. Huh. Can I agree to that? I mean, *really* agree to that? I stare out the window, a feeling of restlessness growing inside me. Maybe I should. Saying no to everything fun certainly hasn't made me happy. "I *do* deserve this," I say out loud. I've had a crap weekend so far, and I deserve one fun afternoon before I hunker down and study for the next several weeks straight.

Marching up the stairs, I hurry to my bedroom to put my mumkini on before I can change my mind.

Once I have it on, I glance in the mirror and consider seeing if I could pop over to a local shop to pick up a burkini.

"No, you're fine. Just do this, Bree. He's not interested in you romantically anyhow, so what does it matter if he sees you in your swimwear?"

It doesn't. So just do it.

I pull my navy T-shirt on over top of my swimsuit, then put on my cropped blue and white gingham summer pants that I bought in a moment of 'I feel pretty.' I stuff some knickers, my bra, and my swim skirt in my bag, and jog down the steps and out the door.

When I walk out onto the driveway, I see Leo wearing blue shorts and a fitted white T-shirt that leaves nothing to my overactive imagination. A backpack is slung over his shoulder, and after a second, I realize he's standing next to an old-timey tandem bicycle. He gives me a little bow. "Ah, Ms. Lewis. Right on time. Your carriage awaits."

"This is the mode of transportation?"

"A bicycle built for two," Leo says with a big grin. "Fun, no?"

I cover my mouth with one hand and I laugh while I shake my head.

Leo holds up one finger. "Improv rules."

Taking a deep breath, I say, "Oh God, okay. Why not?"

"Don't worry. The tires are filled up, and I'll do most of the pedalling—not because you're incapable, but because you're tuckered out."

"Thanks." I stare at him, and for one brief moment, I wonder if I'm in a drunken slumber and have dreamt this entire mostly awful-turned-impossibly wonderful day. "Where are we going?"

"That cannot be revealed until we get there."

"In case we get lost and end up somewhere unintended?" I ask, walking over to the backseat.

"Precisely." He takes my bag from me, puts it in the basket at the front, then steadies the bicycle while I climb on.

My stomach flutters as the bike tilts left and right while he gets on. And we're off and the flutters turn to bubbles of laughter. "I've never done this before."

"Ridden a bicycle?"

"Not a tandem one. You?"

"Never, but the moment I saw it, I knew we'd be good at it." He says over his shoulder as we pick up speed on the hill that leads to the main road.

"Where did you get this?"

"A couple down the street own it—Edna and Phil. I noticed it in their yard, and I asked if I could rent it."

"The Cruikshanks? In the grey house on the corner?"

"Yup."

"They're notoriously grumpy. I can't believe they'd say yes."

"It took some convincing. I had to explain that I'm on a rather meager budget but very much wish to take a very deserving, special lady out."

I blush, glad he's in front of me right now so he can't see how starved I am for compliments. "And that worked?" I ask as we turn onto a paved path that runs alongside the road.

"Only after I told them who the special lady was."

We ride for almost an hour, but I'm not tired in the least, because I'm not really doing much of the work. Instead, I just enjoy the view. To the left, there is a dense jungle. To my right, the ocean. And in front of me, the tightest buns on a man that I've ever seen up close. And I can stare freely because he doesn't have eyes in the back of his head. Not that I *should* stare at something I can't have. It's sort of torturous, like deciding to stand in front of a Cinnabon all day, breathing in that heavenly smell and watching the way the icing melts on the warm gooey bread that's just been pulled out of the oven, but then not letting yourself eat even one measly bite. I could really use a bite of those Cinnabons…

Discipline, Brianna! Discipline, and maybe dig out your vibrator when you get home.

Trying to focus on something other than the hottie in front of me, I play tour guide, pointing out places of interest as we ride. Leo asks lots of questions about what it was like growing up on the island. He listens carefully, has surprisingly insightful responses, and comes out with witty remarks that have me in stitches from time to time. By the time we've reached our destination—Hidden Beach—my face hurts from smiling, and my body is buzzing with lusty thoughts for which I cannot find the shutoff valve.

The small beach, which sits on the east side of the island, is nearly empty, except for a family on the far side having a picnic, and a man walking his dog. It's sort of a secret spot, not known to tourists. The locals who know about it rarely come this time of year, because the surfing is better on the southwest side of the island.

We stop at a spot with a fire pit surrounded on three sides by large tree trunks that have been laid down to use as benches. Leo de-bikes, as he calls it, and holds it still while I get off. The tide is high now, and the waves crash as they come in. The sun is low in the sky, exchanging some of the intense heat of midday for a soft, calm warmth.

"We used to come here all the time when I was growing up. Every Sunday for a picnic."

"Really? That sounds nice."

"It was. There's a cave down the beach that my sister and I used to hide in when it was time to go home. We used to say we'd live in it together when we grew up." My smile fades as the weekend's events come crashing back on me. "It's funny, the things kids believe to be possible."

"Anything and everything."

"You don't seem to have lost that yet," I say. His face darkens slightly, so I quickly add, "That wasn't an insult. I think it's nice."

"Nice, maybe. Smart, no."

"You know how to be a boring adult when you have to."

"Yes, but I hate it," Leo says with a grin. He opens his backpack, takes out two large bottles of water, hands me one, and opens his before holding it up to mine for a toast. "To the Crankshafts."

"Cruickshanks."

"Righto. Them, too."

I have a long pull on my water, exhilarated as the cool liquid slides down my throat. When I lower the bottle, he's watching me in a way that both pleases and alarms me.

"What?" I ask, feeling suddenly self-conscious. "Is my hair all crazy from the wind?"

Shaking his head, he says, "Nope. Quite the opposite." He glances down at my mouth for a second, then back into my eyes again. "It's just nice to see you happy."

"Oh, good. Because I'd hate to have crazy hair," I say, trying to deflect the gooey feeling inside from having *this* man enjoy anything about me at all.

He pulls a towel out of his bag, fans it out, and puts it down on the sand. "You relax. I'll go in search of firewood."

"We're having a campfire?"

"Well, we shouldn't eat the hot dogs cold, should we?"

"You know how to make hot dogs?"

"My parents sent me to summer camp in the US when I was fourteen. I learned all sorts of great things there," he says with a smile that dares me to ask what else he learned. He winks, turns toward the trees lining the sand, and starts toward them.

"Really?" I ask, following him up the bank.

"Yes, really. A camp in the Yellowstone Mountains. My father thought it would toughen me up to live in the wilderness for a few weeks."

"And?" I ask, picking up a piece of driftwood.

"And I managed to get my bunk counsellor to give up his bedroom to me on day two, so instead of sleeping on a creaky bunk bed with a bunch of smelly teenage boys, I had a rustic room with a double bed and my own bathroom."

I laugh, picturing him as a smooth-talking teenager. "I'm almost afraid to ask how you managed that."

"I bet him I could get the Queen of England on the phone to say hi to him," he says as he bends to pick up a few small logs.

My eyes grow wide. "You were able to *do that*?"

"The important thing is that *he* thought I was," he says, standing.

"Who was he really talking to?"

"My mother."

"And she went along with that?"

He shakes his head. "She didn't have to. I called, the butler answered, and I said, 'Hello, Jeeves—' his name is Roger, but I called him Jeeves to get a rise out of him, '—is the Queen home?'"

When she got on the line, I said, 'Your majesty, how are you?' Then after a few niceties, I asked if she may perhaps be willing to speak with a friend of mine from the US who is a big fan of hers."

"Wait a minute. Who's your mum?" I say as we make our way along the trees.

"A rich woman who fancies herself very important. Loves seeing photos of herself in the local gossip mags, so for her, it's not entirely unthinkable that she'd have fans in other countries."

"Wow. What was it like to grow up in your world?" I ask without thinking.

"Cold. Strange. Unrealistic. And lonely."

***

An hour later, the fire is roaring and the coals are 'hot dog' ready. Leo found two long twigs to use as roasting sticks, and my stomach is growling as my wiener bubbles and hisses. A gentle breeze causes the flames to dance along the logs, and the only sounds are the rustling leaves of the trees and the crackling of the fire. It's a calm, comfortable moment, but I can't help being a little sad. I want to ask more about Leo's childhood, but I don't think I can. The moment for that passed without me knowing what to say, but his words ring through my head. *Cold. Strange. Unrealistic. And lonely.*

Suddenly, the grass on the rich side of the tracks doesn't seem so green. I watch him from the corner of my eye as he cooks his wiener. To look at him, you'd never guess he has a care in the world. He's the epitome of freedom, but now that I've had a glance into what's under the devil-may-care façade, I feel sorry for him.

He glances at me for a second, then says, "Go ahead. Ask."

"Ask what?"

"You want to know more about the whole cold-and-lonely comment."

"How could you tell?"

"Because you've been very quiet since I said it," he answers, carefully turning his stick.

"It's just that you come off as this fun-loving guy who's never had a care in the world, and yet…" I stop, not sure how to finish my comment.

"That's because I *don't* have a care in the world. I learned at a very early age that if you don't care about things like impressing your impossible father, you can get by much easier. Especially when you have two highly impressive older brothers."

"Ah, I see."

He rolls his eyes. "Don't pity me, Brianna. Most people have it much worse."

"Do they?"

"Yes. Much better to grow up with a silver spoon in one's mouth than an empty one."

"What about a regular stainless-steel spoon served by people who love you?"

"Like how you're raising Isabelle?"

"No, my life probably seems awful to you," she says. "I meant somewhere more in between. Not *bro*ke, but not disconnected either."

"Your life in no way seems awful to me. You have Izzy and your aunt, who would do anything for either of you," he says. "And my entire family isn't disconnected. My mother tries when she's not too busy getting spa treatments. My brother Pierce and I get on quite well, for the most part."

"Oh, well that's good at least."

"Take what you can get, right?" He deftly lifts his roasting stick away from the fire and pulls a bun out of the bag on the log next to him.

Realizing I'm burning the bottom side of my wiener, I remove it from the fire, and Leo quickly gets a bun out for me and uses it to remove my wiener from the stick.

"Hmm. That's a little charred. Why don't we switch dogs?"

"That's very kind of you, but I don't mind it a little black."

"Ah! Improv rules," he says, holding his perfectly cooked hot dog out to me.

My shoulders drop, and we swap, me feeling guilty to be letting him eat food I've ruined. After adding ketchup and mayo, I take my first bite. "Mmm, that's like heaven in a bun."

"Yup. Who needs money when you can roast hot dogs in paradise for practically nothing?"

"Everyone," I mutter.

Leo stares at me for a second. "Good point. But wouldn't it be nice if one could have an amazing life without it?"

"Like if you lived on a deserted island with a comfortable house and a huge garden with everything you need to eat, and you could make each day what you wanted without having to worry about how to pay your next electricity bill or if you have enough money in your account to buy your daughter that princess castle fairy tent she wants for her birthday…"

"And there were no wankers always one-upping each other about who's got a faster jet or who went on the most exclusive vacation over Christmas…" His voice trails off, and he gives me a sheepish expression. "My examples are crap, really. You're much better at finding things to escape from than I am."

"Okay, that's true."

"Poor little rich boy. Whine, whine, whine." He rolls his eyes.

We eat in silence for a minute, then I say, "Can I ask you something?"

"I have to say yes."

Grinning, I say, "I'm starting to like your rule."

"And I have a feeling I'm about to regret it," he says, tossing his napkin in the fire.

"What are you doing here? Not here on this beach, but here on this island, working as a bellboy and living in a shed? You clearly have more than enough money to live somewhere much better."

"On the contrary, my *parents* have a lot of money. I have nothing," he answers. "And my father has decided he's tired of supporting his ne'er-do-well son."

"But surely you could get a better job? You went to university."

"There are surprisingly few jobs in alchemy these days."

"Alchemy?" I ask, my eyes popping open.

"That was my minor."

"As in the study of how to transform metals into pure gold?"

Giving one big nod, he says, "Let's not forget the quest for the elixir of eternal life."

Tucking my lips between my teeth, I try not to laugh. "What made you want to spend four years of your life studying an ancient, already-proven-to-be-bollocks subject?"

His face twists into a slightly embarrassed smile. "I knew it would upset my father, especially if I pretended to believe I would one day be able to turn scrap metals into riches."

My mouth drops open in shock, and I say the first thing that comes to mind. "You must really hate your father."

"Let's just say I had a lot of pent-up rage, and that four-year period helped to reduce it a great deal."

"Oh, so money well spent, then."

He gives me a broad smile. "Kind of adds something that it was *his* money, doesn't it?"

I burst out laughing. "I honestly don't know whether to be terrified or impressed."

"Be impressed, please," he says with a wry smile. "That took some serious commitment."

As much as I know he wants me to find the entire story amusing, there's something about the way he says please that tells me deep in my bones that he needs someone to approve of him.

Before I can think of the right response, he says, "All right, my turn to ask the uncomfortable questions now."

"Uh oh."

"What was the thing you said that you shouldn't have that got you kicked off the hen's weekend?"

I wince, closing my eyes for a second. "I said her fiancé is an idiot, and that I wouldn't marry a guy like him if someone had a gun to my head."

"Ouch. That's hard to come back from."

"Oh, there's more," I say, holding up one finger. "I told her he's going to drag her down with him, and she shouldn't settle for the first guy who came along, and that she should make something of herself instead of becoming some vapid housewife."

"Whoa," Leo mutters. "You really went for it."

My stomach tightens. "I certainly did. I was extremely drunk at the time, but that hardly matters, does it? I never should have said anything." I stare into the glowing embers of the fire, my eyes stinging with tears. "I just got so defensive, because she and her stupid friends implied that I'm jealous that she's getting married and I'm still single."

"Are you?" he asks gently.

I glance up at him, a flash of anger surging through me. "Why would I be? I have no desire to marry a moron."

"Obviously, but I mean, surely you must sometimes want to share the burdens and joys of parenting with someone. I know I would."

I shrug. "I have my aunt. And I don't need some man to pick up after, so, honestly, it doesn't bother me in the least that men prefer women who look like they stepped off the cover of *Playboy*. I'm a modern woman, and I'm lucky enough to live in a time in history when women can, *and do*, manage to do this on their own."

"Do you really think your looks hold you back from being in a relationship?"

I blush, embarrassed by the question. "No. I'm not in a relationship because I have no interest in one, but before, when I was too young and stupid to know better, I didn't exactly have guys beating down the door to get to me."

"If I had to guess, I'd say it had absolutely nothing to do with your looks, because it certainly doesn't now."

"Oh, please. Men are visual. Looks first and always."

He narrows his eyes at me. "That's not true at all."

"Really?" I ask, giving him a sceptical expression. "Then why do my sister and her beautiful but stupid friends all have fiancés or boyfriends?"

He stares at me for a second without answering, so I continue. "Ha! You can't answer that one, can you? I rest my case."

"That's why," he mutters.

"What's why?"

"You've got this very busy, whip-smart, no-nonsense, soon-to-dominate-the-legal-world thing going on. It's a bit scary." His voice is calm, as though he thinks he's helping me by sharing his opinion instead of pissing me off to no end.

Adopting a mocking tone, I ask, "Like butterfly-scary or much less terrifying, like waking to find a serial killer has you tied up in a room covered in plastic?"

A flicker of amusement crosses his face. "Very clever, but don't try to shift the focus. We're talking about you."

Bugger. That would work on most people. "Excuse me if I don't want to talk about how intimidating I am to the male of the species," I say. "It's pathetic really, that women exist solely for the comfort of their male counterparts. If we have the slightest hint of ambition or a brain in our heads, you men can't get away quickly enough."

"You're going to be quite a success in a courtroom, but your redirection skills won't work on me. I won't be baited into an emotional argument, no matter how sweeping you are in your sexist opinions," he says. "A lot of men—myself included—want a smart woman, one who will challenge us and keep things interesting. You're definitely in that category, no matter how much you wish you weren't."

"What makes you think I want to be in the throw-away pile?"

"Because you do your best not to be noticed, and when someone does show interest, you change tactics from 'please don't see me' to 'get away from me or else.'"

"That's ridiculous."

"What's ridiculous is that you've gotten away with it for so long without anyone calling you on your bullshit."

We stare each other down for a second, my head feeling like it's going to blow, and my heart pounding with anger. He's angry, too, even though he's doing his best to keep his nothing-bothers-me atti-tude going. I'm about to call him on his bullshit when he starts up again with a slight grin. "You do realize you're filled with rage because you've just been told you're smart, attractive, and you'll be a hell of a great attorney."

"That's not it at all!" I snap and push my bare feet under the sand to cool them, trying to think of a good comeback. Nothing. Maybe *he* should be the one in law school. "I'm angry because you're acting like you know me so well, and you don't."

"I never implied I know you. I'm only providing you with objective facts with regard to your attractiveness."

"Well, stop it," I huff.

"Okay," he says simply.

"Good!" Damn him. I cannot afford to fall for a guy like him—one who's going to up and leave in a few months. This man will crush me, and there's not much left of my heart to crush.

"I really didn't mean to upset you," he says, giving me a thoughtful expression.

"Yes, well…you did," I say, still wanting to be in a snit. But as the words come out of my mouth, I realize how insane this all is, and I start to laugh at myself.

After a second, Leo starts to laugh, too, and when we're done, he says, "You really are not like any woman I've ever met—and that's a good thing, in case you were about to accuse me of some nefarious reason for saying so."

"You mean most women don't become absolutely furious when complimented?" I ask, staring into his eyes much longer than would be considered smart.

"Some actually enjoy it." He stares back, then swallows hard as the mood shifts between us to something more…intimate. I look away first, losing our lust-filled staring contest, and when I glance back at him, his eyes are fixed on the ocean. "Speaking of things that are enjoyable, let's take a dip, shall we?"

I blush and shake my head. "You go ahead. I try not to swim within a couple of hours after eating." Or if I'm going to eat in the next several hours. Or if the sun is out…

He holds up one hand, and I know he's going to remind me of our improv rules, but I beat him to it. "Right. Say yes to everything."

"Exactly," he says, stretching out one arm toward the shimmering water. "And at the moment, we're saying yes to a relaxing, refreshing dip in the sea."

He peels off his shirt and tosses it on the log, then looks at me, waiting for me to do the same. Only I'm not moving. Well, nothing but my eyes, which are darting around his torso like a coked-up bee in a flower shop.

"Eyes up here, Ms. Lewis."

My cheeks burn as I tear my gaze away from that sculpted body and to his gorgeous green eyes. "Sorry. I don't know what happened there."

"It's fine, really. It happens to most women. Some men, too," he says nonchalantly. "It's the curse of being naturally muscular."

"How awful for you," I deadpan.

"I'm learning to live with it." He gestures toward the water with one thumb over his shoulder—which incidentally causes his bicep to bulge. Oh, wow. That is a massive bicep. He totally did that on purpose. Bastard.

"Okay, you go ahead, I need a second to get undressed and put my swim skirt on," I say, digging around in my bag.

"You're not going to hop on the bike and abandon ship, are you?"

Turning to him, I say, "Honestly, if I thought I could balance that thing on my own, I'd be saying yes to a solo ride home right now."

"This swimsuit thing is a real deal breaker for you, isn't it?"

"My mumkini? Nah," I say sarcastically. "Totally excited to strip down to almost nothing right now."

"We've already established you're empirically beautiful, so no more excuses. Trust me. You've got everything in exactly the right places, Ms. Lewis. Now strip off your clothes, unless you want to bike home later with soaking-wet trousers."

Well, when he puts it that way, how could I say no? Am I drooling? I think I might be drooling. This is truly pathetic.

I turn toward the trees with my skirt in hand so I can strip down and adjust my boobs without him seeing. While I'm in the bushes, I peek at him. He's standing facing the sea, instead of trying to see me. What a gentleman.

A totally delusional gentleman who thinks I have everything in exactly the right place. Maybe he's severely nearsighted? That would explain it. Or he's a mum-bod chaser. Or he has some sort of cellulite fetish, and he's certain my legs are covered with cottage cheese. Oooh, that's probably it. For my ego's sake, I'm hoping it's the nearsighted thing.

Okay, skirt on. Boobs up as high as they go. Deep breath. Force legs to move.

Nope. They are not listening.

Hmmm…how long will it be until the sun sets? Like an hour?

Oh, just go, Brianna. For eff's sake.

21

You Can't Always Get What You Want

Leo

I WAIT, watching the waves roll in, fighting the urge to turn around and check on her progress. She's so bloody hard on herself, which to be honest, is rather irritating. Here she is, a lovely young woman with some delightful curves falling into the stupid trap of thinking only thigh gaps and stick arms are attractive, when in reality, women are attractive, period. Skinny, curvy, older, younger, they all have something appealing. They're just so much softer, warmer, and more beautiful than the males of the species.

Brianna, especially. The way her eyes light up when she's surprised or amused. Those long eyelashes and her full lips that I can't help but want to feel against mine. I have an idea of how she would feel against me, but I better not think about that because these swim trunks aren't exactly going to hide any obvious signs of my attraction.

A blur of movement to my right interrupts my thoughts, and it takes me a second to realize it's her, running at top speed toward the water.

"Last one in's a rotten egg!" she calls over her shoulder.

Well hello, Ms. Lewis, running in a short purple skirt and halter swim top.

I sprint to catch up with her, hoping that will stop the blood from rushing to a certain area where I don't want it. Seconds later, the warm water splashes against my shins as I watch her dive under the water headfirst.

She comes up a few metres away and turns, her hair slicked back as she laughs. "I win!"

Diving under, I come up right next to her, exhilaration zipping through me from my fingers to my toes. "No fair, I didn't know we were in a race until it was half over."

She stretches her arms out behind her, using them to propel her farther out into the sea. "I still won." Pointing to a buoy, she says, "Race to that buoy. Loser has to do all the pedalling on the way home."

Without waiting for an answer, she takes off, her arms cutting through the water like she's an Olympian. I laugh for a second before I pursue her, wanting very much to catch her, spin her around, and kiss her hard on the mouth.

Damn, she's fast. I think she's going to beat me. I pump my legs with fury, but it's no use. She's got me.

She reaches the buoy first, slapping it before turning to me and cheering. "Victorious! Looks like you'll be pumping, and I'll be riding later."

I stop in front of her and give her a scandalized look. "I'll most certainly say yes to that."

Her eyes fly open. "That came out wrong. I meant you'll be pumping me... No! Shit. Not pumping, *pedalling.* The pedals. Of the bike. I'll be riding the bike, and you'll be pedalling it. Not me."

Closing her eyes, she scrunches up her face for a second. When she opens her eyes, she stares down at the water and says in a small voice, "Yay, I won."

I burst out laughing, and she splashes me while she tries not to laugh.

"You're not going to let that go, are you?" she asks.

"Of course I will. Just not anytime soon," I say, treading water, our bodies dangerously close.

"Bastard," she says with a grin. She splashes me again, and I grab her wrist to stop her and pull her toward me. Her smile fades, and she swallows, glancing at my mouth. "I'm your boss."

"Righto," I say, disappointment crashing over me as I let go of her wrist. "So no pumping you, then," I add with a grin before leaping backward, out of the way of the next splash I know is coming.

She makes a growling sound and follows me as I swim a few metres away from her, then stop so she can catch me. When she gets near enough, she cups her hands and creates a mini-tidal wave, aiming it at my face. Ducking under the water, I avoid it, only to come up behind her. I tap her on the shoulder, and she winces before turning to me.

"Where'd you learn to swim like that?" I ask.

"Here," she answers. "You can't expect to beat an island girl in a swim race."

"Hey, I grew up on an island," I say indignantly.

"In the North Sea? Where the water is freezing most of the year?"

"Only ten months at a time, thank you very much."

"I shouldn't exaggerate, sorry."

"Christ, I wish you weren't my boss."

"Really?" she asks, her voice slightly breathy.

I nod. "Definitely."

"What if no one found out?" she asks, biting her bottom lip.

My entire body reacts to the idea, and I can't help but tuck a lock of her wet hair behind her ear. "Is that what you want, Brianna? Something clandestine?"

"Honestly, at this moment, I think I might," she answers, reaching out and brushing her fingertips against my chest.

"We really shouldn't though," I say, placing both hands on her hips as the tide gently pushes her into me.

Our eyes lock, and she nods, whispering, "Terrible idea."

"Yes, ill-advised and horribly complicated." I lower my mouth over hers, letting it hover there, giving her time to change her mind.

She nods and stretches up a bit, closing the distance between us, her hands now resting on my abs. "It would most likely end in disaster."

"Most likely," I murmur. "Should we do it, anyway?"

"We have to. We're saying yes to everything," she whispers, her chest heaving as she talks.

I stare into her perfect eyes, and in an instant, I feel a surge of something wonderful—unabashed happiness, lust, relief, and excitement all at once. She reaches up as I lower my mouth over hers, ready to let go after so many weeks of wanting her.

"YOOOHOOOO! There you are!" a voice calls from the shore.

We both pull back quickly. I turn to see Jolene standing on the beach with her camera poised in hand. Son of a bitch.

"Is that…your Uber driver?"

"Yes." Regret filling me as I release Bree's waist. "Please excuse me."

22

Whiny, Frustrated Lady Bits

Bree

OKAY, so this just got weird. Leo swam out of the water as though his life depended on it, now he's standing on the beach, dripping wet while he and his Uber driver have an oddly intense conversation. My only guess as to what this is about is that maybe she works for a gossip rag and she just got a shot that will cause a huge scandal for him back home. *Hot Heir to Davenport Communications Slumming it with Chubby Single Mum.*

Oooh! Or maybe he's secretly married, and his wife hired her to keep tabs on him. Now his wife will have the proof she needs to tear up their prenup and take him for millions. I can just imagine the divorce papers, "Reason for Dissolution of Marriage: Infidelity on behalf of the husband with chubby foreign single mum."

Okay, why in my nightmare fantasies am I so hard on myself? Geez, Brianna. Why not future lawyer or successful concierge or fabulous single mum? Note to self: once I pass the bar exam, I need to work on my self-esteem.

I stay in the sea feeling ridiculous as I tread water for a few minutes before deciding to go get dressed. The moment between Leo and I is clearly over which is a good thing, really, even though my lady bits feel like it's the end of the freaking world. Like seriously, if they could talk, they'd be whining more than Izzy when she has to go to bed early on a Friday night. Swimming to the left, I exit the water about one hundred yards down the beach from them, then tiptoe along the sand as though that will make me invisible. I can't help but hear Leo pleading with her and saying something about compassion and humanity and a special circumstance.

Yup. He must be a married sack of crap. I sure know how to pick 'em. My heart sinks to my heels, and suddenly the hot dog I ate is a lead ball in my gut. After a few minutes of writhing and shimmying in the bushes, I manage to squeeze out off my wet swimsuit and get dressed. My skin feels gritty with salt and my insides feel dirty for almost kissing a married man. I desperately want to go home to shower, then crawl into bed and hide under the covers.

The sun has almost disappeared, and as I sit down in front of the fire, I can't help but wish whatever was about to happen in the water had happened (but without the wife waiting for him back home, obviously). Grrrr. How is it possible that my one shot at romance in over five years has turned out to be with a lying, cheating wanker? Well, most likely.

The woman is gone now, and Leo's back at our campfire patting himself dry with his towel, an expression on his face that I can't read. He seems to have the weight of the world on his shoulders as he wraps his towel around his waist and strips off his trunks. I watch him, temporarily forgetting what a dog he is as my lady bits take over my eyes and the rest of me. Oh God, please let that towel slip off so I can see if the south half of him is as impressive as the north.

No! That kind of info would be in no way useful to me. Well, unless he's got a strange schlong or something—like if it's misshapen, or if his balls are so huge, they dwarf his penis. Or if he has a dwarf penis. Oh, not like a little person penis. I would never use the word dwarf to describe a little person. Plus, I once read that they have regular-size penises (or is the plural for penis peni? No, it's penises, isn't it?). Anyway, by dwarf penis, I mean more like a dwarf rabbit, as in tiny.

Jesus, Bree! Stop thinking about penises. That particular penis is likely married so just forget it. He finishes pulling up his grey boxer briefs without incident, so although I don't get to see his Full Monty, I now know he *does* wear undies—sexy man undies at that—which honestly doesn't help my poor lady bits at all because that image is staying put in my sex-starved brain. Once his shorts are on, he tugs at the towel, revealing a very dressed Leopold.

"So," I say, as he packs up his things. "That was weird."

"Yes, I apologize," he says, blowing out a puff of air.

"She's not actually your Uber driver, is she?"

"No, she isn't." He pulls his T-shirt on, depriving me of the view of that body once again.

"Want to talk about it?" I ask.

He makes a low moaning sound, then sits down next to me. "It's a long story, and if I tell you, I'm certain you'll no longer have any interest in so much as riding the bike while I pump."

I smile, and my face heats up a bit in spite of myself. Bugger all, this man has a hold on me. Clearing my throat, I say, "In that case, you should probably know that my very cynical imagination has already come up with two possible scenarios that are quite likely worse than the truth."

Rubbing the back of his neck, he says, "So either way…"

"You're basically screwed."

"Brilliant." He gives me a long stare before he says anything. "I'm not married or in a relationship of some sort, if that's where your mind went."

"Okay, good."

"As you likely know, I have a bit of a…reputation back home for enjoying the good life, and by that, I mean parties, trips, women…"

Nodding, I say, "Go on."

"A few months ago, I committed an egregious error in judgment and slept with one of the heirs to Sweden's throne."

My heart sinks to my stomach. "She's not pregnant, is she?"

Shaking his head, he says, "No, she's neither pregnant nor heartbroken that it wasn't the beginning of a long and happy life together. We both knew where it *wasn't* going from the start, but we weren't exactly discreet about the location or timing of our *getting to know each other.* When the story got out, it was a source of great embarrassment to her family. Not so coincidentally, the King of Sweden decided it was time for their nation to rethink their biggest telecommunications provider."

"Oh, that doesn't sound good."

"Yes, not good at all. My father can ignore any faux pas of mine so long as it doesn't affect his business." He studies the sand in front of him. "His first impulse was to write me off completely, but my mother convinced him to use this as an opportunity to force me to grow up. He had his lawyer draw up a contract in which I've agreed to stay out of the kingdom, get a job and a place to live independently for a period of six months. No booze, no dating, no getting fired or quitting my job, no asking my brother—or anyone else—for money or assistance in meeting the necessities of life. Jolene is the person his lawyer hired to monitor my every move while I'm here. If she can prove I've violated my agreement in any way, I will be permanently and completely disinherited."

My heart thumps wildly. "So did we just ruin your life back there?"

He stares at me for a moment, his expression soft. "Luckily, no. I think she has a bit of a soft spot for me, so instead of taking photos or video of what I think was about to happen, she called out to warn me instead. But if my life had ended up ruined, it would've been my own doing, not yours. I knew what was at stake, but I found myself..."

His voice trails off, and I desperately want him to finish that sentence, but he doesn't. Instead, he says, "You are lovely, Brianna, and if the circumstances allowed for it, I would throw you over my shoulder and take you back out to the sea to pick up where we left off."

"That would be a terrible idea for a number of reasons—not the least of which is that we're well-past caveman days when throwing a woman over your shoulder was considered acceptable behaviour."

"Quite right. I wouldn't really have done that, unless you're into that sort of thing and clearly indicated...wait a minute, a terrible idea for a number of reasons?"

"Boss, employee," I say, pointing back and forth between us. "Single mum with complicated life, man from another country who is not likely to stay beyond six months, I'm guessing."

"All solid points in favour of friend-zoning this relationship."

I nod firmly, pretending my entire body isn't coursing with lust. "Well, good thing Jolene came around when she did."

"Definitely," he says, glancing at my lips. "Because if we'd done what I think we were going to…"

"It would have been a disaster," I say, gazing into his eyes.

"A really long, sweaty, incredibly satisfying disaster," he says in a low tone. Taking a couple of steps toward me, he gives me that look that makes my legs turn to mush. I just start to think maybe he'll decide to risk it all for one night of perfection with me, but then he closes his eyes and exhales sharply. When he opens them, he says, "Employee, boss. Guy who needs to get his shit together, single mum with far too much on her plate. You need to be with someone who has mastered the art of being an adult, and the fact that I was about to do what I was about to do proves beyond a shadow of a doubt that I am no such man."

23

After the Perfect Non-Date Date

Bree

TIME TO FACE THE MUSIC. And by that, I mean I'm on my way to pick up Isabelle at my parents' house. Amber's probably called to tell them what an awful person I am, which will prevent me from making my quick in-and-out stop to grab my child and run.

I pull onto the street where I grew up and drive granny-slow while I try to come up with some way of avoiding the inevitable fight I'm heading toward. So far, all I've got is, "says you" in a saucy tone. Truth be told, I haven't been able to concentrate on much of anything since I got home from the beach and said goodnight to Leo. I laid awake most of the night replaying the entire day over and over. Sometimes, I ran through it while focussing on his voice, his tones, and his words. The next replay was all about his face, his smile, his incredible body. If I could write an exam on my recollection of my time with Leo Davenport yesterday, I'm sure I'd walk out with a perfect score.

I need to stop, but I can't seem to shake him from my mind. It's like I'm drunk on him, even though we haven't so much as kissed each other.

The truth of it—and it's a truth so inconvenient I can hardly stand to acknowledge it—is that I've never felt this way about a man before. Not even Roderick. I'm caught up in Leo like I never thought possible. I want him. All of him. And I'm not just talking about sex, although sex definitely is part of the equation. I'm desperately craving some sweaty sideways salsa time with Leo. The dance, not the food, which would be odd and quite icky if combined with sex. It would possibly burn your skin as well, depending on the spice level, now that I think of it. Anyway, as pathetic as it is, I crave him like he's the Easter chocolate in the cupboard that I don't eat because it belongs to Isabelle.

Unfortunately, the man who has me all hot and bothered (at a time in my life when I really cannot afford to be hot and bothered) has sworn an oath of celibacy. So even if he was up for it—and I think you and I both know he is based on how he acted at the beach last night—he's definitely *not* going to help me shag my troubles away. No matter how much I wish he would.

Speaking of troubles, there's my mum now, standing in front of their white bungalow, watering the flowerbed. She's dressed in a trendy T-shirt dress that displays the thin, tanned legs that could belong to a much younger woman. No one driving by would think she's a nice little old grandma watering her flowers. But then she's not always that nice, and she really isn't old. I made her a grandmother far before she was ready.

I park on the driveway, wishing she was in the house so I could sit here for another minute and try to gather my thoughts. But like most things in life, you don't get what you wish for, you get what you get. In this case, I get a pointed look from my mother as soon as I step out of the car.

"Hello, Mum," I say, dragging my feet as I walk up the sidewalk.

"How was your study-marathon?" she asks, turning off the hose.

What? She's not going after me to find out what happened in Isla del Sol? Oh, I get it. She's just lulling me into a false sense of security before she pounces.

"Good," I lie. "Thanks so much for keeping Isabelle for me. I made a lot of progress."

"Well, your dad and I are here to help. And we love having our Izzy time."

"Where is she, by the way?" I ask, excitement building in me at the thought of a tight hug from my little munchkin.

"In the pool with your dad," she says, setting the hose down on the grass. "She'll be wrinkled up for weeks."

Chuckling a little, I say, "She takes after her mother."

"Your dad and I were just saying this morning how much she reminds us of you." She starts for the back gate, and I follow her, wondering when she's going to begin the inquisition. When she reaches the gate, she turns to me. "I suppose you don't want to talk about what happened between you and Amber."

Now I get it. She wanted to do the pleasant-chat thing in the front garden in case any of the neighbours are spying. "You're right, I don't."

"I tried to warn you."

"I haven't forgotten."

"Then what happened, Brianna?" she asks in a tight voice.

"Drinks were had. Words were said. People were asked to leave."

"When you two fight, it just kills me," she says, blinking back tears. "I was up half the night worrying."

"Try a meditation app and some melatonin." I'm being a brat, but I don't even care.

"Oh, nice," she says, glaring at me.

"Look, sometimes siblings fight. That's why I'm just having the one child," I say with a satisfied grin.

"You're impossible," my mum says, waving a hand at me before turning and opening the gate.

I slip past her and hurry around the house to Izzy, who is looking very regal as she rides a unicorn floaty while my dad pushes her around in the water. When she spots me, her eyes light up. "Mummy! I'm the queen of the sea!"

Striding across the wet grass, I stop at the side of the pool, which comes up to my chest. "How do you do, your majesty?" I say with a formal bow.

"Very welly," she answers, chin lifted as my dad pushes her over to me.

"Hi, Dad," I say as Izzy reaches out and clings to my neck with her wet arms. Not caring if she soaks my T-shirt, I pluck her off the unicorn and swing her around, planting kisses on her chubby cheeks.

"How was your weekend?" my dad asks as he climbs up the ladder to get out of the pool.

"Not as fun as yours, I see," I answer, setting Izzy down on the lawn.

"You're staying for lunch, right?" my mum asks as she holds a towel out for Isabelle.

"I think we should get going. Thanks, though."

"Good call," my dad mutters. "Your mum has invited the above-ground pool salesman over."

Raising one eyebrow, I glare at her, but she doesn't see because she's busy scowling at my father.

"Omar, he's not just a sales guy. He *owns* the company." Turning to me, she adds, "And it's not just above-ground pools. It's patio furniture, barbeques, outdoor kitchens..."

"And I suppose he's single and ready for a committed relationship," I say, rubbing Izzy's hair with the towel.

"Newly divorced. Two kids, so he already understands what parenting is all about," my mum says.

"Newly divorced, you say?" I ask, feigning excitement.

"This one's a catch. Trust me. Someone's going to snag him, and it might as well be you."

"Okay, well, in that case..." I smile down at Izzy. "If you can be dressed and ready to leave in under five minutes, I'll stop at the treat store on the way home."

24

Unwanted Feedback and Tap Water

Leo

"SO HOW'S WORKING LIFE?" Pierce asks, setting his beer down on the table.

"Brilliant, really. The lifting and the stacking…can't get enough of it," I answer, popping a tortilla chip into my mouth.

It's late Sunday afternoon, and I'm at the Turtle's Head Pub, a popular local eatery, with Pierce and Emma. We're seated at a corner table on the busy roof-top patio that offers a lovely view of the sea. My brother has his back to the crowd (not to mention the view) and is wearing his sunglasses despite the fact that we're shaded by a large umbrella. Word has gotten out that the great Pierce Davenport, author of the *Clash of Crowns* series, lives on the island full-time now, so tourists are always on the lookout for him wherever they go—especially the "Crownies," as they call themselves. My brother, not being a fan of "real people" does his best to avoid being noticed.

Emma glances at me, then at the refreshing-looking glass of Sauvignon Blanc in front of her. "Are you sure you don't mind if Pierce and I drink in front of you?"

"That's very thoughtful of you, Emma, but I wouldn't be at a pub if I couldn't control myself around booze and/or women." My gaze shifts to Pierce's pint of Stella which is currently begging to make a liar out of me. Instead, I pick up a homemade tortilla chip and dip it in the salsa dish, trying not to think about all the things that have been testing my resolve lately—not the least of which is a certain woman with whom I shared a most delightful date yesterday.

"Christ, you poor bugger," Pierce says, sounding amused rather than sympathetic. "You're staring at my drink like you used to stare at Tatiana's chest."

"I believe you were the one enamoured with her double F's, not me." I turn to Emma and add, "Tatiana was one of our nannies. Pierce was infatuated with her from age twelve to fifteen."

"Was not," he quips. "That was Greyson."

Emma tilts her head toward me. "Oh, I know who she is, believe me."

"Really?" I ask with a raised eyebrow.

"He's brought her up at least half a dozen times," she answers with a smile in my direction. Her face falls a bit as she peers past me. "Oh, crap. I think we've got a reporter here."

Instead of turning, Pierce picks up his phone and puts it in selfie mode. "What time?"

"Eight o'clock to you," she says, without moving her lips. "Wide-angle lens Nikon on her lap."

Pierce stares at his mobile for a second, then glances at me with a wide grin. "I think she's here for you, Leo."

I twist around and see Jolene sitting at a nearby table. She smiles and raises her bottle of beer in a toast to me. I give her an unenthusiastic wave and turn back to my lunch companions with a sigh. "That's my parole officer," I tell Emma. "She's been on my arse all weekend."

"Oh, wow. Somehow seeing her in person makes the whole thing seem more real," she says.

"Quite," I answer, feeling the weight of the contract bearing down on me. "Don't tell anyone, but this entire experience has been a lot less enjoyable than I expected. I'm only at the halfway mark, and each day, I find something new to miss."

"Such is the fate of a man hell-bent on sponging off his parents," Pierce says, shaking his head as he scoops salsa onto a tortilla.

Emma quickly changes the subject. "Rosy said you're really working out well at the resort."

"Yes, it only took me a few weeks to learn how to be a proper mule," I answer. "But it's kind of her to say that. I wonder if she'd be willing to serve as a reference for me."

"Are you wanting to stay in the hospitality industry?" Emma asks.

"God, no! I meant with my father," I say without thinking. "Sorry, Emma, I didn't mean to offend you."

"Why would that offend her?" Pierce asks. "She's a master chef, not a mule."

"A chef who can't speak for herself?" I ask dryly.

"Apparently," Emma says, rolling her eyes at my brother but giving him a little grin at the same time. "And I'm not offended, Leo. I know being a bellboy isn't your life's dream. I just thought maybe the industry itself would be a good fit for you, since you're so...fun-loving."

"She means irresponsible," Pierce says, leaning toward me and lowering his voice.

"I meant no such thing," Emma says.

"Good God, he loves to talk for you, Emma," I say. "That must get on your last nerve, no?"

"It's not as irritating as a lot of the other stuff Pierce does, so I've decided to let that one go," she answers, trying to hide a smile.

Dipping a chip into the salsa, I say, "Like the amount of time he spends playing with his imaginary friends."

Cupping her hand over her mouth to hide her answer from Pierce, she mouths, "Yes."

"Oh, Christ, please tell me this isn't going to be another afternoon of the two of you bonding via making fun of me," my brother says.

I stare at Emma for a second, then we both nod. "I'm afraid it is," I say, pretending to be sorry.

"You're just going to have to get used to it, dear," Emma adds. "It's sort of our thing now."

"Arseholes, the pair of you," he says with a grin. "Now, Emma made me promise not to bring it up, but apparently everyone at the hotel thinks you're shagging your boss."

Swatting him on the arm, Emma gives him a death glare, which he ignores.

"Oh, do they?" I ask. "Just because we're both single, attractive, and have a searing sexual energy…"

"So you *are* then?" Pierce asks.

"Not that it's any of your business, but, no, we're not shagging." I pick up my sad glass of tap water and have a swig, trying to purge the image of shagging Bree out of my mind. Damn, didn't work. Did it really have to be a no-sex *and* no-booze contract? One surely would have been enough to teach me my lesson. "We're friends, but I'm not about to risk my entire future on a woman, no matter how cute she looks in a swimsuit."

Emma laughs. "Oh my God, so there is some truth to the rumours. You *like* her."

"I also would like to have a sip of that beer," I say, pointing to Pierce's drink. "But if I'm ever to have a life again, I shall have to endure a few more months without that, either."

"Or you could tell Father to sod off and be a free man for the rest of your life and shag whoever you want," Pierce adds offhandedly.

My head snaps back at the suggestion. "I may not be the smartest of the Davenport sons, but I'm not fool enough to give up a life of luxury."

"Life of luxury? Really, Leo? Or is it allowing them to control you until either they die or you do?"

"Controlling me? No." I glare at my brother, anger simmering away in my blood. "I'm not sure if you noticed, but I do exactly what I want, when I want, which is literally the perfect life. And I intend to go back to it as soon as this silly test is over."

"This silly test will never end. You must know that," Pierce says. "This is them painting the boundaries you must live within if you wish to continue to suckle at the financial teat of our father."

"First of all, disgusting metaphor, so thanks for that," I say.

"He's right," Emma adds. "That was one of the more grotesque images you've come out with, which for you, is *really* saying something."

"Second, once I prove our father wrong—which I intend to do—I'll make sure to squirrel away some savings in case he decides to do this again."

"You can't hear how pathetic that sounds?" Pierce asks. "Even when you say it out loud like that?"

"There's nothing pathetic about having no expectations and no responsibilities—"

"No reason to get up in the morning. No purpose."

"Exactly. It's the ultimate in freedom every day. No schedule to keep. No mind-numbing boredom sitting at a desk all day. Just wake up and go wherever the wind blows," I say, staring up at the blue sky.

"Or you could decide you'd rather have a real life—one in which you have hopes and dreams and ambitions and you stand on your own two feet so you can call yourself a man."

"I *am* a man, thank you very much."

"Only as far as biology is concerned," Pierce quips.

The server chooses that moment to come by our table. "Are you ready to order your mains?"

Looking up at her, I say, "They might be. Turns out I'm only a childish side dish."

Her face wrinkles up in confusion. "Excuse me?"

"Nothing. Sorry. I won't be staying for lunch." Standing, I toss my napkin on the table. "Emma, lovely to see you, as always." Raising my voice so everyone can hear, I say, "It's Pierce Davenport, author of the *Clash of Crowns* series!"

Pierce gives me a death glare, and I grin back at him for a second. "Everyone! Literary genius Pierce Davenport in the house! Let's give him a round of applause, shall we?"

The patio is suddenly buzzing with energy as the other patrons start clapping and rising from their seats to get a good look at my brother. Giving him a salute, I say, "Enjoy your lunch," before weaving my way through his excited fans.

That'll teach him.

I stalk out of the pub, giving Jolene a curt nod on my way to the staircase. Once I'm on the street, I storm over to my bicycle and put on my helmet. "Not a man. Fuck him," I mutter, getting on my bike. Pushing off with one foot, I pedal furiously down the street. "Just because I didn't get lucky and write the world's most popular fantasy novels doesn't mean I'm not a man."

***

Isabelle is riding around the driveway on her trike when I arrive home. Today, she's in a swimsuit, a pair of oversized old lady sunglasses, and a big sun hat. She grins and waves at me. "Hi! I'm back from my holiday."

Getting off my bicycle, I give her a small smile. "Welcome home, Isabelle."

"Where were you?" she asks, following me as I walk my bike to the gate.

"Out for lunch with my brother and his girlfriend."

"Oh, did you get ice cream?"

Shaking my head, I sigh. "No, Izzy. Unfortunately, I did not get any ice cream. Instead, I got lectured on growing up."

She gives me a perplexed look for a second. "I like ice cream. It's the best food there is."

"Agreed." I prop my bike against the fence, then turn back to Izzy. "Can I ask you a question?"

"Yup."

"If someone were to say, 'Here, Izzy, I'm going to give you every-thing you ever wanted, and you never have to work, and can just play all day for the rest of your life,' you'd say yes to that, wouldn't you?"

She nods quickly with wide eyes that suggest she has no idea what I'm talking about, but she's onboard anyway. Gotta love kids.

"That wouldn't be pathetic, right? You'd still be a real man—well, in your case, a real girl—if you took it," I say. "Pierce doesn't know what he's talking about," I mutter. "I'm a real man."

I turn to her. "You think of me as a grown-up, right, Izzy? I do grown-up things like mow the lawn and use the washing machine."

"Sort of," she says. "But mostly you don't *really* know how to be a grown-up. You're more like a kid. 'Cept you pee really loud, but Mum says that's cause you're so tall."

What does she know? She's not even five. Besides, who asked her anyway?

25

Rainstorms and Revelations...

Bree

One Week Later

IT'S LATE in the evening. Isabelle is asleep, and I'm washing up the dishes while Dolores fries up a package of emergency bacon. You know, the extra bacon you keep in the fridge when you're running low on bacon. The window in front of me is open to let the smell out, Jerry's bass guitar is thumping out some mellow tune, and I feel a refreshingly cool breeze on my skin as I mindlessly wipe a plate with the soapy cloth. Knickers, Milo, and Puddy Tat sit on the tile floor behind Dolores, waiting patiently for their share as the rain softly falls.

Today, Leo and I had the day off and we spent most of it together getting groceries, running errands, and doing all sorts of other married-couple things—although we prefer to call them totally normal landlady-tenant things so as to remind ourselves of the care-fully constructed boundaries of our relationship. Leo mowed the lawn while I pulled weeds out of the flowerbed, both of us finishing just before a storm blew in. Then we hurried into the house together, laughing as we dodged the huge raindrops, and stood at the kitchen window with Isabelle between us, watching as the earth was pelted with water. The next couple of hours were spent with me studying at the kitchen table while Leo and Dolores played cards and board games with Izzy.

Now, as I rinse the plate, I think about how much Dolores has taken to Leo. She's not normally one to have any use for men, but Leo's different. The two of them get along like a house on fire, sharing private jokes and calling each other Bonnie and Clyde after Dolores *'accidentally'* shoplifted a chocolate bar when they went to the store together the other day.

I hum while I pluck a glass out of the warm water and start to work on it.

"So how long have you and Leo been sleeping together?" Dolores asks from her position in front of the stove.

I whip my head around. "What? We're not *sleeping together*."

She gives me a sceptical look. "But you want to."

"I certainly do not," I answer indignantly, while simultaneously turning back to the sink so she can't see my bright-pink cheeks.

"Oh, please, who do you think you're kidding?"

"No one, because it's the truth. Leo and I have a very nice friendship, and he's very helpful around here, so maybe that's what you're sensing—my gratitude."

"Nope, it's horniness," she says, bending down to give Milo a scratch behind his ears.

"That is...yuck!"

"What yuck?" She stands and puts her hand on her hip. "I'd take a sip from that tall drink of water if I were thirty years younger."

"Just because he's handsome doesn't mean I want to *sleep with him*," I huff, no longer leisurely washing the dishes, but instead scrubbing them vigorously.

"He's handsome, helpful, happy, wonderful with Isabelle, and he very clearly can't take his eyes off you when you're around..." She lifts a slice of bacon with her tongs and lets it drip into the pan before depositing it on a plate. "You'd be insane to let that one get away."

Turning to her, I roll my eyes. "We're not... He's a... There's just no way it would work out, even if I wanted it to, which I don't. The last thing I need is some rudderless dinghy to hang on to while it sinks under the sea."

"He's not a dinghy, and he's definitely not going to sink. He's just getting started, is all."

"What, are you on my mum's side now? Trying to convince me I need a man to be happy?"

"Of course not. I'd never side with that woman," Dolores says, wrinkling up her nose and turning to face me. "Your mum thinks you'd be happy with any man, whereas I know you'll only be happy with *that man*."

"He's the last person I should ever get involved with. He's made it very clear that as soon as his six months are up, he's going home. And since I'm on the verge of having the perfect life here, I'm not about to pack up everything, uproot my daughter, and move halfway across the world for some guy. Not that some guy would ever ask me to because he won't."

"I've seen the way you look at each other. He's the yang to your yin. He's the calm to your storm. He's pretty much your only shot at not turning into me."

I pull the stopper out of the sink, and the water drains loudly. "And what if I want to turn into you? I like you. An independent, feisty—"

"I'm broke and alone, and if it weren't for you, I don't know where I would've ended up."

"Well, I can be you, except with more money, can't I?"

Dolores shakes her head. "You can do better. You can have it all. The career, the family, and the absolutely perfect-for-you partner in life, who seems like the type who'll support you in your dreams, to accept you the way you are, and let you be you."

Does she not know I've been trying my damnedest not to think about any of that? "Yeah, well, that all sounds really nice, Auntie, but the truth is, he's going to leave. If life has taught me anything, it's to examine the facts and live in reality, because living in some sort of hormone-induced fantasy world gets you knocked up and abandoned."

"Roderick was a complete wanker. I knew it the moment I laid eyes on him. But Leo's different. He knows what matters in life—living in the moment, making the best of a situation, caring for those around you. Leo's a good man."

"A good man who's going to leave."

"Not if you give him a reason to stay."

A clap of thunder causes the cats to scatter, all in different directions. I dry my hands, close the window, then sigh and lean against the counter.

Dolores stares me down, clearly waiting for me to say something. I shake my head. "As nice as it would be to have a man who embodies some of Leo's finer traits, it's not going to happen. Not now. Not ever. So please drop it, or I'll be forced to start calling you Naomi Two."

Narrowing her eyes, Dolores says, "You wouldn't."

"Oh, but I would."

"Nasty girl."

"I learned from the best," I say, walking out of the room.

Just as I turn down the hall toward the loo, Dolores says, "The saddest thing in the world is to spend your life wondering what if."

***

An hour later, I flip my pillow over and thump it for the hundredth time, but when I lie back down, it still feels lumpy. I'm too hot, even though the rain has cooled the house down. I can't stop thinking about what Dolores said. What if Leo is the one for me, and all I have to do is be brave enough to tell him how I feel?

The thought makes my stomach flip. I don't think I could handle that much rejection.

But what if he doesn't reject me?

Sitting up on the couch, I tap my fingers on my lap. I'm in love with him. All the signs are there—laughing at everything he says, hanging on every word, sighing happily every time I see him with

Isabelle or Dolores, or the cats, for that matter, the squishy, gooey feeling inside when I think about him.

He is kind of perfect, really. I mean, if he was staying and had a plan for his life, that is. I don't see myself with some party animal who lives off his rich parents. But if he wanted to *stay*, and if Dolores is right and he's just getting started…

I mean, he's only got three weeks left until his contract is over and he's back in his father's good books (or pocketbook, depending on how you look at it). At that point, he can quit his bellboy position and figure out what he really wants to do. More than likely, he's going to get on the first plane that will take him back to Avonia forever. But what if he has a reason to stay? And what if *I'm* that reason?

My heart pounds in my chest, and I feel thrilled and terrified at the same time. I'm going to do it. I'm going to ask him if he'll stay.

Maybe.

But not tomorrow. I should think about it for a few days before I decide…

26

The Lethal Weapon Effect

Leo

"Okay, Jolene, a pleasure as always," I say as I walk toward the front door, having provided my urine sample.

She grunts in response. "Try not to screw up, you've only got less than three weeks left of this whole model-citizen thing. This is when things go sour, right at the end."

I stop and turn to face her. "Really? So in all the father-son contracts you've overseen over the years, it's the last few weeks that are the hardest?"

"Hilarious." She opens the door and moves aside to let me out. "I was talking about the *Lethal Weapon* effect. You know, it's always the day before a cop retires that he gets shot."

"Ah, yes. I'm familiar with the concept, but in my case, there really is no need for worry," I say, stepping out into the hot wind. "I've got my eye on the prize, Ms. Fita, and when I set my mind to something, I never fail. Believe me, when the six months are up, I'll be back home living the good life."

"You sure your eye is on the right prize?" she asks, following me out onto the porch.

"The money, yes," I call over my shoulder as I jog down the three steps to the sidewalk.

"Money won't buy you a quality woman like that lovely landlady. Took me nearly forty years to find Ursula."

My shoulders drop and I turn around to face her. "I'm confused. Is giving life advice part of your job description?"

"That was free of charge," she answers. "I guess I'm just a romantic at heart, and I'm pretty sure your happy ending would be found with her."

Great. Girl talk with Jolene. "As lovely as Brianna is, I'm not the right man for her."

"Sure, not now, but you could be if you stopped letting your parents run your life."

Jesus, first Pierce, now my parole officer? "Thanks for the advice, but I've got it all figured out."

Jolene shakes her head. "You just love to tempt fate, don't you?"

"Yes, fate is my bitch," I answer, mounting my bike.

Chuckling, Jolene shakes her head at me. "All right then, Crazy. I'll be seeing you around."

"Not if I see you first."

As I make my way home, my mind wanders to riding tandem with Brianna, as it does every time I'm en route since our day together. I also think about our date—let's just be honest and call it what it was—when I'm in bed, in the shower, standing next to her at the desk in the lobby, watching her at work or with Isabelle, and pretty much every other minute of the day and/or night.

The real kicker is that for the first time in my stupid life, I'm completely and utterly taken with a woman, and of course, it has to be a woman I have no business wanting. And yet I can't seem to stop myself. I want to know everything about her—what she thinks about every topic under the sun from politics to religion to her favourite book when she was a child. When she speaks, I drink in the sound of her voice and take in her words in a way I've never done with anyone. It's like every cell in my brain is desperate to know her, no matter how many times I tell them to stop.

At night, I lie awake listening for the sound of a knock at my door, thinking about all the things we could do if she'd slip inside silently under the light of the moon. Even though we haven't so much as kissed, I already know it would be incredible between us. A guy can just tell. There's either that whole chemistry pheromone thing going on or there isn't. And with Bree, it's there all the time, even when she isn't. I can immediately conjure the scent of her shampoo and of her skin, the sound of her laugh, the delight in her eyes when she's teasing Isabelle—or me, for that matter. My brain tortures me with it on a minute-by-minute basis, rendering me utterly frustrated and pathetic.

The worst thing is I'm pretty sure she feels it, too. I catch her watching me when I'm loading luggage onto the cart, or mowing the lawn, or hanging my clothes on the line. She seems to find reasons to be near me, whether at home or at work. Little excuses to touch my hand or stand extra close to me at the desk. I do it, too. Yesterday, after our lunch break, I pretended she had something on her cheek, just so I could feel her skin against the pad of my thumb. That tiny gesture has kept me going for almost sixteen hours, but there's only so long a man in love can go on that.

Oh, bugger, I just called myself a man in love, didn't I?

***

"Leo! We've got some customers for you," Mario calls from the front steps.

I hurry out to meet the Jeep, my eyes adjusting to the dark as I reach the sidewalk. In the backseat sits an elderly couple, Mr. and Mrs. Briar, who got on the wrong shuttle bus at the airport and ended up on the northside of the island. They've come all the way from Ireland to celebrate Mrs. Briar's eightieth birthday, so the last thing they needed after such a long journey was several hours on a bus. The driver returned them to the airport but wasn't willing to make the extra few miles to the resort, so Emma's brother, Harrison, picked them up in the Jeep and brought them here.

As soon as Harrison stops, I pull open the back door and give them a little nod. "Mr. and Mrs. Briar, welcome to Paradise Bay. We've been waiting for you." Holding out my hand, I help Mrs. Briar out of the car.

"Well, I should imagine you would be after that fecking bus kidnapped us and took us all over the bloody Caribbean!"

"And I'm sure that's the very last thing you needed after such an exhausting day of travel," I say, taking her by the elbow with my right hand and wrapping my left arm around her back to help her to the bench. "You must be famished by now."

"We ate at the airport, but I could use a good stiff drink."

"Give me a quick minute, young lady, and I'll have you sorted," I say as she sits down. "The wonderful staff at the reception desk are already working their magic to get you checked in as fast as possible. If you like, I'll take your passports up to them and ask them to print out the paperwork, then I'll run it back here for you to sign and bring you your keys."

She gives me a pat on the cheek. "My daughter-in-law said this was a nice place to stay, but I didn't believe her. She's quite the liar."

Unable to stop myself from laughing, I say, "Is she, now?"

I turn back to the Jeep to fetch her husband, but he's already making his way over to us on his own. Harrison walks right behind him, just in case. Out of the corner of my eye, I spot someone standing by one of the palm trees lining the front steps. Pierce is leaning against the tree, staring at me. My heart thumps a bit, the memory of our last conversation popping into my mind. I give him a quick nod, then get back to work.

I hurry around to the back of the vehicle and unload their things straight into a golf cart while Mrs. Briar regales us with stories about her daughter-in-law from hell.

Mr. Briar pipes up after the third horror story. "Christ, woman, she's not that bad. You just hate her because she's a master baker, and you can't even get a pie crust to stay together."

"Oh, is that so? If you don't like my pie, you can just keep your face out of it from now on," Mrs. Briar says.

Did she just mean *her pie*? Can't have, right?

She turns to me with bedroom eyes behind her bifocals. "You look like the type to know a good pie when you see one."

Oh, yes. Yes, she did mean *that* kind of pie.

Reaching up, she pats my cheek. "Such a handsome young lad. If things don't work out with this one, I'll give you a call."

I chuckle, then lower my voice. "How's it going so far?"

"Eh, the first sixty years have been passable, but I'm still not entirely sure I'll stick it out 'til the end."

"You can have 'er," Mr. Briar grumbles, waving his hand at me.

Chuckling, I say, "Let's get you two love birds off to the honeymoon suite, shall we?"

Five minutes later, they're snuggled in the backseat of a golf cart as one of the porters whisks them off to their room for a stiff drink and a big sleep. I walk over to Pierce, who is still standing under the tree out of the light.

"Hiding from the paparazzi?" I ask lightly.

"Why? Are you hoping to rat me out again?" he quips. After a small pause, he says, "I'm waiting for my girlfriend, actually. She asked me to meet her in front of the lobby after her shift. I thought she must have needed to pop by here on her way out, but now I see she had other motives."

"She wants us to kiss and make up," I say.

"Make up, yes," Emma's voice cuts through the quiet evening air. I turn to see her walking toward us in her chef's uniform that looks like it needs a good scrub. "I don't expect you to kiss."

Pierce and I both chuckle as she makes her way over to him and gives him a light peck on the lips. They are disgustingly happy, aren't they?

She wraps her arms around his waist. "Sorry I'm late, darling. The twins got in a bit of a dust up and needed some intervention."

"Twins?" I ask, my curiosity piqued.

"Dishwashing brothers at the steakhouse," Pierce says.

I glance at Emma. "He did it again, didn't he?"

"He really can't help it," she says with a grin. "He just cannot let me answer for myself. Now, get on with it, you two lugheads. Apologize already."

Taking a deep breath, I say, "I'm sorry I told you to fuck off and then sicced a crowd on you."

"Quite right. You were way out of line," Pierce says, jamming both hands in the pockets of his chinos.

Sighing, Emma glares up at Pierce. "And…"

"And what?"

"And don't you have something to say to Leo?" Emma asks in a tight voice.

He rolls his eyes and heaves a large sigh. "You did well there with those elderly people. You're surprisingly good at this job."

Emma puts one hand on her hip and gives him the look.

Glancing at her, Pierce says, "Oh, fine. I guess I owe you an apology for suggesting it would be easy to free yourself from our parents."

"That's very big of you, Pierce, thank you. Or should I thank Emma?"

"Are you seriously trying to push it right now?" he asks.

"Sorry, old habit," I answer, rubbing the back of my neck. "What I meant to say is that I know you were trying to help, and I shouldn't have gotten so angry." Lowering my voice, I add, "Even if you were being a bit of a tosser about the whole thing."

Pierce shakes his head. "Have you not figured out what I was trying to say at the pub?"

"That I'm not a man, and I should tell our parents to sod off."

Shrugging, Pierce says, "True, but have you stopped to consider *why* I would say that?"

"Because you hate them and think me pathetic to allow them to pay for my life."

"No." He raises his voice. "Because unlike you, I know you've got yacht-loads of untapped potential, and it really chaps my arse to see someone with your talent and intellect waste it all."

Oh, that's not what I was expecting to hear. That was rather… nice actually. A little emotional even. I clear my throat, trying to regain my composure. "Well, I wouldn't want to chap your arse. Poor Emma here will be stuck putting some sort of ointment on it," I say with a sideways grin.

"You can try to make light of this, but deep down, you know I'm right, Leo, and it terrifies you." He points a finger at me. "You gave up on yourself years ago, but I never have. I've always known that beneath this act is an extraordinary human being who's capable of so much more."

Well, fuck me. I don't think I can speak at the moment.

He must know this, because he goes on. "I'm not saying it would be easy. It would be bloody hard, in fact. And probably rather terrifying at times. And you'll likely live a very meager existence for a good, long time. And you probably will never have the same—"

"Maybe move on from that bit now," Emma says, cutting him off.

"Good point, love, thanks," he says, glancing at her. Looking back at me, he continues, "But in the end, it would be *infinitely better*."

But this is scary. And I don't do scary—or hard. I don't believe in it. I believe in smart, which is the easiest way to getting what you want. But he is right. Bollocks. "I don't... I've already put in over five months. I'm not going to quit now," I say, sounding utterly lame.

Pierce's face falls, and the hope in his eyes is extinguished.

"Listen, Pierce," I say, taking a couple of steps toward him, desperate to regain some of the approval from a few moments ago. "I'm going to finish this if only to prove to our father I can do it."

"Who cares what that tosser thinks?" he scoffs. "If you're going to finish this thing, Leo, do it for yourself. You're the one who needs to trust you. No one else."

I nod and a small smile crosses my face. "Okay, then. I'll do it for me."

Emma beams back and forth between us. "Now, hug it out, you two sillies!"

We both shake our heads, Pierce saying, "Not necessary," at the same time that I say, "No need, thanks."

"Oh, fine." She looks both exasperated and amused. "I'm just glad you sorted it out. Because even though Pierce has been trying to go all 'tough love' on you, he just can't stop worrying about you."

"That's a wild exaggeration," Pierce says, rolling his eyes.

Ignoring him, she says, "He can hardly sleep."

"Not true, I sleep very well, thank you."

"He goes on and on about it," Emma whispers. "That's because he loves his baby brother very much."

Clearing his throat, Pierce says, "Let's not get carried away. I'm fond of Leo."

"He loves you," Emma says with a firm nod. "More than anyone, except maybe me."

I burst out laughing. "In that case, I should give him a hug."

I close in on Pierce with my arms open, then grab him in a bear hug while he protests vehemently.

"The more you fight it, the longer I'm going to hug you."

"Bastard."

***

Two hours later, I'm driving a golf cart back toward the lobby, having just delivered toothpaste to a family of four. The resort grounds are quiet, with only the sound of the trees blowing in the trade wind. It's a rare calm moment that allows me to process Pierce's words. In my twenty-seven years, I never would've guessed that someone as accomplished as the great Pierce Davenport would think me to be an extraordinary human being who's capable of so much more than I allow myself, but apparently he does.

As I drive along under the moonlit sky, I briefly run through all the steps it would take to free myself of the Bank of Alistair. First, I'd need to tell him to sod off, resulting in weeks of teary phone calls from Mother, who'd be certain she's losing the only person who truly loves her. She'd be wrong about that, but the time and energy to prove it would be considerable. Second, instead of wrapping up my days of menial tasks and mule work in a matter of weeks, I'd guarantee myself years of them—possibly a lifetime.

I suppose, deep down, I've always thought I had something more to offer the world than a good time, but wouldn't it be smarter to find my purpose in life and have money at the same time? I mean, it seems like a rather foolish idea to cut my safety net out from under me, then continue on the trapeze of life, even though it is nice to have one person in my corner who believes I would make it to the other side.

The truth is, I'm not so sure Pierce is right about me. I may be a total failure. And what about Brianna? I'd be lying if I said I didn't want things to go somewhere with her, and I highly doubt that a girl like her would be content to date a guy who's just starting out without a penny to his name. Not that she's a gold digger or anything. I don't mean to imply that. She's just so driven, and she's already got it all together. Why in the world would she wait for me to catch up?

She wouldn't. But she may be willing to date a rich guy who is trying to make something of himself. The smart thing to do is to finish what I started. Then once I'm back in the lap of luxury, I'll have all the time and resources in the world to help get me off in a new direction, hopefully one that will take me along the same path as the woman I love…

27

Butterflies of Desperation

Brianna

AMBER: I *think it's best if you don't come to Mum and Dad's to help with the guest favours today. You're too busy, and we've got more than enough people to get the job done.*

ME: *No, I want to be there. I wouldn't be much of a maid of honour if I didn't help with any of the prep work.*

AMBER: *I'd prefer you didn't come. It's just too awkward right now. Maybe forever. Good luck with your exams. See you at the wedding rehearsal.*

"Shitake mushrooms," I mutter, putting my phone down on the kitchen table and glancing at Izzy. She's too busy devouring a bowl of Choc-puffs for breakfast to notice my non-swear. As much as I was dreading going to my parents' house to work on the party favours, the whole "maybe-forever" bit doesn't exactly sound promising. I stare at my phone, chewing my bottom lip.

"What's wrong?" Dolores asks, crumbling a slice of bacon onto her oatmeal while Milo, Puddy, and Knickers meow at her.

"Wedding stuff," I whisper, walking over to the coffee pot and pouring a second mug.

Not bothering to lower her voice, she asks, "What's the world's most delicate bride upset about now?"

Glancing at Izzy, I give Dolores a there-are-small-ears-attached-to-a-big-mouth-in-the-room look. "She wrote to say it would be best if I don't come by today to help."

Feeding Milo some bacon, Dolores shrugs. "Good. Let Amber and the tattoo sisters take care of that nonsense. You don't have time for it anyway."

"Tell that to my churning gut. She'd prefer not to see me until the rehearsal, which means this whole business will be hanging over my head until then."

"Let her have her tantrum and lick her own wounds for once. It'll do her good not to have her big sister come rushing in to make it all better." Dolores gives me a firm nod. "To be honest, it would have done her some good if she'd heard no a little more often as a child."

The word "child" catches Izzy's attention. "Who?"

"Not you," I say, hoping to distract her from the topic at hand.

"You told me no all the time when I was a child," she says, slurping the milk off her spoon.

Chuckling, I walk over to her, ruffle her hair with one hand, and plant a big kiss on her forehead. "And look at what a lovely young lady you've turned out to be."

"Yup," Izzy says with a big nod.

"Now, don't slurp your milk. Sip it quietly, please," I whisper.

Sighing, I feel a tug of worry pull at my stomach and settle into my chest. My words come back to mind. Moron, idiot, vapid housewife. Oh God. There really is no coming back from that, is there? "Oh, God, why did I say those things about Dane?"

"Because they're true. Now stop dwelling on it," Dolores says. "You've got a far bigger dream to chase than marrying some moron who likes to smash things."

"That's not nice."

"Nice is for pastors' wives and wallpaper, which, if you ask me, are pretty much the same thing. Now, you go study or have a nap or something. Izzy and I have a very busy day planned of finding new bacon recipes, and we don't need you getting in the way of all our creating."

***

I knock on Leo's door and wait for a minute for him to open it. He's shirtless, wearing only a pair of board shorts. He's also fresh from the shower and is rubbing his wet hair with a towel, causing little drops to land on his sculpted chest. I zone out for a second, completely forgetting why I came out here in the first place. He tosses his towel onto the bed and takes a few steps closer to me, raising his right arm up and gripping the doorjamb.

When I finally manage to tear my eyes from his body, I'm greeted by his smug amusement. Letting me off the hook for the undignified drooling, he says, "Hey, you. Aren't you supposed to be at your parents' place tying ribbons onto key-shaped bottle openers?"

Oh God, I want to launch myself into the room and kiss him for days. The way he says "hey, you" is like this sexy combination of delighted and really turned on that just does it for me.

"Bree?" he says with a light chuckle. "You okay?"

I shake my head a bit. "Super great, really. I wanted to see if you need a ride to work later. I'm not going to my parents' after all."

Concern crosses his gorgeous face. "Everything all right?"

"Not really. My sister and I haven't exactly made up yet, so she thought it best if I skip out today."

"That doesn't sound good." Letting go of the door, he turns and takes the two steps it takes to cross to the dresser, then opens the top drawer and pulls out a grey T-shirt. I watch, utterly disappointed as he puts it on.

Stepping inside, I lean against the wall, trying not to imagine him pressing me up against it and planting soft kisses down my neck. Or urgent ones. Or soft, yet urgent ones. Bugger. I'm thinking about it, aren't I? What were we talking about?

My sister. Right. "Yeah, it's not great, but I'm sure we'll sort it out before the wedding. Actually, I'm not sure if that's true. She might not forgive me, and I wouldn't blame her. I'd kill to skip the whole thing. It's going to be so awkward."

"Listen, you wouldn't want a plus-one for the big day, would you?" he asks, rubbing the back of his neck. "For moral support, I mean."

My heart leaps at the thought of having him there with me. Huge step up from Mr. Bananas. "Oh God, I'd never subject you to my entire family. You've met Dolores. Imagine her times three hundred."

"In that case, I definitely want to come. She's hilarious."

I give him a quizzical look. "Why would you even want to come?"

"Because you need a friend, and I'd like to be one," he says, our eyes locking for one delicious second. "But mainly for the free meal. Food is fucking expensive."

I burst out laughing. When I stop, he's giving me a look that could melt my knickers. What the hell? Why not have a handsome, incredible date for my sister's wedding? "I'd love that, Leo, thank you, but only if you're sure. It'll actually help, because everyone is trying to set me up with a total wanker in the wedding party."

If I didn't know better, I'd say his face just flickered with jealousy. But that can't be right, can it?

His face grows serious. "In that case, I definitely have to come. When is it?"

"August eighth," I say, suddenly realizing his six months will be over before then. My heart pounds in my chest. "Are you still going to be here?"

Nodding, he says, "I'll be here."

Act casual, Brianna. Play it cool even though you have the sudden urge to run through the neighbourhood screaming with delight. "Great. Well, I should go get ready for work."

"Okay, see you in a bit."

"Brilliant, yeah," I mumble, trying to force my feet to walk outside. I finally get them going, then turn back to him. "Listen, if you change your mind about the wedding, I'll understand."

"I won't," he says, and there's something about his tone that tells me he means it.

Giving him a small smile, I say, "Right. Free food."

I hurry out into the bright sunlight and let the world's biggest grin cross my face. I stop short of fist-pumping the air and dancing back inside the house, which I'd say is a real sign of maturity. Leo Davenport, world's hottest man, is going to be my date. Suck it, Evander Hammer! And you, too, Mum. I got my own date, and he's hot as hell, and rich AF. Sort of. Not that that matters because I don't fancy him for his money. I fancy him for his everything else. He's sweet and smart and thoughtful and handsome and sexy and caring and amazing with Izzy and sexy—oh, I said that one already, didn't I?

Nothing could spoil this day. This has officially become the greatest day of my life—not counting when Isabelle was born, which was completely overwhelming as far as feeling massive quantities of love goes. But since I didn't just have fifteen hours of horribly painful labour, this day might actually be slightly better in a way. Obviously not as significant, but pretty freaking amazing. The man of my dreams has A) offered to be my plus-one at a wedding, and B) promised he's not skipping town the moment his contract is up.

I don't want to overthink that part of it, because maybe he's only staying for a couple of weeks past the contract, but what if he's staying permanently? Like forever? *Don't even let yourself hope for that, Bree. Just enjoy the moment because for once in your life, you get a win.*

***

"Are you the concierge?"

I look up, only to have a large Styrofoam box thrust at my face. The woman doing the thrusting appears to be about twenty-five based on her face, but her neck's got a good twenty extra years of wear and tear. Her blond hair is pulled back in a tight bun, and she has a severe expression that matches her thick Italian accent.

A short, tanned man stands next to her with the build of a bulldog and a shaved head. He could either be her father or her husband based on his leathery skin. His mouth curves up into a smile I'm sure he believes will melt my knickers. Spoiler alert: it won't. "You are the head concierge, *si*?"

"*Si*, I am," I say, taking the box from the woman. "How can I make your day better?" *And by that, I mean, please flake off, you pushy be-otch.*

"We are the Bianchis. These are one hundred butterflies. You will take care of them," she says. "Then you bring to the beach for us tomorrow when the sun is setting and let them out."

Her husband grins widely. "Yes, we make new wedding vows here at beach tomorrow." His voice is loud, and there's something desperate about the way he's talking, like he wants everyone in the lobby to know what they're doing.

Leo, who clearly has been listening from his spot near the luggage carts, makes his way over to me and smiles at them. "Congratulations, *signor* and *signora*. How long have you been married?"

"Eighteen years," he says, his smile never faltering even though his eyes are screaming for help. "But how you say… I make big mistake, so now we start again."

Glaring at him, she lowers her voice. "*Niente più errori.*"

I don't speak Italian, but based on the way she just mimed slitting her throat with that long, bright gold fingernail, I can guess what the mistake was.

Turning back to me, she says, "You open the box now. Put new… *come si dice*…ice bag on top to stay them cold. They sleep. Then you wake them up and make them fly."

"Uh huh. Uh huh. Sure." I say, nodding quickly, like I take care of dormant butterflies all the time. "And when exactly should I wake them?"

"Two hour before ceremony," she says, holding up two fingers.

"*No, tre ore, giusto?*" Mr. Bianchi asks his wife.

She makes a *tsking* sound and gestures as though she's going to hit him upside the head with one hand. "*Due! Due ore, idiota!*"

"*Va bene. Due ore.*" Looking at me, he says. "Two hours."

Nodding, I say, "Brilliant, yes. And how do I wake them?"

Leo mutters, "We could brew them tiny mugs of coffee."

Folding my lips between my teeth, I stifle a laugh while Mrs. Bianchi glares at both of us.

"Take off ice. They wake up," she huffs, as though I'm even more of an *idiota* than her husband.

"Got it. Remove ice two hours before your ceremony," I say. "Bring box to beachfront. Open box after your service ends and release the butterflies."

Picking up a guest request form, I start to fill it in, giving her a confident nod. "We'll make sure to look after your butterflies. Please enjoy the beginning of your stay with us."

"*Grazie. Grazie mille,*" Mr. Bianchi says, smiling way too much for a man in his position.

When they turn to leave, he tries to touch her arm, but she recoils quicker than Melania Trump. Oh, dear, good luck with starting over, buddy.

Leo, who is standing next to me says, "So, married life, hey?"

"Looks just amazing," I answer, watching them walk out of the lobby. "Do you mind finding a bag of ice and adding it to the butterflies for me?" I glance up at him and see a strained expression.

"Right. Yes. I'll just go get some ice, then open this box and hope no flying insects dart out at me."

"Oh, I forgot. You're scared of butterflies, aren't you?"

"No," he scoffs, shaking his head. "Not scared. I just…hate them with a passion and don't ever want one to fly into my mouth. Or near me, really. Or be shown on the telly. Especially not close up where you can see their disgusting hairy little bodies. But it's not like I have a phobia or something. I mean, *I know* they can't harm me in any way…"

"Oh, well then you're totally fine. That doesn't sound like an irrational reaction at all," I say with a small grin.

"Precisely. Which is why I'm going to go find some ice for my new little buddies here."

"You better take damn good care of those butterflies," Rosy, who has managed to sneak up on us, says, causing us both to start. "Those two aren't just any guests. He's a famous Italian movie producer, and she has her own daytime talk show. This thing has to go off without a hitch, or we'll pretty much lose every Italian traveler for years to come. And you," she says, giving me a pointed look, "can't exactly afford to mess up after the whole studying on the job thing."

Oh, perfect, because this is what I need right now. More insanity to add to my already heaping bowl of crazy noodles. "No problem, Rosy. We're on it."

"Yes, ma'am. We will take very good care of these little sleeping beauties and have them up and ready to delight the Bianchis right on time."

"You better, because if anything goes wrong, heads will roll."

***

An hour later, I'm standing at my desk, discreetly studying tortes when I catch sight of my mother walking toward the lobby.

"Mum, what are you doing here?" I say, hurrying out to meet her. The last thing I need tonight is a scene, and by the expression on my mum's face, she's about to cause one.

"Well, that's a lovely greeting," she says, following me as I rush down the stairs into the night air and out of the way of Leo, who is loading a golf cart with luggage. Out of the corner of my eye, I see him watching us so I take a few more steps along the path toward the parking lot.

I stop near a lamppost, ignoring the moths flitting away near the light at the top. When I turn to my mum, I speak quietly. "I didn't mean to be rude. I'm just surprised to see you here."

"You weren't at the house to help with the guest favours," she says, folding her arms.

"Amber told me not to come. I think she's still upset about the hen's weekend."

"You could say that," my mum says. "And she's not the only one. Quite frankly, I've never been so disappointed in you. You said the most awful things about Dane—calling him stupid and suggesting that he's going to drag her down with him? Then you tell her she's going to turn into some vapid housewife."

Oh God. Amber told Mum *everything*. My gut drops to my toes. "I know. I never should have said any of it. I feel just sick about it."

A couple meanders by holding hands, and my mother lowers her voice so now she's speaking in a quiet rage. "You feel so sick that you've done exactly nothing about it in all this time?"

She's got me there, doesn't she? "At first, I was just giving her some space, then it got past the point of feeling right to approach her. Then it was so close to the day to work on the party favours that I figured I'd do it in person." Now that I say it out loud, it sounds a lot less defendable.

My mum shakes her head in disgust. "You hurt her deeply, and now you're making it seem like you don't even care. Do you know how upset she's been? And poor Dane. You should have seen the look on his face when he heard what you said about him. He really thought you liked him."

Urgh. This just keeps getting worse. "You told him?"

"Of course not," she snaps. "But I was there when Amber did."

My entire body flushes with shame. "I wish he hadn't found out. I didn't even mean it. He's a nice person, and I know he loves her. It's just that I don't want to see her waste her potential." Blinking back tears, I say, "Remember how much she used to love running a lemonade stand when she was little? She used to carry around dad's old briefcase and tell everyone she wanted to be a CEO someday. Even as a teenager, she had that drive to succeed. Then she started dating Dane, and it's like she just dropped all thoughts of having any ambition or her own life."

"Her whole life, all she really wanted was to be a mum. She only said she wanted to be a CEO to get your approval."

"That's not true," I scoff. "She wanted to get her business degree. And she *should*. She could be anything she wants."

"What she wants is to be a wife and a mother. To make a home for her family and look after them. And there's nothing wrong with that," my mum says, and I know the way she's defending it, she's no longer talking about Amber. She's talking about herself. "It's an important calling."

"I know that, but why can't she be both a good mum and a successful businesswoman?"

"I don't want to see both of my daughters working like dogs, trying to be it all and do it all."

"I'm making a good life for myself. Is that really so awful?"

"It's hard. And it's hard to watch your child struggle the way you do."

"I'm fine. And it's only temporary. Things are going to get much easier for me, and it'll all be worth it, because I'll get to spend my life doing work I'm passionate about. I want that for her."

"She can't work as hard as you, Bree. She's too delicate!"

"Do you seriously believe she's *still fragile* because she was born a few weeks early?" I ask, throwing my hands in the air.

"Of course she is. Preemies never catch up."

"That is not true, Mum. She's fine."

"You have *always* resented her for being a preemie. For some reason, you have buckets of sympathy for everyone else you meet, but not even one ounce for your little sister."

"Oh my God, Mother, stop. All I've done my entire life is look after her."

"Except for that time at Long Beach," my mum says in a clipped tone.

"Oh, Christ. Are you seriously going to bring up something that happened when I was ten years old?" I tilt my head back and peer up at the inky sky.

"You scarred her for life. To this day, she can't swim at night." She purses her lips to make her point.

"What a tragedy," I say, anger building in every muscle. "Someday they'll make a made-for-TV movie about her. The Amber Hammer Story: The Epic Tale of the Preemie Who's Afraid to Go for a Night Swim."

My mother glares at me for a long moment before she speaks again, this time in an icy tone. "Your father told me not to come down here, and he was right because you are an absolutely impossible, head-strong girl."

"That's right, I am. And proud of it."

Leo appears in the distance behind my mother. When I glance up at him, he's gesturing with his head toward the lobby where Libby Banks, one of the owners of the resort, is standing talking to a guest. I give him a quick nod, then turn back to my mum and lower my voice. "That's my boss. I need to get back to work, so if there's nothing else, I really must go."

"You're wrong about your sister. You don't know her the way I do. She is fragile. In fact, the last few weeks, she's been very unwell."

"Really? What's wrong with her?" I ask, concern crowding out my anger.

"Her tattoo got infected, and now she's got a horrible scar on her back, which is *definitely* going to show at the wedding. In fact, all the girls are infected. Kandi actually had to go to the hospital every twelve hours for an IV. Amber's an absolute wreck over it."

Okay, please do not judge me, but deep down, there is a very petty part of me that is laughing her arse off. "Well, I'm sorry that happened, but how was I supposed to know?"

"You would know if you bothered to keep in touch with your family."

Sighing, I close my eyes for a second. "Look, I've been trying really hard to be patient about this whole thing, but in case you haven't noticed, the world doesn't revolve around Amber. I have an entire life of my own with important grown-up problems to deal with. There are over three hundred guests booked in right now who are relying on me to be on top of their every want, and when I go home, I have a young daughter who needs me, bills to pay, a home that needs to be looked after, and exams to prepare for."

"Oh God, I know, Brianna. *Everybody* knows about your bar exams, because it's the only thing you ever talk about. Poor me, I have to raise a child, and work, and study all the time so I can be a fancy lawyer!"

"In case you weren't aware, I'm not doing it to upset you. I'm doing it because I have aspirations, which most parents would be proud of, actually." I turn and stalk away from her toward the lobby, then spin back because I'm not done yet. My voice rises out of my chest as my indignant rage builds. "But not you, because the only thing I could do that would be remotely impressive to you is to find some man to take care of me! Well, sorry, but I'm not going to do that, Mum. I'm going to look after myself, thank you very much."

She rushes to me with an urgent expression. "You're making a scene," she hisses.

I'm just about to tell her I don't give a good god damn when there's a tap on my shoulder. I turn to see Mr. Bianchi is standing far too close to my left side. "*Scusami*," he says. "I make check on butterflies. You use enough ice, *si*? But not too much."

I close my eyes for a brief second, then open them and force a smile. "The butterflies are all taken care of, sir, but if you'd like to see them for yourself, I can take you to them in just a moment."

He smiles at my mother. "Is this your mamma?"

"Yes, she is. If you can——"

"Same eyes," he says, grinning back and forth between us. Then he points to my chest. "You got...bigger ones though. Is lucky."

My mother and I both narrow our eyes at him, and I'm pretty sure the two of us could give his wife a run for her money in death glares.

His smile disappears. "I go wait at desk."

"Brilliant," I say. Turning back to my mum, I open my mouth, but she interrupts me.

"I'll let you go so you can take care of the problems that are so much more important than your family, like chilling butterflies."

"It's my job, Mum. It's how I put food on the table for Isabelle. I cater to the whims of every bloody guest that walks into that lobby with their stupid demands. And you know what? I'm bloody good at it, because thanks to you, I've had a lifetime of practice at accommodating ridiculous requests."

"Well, tell me how you really feel, Brianna," she yells, clearly not caring anymore if we make a scene.

"Sure. Why not?" I raise my voice even louder. "This is how I really feel, Mum. I feel like you and dad have babied the shitake mushrooms out of Amber, and the end result is that she's grown up to be a completely incompetent, basically useless adult human being without even a hint of ambition or the ability to take responsibility for anything in her life. You want me to feel sorry for someone who has an infection because she decided to get a tattoo at the dodgiest place in the Caribbean? Sorry, but I'm not going to stop everything and go hold her hand while she takes antibiotics to get rid of a little boo-boo, okay? I tried to tell her it was a bad idea to get permanent artwork on her body by a guy who calls himself Randy Andy, but she didn't want to hear it!" *I'm yelling now. I should totally stop yelling.* "But since Amber's apparently an adult, there's really very little I could do to stop her and her idiot friends from making a huge mistake. Now, unlike you, I have *an actual preschool-aged child*, not to mention three hundred demanding, dumbass guests I need to look after for the next four hours, so if you don't mind, I'll get on with it so I can go home and get three hours of sleep before my daughter wakes up needing breakfast!"

"Fine!" she hollers.

"Fine!"

"I will see you at the wedding," she says dramatically before turning and stalking into the parking lot.

I stand for a moment, watching her, my chest heaving with deep, angry breaths as my brain scrambles to catch up with what just happened. When I turn back to the lobby, I see Leo staring at me, his expression unreadable. Glancing around, I see everyone else, guests and staff alike, are pretending they didn't hear. A deep sense of shame comes over me for handling myself so poorly, and I'm not sure whether I should chase after my mother to apologize or just get back to work. Seeing Mr. Bianchi sitting on the bench near my desk, I decide the best course of action is to take care of him.

***

Things get busy for the next hour, meaning I go straight from a huge fight into please-everyone mode. By the time the lobby is empty again,

I'm so tired, I want to slide down the wall and just sit on the floor until midnight. Leo's been avoiding me, and I can't tell if he's just giving me some space, or if he's horrified with me. Every time I try to make eye contact, he dodges my gaze, and he's kept himself busy polishing the brass poles on the carts for the last ten minutes. They're so shiny, they're stripper ready.

Glancing at the clock, I see it's time for my coffee break. I put the sign up on my desk and tell one of the receptionists, Onika, I'm going on break now. She gives me a slight nod, then escapes my gaze as if I'm a rabid dog, and she's terrified to challenge me. Walking over to Leo, I say, "Break time. Do you want a coffee?"

"You go ahead. I'm going to finish this up first," he says, rubbing a cloth back and forth on the cart he's polishing.

"You don't have to be scared of me," I say with a grin that says what happened with my mum was no biggie. "I'm not going to yell at you or something."

"I know," he answers. When he looks up at me, I see disappointment in his eyes, not fear.

My shoulders slump, and I walk slowly to the breakroom, feeling very much alone. I get myself a coffee, then sit on the couch. I try to have a sip but a lump in my throat stops me from swallowing. I spend the next fifteen minutes listening to the hum of the fluorescent lights and letting tears roll down my cheeks, hoping Leo will walk in and make me feel better. But he doesn't come in and wrap an arm around me and tell me it'll be okay and that my mum was being impossible and poor me for having to put up with her. Instead, he stays away, giving me the distinct impression that I've somehow offended him, too.

28

Can You Break Up with Someone
If You're Not Technically Dating?

Leo

It is 12:04 A.M., and I'm walking the long, lonely road that leads from the lobby to the main road. There, I will catch a bus that will take me to a stop where I have to change buses so I can make my way home. I'll be home sometime after one in the morning, instead of twenty minutes from now, as I would be if I went with Brianna. As sore as my feet are, I couldn't bring myself to get in the car with her, not after hearing what she really thinks of me. I need to distance myself from her until I can leave this godforsaken island.

Luckily, she ran to the loo at the end of our shift, so I took the opportunity to leave a note indicating that I didn't need a ride home tonight. So much better than telling her to her face and having to deal with all the whys and what did I dos?

A gust of wind pushes against me as I hurry along, keeping to the unlit side of the lane in hopes she won't see me when she drives by. I know it sounds dramatic, but for the first time in my life, I thought I had met someone who—and I know this is unforgivably cliché—understood me. But hearing her talk about her useless sister put her true feelings right in my face. She can't respect anyone who lacks the same bottomless ambition she has, which obviously includes yours truly. She also clearly despises anyone who has been coddled or blanketed in the lowest expectations their entire life. All this says is that even though she's clearly attracted to me in a physical sense, she obviously sees me as little more than a bellboy toy.

The unmistakable rattle of her car pulling up next to me causes me to stiffen. Brianna slows to match my gait, and out of the corner of my eye, I see her unroll the window.

"What are you doing?" she asks.

"Did you not get my note?" I ask, giving her only the briefest glance before turning my gaze down the dark lane once more.

"I got it. Have I done something to offend you?" she says in a tone that is somehow both filled with concern and slightly scornful at the same time.

Shaking my head a little, I say, "I just thought you could use a little bit of time to yourself."

"Well, I don't, so why don't you just get in the car?"

"No, thanks. I'll take the bus. I definitely require practice being more independent." Ahead of me, I can see the back of the enormous stone sign for the resort, which means I'm almost at the main road.

"So you *are* mad at me," Brianna says.

I stop and let out a big sigh before turning to her. "Let's just say I caught a glimpse of what you really think of people like me."

We glare at each other for a moment before I turn and step up my pace to get away from her.

Her voice follows me. "What is that supposed to mean?"

Without stopping, I call over my shoulder, "Exactly what it sounds like."

A wave of relief comes over me as I reach the end of the lane and hurry along to the bus stop to my left. She won't be able to follow me here because she'd have to drive into the oncoming traffic. A smattering of Paradise Bay employees wait there—two middle-aged women in resort uniforms sit on the bench chatting. I don't know their names but recognize them as evening shift cleaners. Behind the bench are the twin dishwashers that work in the Brazilian restaurant and create all sorts of problems for poor Emma. At the moment, they seem to be getting along. One of them has two cigarettes in his mouth, and the other one is lighting them, using his hand to block the flame of his lighter from the wind. They turn to me once their cigarettes are lit, and I give them a little nod that says I'm not in the mood for small talk. The one with the cigarettes in his mouth takes one out and gives it to his brother. I try to imagine Pierce or Greyson taking anything I'd just had in my mouth. Nope. Would not happen, which isn't exactly a bad thing.

I pick a spot slightly upwind of the two of them and scan the road for the bus, even though I know from looking at the schedule that it will be another ten minutes before it arrives.

"So this is it, then? You're just never going to talk to me for absolutely no reason whatsoever?" Brianna's voice, which is coming from behind me, catches the attention of my four companions. They all stop what they're doing and turn to stare. Well, isn't this just great?

I spin around to see her on foot, meaning she's ditched her car on the road so we can have it out.

"Seriously, we don't need to make a big deal about this," I say quietly. "I just thought you could use a little bit of time to yourself after what happened earlier."

"No, you didn't." She shakes her head at me. "You're mad at me. You just finished saying you saw who I really am, so don't pretend you're doing me a favour by sneaking off when your shift is over."

"Fine then, Brianna. *I'm* the one that needs a bit of time alone, okay? Can you just let me have that?"

"I want to know exactly what I did that has you so angry. I haven't so much as said one unkind thing to you." Her voice catches. "You don't think I could have used a friend this evening?"

"Not really. You seem perfectly happy doing everything yourself."

"Don't give me that crap, Leo."

The dishwashing brothers make *ooohhh* sounds that I ignore.

"Can we *not* have this discussion here?" I ask quietly.

"Why not? I've already had one fight in front of a crowd today, might as well make it two!"

"I have no intention of fighting with you." My tone is that of the Jedi Knight. *These are not the drones you're looking for.* "Neither of us has done anything directly offensive to the other, therefore discussion at this point is unnecessary."

"What is that supposed to mean—*directly offensive?*"

"Nothing. Just that it's fine, let's leave it well enough alone. We'll start fresh tomorrow and continue our working relationship."

"So you just suddenly decide we're no longer friends—for no reason, I might add—and I'm supposed to simply accept that?" She crosses her arms and narrows her eyes.

"It's not for no reason. It's just not for a reason worth discussing, because there's nothing we can do about it. The truth is, you and I are very different people. In fact, I probably have more in common with your sister than I do with you."

Confusion crosses her face, which irritates me completely. How could she *not know* how badly she offended me earlier? Deciding I don't care about the witnesses any longer, I open my mouth and let it all go. "According to you, your sister is a completely incompetent, basically useless human being without even a hint of ambition, which I believe is an almost exact match for what you said about me when you tried to get me fired."

Her head snaps back. "What? I said that before I knew you. You're nothing like her!"

"I disagree. I've been every bit as coddled as her—more so, in fact. I also have no clue what I want to do with my life other than enjoy it, so I know that doesn't pass the Brianna muster test for ambition."

"That is *totally different*. She's given up on life completely!" Throwing her hands up in the air, Bree says, "She's about to settle for a crappy marriage and resign herself to doing *nothing* with her life."

"How is that different from me? If anything, I'm worse, because I'm going to let my parents bankroll my future instead of my husband," I say, glancing at my bus-stop buddies. "Not that I want a husband or something. Not that there would be anything wrong with that if I did…" I let my voice trail off and shake my head, feeling stupid.

"You just haven't figured out what you want to do, Leo. That's not the same thing as giving up."

"What if I *never* figure it out? Would that make me a useless human being?" I tighten my jaw, already knowing the answer.

"Everyone needs a purpose."

Nodding slightly, I feel my gut harden. "I'll take that as a yes."

"Take that however you want. I don't care," she quips. "I wasn't even talking about you. I was having a private conversation with my mother and you were eavesdropping. So for you to get all high and mighty with me about it is a bit rich."

"*I'm* the high and mighty one? You're the one judging everyone you meet based on your pre-selected criteria. If someone's life goals aren't up to snuff, you toss them aside like you're doing to your sister. So she wants to be a wife and mum. So what? Most people consider parenting to be one of the most important jobs in life."

"But she can be so much more!" Brianna says, raising her voice.

"Like you, you mean? A stressed-out, exhausted, miserable person?"

Our gazes lock, and neither of us say anything for a long, uncomfortable moment. Brianna clears her throat and lowers her voice. "I'm not going to justify my life to someone like you."

"Someone like me? You mean lazy? Useless? Spoiled? Happy?"

"You're not happy. You just keep yourself too busy to think about how pathetic your life is."

"And there it is," I answer, my heart sinking to the sidewalk. "The truth at long last."

Brianna shakes her head. "I didn't mean your life now. I meant how you used to live. *Before.*"

"I have news for you. That's the life I'm going back to as soon as humanly possible."

She stares at me, chewing on her bottom lip. "Is that what you want?"

"Yes...maybe, I don't know." I run my hands through my hair in frustration. "But what I do know is that you could never—" I stop myself before I accidentally use the phrase "love someone like me" because that would be utterly foolish. "You could never respect someone unless they're as career-driven as you are."

"Is that so wrong?" she asks. "Jesus, you and my mum are exactly the same—pretending it's okay for people to go around without any goals in life. Who *does that* even? We're not put on this planet to laze around all day and do nothing with our lives. We're here to accomplish things, to make a difference in the world!"

Her words terrify me, because I know she's right, and I also know I don't have the first damn clue how to even get started. But instead of admitting it, I lash out. "Must be nice to know everything, to work harder than anybody else has ever worked, to have more ambition, more drive than anyone else on the planet. It must feel very good to be you."

"Oh, yeah, it's *fucking wonderful*," she spits out. "Getting four hours of sleep every night, working full time and going to school full time, not to mention being a single mum, and being broke every day of my wonderful, fabulously terrific fucking life. It's just incredible to be me!"

"As much as you'd like to pretend it isn't, you *love* the fact that you work harder than anyone, and that you have it worse than your sister. You might as well just tattoo 'world's greatest martyr' on your forehead." Okay, that was offside. I think I took it too far there because her eyes are filled with hurt which she instantly covers up with rage.

"Oh, that's rich coming from someone who never had to lift a finger the first twenty-seven years of his life! Do you want me to feel sorry for you, Leo? Because you've had six months of slumming it as a bellboy so you can earn your way back into Daddy's wallet permanently?! I thought you were different, but it turns out, you're just another rich, entitled arsehole."

I snort out a frustrated laugh. "God, you're a hypocrite. You hate anyone who has more without having to suffer for it. The self-professed richophobe who wants nothing more than to be rich herself."

"I am not a hypocrite!" she yells. "I don't even want to be rich."

"Right, so you're in law school with the end goal of living the life of a poverty-stricken single mum."

"I *refuse* to apologize for wanting a better life!" She's back to yelling now. "I'm never going to be some rich idiot with a superyacht. I'm going to create a comfortable life for myself and Izzy, and there's nothing wrong with that."

"Spoken like a true rich person—right down to the word comfortable." My words sound as bitter as they taste, and I hate myself for it.

I suddenly feel like I'm suffocating with the humid heat of the night air and the words I can't undo. I want nothing more than to be standing in the cool wind of the North Sea back home. Away from this woman who won't let me pretend. She stares at me defiantly, and I suddenly hate her. She's my father and my horrible brothers dressed in heels. "You think you're so much smarter than everyone else, Brianna, but you're not. *I'm* the smart one because I will always have so much more than you without having to kill myself for it."

"If that's what you really think, I feel sorry for you."

"I don't need to be pitied by *you*."

"Because you're rich and I'm poor," she says, running her tongue along her top teeth.

"Because you're going to miss out on everything good in life while you sit on your pedestal judging everyone you meet. You should see if they'll make you a magistrate as soon as you pass the bar since you're obviously so skilled choosing what's best for everyone else!"

I glare at her, and she glares back, blinking back tears. When she speaks, her voice is filled with a quiet rage. "Fuck you."

With that, she walks away, leaving me with my bus-stop companions.

One of the cleaning ladies says, "Don't worry about it, young man. The makeup sex will be fabulous."

The other three laugh at her joke, but I pretend I didn't hear her. I watch Brianna pull out onto the highway and disappear around the bend, wishing I could take it all back.

29

Butterflies of Doom

Bree

"THERE YOU GO," I say, handing the packet of tickets to the woman in front of me. "The tour bus will pick your party up at two o'clock tomorrow and take you over to the nature preserve. Hold on to these vouchers. You'll need to show them at the restaurant to get your included dinner."

I smile brightly at her, even though inside, I'm a raw, angry, hot mess. She's asking me something that isn't registering for several reasons, including but not limited to: A) I had zero minutes of sleep last night after my fight with Leo, B) he's standing three feet away from me, and it physically hurts to be in close proximity to someone who hates me so much, and C) I don't give a tiny pebble shit about this woman's question.

I wait until she's done yapping, then take a stab at an answer. Nodding, I say, "Yes."

Clearly, that was the wrong thing to say, because she's wrinkling up her nose. "Yes? I just asked you what time the last shuttle comes back to the resort."

"Right. Sorry. I meant nine p.m."

Raising her eyebrows, she says, "Okay, thanks."

"Have fun."

As soon as she walks away, my gut hardens. *Pull it together, Brianna. For God's sake.* I don't want to let on that Leo got to me last night, but if I keep screwing up, he'll know for sure. We're almost two hours into our shift, and I've managed to give him the cold shoulder the entire time. My goal is to say nothing to him for the rest of the night, then follow that with the silent treatment until he gets the hell out of my garden suite and off my island. Not sure if that's possible, but once I set my mind to something...

"Excuse me," Leo says, taking a luggage tag off the desk in front of me. His tone is curt, and when he moves away, he leaves behind the familiar scent of his light cologne that makes my knees go weak. I scold myself for letting him have any effect on me whatsoever, then open my calendar on my computer to check to see what I need to get done this evening.

In red bold letters next to 4 pm, it says, "REMOVE ICE FROM BIANCHI BUTTERFLIES."

"Bugger," I mutter.

"I didn't think you'd resort to name calling," Leo says.

"What?" Bollocks, now I've gone and talked to him.

"You just called me a bugger."

Rolling my eyes, I say, "Did not."

Before he can say "did too," I put up the back-in-five-minutes sign and all but run to the back offices where the butterflies are waiting in the supply closet. Yanking the top off the Styrofoam container, I gather up the ice packs and toss them on the floor unceremoniously.

"Shit, shit, shit," I say, staring at the one hundred extremely dormant butterflies that are meant to be flitting about in approximately twenty minutes on the beach. Grabbing my mobile out of my pocket, I Google "quickly thawing butterflies," but the search proves fruitless.

Think, Brianna, think. You're smart. You can come up with a way to fix this.

Lowering my face into the large white box, I blow hot air on the folded-up insects. "Come on, you little bastards, wake up."

Leo's idea of brewing tiny mugs of coffee comes to mind, causing a pang of regret. I consider asking him for help, remembering how good he is in a crisis, but my pride won't let me.

I continue blowing out in long, hot bursts until I feel like I'm going to pass out. When I touch one of the butterflies, it still feels chilled, and none of them show signs of waking.

Now what?!

A blow-dryer! I snap my fingers and hurry over to the shelf where we keep spares.

I quickly search the closet for an outlet. No luck. I pop the lid on the box, put the blow-dryer on top, and haul arse to the staff room. Two minutes later, I'm blow-drying the butterflies, watching for signs of life. One of them begins to move, wiggling a bit before slowly peeling its wings away from its tiny body. "Come on, little guy. Let's go!"

I glance at the clock and see that I've got under ten minutes. Not cool since it's at least that long of a ride to the beach from here. I am so buggered.

"Never mind. Keep going," I mutter, my words drowned out by the sound of the blow-dryer.

Leo's voice startles me. "Oh, this isn't good."

He stands beside me, staring into the box from as far away as possible. "Weren't these supposed to be flitting around on the beach by now?"

Thanks, Captain Obvious. Abandoning my pride for practicality, I say, "I've still got a few minutes. Go get more hair dryers from the closet and come help."

He nods and hurries out, leaving me alone in what I hope won't be a futile pursuit. A tiny piece of me is relieved to have Leo's help, even though he's turned out to be an awful, whining disappointment. Soon, he returns with three dryers, and the two of us set to work, standing close together while we heat the hell out of these monarch butterflies. The ones on the top layer are really moving now, and out of the corner of my eye, I see Leo gag. I tuck my lips in between my teeth to keep from laughing as he steps as far away as possible and turns his head away from the job at hand.

Shaking his head, he says, "I'm not sure this is such a good idea, Brianna. I think this much hot air is going to be bad for them."

"They can handle it! They live in hot climates!"

"The temperature change is going to be too fast for them. They'll go into shock."

"This isn't like waking a sleepwalker. It won't matter how fast we do this. Besides, we have no choice."

One of the butterflies crawls around and then collapses, looking pretty dead.

"We're killing them." Leo pulls the plugs on his dryers. "Shut those off."

"We can't! We have to wake them up *now*! Some of them will survive, and it's not like anyone will be counting."

"Good God, woman, this is turning you into a ruthless serial killer!"

I glare at him. "Yes, you can add ruthless to judgemental and hypocritical."

"Oh, Christ! Do not make this about last night."

"I'm not! *You* are!"

Suddenly, three of the squirmy little creatures take off, freeing themselves into the staff room. One of them darts past Leo's face, and he screeches like a little girl and ducks before sprinting to the garbage bin and vomiting.

Seriously?

A rush of sympathy flows through me as I watch him retch. "It's okay, they can't hurt you," I say.

Waving over his shoulder, he nods and then vomits again. It takes a few moments for the smell to hit me. Oh God, that's bad. That is… so awful. I feel a surge of liquid moving up toward my mouth and try to swallow it to no avail. It comes out anyway, landing directly in the box.

"No, no, no," I whisper, then puke again, this time, all over the floor. Tears stream down my face as I regain control over my stomach. I shut off my hair dryers and drop them on the table, not daring to peek into the box.

"I can't believe you threw up because of some butterflies," I say, bending at the waist and resting my hands on the table.

"I can't believe you threw up because of some vomit," he answers, lifting his slightly green face toward me.

"Vomit is disgusting. Butterflies are one of nature's greatest achievements."

"Yes, well, nature's greatest achievement is now covered in your sick."

"You're going to have to clean them up," I say, pushing the box toward him.

"I'm not...no." He shakes his head with considerable vigor for someone who's sick to his stomach. "There's no way I can *touch* them."

"And there's no way I can clean up vomit without vomiting." I hold my hand over my mouth and close my eyes.

When I open them, I peer into the box at the mess. "Shit! Fuckity shit fuck." My heart pounds and tears spring to my eyes.

Leo straightens himself, walks purposefully over to the cupboard, takes out a tablespoon, brings the bin over, and starts to scoop vomit out of the bin.

I turn away, holding my hand sideways under my nose. "God, that's bad."

Miraculously, a few of the butterflies make it out of the box, flitting around and depositing puke in my hair before making their way toward the fading light of the window. Then more from the lower layers of the box.

"I think your warm puke woke them," Leo says, flinching.

"Yes, well done me," I answer. "Now, how do we get them back in the box?"

The door swings open, and Rosy walks in, dodging butterflies as her face twists from shock into rage. "What in the hell is going on?"

"They escaped, and they're everywhere!"

The door opens again, and in comes Mario and Todd. "What's all the yelling about?" Mario asks before spotting the obvious. "Oh, Shit. The Bianchis' butterflies."

I give Rosy a weak look. "Maybe we can hold the vow renewal in here?"

· · ·

***

Five minutes later, I'm sitting with a smelly Styrofoam box containing exactly 12 butterflies on my lap while Leo drives like a bat out of hell down to the beach. Neither of us are saying anything, and it's all I can do to fight back the tears that threaten to come out. We reach the spot on the beach where the Bianchis and their guests are, and I don't even wait for Leo to stop before climbing out of the golf cart and running full speed toward them with the box.

Mrs. Bianchi, who is dressed in a white, full-length, extremely low-cut silk gown looks furious while her husband stands next to her mopping his face with a napkin. "See, I knew she would get here. Everything is going to be all right. We let the butterflies go. We start again. Everything fine."

Sweat drips down the back of my shirt by the time I finally reach the centre of the crowd. I set the box down with an expression of a magician's assistant and say, "To new beginnings!" Lifting the lid, I take three quick steps back, grinning as one lonely butterfly bursts out of the box, making it as high as my boobs before dropping onto the sand. Leaning over the box, I see the other eleven lying dead in the box.

Smiling up at the Bianchis, I say, "Could I interest you in some complimentary tickets to the island's aquarium?"

***

The yelling can be heard through the lobby. Mr. and Mrs. Bianchi are in Harrison Banks' office, who has been interrupted at home to deal with the fallout of my screwup. I stand at my desk, pretending to fill in some forms even though my vision is blurred with tears. My head pounds as hard as my heart does while I await the tongue-lashing that is coming my way. Not from Harrison—he's a wonderful and compassionate boss—but from Mrs. Bianchi as soon as she finishes screeching at him.

A mug of hot tea is placed in front of me, and I look up to see Leo standing next to me, his face full of sympathy. "There's nothing that can't be made better by a cup of tea," he says, then tilts his head a little. "I heard that in a movie once, and I thought it sounded comforting."

I nod, feeling completely undeserving of his kindness. "Thank you," I whisper.

"Hey, Leo," a woman's voice comes from the steps. We both turn to see his parole officer, Jolene.

"Jolene, lovely to see you as usual." He says with a little nod. "I thought our next appointment was on Tuesday."

"It is," she says. "I had a strong feeling I should hang out here for a while." She walks past us and takes a seat on the bench in the centre of the lobby. Picking up a brochure for the Island of Eden, she gives Leo a smug grin and then starts casually leafing through the colourful pages.

"Brianna, can I see you in my office, please?" Harrison, who is standing at the entrance to the back offices gives me a grave look.

Mrs. Bianchi brushes past him into the lobby and points at me. "You! You ruined my second wedding!"

Harrison touches her forearm. "Mrs. Bianchi, I'd prefer to deal with this matter in private."

"Why?" she yells. "So that your other guests don't know what terrible place this is?"

"She ruin our second wedding." Holding one finger up, she yells across the lobby at me. "You have one job! She make barf of my butterflies! She is cycle!"

Mr. Bianchi pats her hand, speaking in a soothing voice. "Bella, the word is *psycho*, not cycle. She is psycho."

Nodding at him, she says, "*Sì, sì.*"

Turning back to me, she sets her glare in my direction again. "You are a...*come si dice...*"

"Psycho," her husband offers.

"Yes, psycho, and your boss say he's going to fire you."

My entire body feels numb, and I have the sudden compulsion to vomit. I grip my desk, holding myself up as humiliation courses through me in violent waves.

"You can't fire her for making a mistake," Leo says, his voice angry.

Ignoring Leo and the Bianchis, Harrison gives me a look of regret. "Brianna, please come back to my office for a minute."

Forcing my fingers to let go of my desk, I cross the silent lobby toward my doom. I feel the eyes of everyone on me as my skin prickles with shame. Even the pair of troupials have stopped singing as they peer down from their nest.

I'm about to get fired. For the first time in my entire life. My mind races through everything that has happened. First, the big fight with my mom, then Rosy caught me studying, and based on Harrison's face, I'd say my career as a concierge is ending tonight.

"You should fire me. It was my fault." Leo's voice comes from behind me. "Brianna told me at the start of our shift to take care of the butterflies, and I completely forgot. She thought I had taken care of it, but I didn't. It was my stupid idea to blow-dry them, I'm the one who vomited in the box. So if someone must be fired, it should be me."

I turn, seeing Jolene in my peripheral vision before I come to face Leo. He's standing tall with an air of authority, staring at Harrison. Panic fills me as I realize that if he gets fired, he's giving up his entire future.

"That's not true," I say, glancing at Jolene, who's staring on with wide eyes. Turning to Leo, I lower my voice. "Don't do this. I'm not going to let you give up everything for me."

He stares at me for a moment, but his expression gives nothing away. "I'm doing it because it's the truth, and I wouldn't be much of a man if I let you take the fall for me."

Turning to Harrison, I raise my voice. "He's lying. I'm the one who forgot. He tried to help me, but I messed it all up."

"Fire them both!" Mrs. Bianchi barks out, her eyes wild with excitement.

"That won't be necessary," Harrison says to her before turning back to me. "Brianna, who's responsible for this?"

"I am."

"Only in as far as she's my supervisor." Leo takes a few steps so he's standing in front of me now. "You don't really believe this ultra-responsible woman who has *never* let you down could possibly be responsible for a disaster of this proportion?" He shakes his head. "Come on. Isn't it far more likely the chronic screwup you're quasi-related to, and whom you gave a job to out of pity, did this? The answer is obvious."

Nodding, Harrison says, "It's big of you to take responsibility, Leo, but I'm afraid I do have to fire you."

Giving Harrison a deep nod, Leo says, "Of course. Thank you for the opportunity." Turning to the Bianchis, he says, "I'm very sorry about your butterflies. And Mr. Bianchi, I'm very sorry that you are going to spend the rest of your life with this awful, awful woman."

With that, he turns and walks out of the lobby, shoving his hands in his front pockets and disappearing down the steps without looking back.

30

Definitely NOT Depressed

Leo

I'M BACK, baby. Carefree Leo lives again, thank Christ. After a brief stop at Brianna's to pack my bags and say my farewells to Dolores, little Izzy, and the furry trio, I made my way to Pierce's villa via the Turtle's Head Pub. And I have to say, I've never been happier in my life. Am I about to be disinherited? Yes. Do I care? Not at the moment. Because at the moment, I'm as drunk as Mel Gibson that time he called a female police officer sugar tits.

But even in my inebriated state, I would never stoop to calling a woman sugar tits, especially not a woman of the law. I yawn and roll out of bed, landing on the floor on both knees. "Good thing I can't feel that."

Rising to my feet, I pick up the bottle of champagne that has been sitting open on the bedside table in my brother's guest room since I arrived sometime after six this morning. "Little hair of the dog." I chuckle to myself as I toast the drunk in the mirror. "To freedom."

Ha! Another truly great Mel Gibson line comes to mind—this time from the epic tale of William Wallace in *Braveheart*. "Freedom!"

I chug what's left of the now-flat, warm Cristal, then search around the bed to locate my mobile phone. "There you are, you tricky minx," I say when I locate it under one of the many decorative pillows Emma has thoughtfully arranged on the bed. Oh dear, it's almost two in the afternoon. I should be getting ready to go to the job I don't have anymore.

"To unemployment and a life of poverty," I say, tipping the bottle back again, only to remember it's empty.

Time to go on a booze hunt. Emma has probably left for work by now, and Pierce will be locked away in his office for the next several hours, which will give me ample time to empty their liquor cabinet, then make my way to the nearest bar to keep this party going. Steadying myself, I make my way to the door, not caring that I'm dressed only in my Spider-Man boxer shorts. Mrs. Bailey's seen me in less than this, and since nobody else is home, I might as well dispense with the formality of putting on trousers and a shirt. Come to think of it, I'm not even sure where I left my luggage, but I know I didn't drag it back here this morning. Hmmm…

I walk down the hall, racking my brain for the last location I remember seeing my bags. Was it at the Turtle's Head? Or Captain Jack's Shrimp Tails and Cocktails? The memory of scarfing down a huge plate of greasy calamari with some random tourists I met up with makes me burp. *Note to self: do not think about fried squid.*

Now, what was I doing? Right, getting a drink. I scratch the scruff on my chin as I wander toward the kitchen. What else do I have to do today? Oh, yes, find my lost luggage. I know! I'll drink until I get just as drunk as I was when I lost my bags. That way, I'll be sure to remember where I left them because I'll be in the same state I was when I lost track of them. Brilliant!

I open the mini wine fridge and pull out a magnum of champagne, this time going for a Moët that looks pretty old. Popping the cork, I gulp down as much as I can handle before the bubbles start to come back up, then I do a Napoleon Dynamite dance routine as I make my way outside to soak up some sun, happy to be at one of the most private spots on the island. Yes, it'll be just me and my magnum all day, and please don't think I'm drinking because I need to forget, or I'm devastated at the quick turn my life has taken into being horribly alone and impoverished, because I'm just fine, thank you very much.

In fact, I'm better than fine. I'm Leo Freaking Davenport, the man who always lands on his feet, just like a cat. I'm agile. I'm quick thinking. I'm fierce. And I'm also handsome and charming, so I'll easily be able to find some lovely sugar mamma to bankroll my life if I can't think of some better way to earn a living.

See? I'm a man with a plan. Now, how do you get this fucking door open? Oh, it *slides*. There we go. A blast of hot wind and the sounds of the surf crashing against the shore greet me as I step out onto the deck. I shut my eyes, temporarily blinded by the sun and blue sky.

"Hello, Leo!" Emma says. "We were wondering when you would join the party."

Opening my right eye, I see a small gathering of people standing around holding plates, including Pierce, Emma, and her little brother, Will, who must be back from filming his wildly popular television docu-series, as well as several people I don't know. Oh, and my bosses, Rosy, Harrison, and Libby. It takes me a moment in my booze-soaked state to register the fact that those are my *former* bosses, and suddenly nepotism seems like a terrible idea. Who knew?

"Nice boxers," Will says, holding up a beer.

"Leo, so nice of you to dress up for the occasion," Pierce says in a terse voice. Even though he is wearing his Cartier aviators, I can tell by the set of his jaw he's none too pleased with his little brother.

Glancing down at myself, I realize I have forgotten to put on clothes. "Righto, what exactly is the occasion?"

"Will knowing inform your decision of whether to go with tighty whities or Underoos?" Pierce asks.

"No, I'm happy in my Spideys," I say with a shrug. "I was just curious."

Emma rushes over to me with a glass of orange juice. She smoothly switches it out for my bottle of champagne, then says, "Will has finished his docu-series and is home indefinitely, so we thought we'd have a little get together."

"Well, I hope you don't mind one more friend and fan to help celebrate your suppsess," I say to Will with a firm nod as I put down the glass of orange juice and swipe my bottle off the glass table. "Success," I say slowly.

"Here you are, dear," Mrs. Bailey says, appearing out of nowhere. Well that's not strictly true. I suppose she came from inside the house. I turn and see her standing behind me with a freshly pressed linen shirt on a hanger and some khaki pants, both of which belong to Pierce. "All pressed and ready to wear. I hope you'll pardon the delay."

"You're looking as gorgeous as always, Mrs. Bailey," I say, giving her a kiss on the cheek.

"You always were a most skilled liar."

"True, but not in this case. You are a lovely woman. When are you going to quit working for this wanker and run away with me once and for all?"

Ignoring my nonsense, she deftly removes the shirt from the hanger and holds it open for me. Emma takes my drink, and I slide my arms into the sleeves and begin the process of buttoning the shirt, which is considerably more difficult when one is not sober. "What do you say, Mrs. Bailey?" I raise and lower my eyebrows at her while I fumble with the buttons. "You and me, riding off into the sunset together on a bicycle built for two."

Pierce gives Mrs. Bailey a little nod. She takes it as her cue, handing him the trousers and turning back into the house.

Lowering his voice, Pierce says, "Go back inside."

"Why? Are you embarrassed of your drunken little brother? It's not a big deal, Mr. Stick Up His Arse." Turning to Will, I say, "You don't mind me being a little ahead of the party, do you, Will? You're a footloose and fancy-free sort of ladies man, cool guy."

Will laughs. "If anything, I'd say you're providing the entertainment."

"You and me, mate," I say, pointing to him. "A couple of young bucks with no responsibilities. Let's say we *really* tie one on. We'll get started here and work our way back to the pubs in town, see how many ladies we can pick up along the way."

Without waiting for an answer, I say, "Oh, and I seem to have left my…everything I own somewhere, so I'm retracing my steps until I can find my bags." I laugh wildly for a moment, then point at Harrison, who's holding his adorable baby, Clara. "It's sort of ironic, isn't it? Here I've been employed looking after people's luggage for half a year, and yet I can't keep track of my own." I bust out laughing, but no one joins me.

"Leo, why don't you go inside and have some breakfast, love?" Emma says, her tone full of pity.

"Nah, not really that hungry, to be honest."

Harrison hands the baby to his wife and then strolls over to me. "I'm really sorry about yesterday. I know that can't have been easy for you," he says.

"What are you talking about? What's a little firing between family members?" I slap him on the back a bit too hard, then rub the spot where I smacked. "Sorry about that. Sometimes I don't know my own strength."

"Oh, would you look at the time." Libby hurries over to the glass table, picks up her diaper bag, and slings it over her shoulder. "We need to get Clara home for a nap."

"I hope you're not leaving on my account," I say, gesturing at her with the pants that are still in my hand instead of on my legs.

"Not at all," Libby says with the uncomfortable smile that conveys the exact opposite of her words. "I just didn't realize how late it was getting."

I watch as Harrison and Libby say their goodbyes and disappear around the side of the house. They seem happy—a husband, wife, and their beautiful little girl. Not my way to be happy, mind you, but it works for them. Slinging the chinos over my shoulder, I suck back half of the glass of orange juice and then top it up with champagne. After having a big swig, I smack my lips together. "Yeah, that's the stuff."

Pierce, clearly having had enough of my antics, grabs me by the elbow again and directs me into the house without another word. As soon as we get inside, I come face-to-face with Brianna and Jolene. I focus in on Bree, momentarily dumbstruck by her beauty. I stare at her, trying to decide if I should give in to this desperate compulsion to dip her and kiss her hard on the lips or not.

Not. She can't stand me.

"Have you come to witness the downfall of the world's most childish man?" I say with a nasty grin.

"Are you drunk?" she asks, her face serious.

"Define drunk."

"Yes, he's been going hard since last night, apparently." Pierce takes hold of the pants, swipes them off my shoulder, and holds them out to me. "Your dignity, Leo."

I wrinkle up my nose and point at the pants. "Those are chinos." I giggle, but no one else joins me. "Come on. You two really need to learn to lighten up. Life's too short."

Smiling at Jolene, I say, "Fancy a celebratory drink, Ms. Fita? You caught me breaking the contract, so well done you."

She purses her lips together, her eyes filled with concern.

"Why the long face?" I ask with an even wider grin. "You predicted I'd mess it all up at the end, and you were right, milady. Enjoy the moment. You earned it."

She shakes her head, looking more serious than I've ever seen her. Gone is the sharp edge, and in its place is a disturbing sense of compassion.

"If you're not here to gloat, then why'd you come by? Your contract has been fulfilled. You caught me. I got fired. It's over. Call my father."

"No!" Brianna says. "She hasn't called him yet. We can still fix this."

Shaking my head, I say, "No we can't. It's over."

Jolene narrows her eyes at me. "Did you really lie to save her job?"

"What does it matter?" I ask. "I got fired."

"It *does* matter. *I* should have been the one to get fired, not you," Brianna says urgently. "Why did you lie for me?"

Shrugging, I do my level best to act as though I don't care. "I was going to quit anyway. That job was dreadfully boring." Turning to Pierce, I sway a little bit. "Not a fun person in the bunch." In a dramatic whisper, I add, "Especially not this one." I point at Bree with one thumb to emphasize my words even though I know it's uncalled for.

Brianna takes two steps toward me. "Leo, you can't just throw away your entire future for me."

"Meh, if you ask my brother, it wasn't much of a future anyway."

Ignoring me, she decides she may have better luck with Pierce. "You need to reach out to your parents and tell them what happened. It was *all* my fault. The whole thing. He tried to stop me. I was the one that was supposed to get fired, and Leo lied to save my job."

"Is that true, Leo?" Pierce asks.

"Nope. The person who deserved to be fired got fired," I say, struggling to get my right foot into the trousers.

"Why are you lying to your brother?" Bree asks. "This is insanity. Pierce, you *have* to do something. It's not right. You can't let him lose his inheritance for trying to protect me. If you could just explain to your father that Leo was acting out of nobility, I'm sure he'll understand."

"I don't think you really understand Lord Alistair Davenport," I say, having managed to finally get one pant leg on. "He's been wanting to disinherit me since the moment he found out I was on my way into this world. If it didn't happen now, it would have happened later."

"He's not wrong about that," Pierce says.

"Well, then, *I'll* make him understand. Just give me his phone number. I can convince him. Just let me try," she says, raising her voice in desperation.

"Brianna. Just let it go!" I snap. "I don't want his fucking money."

"Of course you do. You spent six months doing everything right. Everything! Not one drop of alcohol, you showed up for every shift on time, and you did a really great job. You did, Leo," she says, leaning down to try to make eye contact as I struggle with my trousers. "You paid the rent on time. You learned how to cook and do laundry." Turning to Pierce, she pleads, "Please, Pierce. He's tried so hard. He's changed so much. The amount that he's helped me over these past months. He's been an amazing friend and the best tenant anyone could ask for. He mows the lawn and he helps out with my daughter, and he even cleaned up her disgusting vomit one day—"

"After I *made* her vomit," I point out.

Turning back to me, she says, "Leo, I can't let you do this. I just can't let you ruin your entire life for me."

"Believe me, Brianna. I never do anything without my own best interest in mind. I only helped you because I was hoping you'd sleep with me."

"That's not true. You could have slept with me many times over, and no one would have known. But you didn't because you wanted to honour your word."

Damn. She's got me there. "Well, then I did it because I wanted to butter you up in case I ever couldn't pay the rent."

"Why are you lying to me?" she says, tears threatening to spill from her eyes.

"Because it's *what I do*. I lie and I flatter and do whatever I have to do to get what I want. It takes a lot more effort than you'd think, actually," I say with a cavalier smile. "That's the thing about being lazy and having absolutely no ambition, it's a lot of work in the end."

"Stop it. Don't try to make a joke out of this."

"Why not? It's my life, Brianna. If I want to make a joke of it, I bloody well will."

"You're honestly standing there trying to tell me you've done nothing but lie to me this entire time?"

"For someone so bright, it certainly took you a long time to catch on. Although, technically, I guess you didn't because I had to tell you what the game was."

"I don't believe you. I don't believe that this—" she gestures with both hands at me while shaking her head in disgust,"—version of you is the real Leo. The real you was the guy playing superheroes with Izzy and helping me blow-dry those fucking butterflies even though they terrify you. The real Leo is the guy who took me out on that silly tandem bike to give me one perfect day when I was so upset. The real Leo is the man who lied to protect me. So why are you pretending to be someone else now?"

"Honestly, Brianna, I don't know who that guy was. Ask Pierce. This mess of a man who can't even get his own pants on is the real me. I did exactly what I wanted to do yesterday, because the truth is, I've had enough of my father's shit for a lifetime. I *wanted* to be free, so I fucked it all up just like I fuck up everything else in my life."

Brianna takes my cheeks in both hands. "That's not true. You're just drunk right now. You don't know what you're doing."

I stare into her eyes, hating like hell what I have to do. "I may be piss-stinking drunk, but I wasn't yesterday. I know you want me to stand here and tell you I gave it all up for you out of some passionate love that I've been harbouring for you since I laid eyes on you, but that's simply not true. I did the same thing with you that I do with everybody else."

I take her hands and remove them from my face, even though it kills me. "I told you exactly what you wanted to hear and made you feel exactly what I wanted you to feel to get what I wanted. And the moment I no longer needed you, I moved on. Because that's what I do, Bree." I stare at her too long, torturing myself with the sight of the moment when her heart breaks. The selfish part of me wants to wrap my arms around her and tell her she's right about everything. But she's wrong about me. Just like anyone else who's believed in me has been proven wrong my entire life. The kindest thing I can do now is to just let her go and walk away. "You were right about me when we first met. I am just a selfish rich prick who doesn't give a shit about anyone else. I'm not even sorry, really."

She lifts her chin at me. "I don't believe that."

Shaking my head, I say, "For someone who pretends to be so practical, you certainly do have a rich fantasy life in your head, don't you?"

With that, I attempt to walk away, but my left leg gets caught up in my half-put-on pants, causing me to stumble into the beanbag chair. The momentum I have causes my legs to flip over my head, and I do an especially awkward somersault. When I land, I pop up quickly, let my pants drop to the floor, and walk away in only my Spider-Man underwear and my linen shirt. As humiliating as this is, I hope the sight of me stripped of any dignity will make it easier for the woman I love to let me go.

31

Don't You Just Hate It When You're Right?

Bree

I WAIT until I drop Jolene at her house before I allow any tears to slide down my face. "Idiot, Brianna," I mutter as I drive home. I can't believe I thought he might actually love me. I mean, honestly, how stupid am I to think the son of a lord and lady would be even interested in me, let alone have deeply meaningful I've-got-to-sacrifice-everything-for-the-woman-I-love feelings. His words snap through my brain like firecrackers. *"I'm not even sorry." "Rich fantasy life." "I lie and I flatter and do whatever I have to do to get what I want..."*

A sob escapes my chest, and I let it all out, needing to be done with my grief before I reach the house. How could I be such a colossal moron? I knew better, but somehow, I let him suck me in, just like Roderick.

The morning replays in my head—looking up Jolene's address and rushing to her house to beg her to help me, then begging her to come with me to show me where Pierce lives, and begging Leo to admit the truth. Good God, all I've done today is beg. And it got me exactly nowhere. Well, that's not true. It did get me humiliated in a way I've never been before. Wiping the tears from my cheeks, I take a slow, shaky breath. It was all a lie. Every bloody word.

I have a fleeting thought of driving to my parents' house to cry on Amber's shoulder, but then I remember she's not talking to me.

The next few minutes until I reach my street, I allow all the self-pitying thoughts to hang over me—the why me, the it's not fair, the I did the best I could. But then as soon as I pull up in front of my house, I force myself to stop. I won't allow Izzy to see me all messed up over a man. It was hard enough earlier this morning when she woke me up with tears in her eyes because Leo left. "He told me he was never coming back, ever ever."

I managed to hold it together and say all the reassuring mum things I had to about how he'd always be our friend, even if he had to go away, and how we just have to think about the fun we had when he was here, but it didn't work. Her little shoulders slumped as she made her way down the stairs for breakfast. Not even the offer of extra chocolate chips in her oatmeal had helped.

Anger courses through me, replacing my humiliation. Fuck him for hurting my daughter like that. Fuck him for pretending to be this wonderful, caring guy. Fuck me for believing him and letting Isabelle spend any time at all with him.

"Bugger it," I say out loud. *Just forget him. Move on. You didn't really love him anyway. You're just in desperate need of a good shag, but since all men suck, forget shagging or kissing or happily ever afters.*

The only true happiness comes from hard work and accomplishment. So I'll get back to focussing on my career and my bank account, and leave the romance for the chumps of the world. The girls like my sister and her awful friends can have the men, and all the heartache they bring because I am done.

Done for good.

So take that, Leo, you bastard.

32

You Gotta Fight for Your Right to PPPPAAARRRTTTTYYYY

Leo

Three Days Later

TEXT CONVERSATION WITH ALEXANDER BILLINGSWORTH III
ME: *Hey, you old wanker, where are you?*
ALEX: *Swiss Alps this week. Next week is Bali to warm up.*
ME: *Where are you staying?*
ALEX: *Muffy's parents are at their villa, so we're slumming at the Park Vitznau.*

Damn. That's way out of my price range. I'd burn through my entire savings account in under a week at those rates.

ME: *I'm still wrapping things up here, but maybe I could meet you in Bali. I say we go for a really cheap experience for once. All the best girls have no money.*
ALEX: *Is that because you got disinherited?*

Fuck me.

ME: *Who told you that?*
ALEX: *My brother's dating a paralegal at Seth Hughes' office. Is it true?*
ME: *It's complicated.*

ALEX: *Damn. Sorry, bro.*

No, he's not.

ME: *You don't have to apologize. You're not Alistair the Tyrant.*

ALEX: *Won't Bunny help you?*

ME: *That depends on how serious my father is about taking away her wellness fund.*

ALEX: *Sounds awful. Just got to the top of the lift. Good luck with all that!*

"I always knew Billingsworth was a tosser," Pierce says, peering over my shoulder.

"Are you reading my texts? That's the height of bad manners," I say, shoving my mobile into my new cheap shorts (because I never did manage to find my damn bags). I get off the couch and walk over to the mini-fridge in search of an early afternoon Stella, only to find the shelves as barren as those of that little old lady who lived in a shoe.

Pierce sniffs. "I'd say the height of bad manners would be loafing around at your brother's house, sucking down all his booze."

Shutting the fridge door, I turn to him. "So what did you do? Hide it?"

"It was either that or watch you drink all my *Clash of Crowns* royalties."

"Fine. I have enough in my account to buy my own." Barely, but I don't need him to know that.

"In that case, when are you moving out?" he asks, raising one eyebrow.

"As soon as I figure out where I'm going."

"You're welcome to stay here as long as you're doing something with your life."

"I *am* doing something with my life. Enjoying it."

"No, you're not."

"Are too."

"Are not."

"Are too. At least I was until someone hid the alcohol."

"Leo—"

Holding up one hand, I say, "Spare me the you-can-do-anything-you-set-your-mind-to speech. I dropped out of life for a reason. It was too hard."

"Christ, you really are full of horse shit," he says. "Listen, I'm going to tell you two things, and you have no choice but to listen because if you don't, you'll be out on your arse. First, you're clearly miserable without that lovely concierge woman of yours."

"Am not."

"Yes, you definitely are. We all see the moping around you do when you think no one is looking."

"I don't mope!"

"Yes, I'm afraid you do," Mrs. Bailey says, walking through the room carrying a basket of laundry.

"I'm having a blast!"

"No, you're not!" she calls over her shoulder as she disappears down the hall.

I start to speak, but Pierce beats me to the punch. "You're miserable. And in case you've forgotten, you were actually much happier when you had a real purpose in life. Maybe being a bellboy isn't the most glamorous of jobs, but from what I hear and saw, you were good at it, and that's because you like helping people." Shuddering, he adds, "I'm not sure why, but for some strange reason, you do."

"No, I don't."

"God, you're an arse. You're a helpful person, and you bloody well know it. Now, get out in the world and find a way to put that to use so you can get Brianna back."

"The last thing I want to do is—"

"Oh, shut up. You're obviously in love with her, or you wouldn't have given up a fortune for her. She seems to be in love with you, too, so get your shit together, because a woman like her only comes around once, and she's not likely to wait long."

"She's better off without an utterly useless, selfish ne'er-do-well."

"You're none of those things. You are, however, a coward."

"Am not." I give him a bit of a shove for good measure.

Pierce shoves me back. "Are too."

Pushing harder this time, I say, "I'm not a coward. I'm selfish."

"Wrong!" he says, this time taking a quick step forward as he pushes me. "You are not selfish."

"Am so!" I punch his chest.

"Are not!" he says, and the two of us break into a fistfight.

I catch a blow to the chin, then pop him one in the gut. He bends over, moaning, and I immediately feel awful.

I put my hand on his shoulder. "Are you all right? I didn't mean to hurt you."

"Just fine!" he says, grabbing my wrist and attempting to flip me onto my back.

I'm too quick and manage to stop him, but we end up wrestling on the floor in the living room, knocking a vase off the end table. We both get soaked with water and covered in poofy purple flowers, but we're too focussed on besting each other to notice.

Just as I start to get the upper hand, Pierce yells, "Butterfly!"

"Where?" I duck, allowing him to put me in a headlock.

"Get the fuck off me, you arse!" I say in a strangled voice.

"Never." He tightens his hold. "Not until you tell me one thing you're good at."

"Drinking."

Gripping harder, he says, "I will choke you out if I have to, you little bastard. One real thing that you're good at and you could make money at. Now!"

"Nothing!"

"You're smart and kind and you like people," he says, struggling to keep a hold on me. "Now, what are you going to do with your life, you jackass?"

"Sod off, you wanker!" I say, my voice strained with the pressure on my neck.

"One thing, you tosser, or I swear to God, I will choke you!"

I start to see stars, and out of desperation, I say the first thing that comes to mind, "I think I'd make a good teacher!"

He pauses for a second, obviously too shocked to remember his end of the bargain. Tapping him on the arm, I whisper, "Let. Me. Go."

He does, and I drop to the ground on my hands and knees, coughing as I try to get a full breath. I'm covered in sweat and filled with rage at being choked.

"You actually would make a very good teacher," he says with a wide grin. "Good for—"

I stop his praise with a karate chop to his junk. He collapses on the floor beside me, moaning. "What the fuck did you do that for?"

"I'm teaching you not to choke me ever again."

"You bastard," he groans, clutching his crotch with both hands.

"You're the bastard," I say, holding my throat.

"You are!"

"Oh for Christ's sake!" Mrs. Bailey yells, startling us both. "Stop acting like animals before I knock your bloody heads together! Pierce, stay out of your brother's business. If he wants to feck up his life, just leave him to it." Turning to me, she says, "And you, stop fecking up your life, you moron. You're so much better than this, now act like it!"

She spins on her orthopedic heel and stalks out of the room before turning back to us. Pointing at me, she says in a thoroughly pleasant voice, "You should be a teacher though, dear. You'd be quite excellent at relating to the young people. Patient, too."

33

Bar Exams Should Be Written at a Bar

Bree

One Month Later

I'M in the storm before the calm. I hope. With exactly one week until my exams start, and ten days until my sister's wedding, I cannot remember a time when I've been this tired or stressed. Well, tired, maybe. It wasn't exactly smooth sailing when Isabelle was a colicky newborn who cried nonstop for three months. Actually, that was awfully stressful as well, now that I think about it, but I digress.

The point is, the past few days have been shite. Seriously. Between working, studying, and mumming, I'm only sleeping two hours per night. Then my eyes spring open due to a steady supply of adrenaline.

Work has been total bollocks because the bloody computer system goes down at least three times per day, and we no longer have a certain bellboy around to smooth it all over and whip up impromptu parties at will. Not that I want you to think I miss him *at all*, because I don't. In fact, life has been so much better since he packed up and went back to Avonia, or maybe off to the French Riviera, or wherever rich people go when they're bored. I'm sure his mummy is floating him some cash until he finds a way to smooth things over with his father. Whatever, it doesn't matter. What matters is he's gone, so I can get back to my regularly scheduled program of goals, aspirations, and responsible adulting without any stupidly handsome distractions around.

Urgh. I just realized it sounds like I'm obsessing over Leo, but I assure you, I'm not. In fact, I barely think about him at all. Just when I look out my kitchen window and see the empty garden suite. Or when the computers go down. Or when someone needs their bags loaded onto a cart and Leo's not there.

In his place is a very dull new hire named Sidney, whose mouth never fully shuts. Seriously, not even once in the past month. He just stands there in his uniform, breathing loudly and staring off into space. I can just imagine the fun Leo and I would have had talking about him on the ride home after our shift. Leo definitely would have come up with some brilliant nickname for him, like Mouth Breathing Sidney or Sidney Dry Tongue, or… Well, something much better than either of those examples, because funny nicknames were more his thing than mine. Not that we had *things* together. I just appreciated his sense of humour. So what? Let's not make a big thing of it.

Sidney doesn't even have one drop of wit in his entire lanky body, so there's absolutely no point in trying to strike up a conversation with him. Believe me, efforts have been made in this regard, but there is literally nothing going on in his brain. He's good at nodding, following orders, and mouth breathing. He's definitely not the type to exchange glances with when a rude, high-maintenance guest walks into the lobby. Not that I need someone to exchange glances with. In fact, it's better not to have someone like that. Yes, this is definitely better. I can focus so much better on my job this way. Studying too. And my family.

Speaking of family, I haven't seen my sister—or her fiancé and her lovely friends, for that matter—since I was made to leave the hen's weekend early. Whenever I think about facing them at the rehearsal, I break out in a cold sweat. The entire Hammer family probably hates me by now, which is going to make for a super awkward weekend.

They'll be whispering to each other, "There's that awful sister of Amber's who said Dane is a loser. As if *she's* such a catch." Or something else equally mean. Not that I don't deserve it.

Part of me is hoping that Amber or Dane will text me not to bother coming to the wedding. That would be both awful and a huge relief at the same time. To be honest, I've spent way longer than would be considered healthy trying to invent a reasonable excuse not to go. I've even fantasized about breaking my legs so I'm in traction for several months. That sounds better to me than showing my face at that wedding. If I could think of an excuse that wouldn't end in a lifetime of my mum shaking her head and *tsking* at me, I'd actually skip the entire thing—nuptials and all, mail a gift to them and spend the entire weekend holed up in my bedroom.

But that's really not an option, is it? Stupid adulting.

If Leo hadn't abandoned ship, I'd at least have a date for the wedding. A handsome, charming, sexy date. But he did leave. And he's gone forever. FOREVER. Which is exactly why I've forgotten all about him. Which is excellent, because I really need to get back to studying. My dinner break is almost over.

***

One Week Later

"Welcome to the first of your three Caribbean Multi-Island Bar Exams. Over the next two days, you'll be subjected to twelve hours of rigorous testing to see if you've got what it takes to call yourself a barrister. Make no mistake, these exams are designed to crush you, so if you are ill-prepared, you might as well give up now." Our examiner, a woman in her early sixties with a tight bun and black-rimmed glasses, stands at the front of the room staring at the forty sweaty candidates as though she can tell who's going to make it and who won't.

If my shaking hands and light-headedness are any indication, I'm fudge brownied. Aunt Dolores, who walked me to my car twenty minutes ago comes to mind. *"You got this, Bree. You've studied more than anyone in the history of school, you're whip-smart, and you're meant to be a lawyer. Now, go meet your destiny."* Oh, God, I hope she's right.

"The first exam is the Caribbean Bar Multi-island Performance Test. You will have three hours to complete it. Each of you will be given a file and a library with the relevant facts and case law to answer the questions your clients will have. You'll need to work quickly in order to read all of the facts and case law pertaining to your client's situation, then draft your advice in either a memo or email. These packets contain everything you need. As long as you are sufficiently prepared and you use your time wisely, you should get through this morning's tasks. Remember, just like in real life, grammar and spelling count."

The sound of the ticking clock distracts me, and I realize my mouth has suddenly gone dry. I should have brought a water bottle. She's still talking. I should really be listening.

"After this exam, you will have a one-hour lunch break, then you will come back to this room to write the essay exam, which consists of six essay questions. Tomorrow, you will have another six hours of testing. Two hundred multiple choice questions on a wide range of topics. Then comes the most nerve-racking part of the process—waiting for results. Please note, it really does take six to eight weeks to mark the exams, even if you call daily to ask for your results. So don't call or email or show up at the head office with cupcakes or fruit trays or cheese plates. We've got your mailing addresses, so you'll be notified as soon as possible. So I repeat, do not contact us."

She glances around the room with a stern expression. "I will pass out your first packets right now. Do *not* open them until I have started the stopwatch. Good luck, and I hope to see you all practising law very soon."

God, these lights are bright. They're hurting my eyes. Am I sweating? Yes, my palms are damp. Dear Lord! How am I going to hold my pen with sweaty hands? Okay, breathe, Brianna. Calm down. Channel your inner Amal Clooney. Be amazing. Or at the very least, don't fart this up.

34

Lousy Roommates, Mystery Sticky Substances, and Other Wonderful Things

Leo

YOU'RE PROBABLY WONDERING what I've been up to these past several weeks. Maybe you suspect that I've been continuing to lounge around at my brother's, wasting my days and nights drinking and carrying on. Or maybe you think I've found my way to Bali, where I'm sponging off my friends. In either case, you'd be wrong.

It might surprise you to find out I am still in San Felipe, where I intend to stay. I'm not at my brother's luxury villa, but rather in a flat I share with two other guys I work with at the Turtle's Head Pub. And, no, sadly, I am not living my Tom Cruise in *Cocktail* fantasy life, tossing bottles of vodka over my shoulder only to deftly catch them whilst soaking up the adulation of the clubgoers. Instead, I'm a lowly busboy.

For now.

Last Monday, I applied for the University of Santa Valentina's education program, and I've been on pins and needles while I await their answer. Pierce seems to think I'm a shoo-in, but to be honest, I wasn't exactly at the top of my alchemy class, so they may take one look at my grades from the University of Valcourt and stamp my application DENIED in red ink.

I've put quite a lot of stock in the results of my application. It's not just about my future career, but my future happiness. You see, I haven't told Brianna the truth yet. As of this moment, she doesn't know I gave up everything because I'm madly in love with her, or that I'm going to make a go of a good life here on the island, or that I'm even still here. As much as I want to rush to her, I need to have something real to offer her before I take that chance. I need to prove beyond a shadow of a doubt—to her and me—that I have what it takes to be the man she needs.

I know it's risky, and I have the urge to rush to her and lay my heart at her feet at least twenty times a day. But I can't. Not until I know I won't mess up my future and bring her down with me. I just have to trust she won't find someone else in the meantime. And for the moment, I should be safe, because she's busy with her exams. In fact, she's probably sitting down to write the last one right about now. Then this weekend, she'll be busy with her sister's wedding, which honestly does concern me a bit. I mean, there could be an eligible bachelor thrown in her path, and she may just decide to give him a go since she thinks I'm a long-gone loser.

My heart pounds at the thought of it. Maybe I should just rush to her right now. I could wait for her outside her exam, and when she comes out, I could pour everything out right there on the sidewalk in front of the school of law building.

As soon as I finish scrubbing this sticky mystery substance off the kitchen floor. My roommates, who are still sleeping, had last night off, and from the looks of things, they had their own party here. Since neither of them have any intention of cleaning up, and I have no desire to walk in filth, I scrounged around to find a mop and bucket, and I'm doing the best I can with some dish soap and hot water.

My mobile phone rings and my heart jumps. Bugger. It's not Brianna, but my mother on the phone. "Hello, Mum."

"Leo, I've had the most alarming call that you've decided to stay on that dreadful island and that you're working as a *busboy*. Tell me it isn't true."

"Okay, it's not true, Mother."

"So it is true?" she asks, sounding panicked.

"Yes, I'm afraid so, but don't worry, because it's only temporary. I have a plan."

"Thank *God*, because I don't think I can suffer the humiliation of having you work as a busboy on a permanent basis."

Might as well wind her up a bit. It's been a while since I've had any fun. "I'm on a three-year plan working my way up from bellboy to busboy to pool boy, with an end goal of cabana boy—that's where the big bucks start rolling in."

A strangled gasp comes from the other end of the line, and I stifle a laugh while she starts going off. "Pool boy? You think of that as a step *up* in the world?"

"Strictly speaking, no. I suppose the pay's not much above busboy, and the tips are nonexistent, but it really is the only way to get to cabana boy."

"I can't believe this. After everything I've done for you, all the sacrifices I've made! And this is what you want to do with your life?" She moans sorrowfully, then continues. "Never mind. It doesn't even matter, because I've convinced your father to let you have a crack at an intern position at one of the companies. Entry-level, you'd be at the headquarters in Dublin, and you can stay at my cousin Edna's while you work your way up the ladder. It won't be easy, but at least you'll be much closer to home, and in time, I know you can prove to your father you're ready to take your rightful place at Davenport Communications."

"No, thank you," I say.

There's a long silence, while she most likely processes what she's just heard. "Pardon me?" she asks stiffly.

"No. Thank you, though. I really do appreciate the effort on my behalf. The truth is, I do have a plan, and it's a very good one. I've actually applied for university here. I want to be an elementary school teacher."

"A teacher?" she sputters. "But you hated school, and you were an awful student. Absolutely dreadful."

"But I do think I'd love teaching. I love kids, and it's an honest profession, Mother."

"An honest profession that pays nothing," she quips.

"The pay is enough. As crazy as that may sound, I've discovered that having a purpose is as important as cash when it comes to happiness."

After a long pause, Bunny says, "Is this about that woman you were living with? Did she talk you into this?"

"If you're referring to Brianna, I haven't spoken with her in weeks, so, no. Besides, she's not the type to manipulate people into doing what she wants." *Unlike some other people I can think of...*

"This is ridiculous. I'm going to march straight to your father's office and get him. Then the two of us are going to fly down there and pick you up. That's enough of this nonsense. You need to come back home where you belong."

"I am where I belong."

"I'm not going to have one of my sons embarrass the family by working as a *teacher* for the rest of his life."

"I'm afraid you are."

"If you do this, I really will stop helping you, Leo. I swear it."

"Good."

"Good?" she asks. "Did you not hear what I just said? I will *stop helping you*. That means I'm not going to keep begging your father for money on your behalf. You really will spend the rest of your life being broke."

"That's okay. Being broke isn't as bad as all that."

"Are you on drugs right now?"

"No, Mother, I'm not. For the first time in my life, you don't need to worry about me, because I'm finally fine. Now, I need to run. I have to finish washing the kitchen floor before I go to work. I don't want to be late for my shift."

"Seriously, Leo. You must be high. Or is someone holding a gun to your head? Is it that woman?"

"I love you, Mother. I'll come and visit as soon as I can set aside money for airfare."

With that, I hang up and smile, feeling ridiculously proud while I wash the floor. I'm a man. A man with responsibilities and an amazingly full future ahead of him. As long as that future doesn't fall for someone else while I finish getting my shit together...

35

One Day, Twelve-Hours of Testing, and One Brain-Dead Concierge Later...

Bree

"So?" Dolores says when I arrive at home.

"My brain is completely fried. I honestly have no idea how I did," I say, shaking my head. "Turns out, they don't make it easy to become a barrister."

Dolores gives me a mock-surprised look. "Really? That's surprising. All you ever hear about the bar exams is how easy they are."

I grin at her. "Right?"

"Mummy!" Isabelle rushes across the living room and jumps into my arms, kissing me hard on the cheek. "You're done! Now we can play all the time."

I hold her in my arms and plant kisses on her soft cheeks and forehead, then give her a good long hug, my heart squeezing with guilt at the number of hours I've kept her waiting while I study. "I'm so excited that we'll have more time together, my little peanut."

"Me, too!" Wiggling out of my arms, Izzy grabs my hand and gives it a tug. "Come on! Auntie Dolores and I maked a big party for you."

I follow her toward the backyard, my gut tightening at the thought of who might be waiting for me. I can't imagine Amber and Dane being here—not after what happened. But maybe my parents, in which case, we'll do the whole pretend-everything's-fine, ignore-the-elephant-in-the-garden thing.

Oh, or what if Leo's out there? The thought of him on the other side of that door makes my heart race. Logically, I know he's gone, but what if he's not?

I can't see him right now. I'm a total mess. I've been sweating all day and need to brush my teeth and fix my hair. Dear God, don't let him be out there. But also, *do* let him be out there because I so desperately want to see him.

I allow Isabelle to lead me out into the garden, where a table and some chairs have been set up. A small glass vase sits at the centre of the table, filled with random flowers from our beds. Four place settings surround the vase. Four. Izzy, Dolores, me, and…who?

My palms go sweaty, and I glance around for signs of him. The garden suite looks as empty as it has for the past several weeks. He's not here. He's halfway around the world by now.

"Who's the extra chair for, sweetie?" I ask, trying to sound casual.

"Mr. Bananas." Isabelle beams up at me. "Oh damn, I should go get him! He'll be all ready by now." She dashes back into the house, leaving me alone in the yard.

My heart sinks to my heels, solidifying what I already knew deep down. I'm madly in love with a man who is never coming back. I can't get him out of my stupid mind because the longer he's gone, the more I realize he was lying when he said he was only being so wonderful to get what he wanted from me. The truth that I know in my bones is that he is an amazing human being and I pushed him away with my need to judge the world. We could've had a wonderful life together if I hadn't buggered everything up by acting as if I'm the smartest person in every room.

The door swings open and Dolores walks out carrying a tray of food. "We've been cooking up a storm. All your favourites—bacon-wrapped scallops, spaghetti carbonara, and Caesar salad."

She means her favourites. "Sounds amazing." I do my best to seem happy.

"I invited your parents, but they're so busy with the wedding, they couldn't make it," Dolores says, setting the tray down. "But they wanted you to know that they intend to celebrate with you as soon as the wedding's over."

Shrugging as though it's no big deal, I say, "Well, there's really nothing to celebrate today. We don't even know if I passed."

"Yes, we do." Dolores says firmly. She gestures to the tray while giving me an expectant look.

Glancing at it, I laugh when I notice a cheese me sitting on a bed of lettuce.

Izzy bursts through the door and runs down the steps with Mr. Bananas dragging behind her. She points at the blob of cheese and says, "I helped make a Cheese Lawyer Mum. See? You have a fancy suit on and a briefcase."

Wow," I say, staring at the unrecognizable white blob. "That is amazing. You two must have been working very hard all day."

"Yep." Isabelle nods proudly, then sets Mr. Bananas up at on one of the chairs. "Him can sit between us."

"Perfect." I pick up his little hand and give it a shake. "Mr. Bananas, thanks for joining us on this auspicious occasion."

"You sit down and relax," Dolores says. "I'll go get us some wine."

"Oh, yes, please." I do as I'm told, a sense of relief coming over me as I take a seat.

The sun starts to set while we dine on the world's saltiest celebratory dinner. Isabelle chats excitedly about the upcoming wedding and begins the extensive negotiations regarding how late we can stay out so she can dance the night away. Then I give her the it-all-depends-on-your-behaviour speech.

As we move on to the dessert portion—warm chocolate chip cookies with a scoop of vanilla ice cream and bacon sprinkles, I keep the smile on my face, even though on the inside, I feel strangely empty. I'm sure it's just because I'm so tired.

By the time we're done eating, it's dark out, and the bottle of wine is empty. I have a nice warm feeling of being full, of having completed one of the biggest challenges of my life, and of being slightly numb.

Isabelle yawns audibly, and I glance at my watch. "Oh, dear, we better get you off to bed, young lady. We have a big weekend ahead of us."

"Aww, but, Mum..." Isabelle starts.

"Who's this Butt Mum you keep calling?" I say with a wink. "Now, you and Mr. Bananas go get your jammies on, or you'll be too tired to dance all night this weekend."

That seems to do the trick because she disappears into the house without another word while I stand and stack the dishes. "Thank you so much, Auntie. I'll do the cleanup. You go watch *Jeopardy*."

"Don't have to tell me twice." She gets up, then gathers the salad bowl and wine bottle to take inside. Stopping after a few steps, Dolores turns to me. "You should just call him."

"Call who?" I ask innocently.

"Leo. It's painfully obvious that you miss him."

I shake my head. "Why would I miss a big, irresponsible, goofy guy like him?"

"Because you're in love with him," she says. "Besides, he's not irresponsible. He's just more fun than you are."

"Same thing."

"No, it's not, and you know it."

Sighing, I let my shoulders drop. "He's gone. End of story. So any feelings I may or may not have had for him are irrelevant. Not that I did have feelings for him, because I didn't."

"You're a terrible liar. Always were," she says, turning back to the house. "You love him, so the smart thing to do would be to call him, or swipe him on your phone, or whatever you kids do these days..."

I follow her inside. "I don't... Even if I did have feelings for him, it doesn't matter. We're too different. Plus, he left, so——"

"So you need to tell him to come back," she answers, setting the bowl on the counter. "He will."

"No, he won't. He made it very clear that he has no romantic interest in me whatsoever. Which is a good thing, because we're totally wrong for each other. Not in any way compatible."

"Oh, bollocks. He's the yang to your yin. Without him, you have no yang. Is that the kind of life you want?"

"I'm not in need of his yang. I have a vibrator."

She opens her mouth, but I hold up one hand. "Can we not ruin a perfectly wonderful evening by talking about Leo?"

"It wasn't perfectly wonderful," she says, shaking her head. "You would have enjoyed it so much more if he'd been here."

"That's not true. I loved every minute——"

"No, you didn't. But you tried like hell to make it seem like you did, which I appreciate." She pats me on the cheek, smiling up at me. "Such a nice, stupid, cowardly girl."

"I am not!"

"Then call him," she mouths.

"He's gone forever," I say firmly.

"But if he weren't? Like if he showed up right now, would you have the ovaries to tell him how you feel?"

"Sure, Auntie. If he walked through that door right now, I'd rush into his arms and tell him I'm wildly in love with him." My nostrils flare, and I consider opening another bottle of wine. "Okay? Can we drop it now?"

Dolores stares at me for a moment, then says, "On one condition."

"What?"

"You promise you'll call him."

Oh for... "I'm not...no. It's over, much like this conversation." I plug the sink and turn the taps on full blast, then squirt about a week's worth of soap into the water.

"Yup. You're a coward," she says.

I ignore her and get started on the washing up. A moment later, I hear the familiar voice of Alex Trebek. I furiously wash the wine glass in my hand. "I am not a coward," I mutter. "I'm smart."

36

Missing Brides and the
Judgmental Maids of Honour
Who Love Them...

Bree

TODAY IS the official start of the wedding festivities—a day I've been dreading since the horrible hen's party incident. I've been up since before the sun, unable to sleep due to the big knot twisting in my gut. Is there any feeling worse than regret? Because if there is, I don't know what it would be.

I'm currently scrubbing the walls of the garden suite, having stripped the bed and put the sheets in the washer earlier (while trying very hard *not* to notice how deliciously Leo the pillowcase smelled). I've had no time to prepare the suite for a new renter, but now that my exams are over, it seems like the smart thing to do. It rained all night, and the clouds are still hanging overhead, casting a grey, lonely feeling to the world. Or I suppose that's just me and my dramatic I'll-be-alone-forever state of mind.

Dolores and Izzy are still in their jammies watching *Doc McStuffins*, which is giving me some much-needed time to think of how to gracefully handle the wedding rehearsal. I plunge the rag into the bucket of hot, soapy water, then wring it out and get started on the windowsills. So far, I'm making a lot more progress with the cleaning than I am with figuring out how to handle this weekend. I've thought of attempting to get my hands on an invisibility cloak a la Harry Potter, and/or hiding behind Isabelle the entire time, but since invisibility cloaks don't exist in the muggle world, and Izzy's not quite four feet tall, it would prove somewhat difficult.

A knock at the door interrupts my pondering, and when I open it, Dane is standing on the other side, filling the entire doorframe, his thick eyebrows knitted together, and his face slightly damp and pale.

"Dane, are you all right?"

He shakes his head. "No, actually. I'm trying to find Amber. She called off the wedding."

"Oh my God, what happened?" I ask, stepping aside to let him in.

"We had a big stupid fight last night about her not wanting to change her name. Now I can't find her. I've been looking everywhere for her this morning, and I thought maybe she'd have come here since you hate me, too."

Oh, ouch. I deserved that one. "I don't hate you, Dane."

"You certainly don't like me." He stuffs his hands into the front pockets of his jeans.

I close my eyes for a second. When I reopen them, I say, "I wish I could take back what I said. I cannot tell you how sorry I am."

"Because you don't mean it, or because you wish you hadn't said it?" He holds up one hand. "You know what? Don't answer that. I think it's better if I don't know." Raking his hand through his hair, he says, "It probably doesn't matter anyway."

"It does matter. What I said had nothing to do with you, actually—"

"Even the bit where you said I'm a moron and I'll drag her down with me?"

Urgh. Right. That part. My face grows hot with shame. "To be honest, even that part. I know it's not a good excuse, but I was really drunk at the time, and I've been worried about her not wanting to have her own career. But honestly, it's nothing to do with you as a person. It's just... I thought she was giving up on her dreams." I ramble on while he watches me, his face full of scepticism. "I meant the dreams that don't have to do with marrying you and having children. Her *other* dreams. Anyway, I am so, so sorry, Dane."

He stares at me for a moment, he then tilts his head. "Okay."

"Okay?" I ask, my heart daring to lift in relief.

Shrugging, he says, "Yeah, it's okay. Everybody says dumb shit when they're drunk."

"Thanks, Dane," I say, giving him a grateful smile. "Now, let's say we find your bride. Did she leave any clues of where she might have gone?"

Shaking his head, he pulls his phone out of his pocket. He swipes the screen and shows it to me.

I'm sorry to do this to you, but the wedding is off. I don't think we want the same things out of life, and it's better if we realize it now than later. Please don't try to find me. I've made up my mind, and it will only make it harder for both of us.

"All this over her not wanting to become Amber Hammer?" I ask, handing the phone back to him.

Dane sighs, rubbing the back of his neck and looking like the most upset man in the world. "For some reason, I thought it sounded so nice, but I can hear it now. Stupid, Dane. Stupid. To risk what we had together over something so dumb."

"Okay, I'm not going to agree or disagree with you, but I will say this isn't the hill for either of you to die on. Not when you're as in love as the two of you are."

Dane swallows hard. "Exactly. I want to spend the rest of my life with her whether she wants to become a Hammer or not. She's the only woman I'll ever love, Bree. I need to find her."

Snapping my fingers, I say, "I think I know where she might be."

***

I pull into the Hidden Beach parking lot, a wave of relief coming over me at the sight of Amber's car. The entire ride over, Dane's been sniffling and letting the odd sob escape his chest while he stares out his window so I won't know he's crying. The old me would be thinking, 'hey, genius, you're not fooling anyone' but the new me just feels bad for the poor guy.

Parking, I take the key out of the ignition and turn to Dane. "Why don't you wait here and…compose yourself while I go see if I can warm her up a bit for you?"

Nodding, he gives me a hopeful smile. "Thanks, Bree. I really appreciate it."

It takes me nearly fifteen minutes of walking along the beach to find the hideaway cave. The rain spits down at me, and the wind howls, causing sand to stick to my now-wet pants. It's a miserable day to be out here, which is kind of fitting since it's been a miserable day for Amber and Dane so far. And for me, if I'm really honest, because coming back to Hidden Beach reminds me of a certain man I'm refusing to think about. And all this talk of marriage and love is making me entirely too aware of the fact that he's gone for good.

When I reach the cave, I crouch so I can make my way inside. It takes a moment for my eyes to adjust to the dark. Amber sits on a log at the back, a pile of twigs in front of her on the sandy floor. She looks up at me. "Oh great. Are you here to say you told me so?"

"No. I'm here to apologize."

"Oh," she says, taken aback.

"I'm sorry, Amber. I was a total shit on your hen's weekend. I had no right to say what I did. This is your life and it's not for me to decide how you spend it."

"Took you long enough to realize it."

"That's a fair point." I keep my head ducked while I make my way over to her and sit down with a heavy sigh. "This cave is much smaller than I remember."

"Right? I thought I'd be a lot more comfortable but it's cold and damp and I forgot to bring matches. Stupid."

I put my hand on top of hers and give it a little squeeze. "I don't think we ever once remembered the matches."

She chuckles at the memory but says nothing.

"I heard you called off the wedding?"

"I'm sure you're secretly thrilled," she says, pulling her hand away from mine.

"I'll be happy if this is what you really want."

"It is. I can't marry a controlling jerk like him."

"In all the years I've known Dane, I never once would've thought him to be controlling."

"Well, you weren't at his house last night when he was going on and on about how important it was that I become a Hammer. What if I want to be a Lewis?"

"Or a nail, for that matter?" I ask with a small grin that she doesn't return. "Okay, too soon. You sure this isn't maybe a case of cold feet?"

Shaking her head, she says, "I'm sure. I thought I knew what I wanted, but it turns out I didn't." Her voice cracks, and she goes on. "It's for the best really because now I can figure out what I really want to do with my life. Maybe I'll go to med school or something."

"You faint at the sight of blood."

"Well, I'm sure there are loads of doctors who can't stand the sight of blood."

I laugh, and this time, she joins me and then rolls her eyes at herself.

"Listen, if you want to be a blood-hating doctor, I know you can do it, hon. You're smart, and you've got buckets of potential. But are you sure you have to give up one dream for the other?"

"I already did," she says, dissolving into tears. "Oh God, Bree, I love him so much! I'm just so confused and scared, you know?"

"I know, sweetie. And from what I understand, that's totally natural." I wrap an arm around her shoulder. "It's not too late. Only three people know you cancelled the wedding. Two are in this cave and one is sitting in my car, trying very hard not to cry."

Her bottom lip quivers. "Really?"

"Really. He said he doesn't care if you change your last name to Hammer or not. In fact, he'll even change his last name if it'll mean you change your mind."

"Did he say that?" she asks, wiping the stream of tears off her cheeks.

"Not in those exact words, but if that's what you want, I could broker the deal for you," I say. "He's desperate, Amber. I don't know exactly what happened last night, but he's absolutely never going to stop loving you."

"It's just that... I've been thinking about what you said about me having a purpose and a life, and I feel so mixed up because maybe I should want to go back to school so I can have a big, fancy career. I mean otherwise, what kind of example am I setting for our kids? I mean, if we have kids, that is."

"You'll be teaching them that it's important to know who you are and what matters in life," I answer.

Amber gives me a sceptical look. "You're just saying that because you feel bad that you might have actually broken us up."

"I'm saying it because it's true, Amber. You know who you are, you always have, whereas I've just been trying to figure it all out and pushing everyone who matters away in the process."

She stares at me, clearly trying to figure out if I'm sincere or not.

"I spent my entire life trying to be this perfect person and making myself miserable in the process. The truth is, I'm always so worried about everybody else judging me that I have done my damnedest to beat them to the punch."

"That's not true." Amber sniffs. "You *are* perfect, which is why you probably feel justified to judge everybody else."

"Well, being a total Judge Judy isn't exactly a good quality in a human being."

"Unless you're the real Judge Judy," she says.

"Exactly. It's being an amateur Judge Judy that's ill-advised." I rest my head on her shoulder. "Then you just end up hurting the people you love. I'm so sorry, Amber. I apologized to Dane, too, and I really mean it with my whole heart."

"Thanks." She sniffs. "That means a lot to me."

We give each other a long, squeezy hug, a wave of happiness coming over me. When we pull back, I say, "I envy you, Amber. Not just because you already found the love of your life, but because you have this strong, certain vision of your life. It's not the right one for

265

me, but it's the right one for you, and you've always known it. And that's a good thing."

"But what about everything you said about how Dane was just going to drag me down with him?"

I wince, shaking my head vigorously. "I should *not* have said that. It's not true. He's a good guy, and he just wants to make you happy, whatever that means. And at the end of the day, all that really matters is whether *you* want this life for yourself. Don't listen to me or Mum or anybody else who tries to tell you how you should live. The truth is, none of us have the answers. I think we're all just making it up as we go along and hoping for the best."

"Even you?"

"*Especially* me. Now, what do you say? Do you think you've kept that man of yours waiting long enough?"

Amber nods, fanning her face with her perfectly manicured hands. "How do I look?"

"Beautiful, as always." I stand and hold both hands out to her to help her up. "I'm so sorry if I made you question yourself. I had no right to do that."

"It's okay. I know you just want the best for me."

"I do," I say, taking her cheeks in both hands. "But what I failed to realize is that you're not some little kid anymore, needing your big sister to tell you what to do. You're an adult, and *you* know what's best for you."

Her face twists up into an ugly cry, and she reaches for me, sobbing as she wraps her arms around me and pulls me in for a monster hug. "I'm so sorry about what happened," she says.

"I'm sorry, too. I never should've come on the trip. Not when I knew there was about an 80% chance I was going to spoil the fun."

"No, it's my fault," she says, shaking her head. "I shouldn't have been so pushy about everything. You were right about Randy Andy. We were all so infected. We should have listened to you."

Smiling through her tears, she says, "I missed you so much these last few weeks, and it made me realize that I need to accept you for who you are. You'll never be fun or exciting, but that's okay because you're so much more than that. You're smart and talented, and you're going to be wildly successful, and I'm really proud of you."

A lump forms in my throat. "Thanks, sweetie. I really needed to hear that."

We walk arm-in-arm down the beach, catching up in that we-need-to-talk-fast-because-there's-so-much-to-say sort of way. Amber tells me in excruciating detail about their tattoo infections and about the rest of the hen's weekend, which turns out to have been a total bust with Kandi and Valerie getting into a huge row which got them kicked out of a restaurant on Saturday night. Then the entire party spent Sunday alternating who could use the bathroom to get sick in. I tell her about the horrible, sweaty bar exams and the butterflies and Leo, and that I think I may have ruined the best thing that ever happened to me—aside from having the world's best sister, and Izzy, and hopefully my career, if it happens.

By the time we reach the parking lot, the sun is out, and all feels right in the world. Well, almost everything anyway. Amber rushes ahead to Dane, who is leaning up against the side of my little Corolla with his head hanging down and his arms crossed. She calls out his name, and he turns, his face instantly breaking into a look of pure joy as he holds his arms out to her. I hang back on the beach, feeling very much the third wheel as I give them time to reunite and reassure each other that they'll be just fine.

I turn and face the sea, suddenly realizing I am in the exact spot I was when Leo brought me here. Regret blooms, crowding out any joy I felt at helping my sister and Dane sort things out. The truth is, Leo was right. I've done a spectacular job of judging my way out of what could have been a wonderful life. *I'm* the reason he left. He didn't leave because he's irresponsible. He left because I didn't give him a reason to stay.

37

Sisters and Their Misters

Bree

I ARRIVED AT MY PARENTS' house at 5 a.m. to have my hair and makeup done and was greeted by a mostly silent bridal party, all of whom are sporting matching bandages on their upper backs in place of Celtic sisterhood hearts.

Now, as we stand at the back of the large cathedral where over two hundred guests wait to catch a glimpse of my little sister, I feel completely choked up with emotion. I'm overcome with happiness for her, but at the same time, I've never felt so alone in my life.

Kandi, Quinn, and Valerie all line up, shoulders back, ready to make their grand entrances. Bruno Mars "I Think I Want to Marry You" starts, and the three make their way up the aisle in a coordinated dance routine that is slightly shocking, kind of inappropriate, and definitely very attention-grabby. It's sort of flash mob meets strip club, except in a church.

Isabelle stands in front of us, watching and waiting for me to give her the okay to go. Our poor dad stands next to Amber, looking as nervous as a one-armed squid in a shark tank. He takes a handkerchief out of his pocket and mops his brow, then pats Amber's hand.

"You look just beautiful, sweetie." Turning to me, he says, "You, too, Breenut."

"Thanks, Dad," Amber says, tearing up and fanning her eyes with her hands.

"He's right," I say. "You're absolutely stunning, Amber. Dane is lucky to have you."

Her face falls for a second, and I quickly add, "And you're lucky to have him, too."

I turn to the front and am just about to tell Isabelle to go when my heart starts to pound so hard I can hear it in my eardrums. Leo is standing in the last pew, smiling at me and looking ludicrously handsome. My knees go weak, and I'm momentarily unaware of what my body and face are doing. It must be noticeably stupid though because Izzy tugs at my hand and says, "Mummy, why is your mouth hanging open?"

Not breaking eye contact with Leo, I say, "Yes, sweetie. It's your turn."

"What?" she asks.

I glance down at her, my entire face hot with embarrassment. "Sorry, what?"

"Okay, Izzy, you can go now," Amber says, tapping her on the shoulder.

She whips around to face the crowd, holding her shoulders back, ready to lap up the attention as the world's cutest flower girl. Spotting Leo, she waves with abandon. "Hi, Leo! You maked it!" Turning back to me, she says, "Mummy! Leo's here!"

I feel my face go flush again, and I nod quickly, gesturing for her to get going. Taking a deep breath, I start up the aisle, praying I don't trip and make a fool of myself. When I'm almost at Leo's pew, I whisper, "What are you doing here?"

He mouths, "I promised."

I shake my head and chuckle a little, then hear him say, "You're beautiful, by the way," as I pass by. And suddenly, I'm pretty sure I could float the rest of the way up this aisle without need of my feet.

. . .

***

I stand at the front of the church next to Amber, holding her large bouquet of white roses and lavender hydrangeas, along with my smaller, matching flowers. She and Dane are holding hands and are repeating their vows. I have fallen into an annoying habit of glancing at the very back where Leo is every chance I get, like right now. Yup, he's still dangerously handsome in that black tuxedo.

He smiles up at me in a way that makes me feel like the only woman in the world, and I start wondering all sorts of very unhelpful things, like what would it feel like to kiss him, and what would it be like to wake up with him next to me every morning, and could he possibly ever love someone like me…

"…For all the days of my life," Amber says in a very shaky voice.

I glance back at my sister, checking to see if she needs anything, but noticing that she's got everything she ever wanted right in front of her. He's holding both of her hands, and his eyes are filled with tears that reassure me he means this every bit as much as she does.

The minister smiles at the happy couple. "Having exchanged symbols of your undying devotion and vowed before God and everyone you know to remain true to each other, you are now bound together in holy matrimony."

Glancing at Leo again, I tell myself whatever I'm feeling is just from being at a wedding. I remind myself to think of the Bianchis and how miserable they are. That's real. Looking down at Isabelle, I smile at her little face. She's real. And how she got here is also real. Leo is not real. He's just here because he said he'd show up. Which makes him kind of perfect, considering that he still came to support me, even after everything that happened between us. And everything that *didn't* happen, for that matter.

My eyes divert back to him again without my permission. Frick. I am never going to get over this man, no matter how long I live.

***

. . .

The ceremony ends, and I follow Mr. Hammer and Ms. Lewis-Hammer out of the church. I'm reluctantly holding on to Evander's forearm since I've been paired up with him for the processions. He's talking away about something, but I can barely hear him over the sound of Robbie Williams and Lily Allen singing "Dream a Little Dream" over the speakers. I make the odd mm-hmm sound while I focus in on Leo the entire time.

The late-day sun greets us when we step out of the air-conditioned building, and Evander and I take our place in the receiving line, pose for photos, and greet relatives and old friends for the thirty minutes it takes for the church to empty. Isabelle spots Leo and disappears through the legs of the crowd, and soon she's jumping into his arms and hugging him with her death grip around his neck. He beams and hugs her back, then finds me across the courtyard and makes eye contact so I'll know he's got her.

I'm desperate to get out of this damn line so I can talk to him, but I can't seem to slip away, because just when I think I'm in the clear, another friend of my mum's pops up with a *nice, young man* I should meet.

Finally, the crowd thins out, and I make a beeline for Leo, who is now crouched down, teaching Isabelle how to make her thumb disappear. She laughs wildly when he does it, then deftly makes it reappear again. She spots me and says, "Mum! Leo's teaching me impressive party tricks."

I laugh. "Well, that's very nice. Say, I think Auntie Dolores has some of your favourite cookies in her purse. She's right over there with Grandma."

Looking up at Leo, she says, "Want one?"

Leo nods, and Isabelle takes off on her mission, leaving us alone. But now, I suddenly feel terrified. I have no idea what to say or why he's here or what any of this means. Or if it means anything at all, really. I also seem to have forgotten how to stand casually while wearing heels and a fancy dress. I fidget, trying out various arm positions and leg stances while Leo watches.

"Are you all right?" he asks.

"Yes, of course. Wonderful, actually," I say, then I panic. "But not too wonderful or something. Just the right amount." *Shit.* "I thought you went home."

Shaking his head, he says, "I had better reasons to stay."

Oh my God! Could he mean me? No, do not get your hopes up. "Cool. That's…" Insert casual shrug. *Do not wrap your arms around his neck and kiss him.* "Cool. Yeah."

"I hope you don't mind me showing up. I should have texted or something, in case you found another date," he says, seeming a little awkward.

"No, I didn't find another date," I say, sounding stupidly desperate. *Calm down, Bree! Do not blow your one chance at happiness because you don't know how to play it cool.*

Smiling at me, his eyes flick down to my lips for a second, then back up. "I'm glad."

"Bree! We gotta go!" Kandi calls from the parking lot where the limo is waiting.

Leo and I both turn to look, and I give her a little annoyed wave. "Okay, I guess I need to go for photos now."

"Brilliant, yes. See you at the reception, then?"

I nod. "See you there. Unless you change your mind about coming or get a better offer or something. Whatever. I'm breezy."

"No, you're not. But that's okay. I like you the way you are." He reaches up and tucks a lock of hair behind my ear. "And I will be there."

"Right," I say, my voice going all breathy. "Because of the free meal."

Chuckling, Leo says, "Exactly."

"Bree! Move it!" Valerie calls, causing me to snap out of my Leo-induced haze.

"Okay. I'll see you then."

"Good, because I have some very important things to discuss with you," Leo says.

"Brianna!" This time, it's my mum doing the shrieking.

I hurry off, turning no less than three times to smile at him over my shoulder. When I get in the limo, I stare out the window, my entire body both numb and buzzing with excitement at the same time as I wonder what the very important things are he needs to discuss with me.

***

It's evening now. The toasts have been given, the meal—lobster and chicken with rice pilaf and grilled veggies—has been eaten. The first dance has happened, which if you ask me is just plain awkward—two people swaying side-to-side while four hundred eyes watch their every move for three minutes and forty-one seconds. Well, in our case, three hundred ninety-nine. Uncle Dave lost his left eye in a terrible rescue cat incident back in 2009.

I've had just enough champagne to not care that my mum is trying to set me up with anything with a penis despite the fact that Leo's here as my date. My date, who, incidentally, I haven't had so much as twenty seconds alone with since... Well, since he moved out really. At the moment, I'm standing next to the bar while Isabelle and Leo bust a move on the dance floor. Dolores and Izzy are so thrilled to see him, they haven't left his side once since the church service, but there's something about the way he looks at me that is giving me some very hopeful feelings. It's sort of an 'I want to get you out of that dress and do all sorts of delicious things' to you look, which coming from any other man would earn him a kick to the business, but from Leo, oh my...

I take the opportunity to go to the ladies' room to freshen up.

My mum stops me at the ballroom entrance. "The bellboy? Really, Bree, you can do so much better."

"I'm not so sure about that, Mum, but it doesn't matter anyway, because we're just friends. He came as a courtesy."

"Well, his presence here isn't exactly convenient. Do you know how many eligible men there are here?" she asks in a hushed tone.

"That's why I invited him," I say. With that, I push open the door and walk into the bathroom, happy as silence fills the air when it swings shut behind me.

Walking over to the sink, I turn on the water to wash my hands. Aunt Dolores comes out of one of the stalls, her dress still hiked up above her navel while she struggles with her nylons. "So? Did you tell him yet?"

"Tell who what?" I ask, even though I know what she meant.

"Your hot date that you love him."

"First of all, I don't even know if I love him. Second, he may just be here as a friend, which would make it super awkward were I to start professing my love to him."

"Knew you didn't have the ovaries," she says, clicking her tongue as she washes her hands.

The bathroom door swings open, and Valerie and Kandi stumble in, both looking worse for wear.

Valerie points at me. "There she is! Bitch One!"

Kandi giggles as the two of them lean on each other. Suddenly, she straightens up. "Is that hottie your boyfriend?"

"We're just friends," I say.

"Nice, because I've been thinking about breaking it off with Jared, and that sweet slice of man cake would make a perfect rebound."

"Oh, he's not on the market for rebounds," I say, feeling a surge of protectiveness.

Pouting, Kandi says, "Why not?"

"He's…extremely religious. He doesn't believe in sex before marriage," Dolores says with a smug smile.

Kandi shrugs. "Oh fine. I'll stay with Jared then."

38

The Part Where the Guy Gets the Girl...He Hopes

Leo

"MUMMY, I want you to dance with Leo!" Isabelle jumps up and down, holding both of our hands. "Everything I Do, I Do it For You" has just started—a wedding reception must.

Bree grins up at me in that cute, uncertain way she has about her. "Only if you want to. We could wait for a fast song or something from this millennium if you'd prefer."

"Not a chance. I'm a huge Bryan Adams fan. Besides, I've been waiting for a proper chance to talk to you since I woke up this morning." I take her hand in mine, and together we find a spot among the twenty or so other couples slow dancing.

Placing my right hand on her back, I lift my left hand into the waltz position and try not to let it affect me when she moves closer. She slides her hand into mine, then places her other one on my shoulder. Something about this feels exactly right, and I'm suddenly filled with the desire to confess my feelings and my hopes for the future all at once. But this is one of those moments you have to take slow. You have to make it count. "Have I mentioned how stunning you are yet?" I ask, smiling down at her.

She blushes and looks away for a second. "I think you used the word beautiful earlier."

"That too." I pull her a little closer and direct us toward a door that's been propped open in the corner of the dance floor. I dance us outside into the dark, warm evening so we can be alone. "I have a confession to make."

She looks up with fear in her eyes, although she nods bravely. "Okay."

"I lied to you when I said everything I said was a lie. Everything before that was the truth." My heart pounds in my chest, and I struggle to get a full breath. "The thing is, I'm absolutely, madly in love with you and have been since I laid eyes on you. But the problem is, for every ounce of love, there exists an equal measure of fear that I'm going to fuck it all up entirely for you and Isabelle. I'm not used to having anyone trust me the way you do. Well, did. The truth is, nothing in my life has mattered the way you do, which is just awful because I'm no longer able to continue as a devil-may-care guy. Because I do care. And now that I feel this way, the only future I can imagine has you and Izzy in it."

I stop rambling and just stare into her beautiful eyes, momentarily stunned into silence. My heart squeezes, and I know I have to go on, or I'll lose her forever. "I got scared, Bree. Scared that if I stuck around, I'd end up hurting you both, and I just couldn't have that. So instead of telling you the truth, I told you a bunch of horrible lies so you'd give up on me. Then I ran like an idiot. And I'm so sorry, Brianna. I am. If you never trust me again, I'll completely understand. In fact, it would make good sense if you told me to sod off and leave you alone forever."

She does this sceptical little nod that says she agrees with that last point. "Yes, I'd be smart to say we're through, wouldn't I? I mean, how do I know you're not saying exactly what I want to hear so you can get something from me?"

Nodding quickly, I say, "You're right. That's exactly what I'm doing."

Unmistakable disappointment crosses her face, so I continue

before she can pull away. "I'm saying what I think you want to hear so you'll spend the rest of your life with me."

Tears spring to her eyes, and she smiles up at me. "Manipulative bastard."

"Right? It's like an illness. I can't seem to stop myself," I say, lowering my face to hers, wanting very badly to brush my lips against hers.

Instead, I give her a spin, then pull her back into my arms. "If you do decide to do the foolish thing and agree to spend your life with me, there are a few things you need to know upfront. First, I'm very poor, and I live in a terrible flat I share with three other disgusting guys. Second, I'm currently employed as a busboy at the Turtle's Head, but I won't be forever, because for the first time in my life, I have a plan. I've applied to Santa Valentina University's Faculty of Education. I want to be an elementary teacher."

Brianna gives me a huge grin. "That's brilliant, Leo. You'll be an amazing teacher."

"I know," I say, which earns me a laugh. "And just the thought of it makes me feel like a better man. Like I do when I'm with you. You've given me a purpose, and you were absolutely right because without a purpose, this whole stupid life is utterly pointless."

Swallowing hard, I go on, adrenaline coursing through me. "So what do you say? Could you wait for me while I become the man you need me to be?"

Her face falls, and she bites her lip. "No."

My entire body goes numb, and my mind scrambles for a response.

Brianna sighs heavily. "The thing is, I don't want to wait anymore. I've done enough waiting for my life to get started. And I feel pretty certain that the man who looked after Izzy so I could study, and cleaned up when she was sick, and gave up his fortune to save me, is already the man I need him to be. More even."

She lifts herself up onto her tiptoes, closing the distance between our mouths, and whispers, "I want to be with you now."

She kisses me hard on the mouth, and my entire body reacts with an elation I've never felt before, because kissing the right woman is *so much better* than kissing just any woman. Her lips on mine are perfection. We stop dancing, and I pull her closer, hugging her tightly, and lifting my hands into her hair while our mouths move together, saying everything that's left to say.

***

"Oh, they're both out cold," Brianna whispers, looking in the backseat at Dolores and Izzy. It's after two in the morning, and we've just pulled up in front of the house after a night of dancing and me having the pleasure of seeing Bree let go and have a good time for once.

I turn to see Izzy and Dolores both sound asleep with their mouths open wide.

"How about if you carry your aunt up, and I'll take Izzy?" I whisper, handing her the keys to the car.

Bree stifles a giggle and gets out of the car. She opens her aunt's door so she can gently wake her. I get out and open Izzy's door, then unbuckle her and carefully lift her out of her car seat and into my arms. She's warm and small as she snuggles her face into my shoulder. Beautiful little thing.

Five minutes later, Bree follows me down the stairs. "So this is my bedroom," she says, pointing to the couch.

"Not exactly private."

She shakes her head. "Not really."

Snapping my fingers, I say, "I may be able to score a nice little garden suite for the night, if you're interested."

Bree giggles softly. "I'm in. You check with the landlady to see if it's available. I'll let my aunt know I'll be gone."

***

Brianna unlocks the door to the suite and pulls me inside. Shutting the door with my foot, I wrap my arms around her and kiss her with everything in me. Oh my God, this is some amazing kissing.

She moans and moves her hands up and down my back, then to my bottom, which she gives a firm squeeze. My, she's a feisty girl. Just my type. Leopole is now wide awake and incredibly excited as the blood leaves my brain and heads south. I pull back, leaving us both panting wildly. "We can't. You've been drinking. It wouldn't be right."

"Three glasses of champagne that wore off hours ago. I'm completely sober."

"Are you sure?"

"I'm one hundred thousand percent sure," she says, kissing me again. "I want you now. I want to show you what it feels like to be with a woman who believes in you, who wants you for *you*. Not your money, not your name, not your body. You."

"Oh, that was good. You're going to win every case," I say, lowering my mouth to hers and kissing her hard. She parts her lips, allowing room for more, which I take, as my hands roam over her waist and to her lovely, large breasts. Oh, yes, those feel as amazing as I knew they would.

I unzip her dress and push the straps off her shoulders, watching as it falls to the floor, then I take a second to drink her in with my eyes. "Wow," I whisper. "You're incredible. We should have done this much, much sooner."

We frantically undress each other, clothes flying all over the tiny room. When we're done, she bites her bottom lip as she stares unashamedly at my nude body. A tiny whimpering sound escapes her chest. "Oh, yes."

We rush together, our naked bodies melding in one lust-filled form. Lifting her up by her bottom, I hold her against me as she wraps her legs around my waist, our mouths acting as a preview for coming attractions.

I carry her over to the bed, put her down, kissing her neck and working my way to her breasts. I take my time here, fully enjoying their fullness before I move even further south, planting soft kisses on her tummy and parting her legs with my hands as I kneel on the floor in front of her.

"I don't have any condoms, so I think it best if we…do other things," I say, Leopole not understanding the message at all.

Leaning on her elbows, Bree bites her bottom lip. "You don't?"

I shake my head. "I have never been more upset about not purchasing something in my entire life." I look her over again, running my hands up her sides and back down again to her knees. "But I promise you'll have a good time anyway."

"Okay." She nods. "Then your turn."

"Yes, please."

***

"Well, that was…incredible," I say, kissing her on the forehead.

We're now lying together in my small bed, recovering from hours of no-sex sexy time. The sun is starting to come up, giving a pink glow to the room.

"You are so skilled…and generous in your attention to my happiness," she answers, her voice raw from panting.

I turn onto my side so I can take her in like this—happy, relaxed, satisfied. Her cheeks are flushed, and her hair is draped over my pillow, and she has never looked lovelier to me than right now. Tracing her breasts with my finger, I say, "You are a remarkable woman, Bree. I'm so glad I tricked you into spending your life with me."

She laughs, then reaches up and runs her fingers over the stubble on my jaw. "I should get back inside before Izzy wakes up."

I nod. "Righto."

"Say, you wouldn't want to go to a gift opening in a few hours, would you?"

"I'd like nothing more."

39

Life is Beautiful

Bree

"GOOD GOD, there are a lot of naked lady statues here," Leo mutters, holding his flute of plain orange juice in front of his mouth.

We're back at the senior Hammer residence, but this time, instead of Mr. Bananas as my plus one, I've got a very handsome, charming, incredible-in-the-sack-even-though-I-didn't-actually-have-sex-with-him man.

We're standing at the back of a semicircle of chairs facing Amber and Zidane, who both look happy, if not bleary-eyed from being out late last night, drinking in every last drop of their wedding reception. And by that, I mean, based on Dane's face, every last drop of booze behind the bar.

Kandi is sitting to the right of my sister, like a dutiful bridesmaid, writing down all of the gifts, as well as who they're from, in a little wedding notebook. Valerie, who's sitting next to her, is in charge of putting all of the wrapping paper into recycling bags and folding up the gift bags. Quinn takes each gift from Valerie and passes them to Dane's mum, where they begin the rounds so everyone can ooh and aahh over the plethora of stemware, heavy, expensive cutlery, and thick linens. The off-duty groomsmen sport sunglasses and slouch down in their lawn chairs, and it's not entirely clear whether any of them are actually awake or not. Isabelle is busy helping her auntie and new uncle open the presents and thoroughly enjoying being the centre of attention.

Amber has just unwrapped a wooden handmade sign that says "Welcome to the Hammer Residence. Love lives here." She smiles, tearing up as she stands to hug whichever one of Dane's buff, moustached relatives made it for them. Normally, I'd find the whole thing sappy, if not amusing, because of the whole "Hammer Residence" thing, but today, I think it's kind of sweet.

This afternoon's cheese people platter is a near replica of the original Dane and Amber, except this time, Amber's not sporting a veil.

But somehow, the cheese people platter doesn't annoy me today, neither do the bridesmaids or groomsmen or even my mum, who gave me the once-over when she saw me in my comfy maxi dress and flip-flops. Nothing could bother me this morning, because, well, I suppose you know, because, well…sexy time.

But it's not just that, it's also knowing I very likely will be spending my future with literally the most thoughtful, generous, fun man I've ever met. Not to mention the best-looking, most charming man here. Kandi, Valerie, and Quinn keep glancing at him, then looking at me, their expressions screaming mismatch. But I don't care, because it's a lovely day, the wedding is finally over, my exams are done, and life is beautiful.

Last night was literally the best night of my life. Up to this point, my only sexual experience was Roderick, who, upon comparison, turns out was a completely selfish lover. Wham, bam, knocked me up and ran.

"Can I get you another drink?" Leo asks, smiling down at me.

"I'm good, thanks." And I am.

The happy couple reaches the bottom of the present pile—thank God—and Izzy comes rushing over to Leo and takes his hand. "Come see the dolphin statue."

"A dolphin? Does he have any clothes on?" Leo asks her.

Isabelle wrinkles up her nose in confusion. "Dolphins don't wear clothes, silly. Come on!"

"Excuse me, Brianna, it appears I have an ocean-dwelling mammal to meet."

I watch as they stroll hand in hand, my heart squeezing at the sight. Smiling to myself, I think about the future that lies ahead—a future with him in it, and I can't imagine anything more wonderful.

Epilogue - We Did it Our Way...

Bree

Six months later

Leo and I stand in front of our not-too-big, not-too-small, canary-yellow two-storey house that I've had my eye on for years. We snapped it up the same day it went on the market, which incidentally was a month after our wedding.

As it turned out, Leo was able to make a most compelling argument for getting married right away. He did, after all, give up his fortune for me, then made it his life's goal to shed his cocoon of luxury and become a full-fledged, responsible-yet-still-wonderfully-fun adult. Plus, we were both getting sick of using Kevlar Condoms with double the thickness and triple the spermicide. Their slogan is "The tank of condoms. Nothing's getting through these babies...especially babies." We're still using protection, but not quite as much, which is a huge bonus of being married.

Leo proposed the night he received his acceptance letter for university. He borrowed the tandem bicycle and recreated our perfect date together. Over a bottle of wine at Hidden Beach, he convinced me without a shadow of a doubt that I, Brianna Lewis, deserve to be loved. That I am enough, just the way I am, and he's the man to do the loving. He slid a beautiful, but sensible, blue apatite and copper engagement ring on my finger, and we sealed the deal with some skinny dipping in the ocean as the sun set.

And now, we're here, standing perfectly still for a moment, listening to the sounds of the trees rustling in the breeze and the gulls flying overhead. Our little house isn't waterfront, but it's close enough that you can smell the salty air from here, and there is a view of the water from the small balcony off our bedroom, where we will someday have a couple of cozy reading chairs. The house has a nice, big yard and a detached two-car garage with a lovely, well-appointed granny suite above it where Aunt Dolores will live.

"I can't believe this is ours," I say, taking it all in. "Are you sure you're not going to miss the life of Riley?"

"I honestly can barely remember it, but what I do recall seems utterly empty." He slips his arm behind me and pulls me toward him for a lingering kiss that makes my toes curl and my entire body warm up. "This is my real life, with you and Izzy. And Aunt Dolores and her cats."

"Oh, Christ, take it inside, you two." Dolores shakes her head as she brushes past us, lugging a pet carrier containing Milo. "Come on, Milo, I'll show you to our new home above a stinky garage."

Leo and I exchange a look and then laugh quietly. Dolores and change aren't exactly friends, but underneath the grumbling, I know she'll be happy to have her own space again, even if it is above a not-at-all stinky garage.

The sound of a car pulling up catches my attention, and I turn to see my parents in the front seat of their Subaru, Dane and Amber in the back seat, waving.

They climb out, and I rush over, genuinely happy to see them. Hugs are given, and hearty handshakes are exchanged.

"Well? What do you think?" I ask my mum, pointing to the house.

"It's just perfect. Plenty big enough to add some brothers and sisters for Isabelle."

"Mum, we just got married. We don't want to rush into——"

"We'll get right on it," Leo says, dipping me back and giving me a big, wet kiss. I laugh, slightly shocked as he lifts me back up to standing. Winking at me, he says, "I would absolutely love to be a stay-at-home dad while my very important wife goes off to work every day. And then, when our kids are old enough to go to school, I'll be there every day, in case they need me."

"Stay-at-home dad?" my dad says, wrinkling up his nose.

"That's very forward-thinking of you, Leo," my mum says. She's been trying to be the epitome of supportive ever since she found out that Leo's gone back to school to become a teacher. Well, it also probably helps that his brother is Pierce Davenport, and that Leo likely will inherit some of his parents' fortune someday.

Another car pulls up, and Pierce and Emma get out. Pierce claps his hands together and says, "I hear there is unlimited pizza and beer for anyone willing to move a few boxes."

"I said there will be pizza and beer. I never once used the word unlimited." Leo says.

"Are you sure?" Amber asks, joining in on the fun. "Because I was sure Brianna's text said unlimited."

"I'm a lowly uni student."

"But she's a fancy lawyer," Pierce says, pointing to me with one thumb. He turns his gaze to the house, then gives a firm nod and looks at Leo. "Well done, you two. Well done. Not to get sappy, but I'm proud of you."

"Oh, that was sappy. Don't ever do that again," Leo says, shaking his head and wrinkling up his nose a little, even though he's beaming at the compliment.

"Just once more, I promise," Pierce says, looking at me. "Brianna, a long time ago, Leo told me that when he met the right woman, he'd do whatever it took to keep her. I'm so glad that woman was you."

My chest swells with emotion, and I fight back tears.

"Come on, then," Pierce says. "These boxes won't unload themselves."

I take a moment to watch as the scene unfolds—Izzy chasing

Knickers through the grass that needs mowing, and my family, and Emma, and Pierce helping us to start our life together.

Even though we have a long day ahead, I've never felt this happy, this settled, this hopeful. Not ever. But now, as I watch my wonderful husband carry my favourite armchair up the sidewalk, I laugh out of pure joy. He's the type of man who will let me be who I need to be, he'll support me in whatever I want to do, and he'll keep me laughing when things don't go my way.

Together, we're creating a truly rich life—the kind of fairy tales, even though there is no castle. Instead, we've got a just-right house, two busy working parents, one crazy bacoholic aunt, three surly cats, and one little girl who will never have to wonder if she's loved.

The Beginning...

The Benavente Islands Law Association

Certificate of Admission

as of November 15, 2020

BRIANNA LEWIS

was duly admitted and licenced to practice as a Barrister and Counselor in the Benavente Islands as well as the Kingdom of Avonia.

Fred Armitage

Attorney General of the Benavente Islands

Melisa McCarthy

Santa Valentina Court Clerk

Afterword

MANY THANKS FROM MELANIE

I hope you enjoyed Leo and Bree's story. I hope you laughed out loud, and the story left you feeling good. If so, please leave a review.

Reviews are a true gift to writers. They are the best way for other readers to find our work and for writers to figure out if we're on the right track, so thank you if you are one of those kind folks out there to take time out of your day to leave a review!

If you'd like a fab, fun, FREE novella, please sign up for my newsletter at www.melaniesummersbooks.com.

All the very best to you and yours,

Melanie

Available Now

ROYALLY CRUSHED

~ A Crazy Royal Love Romantic Comedy, Book 1 ~

A wildly funny, ridiculously romantic spinoff from best-selling author Melanie Summers...

Princess Arabella of Avonia has spent her first twenty-nine years in an endless loop of high teas, state dinners, and the same five conversations. Every minute of her day is planned by someone else. From what to wear to what to eat, the royal handlers keep her on a tight leash. To make matters worse, they've extended their duties to include finding her a suitable husband before she turns thirty. Desperate for an out, she sneakily signs up to co-host a new nature docu-series, starring Will Banks, the man dubbed McHotty of the Wilderness.

Will has ladies all over the globe lining up to meet him until a hot, new adventure show comes on the scene, and his ratings take a nose-dive. Producers decide an emergency change in format is in order. Enter Princess Arabella. The pampered and proper royal is the perfect foil to Will's rugged outdoorsman.

It's hate at first sight, but their on-screen loathing makes for great television. Surprisingly, when the cameras stop rolling, these two finally see each other's good sides. Can these opposites find their forever in each other's arms, or will their differences be their undoing?

Coming Soon

RESTING BEACH FACE

~ A Paradise Bay Romantic Comedy, Book 4 ~

Melanie Summers welcomes you back to Paradise Bay for a ridiculously romantic, laugh-out-loud tale of reluctant homecomings, lost loves, and second chances...

Yoga instructor, Hadley Jones, has loved Chase Williams since high school. Fifteen years later, she still does. And while he hasn't popped the question yet, she knows it's only a matter of time. Little does Hadley know Chase has been busy making wedding plans—just not with her.

Heath Robinson left the Santa Valentina Islands the first chance he got. He's about to be named CFO of a fortune-500 company when he gets a call that has him boarding a plane home. Now, instead of sipping whiskey sours with the big boys, he'll be watching his bed-ridden mother sip from a juice box. His plan is to help her recover from her moped accident as quickly as possible so he can get back to his real life—hopefully before he runs into the girl who crushed his heart, Hadley Jones.

Will Hadley realize that Heath is the real man of her dreams? Will Heath forgive Hadley? Will his mum ever ride a moped again?

Find out in this delightfully funny tale of life coming full circle! Resting Beach Face is sure to leave a smile on your face.

About the Author

Melanie Summers lives in Edmonton, Canada, with her husband, three kiddos, and two cuddly dogs. When she's not writing, she loves reading (obviously), snuggling up on the couch with her family for movie night (which would not be complete without lots of popcorn and milkshakes), and long walks in the woods near her house. Melanie also spends a lot more time thinking about doing yoga than actually doing yoga, which is why most of her photos are taken 'from above'. She also loves shutting down restaurants with her girlfriends. Well, not literally shutting them down, like calling the health inspector or something. More like just staying until they turn the lights off.

She's written fourteen novels (and counting), and has won one silver and two bronze medals in the Reader's Favourite Awards.

If you'd like to find out about her upcoming releases, sign up for her newsletter on www.melaniesummersbooks.com.

Special Thanks

I am forever working at a ridiculously fast pace, which means I need a LOT of help to keep things flowing. Time to acknowledge the many people who have made this book possible, including:

- You, my lovely reader friends, without whom, all of this playing around with imaginary friends would mean people would look upon me with a mixture of pity and fear. Instead, I get to call myself an *author*, which has a markedly better reaction,
- Kristi Yanta, editor extraordinaire who took the skeleton of Leo and Bree's story and said, "Here's how to make it complete,"
- Heidi Shoham, the gif-toting line editor,
- Melissa Martin, an amazing proof-reader/copy editor, and wonderful friend,
- Janice Owen, a terrific and patient proof-reader who taught me a lot of neato stuff,
- My Chick Lit Think Tank Pals: Whitney Dineen, Tracie Banister, Kate O'Keeffe, Virginia Gray, and Annabelle

Costa, for sharing their knowledge and cheering each other on as we write, edit, release, repeat,

- Tim Flanagan, my marketing, maps, formatting, print covers, and other graphics genius who took my crazy fun idea and made it happen,
- Christine Miller, my author assistant, who keeps my social media stuff going while I'm lost in Paradise Bay,
- My oldest and dearest friends, Nikki Chiem and Karlee Chance, who are always there for me no matter what,
- My mom, who helps out SO much around here (including with proofreading) so I can work, especially when I'm under a deadline,
- My dad, who I miss every day and whose unwavering faith in my abilities will go with me wherever life takes me,
- My kids for bringing humour and hugs to my days,
- And, last by certainly not least, my husband and best friend, Jeremy, for always supporting me and being such an inspiration when it comes to both romance and comedy.

Thank you to all of you from the bottom, the top, and the middle of my heart!

You mean the world to me,
Melanie

Made in the USA
Las Vegas, NV
04 October 2021